The Emerald Affair

ALSO BY JANET MACLEOD TROTTER:

The India Tea Series

The Tea Planter's Daughter – Book 1

The Tea Planter's Bride – Book 2

The Girl from the Tea Garden – Book 3

The Secrets of the Tea Garden – Book 4

HISTORICAL

In the Far Pashmina Mountains

The Jarrow Trilogy

The Jarrow Lass

Child of Jarrow

Return to Jarrow

The Durham Trilogy

The Hungry Hills

The Darkening Skies

Never Stand Alone

The Tyneside Sagas

A Handful of Stars

Chasing the Dream

For Love & Glory

The Great War Sagas

No Greater Love (formerly *The Suffragette*)

A Crimson Dawn

Scottish Historical Romance

The Jacobite Lass

The Beltane Fires

Highlander in Muscovy

MYSTERY/CRIME

The Vanishing of Ruth

The Haunting of Kulah

TEENAGE

Love Games

NON-FICTION

Beatles & Chiefs

The Emerald Affair

Book 1 of the Ray Hotel Series

JANET
MACLEOD TROTTER

This is a work of fiction. Names, characters, organizations, places, events, and incidents are either products of the author's imagination or are used fictitiously. Any resemblance to actual persons, living or dead, or actual events is purely coincidental.

Published by Lake Union Publishing, Seattle

www.apub.com

ISBN-13: 9781542041188
ISBN-10: 154204118X

Cover design by Lisa Horton

Cover photography by Richard Jenkins Photography

Printed in the United States of America

To all my lovely great-nieces and great-nephews: Molly, Lyra, Ylva, Luke, Ally, Jake, Harrison, Corbyn and Landon. May you continue to enjoy stories!

The Civil & Military Gazette, February 1919

FOR SALE

Fully licensed premises and well-furnished hotel with electric lighting

known as

THE RAJAH HOTEL (locally as "the Raj")

Situated in Nichol Road, Rawalpindi,

Northern Punjab, India

Presently in the occupation of Mr. James Littleton

The Premises comprise:- grand reception hallway, dining-room for 30 guests, 2 sitting-rooms, 12 bedrooms (some with wash-hand basins), 3 bathrooms, 6 W.Cs., courtyard, gardens to front and rear, manager's bungalow, servants' compound, kitchens, washhouse, drying green, stables (motor vehicle by negotiation – four-seater Clement Talbot)

For further particulars and price, apply in writing to Mr. J. Littleton.

****

Chapter 1

Ebbsmouth, Scotland, May 1919

As the train taking Esmie McBride south from Edinburgh slowed, Esmie's heartbeat quickened – half in excitement, half in dread – as she craned for a view of her old home town. She hadn't been back in nearly three years, owing to serving abroad as a nurse during the recent war. Nervously, she fingered tendrils of her brown hair and pressed her button nose against the window. The pinkish stone of the harbour cottages glowed in the late spring sunshine and the sea beyond sparkled as white-capped waves broke against the harbour wall. The Anchorage jutted out over the cliff like a brooding eagle, a gothic tower that had until recently been a temporary hospital where Esmie had spent a few months nursing in 1916. Her best friend, Lydia Templeton, had written to tell her that the last of the convalescent patients had been transferred and elderly Colonel Lomax and his eccentric daughter were once again in full residence.

Dear Lydia! Esmie's spirits lifted to think she would be staying with her old school friend and her hospitable parents. Lydia's amusing gossip was just the antidote she needed after her gruelling work with the Scottish Women's Hospitals on the battlefronts of Serbia and Russia. She felt so much older than her twenty-five years. Bubbly Lydia would make her feel young and carefree again.

Suddenly she caught sight of her old home on the clifftop – a white-washed house with black doors and window frames – where she had lived with her father after he took the job of school doctor at St Ebba's School for Girls. Tears prickled her eyes. The garden was overgrown with brambles and the swing he had made for her in the boughs of the apple tree had gone. But this hadn't been her home for over ten years. She felt a familiar stab of loss for her beloved father, who had left her orphaned at fourteen years old, her mother having died when Esmie was five. The nearest she had to a home now was the psychiatric hospital at Vaullay in the Highlands where, for the past year, she had nursed and lived with her kind guardian, Dr Isobel Carruthers.

Then the train was past her former home and her old school came into view with its jumble of slate roofs and tall chimneys. Esmie's stomach lurched. She would have to visit the Drummonds, who ran the school. Whenever she thought of them and their son, David, she was consumed with a mix of guilt and remorse. Would they look at her with accusing eyes? Or worse: would they smother her in kindness and sympathy? She couldn't put off meeting them in person for much longer. But not yet.

With a hiss, the train came to a stop in the station.

Lydia was waving from the barrier, unmistakable in a fashionable spring coat and jaunty hat perched on her coils of blonde hair. She'd commandeered a porter to help Esmie with her case, even though it was small enough for Esmie to carry herself.

'Dearest!' Lydia squealed, grabbing hold of Esmie in a hug. 'My golly, you're as thin as a rake. Mummy will absolutely insist that Cook force-feeds you. Mind you, the new fashion is all about being thin – so lucky you! Makes your lovely grey eyes look huge too.'

Esmie laughed. 'What nonsense you talk! I can't tell you how much I've missed it. And you are looking as beautiful as ever.'

Lydia looked pleased and slipped an arm through her friend's. They walked out of the small station with the porter in tow.

'We are going to have so much fun. Us Templetons are going to spoil you rotten and you're going to tell me about all the foreign soldiers you've met and hearts you've broken—'

Lydia stopped abruptly and peered at Esmie with round blue eyes. 'Gosh, I'm sorry. I'd forgotten about David. I didn't mean to be disrespectful. We're all terribly sorry about him.'

Esmie's insides clenched. 'Yes, I know. You don't have to apologise.'

'Awful business,' said Lydia, 'and so near to the end of the War. Just not fair.'

Esmie felt the blood drain from her head and thought she might faint. But Lydia was quickly steering her towards an open-topped car parked at the station entrance and pushing her into the passenger seat. Her friend slipped into the driver's side, hitching up her skirt and showing a flash of shapely legs.

'Has Dickson the chauffeur retired?' asked Esmie.

'No, he still works for Daddy. But I like to drive myself these days.' Lydia grinned. 'All that time in the transport corps driving generals around hasn't been wasted.'

'Trust you to get the generals and not the army's washing,' Esmie teased.

'Absolutely!' Lydia agreed. 'But the highlight of my war was going to America to fundraise for the Scottish Women's Hospitals.'

'That was very brave of you to cross the Atlantic,' said Esmie. 'Aunt Isobel said you did a wonderful job.'

'Did Dr Carruthers really say that?' Lydia asked with a smile. 'Do you think the great Dr Inglis thought that too? She encouraged me to go, you know?'

'I'm sure she did. She couldn't have supplied all those hospitals without your efforts.'

'I wish I'd been able to tell her about America in person,' Lydia said. 'It was tragic her dying so suddenly.'

'Not so sudden,' Esmie said. 'She knew she had cancer for months but didn't tell us. She drove herself to the very end.'

'And you were with her on the return from Russia?'

Esmie nodded. Sadness washed over her as she thought of the death of the heroic Edinburgh doctor who had taken her female staff all over the Continent to help Britain's allies when their own government had spurned the offer of women medics. After the horrors of the Serbian Retreat in 1915 and a gruelling year of unrelenting nursing on the battlefronts in southern Russia and Romania, Dr Inglis and her women had finally been defeated by the chaos of revolution in late 1917. Avoiding the killings and anarchy, the women had only just escaped from the Arctic port of Archangel before it became ice-bound for the winter. Elsie Inglis's death, which followed swiftly after, had brought an end to Esmie's involvement with the Scottish Women's Hospitals.

Worn out and dispirited, Esmie had retreated to Vaullay to be cared for by her guardian. Isobel Carruthers, an old friend and colleague of her father's, was the nearest Esmie had to a parent. With affection, Esmie called her Aunt Isobel. There, in the soft air of the Highlands, close to her childhood home and far away from the guns and bloodshed, she had recovered her zest for life. In what turned out to be the last year of the War, Esmie began to help nurse the psychiatric patients, some of them soldiers suffering from shell shock. And as the War had turned in favour of the Allies, Esmie had known the time had come to be honest with David . . .

'Don't look so glum,' Lydia cried, breaking into her thoughts. 'I didn't mean to make you sad. We're simply not going to think about unhappy things. We're going to talk about the future and drink cocktails and play tennis and I'm going to teach you to dance to ragtime music. I brought some recordings back from America for the gramophone.'

As they sped along the country lanes out of Ebbsmouth and towards Templeton Hall, Lydia regaled her with tales of her time in New York and Chicago and the drama of crossing the Atlantic dodging enemy submarines. She made light of it but Esmie knew that Lydia had taken great risks to travel to and from America. She liked that about her friend; hiding her courage under a nonchalant manner.

'And dear Harold is back from India,' Lydia said with another sudden change of subject. 'You remember Harold Guthrie? His father was the stationmaster. Harold read medicine at Edinburgh – went out to India as a missionary doctor but also did a stint in Mesopotamia during the War.'

'Was he the red-haired one who was sweet on you?' Esmie asked. 'A few years older than us?'

Lydia laughed. 'That's the one. Not so much red hair now though – he's gone a bit thin on top. Mummy says wearing a solar topee in the heat makes the hair rub off. Daddy says that's nonsense.'

'Whereabouts in India was Harold working?'

'Oh, somewhere incredibly hot and dusty and dangerous,' said Lydia with a wave of her hand. 'Lots of Pathans sticking knives into each other.'

'The North-West Frontier?' Esmie asked with interest.

'That could be it. Anyway, Harold is still a sweet man.'

'And are you still interested in him?' Esmie asked.

'Heavens no! To be honest, he can be a bit of a bore about his mission work – and now he's fussing about some war that seems to have broken out with the Afghans. But he's bringing a friend of his over for tennis this afternoon. Guess who it is?'

Esmie could hear the excitement in Lydia's voice. 'Douglas Fairbanks?' she joked.

Lydia laughed. 'Just about – he's as dishy as a film star. Captain Tom Lomax!'

'The colonel's son?' Esmie asked in surprise. 'I thought he was soldiering in the wilds of Afghanistan or somewhere.'

'He was,' said Lydia, 'but he's home at The Anchorage now. Another hero from Mesopotamia.'

'But he's married, isn't he?' asked Esmie. 'I remember we sneaked out of school on their wedding day to watch them come out of the church.'

'He's a widower,' said Lydia with a conspiratorial wink.

'Poor man,' said Esmie.

Lydia adjusted her expression. 'Of course it's very sad – she died before the War – some horrid disease in India. But Harold says the captain doesn't talk about her anymore.'

'What about that wine importer with the vineyards in France you mentioned in your last two letters? The one who's been dining you all over the county,' Esmie asked. 'You sounded keen on him.'

'Colin Fleming?' Lydia answered. 'Yes, he's nice – and has plenty of money – but he's away in France at the moment. Besides, Colin's not nearly as handsome as the captain.' Lydia glanced at Esmie and smirked. 'I've always had a weak spot for a man in an officer's uniform.'

Esmie gave a wry laugh. 'To be honest, I'm just thankful to see men back in civilian clothes.'

They turned off the narrow road and passed through a gateway. Esmie's heart lifted as they drove up the familiar drive lined with well-trimmed beech hedge and gleaming white Templeton Hall appeared before them. Despite its grand name, Lydia's home was more of a sprawling modern villa, with French windows and balconies and a portico covered in climbing roses that was large enough for a car to pass under so that passengers could alight and enter the house without getting drenched by rain.

Baxter, their ageing butler-cum-footman, was ready to open Esmie's door.

'Miss Esmie, welcome back,' he greeted her, with a smile that revealed large gaps in his rotten teeth.

'Thank you, Baxter. It's lovely to be here,' Esmie said, getting out of the car and shaking his hand.

As the butler went to get Esmie's case, Lydia suppressed a giggle and murmured to Esmie, 'Daddy had dentures made for Baxter but ever since they dropped into Mummy's soup he's refused to wear them.'

As Esmie watched him struggle up the front steps with her suitcase, she had to resist the urge to take it from him, knowing how offended he would be. Arm in arm, the two friends entered the house.

Sun streamed in at large stained-glass windows and threw patterns of vivid colours across the tiled hallway. Esmie breathed in the smell of warm wood and beeswax polish and felt a rush of nostalgia for her girlhood and friendship with Lydia. Everything about Templeton Hall had been built for comfort; from its modern plumbing, roomy bathrooms and electric lighting to its upholstered walnut furniture and well-sprung beds. As a young woman, Lydia's mother had travelled on the Continent and returned with a passion for Art Nouveau and its sensuous, curvaceous style. Her home reflected her tastes.

The house was full of beautiful cabinets of pale wood, gaudy jardinières of tropical ferns, curving banisters of intricate ironwork and lampstands in the shape of half-naked nymphs. Everywhere was flooded with light through the many windows which gave views onto the sheltered garden and distant glimpses of the North Sea. Yet it was a family house with a downstairs porch crammed with sporting equipment and old gum boots and a drawing room full of family photographs where dogs were allowed to curl up on the Persian rug in front of the inglenook fireplace.

'Daddy's away in Newcastle today,' Lydia explained, 'but he'll be back at teatime. He's dying to see you.' She stopped and called out, 'Mummy, we're here!'

'In the conservatory, darling!' Minnie Templeton answered.

Lydia rolled her eyes. 'She'll be hacking the poor rubber plants to death. No patience with plants whatsoever.'

Lydia's mother bustled out of the glass-roofed room, her round face flushed puce below immaculately pinned fair hair. She dumped her basket of dead-headed flowers and threw out plump arms.

'Esmie, sweet girl! Come and be kissed!'

Esmie, a head taller than Minnie, responded with a hug. Minnie felt soft and smelt of roses. Esmie's eyes smarted with emotion. 'Thank you for inviting me to stay, Mrs Templeton.'

'Goodness, girl!' Minnie exclaimed. 'You don't need to wait for an invitation. We love having you here any time you want.'

'That's what I've been telling Esmie for months,' agreed Lydia. 'It's high time she got away from all those loony inmates and had some fun.'

Esmie winced at her bluntness. 'We don't call them lunatics anymore,' said Esmie. 'They're psychiatric patients.'

'Well, whatever you want to call them,' Lydia said with a dismissive wave. 'You've done your bit and now we're going to help you look for a husband. You and I will be left on the shelf if we don't do something about it jolly soon.'

Esmie laughed. 'You're still only twenty-four.'

'Twenty-five next month,' said Lydia with a shudder.

'Hardly old, my darling,' said Minnie.

'You were married and had given birth to Grace at my age, Mummy,' Lydia pointed out.

'Yes, but you modern girls have been doing your bit for the War.'

'Precisely,' said Lydia, 'and the War has left us with a lot less choice than your generation had.'

Esmie tensed, thinking of David. Once again she agonised over how his parents must be grieving for their son. Minnie caught her look and touched her arm.

'Jumbo and I were so sorry to hear of David's loss,' she said. 'Lydia says you've been very brave about it.'

Guilt gripped Esmie at her concern. She didn't deserve it. 'It's the Drummonds who should have our sympathy – losing their only child,' Esmie said. 'How— how are they taking it?'

Minnie sighed. 'Badly, so I hear. I never see Maud Drummond these days – keeps to the house and refuses all invitations. Jumbo has been for walks with William on a few occasions but he's a shadow of his former self.'

Esmie felt leaden at the news. David's father had always been a vigorous man with a gregarious nature. Some of Esmie's fellow pupils had been in awe of their headmaster, with his booming voice and bushy grey beard, but she had always liked him. After all, William Drummond had been her father's closest friend and he had shown her particular kindness and leniency following her father's sudden death, keeping her on as a pupil and waiving the school fees.

'I must go and see them,' Esmie said. 'I feel bad that I haven't. I've written, of course.'

'Well, you've been a long way away and busy with your work,' said Minnie generously.

Lydia took Esmie's arm and steered her towards the stairs. 'Plenty of time for duty visits another day,' she said. 'But right this minute we're going to get you settled into your old room and freshened up before lunch. Harold and Captain Lomax are coming over at three so we'll need to sort out some tennis clothes.'

'Luncheon in half an hour, girls,' Minnie called after them.

Esmie glanced over her shoulder and smiled. For a moment it was as if the terrible years of war had never existed and they were once again the young friends whom Minnie had loved to spoil and fuss over – girls who had nothing more serious to worry about than the next delicious meal or game of tennis.

Lydia peered into the wardrobe where the maid had hung up Esmie's clothes. 'You can't wear that,' she declared, pulling out the offending garment and tossing it onto the floor.

'What's wrong with it?' Esmie asked, picking up the old tennis skirt. 'It's just a bit faded.'

'It's the colour of sandbags,' Lydia retorted, 'and about as fashionable. You'll have to borrow one of mine or Grace's until we can order a new one.'

'I can't really afford—'

'Well, I can.' Lydia cut off her protest. 'We're simply going to have to renew your entire wardrobe, as far as I can see. Have you really bought nothing new since before the War?' She hauled a dress off its hanger. 'I'm sure you used to wear this when we were still at school.'

'I did,' said Esmie. 'But it cost Aunt Isobel a lot of money and I've only worn it on special occasions.'

'Maybe if we have a Victorian-themed fancy dress party I'll allow you to wear it,' said Lydia with a wink, dropping it onto the growing pile of discarded clothes.

Esmie laughed. 'I'll just put them all back in the wardrobe when you've left the room.'

Lydia gave her a cross look. In an instant, she was gathering up the small heap and marching to the window.

'Don't you dare!' Esmie cried, scrambling to her feet.

'I dare!' giggled Lydia, throwing open the casement window.

Esmie dashed to stop her but Lydia was too quick. She hurled the clothing out of the window. Esmie peered out, stunned at the sight of her clothes scattered over the flowerbeds and bushes below.

'All gone,' announced Lydia.

Speechless, Esmie looked at her friend and then out of the window again. She should have known Lydia would be provoked by her challenge into doing something devilish. Suddenly Esmie began to laugh. Then Lydia was laughing. Soon they were both doubled up and clutching each other with mirth at the absurd sight of Esmie's clothes strewn outside.

When Lydia had regained her breath she said, 'Come on, we'll see what's still hanging in Grace's wardrobe – you're about the same height as my sister.'

By the time the afternoon guests arrived, Esmie was dressed in a flouncy white tennis dress and petticoats that had once belonged to Lydia's sister Grace. Older than Lydia by six years, Grace had left home for finishing school in Switzerland before the War and never returned to live at Templeton Hall. Instead, she had met and married a Swiss financier and settled in Zurich. The sisters had constantly bickered and had never been close; Grace had always thought Lydia spoilt and childish, while Lydia had complained at Grace's bossiness and lack of fun.

Esmie felt overdressed in the extravagant lacy outfit and was resisting Lydia's attempts to put mother-of-pearl combs in her unruly hair when they heard the toot of a car horn.

'That'll be Harold,' Lydia said in excitement, losing interest at once in styling Esmie's hair and dashing to her cheval mirror. 'How do I look?'

'Very pretty,' said Esmie. 'As ever.'

'You're not just saying that?' Lydia frowned at her reflection, twisting from side to side to view her hourglass figure. Her new tennis skirt showed her trim ankles and calves, while her blouse was tailored to show off her curves and slim neck. On her head she had pinned a fetching straw boater. Hats suited Lydia.

'The captain will be captivated,' Esmie assured her.

Lydia gave a gleaming smile of near-perfect teeth, patted her blonde hair and said, 'Come on then – into battle!'

They found Minnie on the terrace fussing over the new arrivals. The two men, dressed in flannels and blazers, were already sitting in cane chairs and sipping lemon cordial in the shade of a large canopy. They sprang up as the young women appeared. Dazzled by the sun, Esmie put up a hand to shade her eyes and squinted at them. But they were still sun-blurred shadows, one a head and shoulders taller than the other.

Harold stepped into the sunlight and Lydia brushed his cheek with a kiss that made him blush. He was stockier than Esmie remembered and his face was lined and ruddy from years in harsh sunlight. He could only be in his early thirties but looked ten years older. Yet when he smiled he looked suddenly boyish and handsome. As he shook her hand firmly, she recalled how Harold had been kindly and ever patient with Lydia and Grace's teasing.

'How are you, Miss McBride?' asked Harold. 'I've heard such wonderful reports of your work with the Scottish Women's Hospitals. Ministering angels. I knew your guardian, Dr Carruthers, when I was training as a doctor. Wonderful woman.'

'Yes she is,' agreed Esmie. 'I didn't know you knew her.'

'Before the War,' Harold explained, 'she took me round the slums of the Canongate in Edinburgh. Wanted me to see the poverty on our doorstep and understand that you don't have to travel halfway around the world to be of help to people. I don't think she approved of my missionary zeal to go and convert Indians.'

'But you went to India anyway,' Esmie said with a quizzical look.

'I did indeed,' Harold admitted. 'Of course once I got there, I realised my job was ninety-nine per cent about healing the sick. I don't think I've converted a single soul to Christianity.'

'Harold, that's enough talk about religion,' said Lydia. 'Introduce us to your friend.'

'Of course,' Harold said hastily. 'This is—'

But Lydia had already turned to the taller man and was holding out her hand. 'Pleased to meet you, Captain Lomax. And welcome to Templeton Hall.'

'Delighted to meet you, Miss Templeton,' he replied in a deep voice with the trace of a Scottish burr and the huskiness of a smoker. 'Harold is a great admirer of you and your family. I once met your sister Grace at a hunt ball.'

'Well, we won't hold that against you,' quipped Lydia.

'Lydia!' Minnie chided.

The captain gave a surprised chuckle. As he stepped towards the women, Esmie saw his face full-on for the first time. She stifled a gasp of astonishment. She'd forgotten how handsome he was, with his shock of dark hair and lean, handsome features. He glanced at her over Lydia's shoulder with startlingly blue eyes that assessed her through dark lashes. As girls on the cusp of womanhood, Esmie and Lydia had gazed at the colonel's son from afar – on the few occasions he came back from boarding school and then officer training – and had admired his tall good looks and athletic build. But Esmie hadn't seen Tom Lomax for years and hardly knew him, so her reaction surprised her.

Lydia turned and waved Esmie forward. 'And as you probably realise, this is my best friend, Esmie McBride.'

'Miss McBride.' Tom smiled and shook her hand.

Esmie stared at him. He looked at her puzzled and then turned his attention back to Lydia. Esmie realised with embarrassment that she'd been gazing at him, tongue-tied, and hadn't returned the captain's greeting.

It didn't seem to matter. Lydia was steering him into a seat beside her and questioning him about his brave deeds in the War. Tom seemed embarrassed by this and shrugged off her adulation.

'A lot of boredom in the heat,' he said. 'The real heroics were done by the quartermasters and the water-carriers – the men who really keep an army on the march. I was less than heroic, believe me.'

Lydia laughed. 'Your modesty is very attractive, Captain Lomax. But I've already heard from Harold about how you helped liberate Baghdad.'

'My good friend Guthrie has always been prone to giving the credit to others,' said Tom. 'While I was safely behind the guns, he was out tending to the wounded in the field.'

'I'm sure you both did your bit splendidly,' Minnie said. 'But tell us, Captain Lomax, what is it like being back at The Anchorage? Are you getting the place back to normal now that the patients have gone?'

'My sister, Tibby, is attempting to,' Tom replied. 'But the castle still smells like a hospital no matter how many armfuls of flowers she makes me carry inside. Yesterday she had me and Harold all over the countryside cutting hawthorn blossom from the hedges. And something else that smelt like cat's pee.'

Lydia spluttered with laughter. 'Poor you!'

'Your sister has the right idea,' said Minnie kindly. 'You can never have too many flowers in the house. She'd be very welcome to come and help herself to some of ours.'

'Yes,' Lydia encouraged. 'You must bring your sister over here. Mummy grows the most sweet-smelling flowers in the county.'

'Judging by the delicious scent around us,' Tom said, 'I have to agree.'

'And how is your father?' asked Minnie. 'Does he keep in good health?'

Esmie saw a frown flit across Tom's brow. He gave a soft grunt. 'My father is in rude good health, thank you.'

Esmie thought back to her few months of nursing at The Anchorage. The old colonel had been bad-tempered and constantly harangued her and her fellow nurses. One minute he was calling them lazy and the next accusing them of molly-coddling and overindulging the patients. 'Shirkers the lot of them,' he used to grumble. 'Send them back to the Front. My daughter, Tibby, has more courage in her little finger than these weaklings. Drives lorries in France, don't you know?' Esmie could not remember the colonel ever mentioning his son, Tom.

Tom shifted in his chair and began jiggling his leg. 'Would you permit me to smoke, Mrs Templeton?'

'Of course she would,' Lydia said at once. 'Mummy doesn't mind a bit. Would you like one of Daddy's Turkish ones?'

'No thanks,' said Tom, reaching into the pocket of his white trousers and pulling out a battered silver cigarette case. He offered them round but everyone refused. They watched him light up, inhale deeply and blow out smoke.

'How about we get on with our game of tennis?' Harold suggested.

'Yes, let's,' Lydia agreed, jumping to her feet and leading the way. 'It's all set up. I think we should play mixed doubles, don't you?'

Harold smiled. 'Splendid. Can I partner you, Lydia?'

She hesitated. Esmie thought her friend was about to refuse, but then she beamed at the doctor. 'Of course. If you're as good as I remember, then we'll have an unfair advantage.'

Harold laughed and reddened at the compliment. They went ahead, Lydia reminiscing about tennis games before the War. Tom fell in beside Esmie.

'I hope you're a good player, Miss McBride, because I'm very rusty.'

Esmie's pulse quickened at his sudden attention. Her throat felt tight and her voice came out as a croak.

'I'm afraid I'm average.'

'I doubt that,' he said.

She shot him a startled look. What did he mean? Was he talking about tennis or was he teasing her? Her cheeks were burning. She wanted to make a witty riposte but couldn't think what to say. She was baffled by her sudden gaucheness in his presence. Was she inhibited by Lydia's interest in the captain? Her friend might be showing Harold attention at that moment but Esmie knew that she was just being friendly. She could tell that Lydia had been instantly attracted to Tom too; the minute her friend had stepped onto the terrace to greet him she had begun to flirt with him.

The grass court was in full sunshine and, unusually, there was no sea breeze. Bees droned and the air was pungent with the smell of lilac blossom and wild garlic. Esmie, constricted by her long skirts and high-necked blouse, was hot before they even started to play. How she wished she was still in her old tennis skirt that she had shortened to allow her to run more freely.

She hurtled around the court, getting in Tom's way and mistiming her shots. They quickly lost the first four games.

'How about you stay close to the net and I'll cover the back of the court?' he suggested.

After that, they won the next two games but then Lydia began targeting Esmie as the weaker partner and swiftly won the first set. Harold, she noticed, was much more competitive than his friend and made a good partner for Lydia who was just as eager to win. Their opponents won the second set without conceding a game. Esmie kept apologising to Tom.

'I appear to be the rusty one. Sorry.'

'Don't be,' he said. 'It's just a game.'

'During the War I used to dream of being here and beating Lydia at tennis,' Esmie admitted ruefully, pushing messy tendrils of hair behind her ears. 'Now I can't wait for tea to stop play.'

Tom smiled and murmured, 'I hope they give us something stronger than tea after this ordeal.'

Esmie laughed. 'If Mr Templeton returns you'll be in luck.'

'What are you two finding so amusing?' Lydia called. 'I don't think you're taking this at all seriously.'

'Do you want to take a break for some juice?' Harold asked.

'Perhaps we should change partners?' Lydia suggested. 'Let's give them a chance, Harold.'

'Shouldn't we finish this match first?' he said with a look of disappointment.

'Poor Esmie looks exhausted,' said Lydia, already walking towards the other end of the court. 'Come on, Esmie; we'll swap.'

Tom raised a quizzical eyebrow. Esmie gave him an apologetic shrug and did as she was told. She could tell that Tom didn't care about the outcome of the match.

After that, the sides were more evenly matched. Esmie followed Harold's hissed suggestions and encouragement and her serving became more accurate. The game grew fast-paced. Lydia and Tom moved around the court as if they had played together often, each anticipating the moves of the other. Esmie thought what a strikingly good-looking couple they made, with Tom's dark Lomax looks and Lydia's fair beauty.

The set was neck and neck when a shout rang out and Esmie missed her return shot. Jumbo Templeton bowled around the corner with two yapping terriers at his heels. He was even more portly than Esmie had remembered, his bulky body straining at the seams of his brown suit. His jowly face under his fedora creased into a smile of delight on catching sight of his guests.

'Esmie, my dear! So sorry not to be here when you arrived.'

She went to greet him and they kissed cheeks. The dogs, Bramble and Briar, growled and jumped at her jealously. She had never taken to them, nor they to her.

'Daddy, you're interrupting our game at a crucial moment,' Lydia admonished.

'Oh dear, am I?'

Esmie smiled. 'No, you've come just in time to save me from complete humiliation.'

'Harold, dear boy!' Jumbo clapped the doctor on the shoulder as he shook his hand. 'And Captain Lomax. Welcome to our home.'

'Thank you,' said Tom as they also shook hands.

'I've been told by my wife to say that tea is being served on the terrace,' said Jumbo. 'But if you need a few more minutes . . .'

'Tea sounds wonderful,' Esmie answered, wiping her brow with a handkerchief. 'I think Harold and I will concede the final set to Lydia and Captain Lomax. What do you say, Harold?'

Harold bowed gallantly in agreement.

'Oh, I suppose we *were* about to beat you,' said Lydia, turning and giving Tom a broad smile. 'Follow me, Captain Lomax. You are about to taste the best Victoria sponge cake this side of the Border.'

He grinned and held out his arm to her. 'A bold claim indeed.'

A leisurely tea led on to pre-dinner drinks. Neither of the young men seemed in any hurry to leave and the Templetons pressed them to stay for dinner.

'We can hardly go into dinner in our tennis whites,' Harold said. 'Should we go home and change first?'

'We don't stand on ceremony here,' said Jumbo.

'You are quite acceptable as you are,' Minnie agreed. 'Unless you would feel happier changing for dinner?'

'I'm perfectly happy as I am,' said Tom, taking a large gulp of his whisky. 'It's a relief to find such refreshingly unstuffy attitudes. The Army would have you changing five times a day.'

'Bit of an exaggeration, Lomax,' laughed Harold.

'Four times then.' Tom grinned and drained off his whisky.

'Well, Esmie and I hold to higher standards,' said Lydia, standing up. 'We shall certainly be changing for dinner.'

'Thank goodness for that,' Esmie murmured. As she made to follow her friend, she caught Tom's amused expression.

'Oh, by the way, Minnie dearest,' said Jumbo. 'As I was coming over from the kennels, I saw Ivy gathering up clothes from the bushes. Any idea why?'

Lydia and Esmie exchanged glances and burst into laughter.

'We'll explain later,' said Lydia, pulling Esmie with her.

As they left, Esmie heard Minnie sigh happily and say, 'Isn't it fun having the girls back together again?'

The men chorused in agreement, and Jumbo ordered Baxter to refill their glasses.

All through dinner Esmie and Harold swapped stories about their work and experiences during the War and Esmie's current work at the psychiatric hospital at Vaullay. She found his tales of the North-West Frontier fascinating, though the current situation was troubling the doctor. No sooner had he left on leave than the Afghans had started raiding over the border. All the time she was aware of raucous conversation at the other end of the table between Lydia and Tom but Harold monopolised her, eager to hear all about the Scottish Women's Hospitals.

'Tell me about your time in Serbia,' Harold said. 'You must have had such courage to endure that terrible retreat with the Serbian army over the mountains to Albania.'

He was surprisingly easy to talk to. Even though she had only ever spoken of it to Aunt Isobel, who had been in Serbia with her, Esmie found herself easily telling him about what had happened.

'It wasn't just the remnant of the army the Serbs were trying to save,' she told him. 'Belgrade had fallen and there were literally hundreds of thousands of people trying to escape – it was like a nation going into exile.' She shuddered at the memory of the desperate hordes of people, their carts and horses mired in the mud, camping out each night as the temperatures plummeted. 'And it was the worst time of year to be travelling. It took weeks to reach the mountains and when we did the snow had come and people were already starving. Some locals let us sleep in their barns and shared a little milk but others chased us away, too frightened for their own survival to help. We did what we could to save people – binding up their frostbitten feet with sacking and bartering for food with what few possessions we had left – but we were only thirty nurses and our efforts were futile.'

'It must have been truly terrible,' Harold sympathised. 'But I don't believe your work would have been in vain. You must have brought great comfort to those you helped.'

'The Serbs were such spirited people,' said Esmie, grateful for his kind words. 'A small nation like us Scots and equally as proud. I saw soldiers kiss their cannons and roll them into icy rivers rather than surrender them to the enemy. And the young boy conscripts that they were trying to save – they suffered terribly – and most of them perished. It was all so heartbreaking.'

Esmie broke off, the memory of the dying children too harrowing to put into words. She quickly changed the subject and asked Harold more about India instead. It was only when the Templeton parents announced they were retiring to bed that Esmie was able to join the others. Lydia, in high spirits, got Tom to carry the gramophone out onto the terrace where she kicked off her shoes and showed them how to dance to ragtime.

Harold, baffled by the dance, collapsed panting into a wicker chair.

'Enough,' he cried, 'it's giving me indigestion.'

Esmie sat down too, exhausted by the long day. Lydia was laughing hysterically at Tom's exaggerated moves. When the record finished, Lydia told Tom to wind up the gramophone and play it again. Instead, he fumbled for his cigarettes, swaying unsteadily as he lit a fresh one, and Esmie realised he was quite drunk. Lydia pinched the cigarette from him and took a long drag. Tom laughed and lit another one for himself.

Esmie turned to Harold.

'Tell me more about India. Will you be returning soon?'

He hesitated. 'I'm due back off furlough in September but this new conflict with the Afghans is very worrying. Our local Pathans might feel they have to join forces with their Afghan cousins.'

'Your wily Pathans are the ones who are fuelling the fighting,' Tom said, startling Esmie; she hadn't realised he was listening in to their conversation. 'Deserting their Indian regiments now that war is over and taking Indian Army weapons with them.'

'That's purely rumour,' said Harold.

'Ah, Guthrie, you are an incurable romantic when it comes to your Pathans – they're all noble savages in your eyes.'

'Not true, Lomax. But I do feel responsible for my people at Taha and worry about them.'

Esmie could see the subject was agitating Harold and wished she hadn't raised it again. 'I hope you'll get reassuring news from the mission soon, Dr Guthrie.'

'Don't worry,' said Tom with a mirthless laugh, 'we'll drop a few bombs on Kabul and send in the Gurkhas to do our dirty work and it'll all be over in a jiffy.'

There was an awkward pause.

'Does it get very hot during the summer at the mission?' Lydia surprised Harold with her sudden question. Esmie knew it was because Lydia didn't want the evening spoilt with talk of the conflict in far-off Afghanistan.

Harold looked at her nonplussed and then recovered his poise.

'Yes, scorching,' he replied. 'It's semi-desert at Taha where I live. But sometimes I get away for some R & R to Murree in the hills when it gets unbearable.'

'Don't believe him,' Tom said. 'Guthrie hardly ever takes local leave. Works himself too hard – always has done. He was like that at school too.'

Lydia blew out smoke and arched her eyebrows in amusement. 'And you weren't, I suppose?'

'I was a hopeless scholar,' Tom admitted. 'Harold wrote half my essays but I failed most of my exams. Father decided that only the Army and India would be the saving of me.'

'Which it obviously was,' said Lydia.

Tom gave a short laugh and reached for the half-empty whisky decanter. 'Well, it got me out from under my father's feet, which was a relief to both of us. Mind if I help myself to another nightcap?'

'Of course not,' said Lydia. 'Pour me one too, will you?'

Esmie was surprised; Lydia had always dismissed whisky as an old man's drink. Her friend clinked glasses with Tom, took a swig and tried not to grimace.

'I bet you enjoy the soldier's life,' Lydia said with a coquettish smile. 'All those mess dinners and playing polo and chasing tribesmen. A boy's dream, isn't it?'

'You're right, of course, Miss Templeton,' he said. 'It's one long bloody good picnic.' Tom raised his glass. 'To the Army and all that's left of it!' Then he drained his drink.

Lydia laughed and copied his gesture. Esmie glanced at Harold and saw his look of concern. She didn't think Tom had been joking and heard the suppressed anger in his words. He seemed to be spoiling for an argument.

Harold stood up. 'Lydia; thank you so much for having us to dinner – it's been splendid – but I think it's time we left you in peace.'

'Oh, but we haven't finished dancing yet,' Lydia cried.

'Perhaps another evening,' Harold said.

'Don't spoil the ladies' fun,' Tom protested.

Harold looked undecided. Esmie came to his aid.

'I'm totally exhausted too – I had such an early start. Let's leave more dancing till tomorrow.'

'What a spoilsport you are,' Lydia complained.

'No, we must do what Nurse McBride orders,' Tom said in mock obedience. 'She's the expert on what's best for our health. Plenty of rest, isn't that right?'

Esmie eyed him. 'Yes, rest is essential.'

'Rest and fresh air,' said Tom. 'I heard you over dinner. Do what the Boches do. Drink mineral water and chop wood, wasn't it? Healthy outdoor activity is the key to a fit body and a sound mind.'

Esmie was irritated by his sarcastic tone. Why was he needling her? She had no idea Tom had overheard her talking about Isobel Carruthers' enthusiasm for treating the mentally ill with Dr Lahmann's *Luftbad* – 'the Air Bath' – a therapy popular in pre-war Germany.

'Why should it matter that it's a German idea?' she challenged. 'It seems to work for some patients and that's what matters – especially for those suffering the effects of shell shock. They get relief from being outdoors and doing activities such as walking and swimming, and keeping occupied with physical tasks that also give them a sense of worth. Such as chopping wood.'

Tom was reaching for the decanter again. Harold put a hand on his arm.

'Don't you think you've had enough?'

'Just a wee one for the road,' said Tom, shrugging him off. 'This is the way simple soldiers like me get a good night's sleep.'

He reminded Esmie of some of her patients who had turned to liquor to try and blot out their memories of war. She could only imagine what horrors he must have witnessed in four years of slaughter – and he had lost a young wife too before that. Yet no one mentioned Mary Lomax. She felt a pang of pity for the man.

'Whisky's more likely to keep you awake, Captain Lomax,' Esmie said more gently. 'I could recommend an elixir if you have trouble sleeping.'

He laughed. 'There's no need. I'm not one of your lame ducks, Nurse McBride.'

'Not lame ducks,' Esmie said, bristling. 'They are men who are suffering deep mental pain – and they deserve just as much care and attention as if they had physical injuries. Given time, many of them will recover well. I've seen it happen.'

'At The Anchorage no doubt?'

'Yes, at The Anchorage.'

'And how do you know they weren't a bunch of cowardly shirkers?' he demanded. 'If we'd all decided to convalesce and go for nice walks, we'd have lost the War.'

Esmie sparked back. 'You sound just like your father. He pooh-poohed what we were doing too but we nursed many back to health and active service.'

'I'm nothing like my father!' Tom snapped. 'But the old man had a point. I knew men who claimed shell shock who were nowhere near the guns.'

'It's not just proximity to gunfire that causes mental stress – we know that now. Other things can trigger it like the death of a close comrade or bad news from home—'

'Goodness, Esmie!' interrupted Lydia. 'What a grim topic of conversation. The poor captain won't want to come back.'

Esmie bit back a retort; it was he who had provoked the argument. But she shouldn't have allowed him to rile her – or compared him to his father knowing it would probably goad him.

'I'm sorry, Captain Lomax,' she said.

Tom's stern look vanished. 'No, it is I who should apologise. Forgive my boorish behaviour, Miss McBride.' He turned to Harold. 'Guthrie, take me home before I cause any more offence.'

'No offence taken,' said Lydia quickly. 'And you will call again, won't you? Bring your sister – I'd like to meet her.'

The men said their goodbyes and climbed into Harold's car. Lydia waved them away. Esmie, tired out, longed for bed. She began clearing up the records.

'Oh, leave all that,' said Lydia. 'The servants will see to it.' She led them indoors.

Lydia, smelling of whisky and cigarette smoke, followed Esmie into her bedroom and threw herself down on the bed with a sigh. 'It's wonderful to have you here again. It's just like old times, isn't it?'

Esmie thought how it could never be like before – those innocent times were like a distant dream – and she had changed too much. But she nodded in agreement. 'It's wonderful to be here.'

'And I'm so pleased to see you getting on well with Harold,' said Lydia. 'You've got so much in common with you being a nurse and him a doctor.'

'He's very fond of you though,' Esmie pointed out.

'And me of him,' said Lydia. 'But we're not a good match – Harold is too serious and not very good-looking.'

Removing the neat pile of clothes retrieved by the maid, Esmie sat down and stifled a yawn, hoping that Lydia wasn't embarking on one of her long midnight chats.

'Whereas Tom Lomax is very handsome,' Lydia continued. 'And he makes me laugh. Do you think he likes me too?'

'He seemed to be enjoying your company a lot,' said Esmie.

'Yes, he did, didn't he?' Lydia giggled and sat up. 'I'll send over an invitation tomorrow – and press him to bring that strange sister of his. Harold says the captain is very close to her; they're twins, you know.'

'No, I didn't know. From what I remember of Tibby, they don't look alike.'

'No, thank goodness,' Lydia smirked. 'If the weather holds we can go for a picnic or out in Daddy's boat. You can keep Tibby in conversation while I get to know the captain better.'

Esmie laughed. 'You'd do better inviting your mother along so she can talk about flowers to Miss Lomax.'

'Certainly not. I don't want Mother around while I set about seducing the captain.'

Esmie's eyes widened. 'Is that what you're planning to do?'

'Yes,' Lydia said with a grin. 'I decided the minute I saw him – I'm going to be the next Mrs Thomas Lomax.'

'Lydia, you hardly know the man!'

'I know him enough to like what I see,' she retorted. 'And I'm certainly not going to sit around Templeton Hall turning into an old maid like some pathetic Miss Havisham.'

Esmie was shocked by her friend's calculating attitude and she was far from sure that Lydia would be good for the troubled captain – or he for her. But Esmie kept quiet. Lydia was tipsy and might have changed her mind by the morning; her whims came and went quickly.

'You're not to pick arguments with him,' Lydia said. 'And don't be standoffish. You were quite rude when you were first introduced.'

Esmie blushed, remembering how her physical reaction to first setting eyes on Tom was like receiving an electrical shock. 'Sorry, I didn't mean to be.'

'I want us all to get on like a house on fire. Me with the captain and you with Harold.'

Esmie rolled her eyes. 'When did you become such a matchmaker?'

'Needs must,' Lydia said with a wink.

Esmie was adamant. 'I'm not going to marry Dr Guthrie just because you say so.'

'Darling Esmie,' Lydia said, her look suddenly concerned. 'You can't go on grieving for David forever – you deserve a little happiness and fun.'

Esmie's insides clenched with guilt. She hadn't been thinking of David.

'It has nothing to do with David,' she said. 'I'm just not attracted to Harold Guthrie – nor he to me.'

'Give it time,' Lydia replied. 'I think you'd be perfect for each other. Then when I go to India as the captain's wife, my best friend will be there too.' She grinned up at Esmie.

Esmie held out a hand and hauled Lydia to her feet, steering her out of the room. 'I'm not going to marry Dr Guthrie. Now go to bed.'

'Don't be a spoilsport,' said Lydia.

Esmie smiled and gently pushed her into the next-door bedroom. 'Good night, sleep tight.'

'Don't let the bed bugs bite,' Lydia finished the phrase they had used as girls.

Esmie closed the door and padded back to her room.

She thought sleep would come quickly but her mind whirred with the events of the day. Lydia's rash plans had shaken her. Marriage to Harold was a non-starter as far as Esmie was concerned. He was kind and attentive but a little bit too earnest. She admired the doctor for his dedication to his Pathan patients but she felt no attraction to him, unlike the darkly good-looking Tom Lomax.

Esmie's pulse quickened as the captain intruded into her thoughts again. If Lydia had set her heart on winning the colonel's son for her husband, then Esmie should leave well alone. Lydia was used to getting what she wanted. Besides, the captain was obviously as irritated by Esmie's work and conversation as she was at his off-hand manner when drunk. They didn't particularly like each other.

Sighing, Esmie kicked off the bedclothes and waited for sleep.

All about her was suffocating snow. The air was so cold it hurt to breathe it in. Beside her, the two boys she had tucked under the crook of her arm were sleeping, their uniforms in tatters and their soft hair encrusted in snow. A noise had woken her. A bird screeching. But when Esmie tried to sit up, she couldn't. Her ears rang with the discordant sound until Esmie realised it wasn't a bird but the screams of a woman.

'My baby, my baby!'

Esmie struggled onto numb feet and reached out for the distraught woman. 'Give her to me – I'll warm her up.'

But as soon as she took the frozen bundle from the woman, Esmie realised with horror that the baby was dead. She staggered back to the sleeping boys. She must wake them up and get them moving so that they didn't freeze to death too. They stared up at her with lifeless eyes, frost glinting on their lashes. Esmie tried to scream but no sound would come. All she could hear was the keening of the grief-stricken mother . . .

Esmie lurched awake, heart pounding. She stared around in panic. Where was she? It took a few terrifying moments to realise she was in the safety of her old bedroom in Templeton Hall. Relief engulfed her. The nightmare receded. It left her trembling and gulping for air. It was always the same bad dream; the horror of touching the dead baby, the screaming of the mother and the panic of trying in vain to revive the frozen boys.

Esmie put her hands over her mouth to smother a sob. It must have been talking to Harold about Serbia and the retreat over the mountains of Montenegro that had triggered off the nightmare. She hadn't been plagued with it for weeks and had hoped the traumas of the past were finally diminishing. She took deep breaths to calm herself.

Padding to the window, Esmie peered out at the tranquil garden lit by early morning light. Perhaps it was the argument with Tom Lomax about the effects of shell shock that were to blame for her disturbed sleep. She wondered if he had a sore head this morning and whether he would remember their fractious argument, and thought probably not. He would no doubt be still sleeping off his hangover. Well, let him deal with his demons as he saw best; she would not judge him or interfere. She knew what complete exhaustion from war was like. Only the care of Aunt Isobel and time in the Highlands had helped heal her own mental wounds as well as restore her vitality. She knew though that she was not the same carefree young woman as before the War.

Yet the War was over and she'd survived it where good men like David Drummond had not. Esmie felt the familiar gnawing pain at the thought of the Drummonds' son.

'Live your life to the full, dear Esmie,' Isobel had urged her. 'And that will be your way of honouring David's memory.' Esmie had promised that she would – and privately she hoped that by doing so she might in some small way make up for letting David down.

Chapter 2

Tom shot awake at the sound of a gun going off. He had no idea where he was. He sat up, heart thudding. They were under siege. Moments ago, he had been fending off snipers hidden behind a ridge of black rock . . .

He looked around him in confusion; it must have been a dream. He was in his bedroom in the tower of The Anchorage, its walls crowded with his amateur watercolour paintings and the sound of the sea crashing on the cliff below. The noise came again; an exhaust backfiring. Tibby must be going out.

Tom sank back. But his relief was short-lived. The sudden movement made his head throb as pain shot through his temples. Daylight hurt his eyes. The scar across his left shoulder from an old sniper wound ached more than usual. Why did he feel so ill? He squinted at the trail of discarded clothes across the threadbare carpet. Shreds of memory began to surface.

'Oh, God!' he groaned, pressing the heel of his hands to his sore head.

The Templetons' dinner party. He remembered the drinks before dinner and the meal – or some of the meal – and copious amounts of Jumbo's claret and whisky. Lydia had found him amusing; at least he remembered her laughing a lot. And hadn't they danced? He had a vague memory of a gramophone and Harold red-faced and sweating.

And Lydia's friend with the attractive eyes . . . Had he argued with her? Yes, he had. Why on earth would he do that? She didn't like him – he'd been aware of that the moment they'd been introduced – though he had no idea why she should take against him. She'd reluctantly partnered him at tennis and hadn't been very good.

Amy? Ellie? Esmie; that was it! Esmie McBride, daughter of the late Dr James McBride, a hale-and-hearty man who'd once reset Tom's broken arm when he'd fallen out of a tree. She was one of those modern girls who did what she wanted. Harold had told him how, unmarried, she'd gone abroad as one of Dr Inglis's medical women and put her life in danger. She'd been on the infamous Serbian Retreat. And she'd been engaged to David Drummond – or so Harold had thought – but the gentle, upright David had died right at the end of the War.

Tom sighed. No wonder Esmie held him in such little regard; he had none of David's good qualities. She must resent him surviving the conflict when her intended had not. Damn the War!

Gingerly, he sat up again and swung his legs out of bed. They'd argued about nursing – something about shell shock – and he'd been deliberately rude. She'd looked at him with knowing eyes as if she could read his thoughts and offered to source him some sort of sleeping draught. He didn't need her help or want her pity. It might be fashionable to go in for psychoanalysis but he would have none of it.

'You sound just like your father.' Esmie's stinging words came back to him. How that had annoyed him! His father was a bully and a snob; whereas he cared nothing for social standing. Yet in Esmie's eyes he was the privileged son and heir to The Anchorage. She probably thought he was wealthy and didn't need to work – just played at being a soldier – while she had had to go out and earn her own living, with her mother long dead and no father alive to support her. Perhaps that was why the nurse had taken against him; envy at his titled position.

Tom hauled himself out of bed and shivered. Even in this spell of good weather, his turret room was damp and draughty. In winter, ice formed on the inside of the narrow windows. Yet there were times in the broiling heat of India's hot season when he had yearned for this dank room and a cold sea fog to chill his bones.

He stripped off, relieved himself into the chamber pot and then plunged his head into a basin of cold water. The nearest bathroom was two floors below. On his return home, Tibby had warned him he would have to start emptying his own pot and filling his own water jug as they could no longer afford a chambermaid. As part of new economising measures, his sister had appointed herself as housekeeper and declared, 'And I'm certainly not going to be your pot-wallah or whatever you call maids in India.'

'Sweepers,' Tom had chuckled.

He stood in an old tin tub, poured the remains of the water over himself, towelled himself vigorously and then lit the first cigarette of the day. Wrapped in a towel, he sat smoking and thinking of Lydia. Now, there was an attractive girl; pretty face and gorgeous figure. The Templeton daughter was good fun, keen at sport and uncomplicated – she'd been openly flirtatious and he'd been flattered by her attention. He'd forgotten how pleasant banter with a beautiful woman could be. Not since Mary . . .

Tom ground out his cigarette. He would not allow himself to dwell on the past. From now on, he was going to look forward to the future. As he dressed, he wondered if he had made any arrangements to see Lydia again. He couldn't even remember getting home but assumed Harold had dropped him off. Good old Harold. He didn't deserve such a faithful friend. He'd go over to the Guthries' place later and apologise for getting so drunk, and find out if he needed to make further apologies to the Templetons – and Esmie.

Harold had seemed quite taken with the nurse – they had talked non-stop all through dinner. He suspected Harold had once thought romantically about Lydia – not that he'd ever said so as they didn't really talk about affairs of the heart – but it was obvious that Lydia wasn't interested in his friend. Besides, Harold would always put mission work before marriage. He had once said that it wouldn't be fair to take a wife into such a dangerous place as the North-West Frontier, so he had resigned himself to bachelorhood.

Since word had filtered through that the Afghans had started raiding into British India, the lawless borderlands would be even more hazardous. Yet Tom thought Esmie might be one of those rare British women who could handle living in such a harsh terrain with the ever-present danger of martial tribesmen.

For a moment, he thought about the slim young woman in the tennis whites, with her tendrils of flyaway hair that wouldn't stay pinned back. She had a sweet nose with a dusting of freckles but it was her grey almond-shaped eyes that were striking – or were they blue? The greyish-blue of the sea at Ebbsmouth on a cloudy day. He shook the thought from his mind and came to a resolution.

Today would be the day he confronted his father about the future. He had put it off for too long. Tom strode to the door, took a deep breath and clattered down the stone spiral staircase in search of the colonel.

Tom's nerve failed him and he decided he needed breakfast first to fortify him for the ordeal ahead.

While he was eating scrambled eggs – Tibby had shown him how to make them – his sister returned from the shops, staggering in with two hessian bags of vegetables. Tom jumped to his feet.

'You should have let me do that,' he said, taking one of the bags.

His sister gave a snort of amusement as she dumped the other on the table. 'Judging by last night, Tommy, I doubt you were in any state to help this morning. I had to help Harold get you upstairs without waking the old man.'

Tom grimaced. 'Sorry. Was I really that bad?'

She gave a hearty laugh. 'You were singing about Tipperary and jabbering about ragtime. And you tried to show me some dance steps but kept falling over. All quite entertaining.'

'Did I wake up Papa?' Tom asked, cringing inside.

'Luckily he's as deaf as a post,' said Tibby. 'Never heard a thing.'

'Thanks, Tibby,' said Tom, swinging an arm around her shoulders and planting a kiss on her rosy cheek.

She wiped it off and pushed him away. Shrugging off her long coat but keeping on her battered khaki hat, she busied herself unpacking the shopping.

Tom scrutinised his sister. 'Tibby, are you wearing my old polo jodhpurs?'

'Yes; what of it?'

'Bet that surprised the grocer.'

'I doubt it. He'd be more shocked if I walked in wearing a tea dress and a feathered hat.'

Tom chuckled. 'Well, you're welcome to them. I shan't be needing them again.'

Tibby paused and regarded him with round hazel eyes. 'Meaning?'

Tom hesitated. The only person who knew of his radical plan was Harold. He wanted to confide in Tibby – he nearly always did – but he was wary in case she tried to talk him out of it. She hated scenes between her brother and father. She was so much better at handling the colonel than he was. She coped with whatever life threw at her with a dogged spirit that he could only admire. Even the death of their mother when they were ten years old had not subdued Tibby for long, whereas his grief had been acute. For years he would bury his head under the bedcovers and cry silently for his beloved mother.

'You'll find out soon enough,' Tom answered. 'Is Papa in his den?'

'He was when I went out,' said Tibby. 'What are you up to, Tommy? You're not going to upset him, are you?'

'Stand by with the iodine and bandages,' Tom joked, but his stomach curdled with nerves.

'You haven't finished your eggs.'

'Not hungry,' said Tom.

'Oh, no,' Tibby said in dismay, 'that means you *are* going to upset him. Tell me what it is.'

Tom was striding to the door. 'You won't change my mind.'

'Tommy!' she called after him.

Swiftly, Tom took the stairs to the main hallway and swung through the green baize door that divided the servants' quarters from the family domain. The dining room was still cluttered with iron bedframes from its time as a hospital ward, though he and Tibby had made an effort to refurnish the drawing room and bring it back into use. All through the War, the colonel had clung on to the large downstairs library as his living quarters, from where he could observe the nurses wheeling invalids around the garden and shout at them if there was too much fraternisation.

These days the octogenarian Archibald Lomax, crippled with arthritis, emerged from his 'den' only for a morning perambulation round the grounds and a nightcap with Tibby in the drawing room before bed. Their old housemaid, Miss Curry, came in daily to wash him and serve him breakfast and lunch, leaving Tibby to arrange his evening meal. Tom had passed the lugubrious woman on the back stairs, clutching a pile of the colonel's washing, and given her a cheerful, 'Morning, Miss Curry; beautiful day!' To which she had shaken her head and predicted, 'It'll rain before the day's oot.'

Tom stood outside the library door and tried to calm his breathing. How often as a boy had he hesitated here, summoned by his father, bracing himself for punishment of some minor misdemeanour? His buttocks tingled at the memory of the regular beatings, yet he had long forgotten what they had been for.

He took a deep breath and knocked on the door. There was no answer. Tom rapped louder.

'Yes?' his father barked. 'Come in!'

As Tom entered the darkly panelled room, a familiar fetid smell enveloped him; toast, incontinence, dusty books and smoke from the coal fire that was kept alight throughout the year. The colonel, his back to the door, sat hunched over a vast table by the window, contemplating an array of metal toy soldiers. His shoulders looked shrunken in the large captain's chair, his neck thin under wispy grey hair, and the hand that held up a toy lancer to the light was veined and tremulous. Tom felt a twinge of pity. How vulnerable and alone he looked; an old man who had married in middle-age but outlived his young wife by twenty-three years.

Then his father swung round in his chair and his gaunt face, framed in white side-whiskers, puckered in a frown.

'Oh, it's you. What do you want?'

Tom's heart began to thud. 'A moment of your time, sir.'

Archibald pursed his lips. 'Can't you see I'm busy, boy?'

Tom gripped his hands behind his back. They were slippery with sweat. 'Obviously very busy,' he muttered.

'What was that? Speak up, for God's sake!'

Tom raised his voice and took a couple of steps forward. 'It won't take long, Papa.'

'Very well.' The colonel put down the toy soldier and gave him a sour look. 'I suppose you're after more money but I can't raise your allowance. You'll just have to draw in your horns like Tibby has or pay your own mess bills.'

Tom hid his irritation. Had his father forgotten that he'd stopped his meagre allowance eight years ago in disapproval of Tom marrying? '*No officer should marry before thirty*,' his father had declared. Aged twenty-five, Tom, in a rare act of defiance, had secured the permission of his commanding officer and married Mary Maxwell, his childhood sweetheart.

'I'm not asking for money,' Tom said. 'I'm not asking for anything.'

'What then? Are you wanting to marry again? Can't leave it too long. High time you got on with providing an heir for The Anchorage.'

Tom winced at the tactless words. With such lack of charm, how had his father ever won his mother's heart?

'No, I have no plans to marry again – not yet at least.' Tom wondered if he would ever be ready to replace Mary or risk losing someone so dear. He never wanted to experience that much pain again.

'Well, spit it out,' his father said.

Tom swallowed. 'I—I've come to a decision, sir. About my future. Well, it's already decided. This is just to let you know. It's not just spur of the moment. I've thought about it a lot – thought it through – and I know it's the right thing – for me, at least.'

'Stop talking in riddles, boy. You never can get to the point. Always waffling on, just like your mother. Thought what through?'

Tom's chest thumped. 'I'm leaving the Army – I've resigned my commission.'

Archibald cupped his hand to his ear as if he'd misheard. 'What was that?'

'I'm not going back to the Peshawar Rifles,' Tom said.

His father gaped at him in utter disbelief. For a moment he was speechless, and then he was pushing himself to his feet with a roar.

'You've done *what*? Is this one of your damnable pranks?'

'No,' said Tom, standing his ground. 'I'm no longer in the Army. My days of killing are over.'

His father advanced towards him, his face turning crimson. Even at eighty, the colonel was as tall as his son. He glared at him with pale blue eyes.

'Why?' he demanded. 'Have you been cashiered?'

'No, sir, I've done nothing wrong but I've had enough of soldiering.'

'Done nothing wrong?' Archibald cried. 'No Lomax has ever resigned his commission – *ever*! And for nothing. It's shameful!'

Tom bunched his fists at his side, trying to stay calm. A familiar wave of humiliation washed through him. But he would not be cowed.

'I've done my bit for king and country, Papa. I've done what you wanted – followed in your footsteps in the Rifles. But I've had enough. I'm going to do something I want now.'

His father was shaking with rage. 'You ungrateful boy! I pulled strings to get you into my old regiment – your grandfather's regiment. He fought in the Mutiny – I fought in Afghanistan. You can't just turn your back on all that family history and honour. And to do what? Don't think you can lounge around here spending my money. I've let you grow soft. You don't have the backbone for India. You're weak and foolish like your mother – always have been.'

Tom felt anger pump through him. 'I hope I am like my mother. She would have understood. And I'm not turning my back on India,' said Tom. 'I'm buying a hotel in Rawalpindi.'

Archibald exploded. 'Pindi! A hotel? You're going to be a bloody *box-wallah*?'

'Yes, and why not? It's an honest trade – providing food and shelter and a bit of good cheer. Better than running around playing hide-and-seek with the Pathans.'

'How dare you?' his father cried. 'You dishonour all the brave men who have sacrificed their lives to keep India safe from those brigands and murderers.'

'And what is honourable about bombing men on horseback from the air?' Tom said scathingly. 'Because that's what the future of warfare on the Frontier will be like from now on.'

Archibald's look turned glacial. 'All I ever wanted was a son to make me proud – to make the Lomaxes proud – but you have been nothing but a disappointment to me. Tibby should have been the boy – she has ten times your spirit.'

'I agree,' Tom said, holding his father's gaze.

'If you go ahead with this tawdry little business venture, I'll disinherit you,' Archibald threatened. 'Tibby will get everything.'

Tom smiled. 'Go ahead – she's welcome to it.'

The colonel raised his hand and slapped Tom's face hard. They glared at each other. Tom fought down the urge to punch his father back. Just then, Tibby rushed in.

'What's all this shouting?' she demanded. 'You've set the dogs barking.'

'Get him out of here!' Archibald bawled.

Calmly, Tibby steered her brother through the doorway. 'Tommy, make yourself scarce. I'll see to Papa.'

Tom didn't trust himself to speak but he probably didn't need to. Knowing Tibby, she would have been listening at the keyhole, ready to intervene. Behind him he heard his sister cajoling their father back into his chair with soothing words. Tom marvelled at her patience and good humour. Clattering out of the castle, he fled into the fresh air. He was furious at being treated like a wilful child and yet elated that he was standing up to his hateful father. Tom punched the air and set off down the drive.

Chapter 3

Esmie was writing letters in the drawing room when Harold's car appeared on the drive. She noticed with alarm that Tom was in the passenger seat. He leapt out of the car, brandishing an enormous bunch of what looked like twigs and wild flowers.

Lydia appeared from the terrace where she'd been half-heartedly throwing a ball to Bramble and Briar, waiting for something more exciting to happen. Esmie saw her greeting them with a wide smile as Tom thrust the strange bouquet into her arms. Lydia laughed and turned, pointing at the drawing-room windows. She caught sight of Esmie and beckoned her outside. Reluctantly, Esmie abandoned her letter writing.

'Captain Lomax has come to apologise,' Lydia told Esmie as she joined them on the terrace, handing her the wild flowers. 'I told him there was absolutely no need.'

Tom gave Esmie a wary glance. 'My friend Guthrie tells me otherwise. And from what I recall of last night, I was unconscionably rude, Miss McBride. Please forgive me.'

He looked suddenly boyish and unsure.

Esmie nodded and smiled. 'Apology accepted, Captain Lomax.'

He grinned in relief. 'Thank you.'

'Good,' said Lydia. 'Now that that is sorted, we can have some refreshment.' She rang the bell on the table and when Baxter appeared, she ordered lemonade and shortbread. 'And take the flowers away and put them in water, please.'

As they settled into cane chairs, Lydia turned to Tom. 'I tried ringing you at The Anchorage to arrange a boat trip. Got your sister Tibby. She didn't know where you were but thought you'd probably be with Harold. What have you boys been up to?'

Esmie saw a look pass between Tom and Harold.

'Guthrie has come to my aid as usual,' said Tom. 'I had rather a big disagreement with my father this morning. I'm going to stay with Harold for a couple of days until things simmer down.'

'Oh dear,' said Lydia. 'Can we ask what about?'

Tom shrugged. 'I don't want to bore you with our family squabbles.'

Lydia grinned. 'I never find family squabbles boring. Domestic harmony can be far more tedious.'

Tom gave a surprised laugh.

Harold said, 'Why not tell them. It's nothing to be ashamed of.'

'Yes, do,' encouraged Lydia.

Tom scratched his chin. 'Very well. My father is rather annoyed because I've resigned my commission.'

The women stared at him.

'You're no longer in the Indian Army?' gasped Lydia.

Tom shook his head. Esmie saw Lydia trying to hide her shock as she absorbed the news and her dream of being a captain's wife suddenly vanished.

'But why?' asked Lydia. 'I thought you loved the soldier's life?'

'No, not really,' said Tom frankly. 'It was what my father wanted for me. Then with the War . . . Well, I've had enough. It's time for something different.'

'So what will you do instead?' Lydia probed.

'I'm buying a hotel in Rawalpindi in northern Punjab. It's a very pleasant town with a large army cantonment and plenty of social life. I think I can make a good business of it.'

'You'll be a splendid host,' said Harold.

'And it's near the hills so I can get away for a spot of *shikar* from time to time.'

'*Shikar*?' Lydia queried.

'Hunting game and shooting birds,' Tom explained. 'It'll be a grand life.'

'Goodness, a hotel,' Lydia said. 'It all sounds rather glamorous.'

'Well, I'm not sure about that . . .' Tom shrugged.

'Oh, Daddy knows lots of hoteliers who have made pots of money – it's all about location and clientele.'

Esmie smiled to herself. She admired her friend's unfailing optimism, undaunted by this sudden turn of events. Lydia, with her style and engaging manner, would make an excellent hotelier's wife; as long as someone else was employed to do the hard work.

'My needs aren't great,' said Tom. 'I just need enough for a comfortable life in India – and not to have to rely on my father.'

'Oh, I'm sure Colonel Lomax will come round to the idea given time,' said Lydia.

Ivy appeared carrying a tray of drinks. They paused while Baxter supervised the maid and handed around biscuits. When the servants had gone, Lydia took up the conversation again.

'And what does your sister think of your bold plan?'

Tom looked embarrassed. 'I'm afraid I hadn't discussed it with her before I told Papa. She told me to make myself scarce. But Tibby takes everything in her stride. If I told her I was going to the desert to live as a hermit, she would wave me off with a bag of provisions and tell me to keep my head out of the sun.'

Lydia laughed. 'Well, I hope you won't be going to that extreme to get out of your father's way.'

Harold suddenly turned to Esmie and asked, 'What do you think of Lomax's venture, Miss McBride?'

Esmie felt herself colouring. 'I—I have to admit I'm a little surprised – but I think it's a brave thing to do.'

'Brave?' Tom said with a grimace. 'My heart always sinks when people call me brave – it usually means they think I'm being foolish.'

'Not at all,' said Esmie with a smile. 'I too have experienced the occasional tongue-lashing from the colonel. I think it's admirable that you are standing up to your father and doing what you want to do. I hope it's a great success. I congratulate you, Captain Lomax. Do we still call you Captain?'

'Of course we do,' Lydia said at once. 'The military can keep their rank even after they retire, isn't that so?'

Tom gave a wry smile. 'I suppose we can but I'm not sure I want to.' He flashed a look at Esmie. 'Thank you, Nurse McBride. I'm glad it meets with your approval. My equivalent of chopping wood, perhaps?'

'Don't tease her,' said Harold.

Esmie held Tom's look. 'I'm sure running a hotel will be an excellent therapy for an ex-soldier,' she replied. 'Just be careful not to drink the profits.'

'Esmie!' Lydia admonished. 'Don't be so impertinent.'

Tom laughed loudly. 'Touché, Nurse McBride – I deserved that – and Guthrie has already said much the same thing.'

Harold nodded in agreement.

Lydia said, 'Let's have a celebration! A drive in the country and a picnic tea. We can take my car – it'll take all four of us.'

'I haven't actually bought the hotel yet,' Tom confessed. 'We're still agreeing terms.'

Lydia waved away his caution. 'I'm sure that's just a formality.'

'A picnic would be nice,' said Esmie. 'How about going to the beach and we could swim. The sea was looking so inviting this morning.'

Lydia rolled her eyes. 'Esmie's always been a sea-bather – quite mad. But if you gentlemen would like a swim then we can go via Harold's to pick up bathing costumes.'

Driving south, they stopped at a wide beach easily accessible from a farm track. Esmie threw off her bathing robe and ran yelling into the sea. The men followed; both were strong swimmers and struck out into deep water. Esmie noticed a scar on Tom's left shoulder, purple and jagged in the cold. It looked like a bullet wound that had been badly sewn up and she wondered if it gave him pain. But given his testiness when talking of war or the army, she decided not to ask.

The sea was still icy from winter and they did not linger. Lydia, with her frock hitched up into a belt, stood at the water's edge with towels, shouting encouragement.

Esmie went behind a rock to change back into her clothes. When she emerged, feeling invigorated, the others were lounging on tartan rugs munching cake. Tom was studying her. She glanced away quickly, flustered by his scrutinising look. Harold poured tea from a vacuum flask into a beaker and handed it to Esmie.

'Brava, Miss McBride! First in and last out. You put us men to shame but we've grown used to bathing in warm water in India.'

'Can you swim in Rawalpindi?' Lydia asked in interest. 'Isn't it a long way from the sea?'

'Yes,' said Tom. 'But some of the well-to-do have pools – tanks of water – where we can cool off in the hot weather.'

Lydia smiled. 'Sounds divine, doesn't it, Esmie?'

'I'd prefer swimming in rivers or lochs,' said Esmie.

'Then you'd love Kashmir,' said Tom. 'The Dal Lake at Srinagar is like swimming in a paradise garden.'

For a moment, their eyes met again. Esmie saw something in his look – yearning or sadness – and then he turned his attention back to Lydia.

'Gosh, I'd love to go there,' said Lydia. 'India sounds so romantic.'

Harold grunted. 'It's not all paradise gardens and maharajas – that's for the few. Life for most Indians is very tough and it can be hard for the British too, despite the luxury of the cantonments. Some of them never get used to the heat and find it all too alien.'

'We don't all live in primitive mud huts in the *mofussil* like you, Guthrie,' Tom teased. 'Pindi is a world away from Taha.'

'Oh, do tell us more about it, Captain Lomax,' Lydia enthused.

Tom began to describe the town nestled on the Punjab plain below the foothills of the western Himalayas, its leafy cantonment divided from the narrow-laned old city by the meandering Leh River. Esmie saw how his eyes shone with enthusiasm as he talked about the place.

'The Mall is wide but shaded with trees – early morning rides are excellent, especially in the cold season. And Topi Park is a charming wild area just on the edge of the army cantonment. Pindi's old quarter is fascinating – tall buildings that are so close together they keep the lanes shadowed and cool. You can hear the singing from the temples right across town . . .'

'But what is the housing like for the British?' Lydia interrupted.

'It's very good – bungalows with large gardens.' He gave a dry smile. 'Not the size of Templeton Hall, of course, but quite comfortable.'

Harold joined in. 'In the cantonment you would think you were in a British town – it has all the same facilities – post office, banks, shops, churches. There's even a Scots Kirk.'

'Yes, there's often a Scottish regiment stationed in Pindi,' said Tom. 'They make the town lively during Christmas Week and Hogmanay – always dances and parties going on. Then there's Race Week in February with competitions and polo matches.'

Lydia's eyes lit up. 'And is tennis played too?'

Tom nodded. 'Plenty of tennis at the Club. And cricket.'

'And there's a golf course,' said Harold.

'I love golf,' cried Lydia. 'Daddy's been teaching me. This Rawalpindi of yours sounds idyllic – like the best of Britain except in permanent sunshine.'

'It can rain cats and dogs when the monsoon comes,' Harold warned. 'And it gets extremely muggy from May onwards. That's why people head for the hills – even the regiments.'

'Except for dedicated men like you, Harold,' said Tom, 'who stick it out in the heat.'

Esmie raised an eyebrow quizzically. 'And hotel owners?'

He smiled wryly. 'I suppose so, yes.'

'Not the owners,' said Lydia. 'That's what managers are employed for. It's all about delegating responsibility but keeping a tight rein on the purse strings. That's what Daddy would say.'

An awkward silence followed. Esmie saw a flush creep into Lydia's cheeks as she realised she might have been too presumptuous.

'Of course that's entirely up to you how you run your hotel, Captain Lomax,' Lydia said hastily. 'It was just an observation. You should talk to Daddy about it. I'm sure he'd be happy to give you advice on being a successful businessman.'

'Thank you,' said Tom. 'It would be helpful to speak to someone who knows about these things. My family have little experience of commerce.'

'Your family run an estate,' Lydia pointed out. 'I imagine it's much the same. Keeping an eye on the servants, that sort of thing.'

'What's the hotel called?' Esmie asked.

'The Rajah,' said Tom. 'Except everyone calls it the Raj. Years ago the last two letters fell off. They fixed up the sign again but by then the nickname had stuck.'

'The Raj,' murmured Lydia. 'I think it sounds rather grand.'

'Not the grandest in Pindi by any means,' Tom admitted. 'The famous one is Flashman's, just off the Mall.'

As Lydia pressed Tom for more information about Rawalpindi society, Esmie's mind wandered. She knew little about India apart from what she had gleaned in geography lessons at school and the headmaster's scrapbook of newspaper cuttings about a royal visit there in

1910 – lavish pageants of princes on elephants, reviews of troops and tiger hunts. It hadn't really interested her and it didn't match up with Harold's description of his mission work in Taha. His talk of a peasantry eking out a living from a harsh land, their hospitality and good humour, had reminded her of the Gaelic-speakers she had grown up amongst in the Highlands.

She had been impressed by Harold's sense of purpose; saving lives and living in simplicity. She could understand the appeal of such a life; her work with the Scottish Women's Hospitals had had a similar intensity. In dusty, fly-blown camps, they had lived for the moment. Despite the gruelling nursing of casualties, they had found time to relish the simple pleasures; a river swim, a sing-song after dark or a snatched lie-down with a book in the shade of a tumbledown wall. Was she perverse in missing those days of comradeship and endeavour? The War had caused untold misery and devastation – countless numbers had been lost – and yet amid the hellishness she had felt intensely alive . . .

Esmie shivered. The wind was now coming off the sea and was strengthening.

'You're cold, Miss McBride,' said Harold in concern. 'Perhaps it's time to go.'

Esmie dragged her thoughts back to the present. 'Yes, I am a bit.'

'Stayed in the sea too long,' Lydia rebuked.

Tom was looking at her quizzically. Esmie hoped she hadn't appeared rude by letting her mind wander while he had been talking.

As they packed up, Lydia made arrangements for them all to go out in her father's boat the next day.

'Do you like to fish, Captain Lomax?' she asked.

'I love it,' he said eagerly.

Lydia smiled. 'Then we'll fish from the boat. As long as I'm not expected to touch the slippery things.'

For the rest of the week, while the good weather lasted, Lydia organised Esmie and the men into a non-stop round of activities and social get-togethers. They fished and picnicked, played tennis and croquet, went riding on horseback and for runs in the car. When the weather broke and rain set in, they took the train to Edinburgh and went to a tea dance. The four friends were soon on first name terms. Postcards of the French Riviera that came from Colin Fleming went unanswered; Lydia's attention was completely focused on Tom. She encouraged Tom to invite Tibby round to Templeton Hall and help herself to cuttings from their hothouses.

'She's very odd,' Lydia said to Esmie after Tibby's first visit. 'Do you think she ever takes off that awful old hat or does she sleep in it?'

'I think she's good fun,' said Esmie. 'And Tom seems very fond of his sister.'

'Yes he does – that's why I'm paying her attention – to impress him.'

'So, you're not put off by his hotel venture?'

'I can't pretend I'm not a little disappointed he's not going to climb the ranks in the army,' Lydia admitted. 'But I'm not one of those stuck-up girls like my sister who think you shouldn't marry into trade. Daddy made his money that way and I like all the luxury it brings. Besides, Tom won't be trade – just one of the gentry dabbling in a hobby which happens to be a hotel.'

'If his father carries out his threat to cut him off without a penny then Tom will have to rely on the Raj Hotel for a living,' Esmie cautioned.

Lydia gave her an astonished look. 'That's not going to happen. I'll win the old boy round, just you see.'

Esmie was enjoying this time of leisure; her companions were amusing company and she hadn't laughed so much in ages. It touched her to see how deep was the friendship between Tom and Harold. They had grown up together, gone to the same boarding school in Perthshire and both ended up in India a day's journey from each other. Tom made jokes at his friend's expense which Harold laughed off good-naturedly, yet it was obvious how much Tom admired the young doctor.

Esmie knew that her Aunt Isobel wasn't expecting her to hurry back to Vaullay and Lydia was insisting she stay for at least a month. But she was plagued by guilt that she hadn't yet been to see the Drummonds. She knew that they would be busy with the school summer term and Lydia kept discouraging her from visiting. 'It'll spoil my plans for the day,' she had chided. 'You can go one Sunday evening, when there's nothing much to do, can't you?'

After two weeks of mounting self-reproach, Esmie knew she could no longer delay a visit. She sent a note round to the Drummonds asking if she could call on them. No invitation came back. Her anxiety was tinged with relief. Perhaps she wouldn't have to face them. Then she felt ashamed. If Tom had been brave enough to stand up to his martinet father, then she should not shirk facing David's parents. And they might find comfort in talking to her about their son; they deserved whatever solace such a visit could bring. So Esmie wrote again. This time, William Drummond wrote back apologising for not responding sooner – he'd been away – and inviting her round for tea the following Saturday.

'I was going to organise a tennis match on Saturday,' Lydia said in dismay.

'Ask Tibby to make up a four,' suggested Esmie.

Lydia sighed. 'I suppose I could.'

As the day drew near, Esmie's dread mounted. Late on the Friday evening, after the Templetons had retired to bed, Esmie and Lydia sat on the swing seat of the upstairs balcony, where they had often gone to share girlish secrets long ago. The swing creaked as they swung gently back and forth. Lydia had been talking excitedly about a trip to the races she was planning for June, which was fast approaching.

'You're not listening, are you?' Lydia accused. 'What's bothering you? Is it the Drummond visit? I'm sure they'd understand if you called it off. They probably don't want to keep being reminded anyway.'

'Can I tell you something?' Esmie asked.

'Of course you can.' Lydia turned to scrutinise Esmie in the twilight.

'I *am* worried about seeing the Drummonds – because I can't bear it if they're kind to me. I feel such a fraud. So guilty about David.'

'What on earth do you mean?' Lydia was nonplussed. 'Guilty about what?'

'That I never loved him – not really – not the way he wanted me to.' Her chest tightened. 'I should have told him long ago, at the start of the War, but I didn't have the heart. He signed up so quickly for the Scottish Horse that it seemed cruel to take away his hope. Not that we ever actually talked about marriage.'

'So you were never officially engaged?' Lydia asked.

Esmie shook her head.

'So what are you feeling guilty about?'

'Last October – when the War was swinging in our favour – David wrote to me from France proposing marriage. I wanted to wait until I saw him again so I could let him down gently, so I wrote back putting him off – saying we could talk about it when he got home.'

'And?'

'He wrote again and said he had to have my answer and that saying yes would make him the happiest man in the world. But I couldn't pretend I loved him, so I told him I couldn't marry him – not ever.'

Lydia pressed her. 'And did David write back? What did he say?'

Esmie hung her head, her throat tight with tears. 'Nothing. The next thing I heard was that he'd been killed – two weeks before the Armistice.'

'So he might never have read your letter turning him down before he died?'

Esmie said tearfully, 'I don't know. It's possible he didn't. But I wish with all my heart I'd never sent it. He was such a kind, gentle fellow – he would have done anything for me – and yet I told him I didn't love him. How awful if it was the last letter he got before . . .'

'Well, he forced the issue,' said Lydia, sitting back. 'It would have been worse if you'd said yes and then broken off with him later. You've got nothing to be ashamed about. You didn't lead him on. He just misread your feelings for him.'

'I suppose so,' Esmie said hesitantly.

Lydia was adamant. 'It's not your fault David died so near the end of the War – it's just bad luck. So stop feeling guilty.'

Esmie gave her friend a grateful look. 'Thank you. You've always been good at making me feel better.'

'That's the spirit,' said Lydia. She stretched and yawned. Beyond the balcony darkness had fallen. In late May the night would be brief and daylight would soon be seeping into the sky. Lydia stood and pulled Esmie to her feet.

'Come on, bed. Tomorrow you can keep your visit brief. Give your condolences. Duty done. Then you don't have to think about David and the Drummonds again.'

Chapter 4

For the first time in nearly three years, Esmie stood on the doorstep of the Headmaster and Headmistress's house, heart thumping. Countless times she had entered here; first as a bewildered seven-year-old clutching her father's hand and later as an orphan regularly invited in for tea by the hospitable Drummonds. All was familiar; from the uneven sandstone steps worn down by generations of passing feet, to the heavy outer door that was always left open. The ivy over the lintel had grown more profuse but otherwise the house looked just the same.

She had a sudden keen sense of loss for her long-dead father, remembering how he would ignore the brass bell and stride up to the inner door, knock on the glass and go in before anyone answered. '*Hello! Is Drummond in his lair? Or the fair lady of the house?*'

Esmie took a calming breath and pulled the brass bell. Its ringing echoed and died. A young maid she didn't recognise answered its call and showed her into the drawing room to wait for her hosts.

Esmie's heart pounded faster. The room was in half-darkness, the yellow blinds pulled down to allow only muted sepia light to penetrate. There was a musty smell of neglect – a room no longer in regular use – that made Esmie feel queasy. The heavy gilt-framed paintings of stags and mountains that Esmie had loved because they reminded her of Vaullay, were shrouded in black gauze. Only a portrait of a man in uniform that hung over the unlit fireplace was uncovered. Peering closer,

Esmie gasped. It was David, though an older and more severe version than she'd ever known, his mouth unsmiling and his look resolute.

Esmie turned away, searching for the familiar. The piano that David had loved to play had been pushed into a corner. Its lid was shut and no music lay scattered across its top. The card table in the window – where they'd played during wet winter afternoons – was gone. In its place was a pedestal holding a vase of wilting flowers and a framed photograph of David in his graduation gown. His gaze was serious but there was a hint of a smile on his lips. Esmie's eyes prickled with tears; this was the David she remembered. Yet within a month of the photograph being taken, war had been declared and his ambitions in the law put on hold.

The door opened and Esmie swung round. William Drummond came hurrying in. He was the opposite of her father in looks; thickset, bearded and with brown beady eyes behind gold-rimmed spectacles. But just seeing him again conjured up her father too. They had been the best of friends – walking companions who had put the world to rights and shared a love of the countryside.

'My dear!' William took hold of her hands and squeezed them.

She wanted to kiss him on the cheek but felt inhibited. He may have been her father's closest friend in Ebbsmouth but he had also been her headmaster and classics teacher. So she smiled and said hello, her voice husky.

'Please sit down.' Guiding her into a bulky oak chair, William sat down opposite. Between them, a small table was covered in a white linen cloth. 'Tea's on its way and Maud will join us shortly. How are you?'

'I'm well, thank you. Lydia and her parents are spoiling me terribly.'

'I'm pleased to hear it. And Dr Carruthers? Has she settled back in Vaullay for good?'

'I'm not sure. She has great plans for the hospital so perhaps she will. She misses Edinburgh and her friends though.'

Sadness clouded his face. 'I imagine Edinburgh is not the same place as before the War. With Dr Inglis gone and . . .'

Esmie gripped her hands in her lap to stop them shaking. 'I'm so very sorry about David.'

William cleared his throat. 'Yes. You wrote such a kind letter. Thank you.' Abruptly he stood up and went to the door. 'I'll just make sure about tea. The new maid, you know . . .' He disappeared from the room.

Esmie felt clammy and hot, yet she shivered in the gloom. The room was a shrine to the Drummonds' lost son, yet she felt David's absence acutely.

After long minutes, William returned with his wife, followed by the maid who cautiously carried in a large tea tray that she plonked down on the table.

'Mrs Drummond.' Esmie stood up and went to greet her old headmistress, shocked at how old she looked in her black mourning dress. Her hair had turned completely white and deep lines were etched across her brow. Her once plump face sagged and looked colourless against the severe black of her clothing. In charge of the pupils' health and morals, Maud Drummond had always been a little intimidating. Esmie tried to dismiss the feeling that she was fifteen again and about to be admonished for untidy hair.

Maud gave her a strained smile.

'Isn't it lovely to see Esmie again?' William said, his voice falsely jovial. 'Just like old times.'

Maud, ignoring his remark, hovered over the young maid as she poured out the tea. 'Try not to splash it in the saucer, lassie.'

The nervous girl slopped the tea over the cup.

'Would you like me to pour?' Esmie offered.

'Maisie has to learn,' answered Maud in a tight voice.

As Maisie began handing out the tea, Esmie stifled a gasp. There were four cups poured and four plates holding slices of gingerbread. Surely the fourth place couldn't be for David?

Maud caught her look. 'Yes, in memory of David – gingerbread – his favourite.'

'Yes, it was,' said Esmie, still looking aghast at the extra place set for their dead son. 'I was just saying before to Mr Drummond how sorry I was about David—'

'Gingerbread without butter,' interrupted Maud. 'Doesn't need butter if the cake's fresh. We used to send him gingerbread when he was at the Front, didn't we, dear?'

William nodded.

'Very popular it made him with his fellow officers,' Maud said.

'I'm sure it did,' Esmie agreed.

Maisie shot her a glance of sympathy before hurrying from the room. Esmie took a sip of tea; her insides were too knotted to eat the cake.

'What he liked best though was getting letters,' continued Maud. 'Any news from home was better than any gift we could send. Red-letter days, David called them.'

'And he was a good letter writer himself,' said Esmie.

Maud gave her that direct assessing look that used to unnerve her as a schoolgirl; the woman had always seemed to know what her pupils were thinking. Esmie flushed under her gaze.

'Did David write to you a lot, Esmie?'

'From time to time, Mrs Drummond. More than I did, I'm afraid.'

'Well, it must have been more difficult for you,' said William generously. 'You were so often on active service – nursing at the battlefront. David spent most of the War in tedious postings in England, ferrying the wounded to hospital.'

'He spent the last year of the War in France,' Maud said, her tone suddenly indignant. 'Nobody could have done more for his country than our dear boy.'

'Of course not,' said William with a pained expression.

Esmie searched for something to say. She nodded at the portrait above the mantelpiece. 'It's a fine painting. When did David sit for that?'

William glanced at his wife, perhaps wary of speaking first.

'He didn't sit for it,' said Maud. 'We had it done from a photograph – one that was taken when he was last on leave.' She gave a wistful smile. 'It was last September. We had a lovely week of weather. David did all the things he enjoyed most – swimming off the rocks, playing the piano, reading.' She glanced at Esmie. 'You know; the sort of things the pair of you used to do together.'

Esmie felt as if a large stone was blocking her windpipe. She nodded.

'He was full of optimism,' Maud said, gazing back at the portrait. 'Planning what he'd do when the War ended. Practise law in Edinburgh. Have a holiday first. Go and visit you in Vaullay. But then you must have known all that if he wrote to you often.'

Esmie's cup rattled on its saucer as she placed it back on the table with a trembling hand.

'I'm glad he had a happy leave,' she said.

'So am I,' Maud said, her eyes filling with tears.

William nodded.

They sat in silence as the clock ticked towards four thirty. She had been there barely twenty minutes, yet it seemed an eternity. The grief in the room was palpable. Esmie couldn't bear to think what life had been like for the Drummonds these past seven months.

'Do you remember the time David brought that injured bird home?' Esmie asked softly. 'And Cook wanted to throw it to the cat but David kept it in a box in his room and wouldn't let anyone touch it.'

'He was always good with birds and animals.' William smiled.

'And every morning we expected the bird to have died in the night but it hadn't,' Maud recalled.

'He nursed it back to life,' said Esmie, 'until one day it just flew away. And then he cried and laughed at the same time because he was happy he'd made it better but sad it had gone.'

'Always a sensitive soul,' said William.

'He felt things more deeply than we ever did, that's all,' said Maud. 'It wasn't a weakness.'

Esmie coaxed them into more reminiscing. Briefly Maud's bleak mood seemed to lift a fraction and William laughed at silly anecdotes. As the clock chimed five, Maud said, 'Mr Drummond has to give a tutorial in a few minutes.'

'Goodness, I quite forgot,' said William.

Esmie got to her feet, relieved to be going. 'Thank you so much for the tea.'

The Drummonds stood too. 'It was good of you to come, my dear,' said William. 'Wasn't it, Maud?' When Maud didn't respond, William filled the pause. 'It's comforting to speak to someone who knew David as well as you did – and cared about him. We did so hope that, in time, you would become a dear daughter-in-law.'

Esmie felt her throat tighten with emotion. Did they know about David's proposal to her? Perhaps he had told them of his intentions on his final visit home. She was desolate that she would never have been able to fulfil their wishes had their son lived. She forced herself to ask. 'Did you hear from him after his last leave before he . . . died?'

'We have a precious letter,' said Maud, 'that told us how much he'd enjoyed being at home. It's the only thing that gives me comfort – to know we'd made him happy on his last visit.'

Esmie's pulse began racing. 'And did his C.O. return any letters from me with David's things?'

'Oh, the letters!' William cried. 'It quite went out of my head. Of course you must have them back. Maud, dearest, they're in your bureau, aren't they?'

'If you're sure you want them?' Maud asked.

'Please,' Esmie said.

Maud crossed the room to a corner in shadow and pulled down the lid on her writing desk. She opened the middle draw and retrieved a small bundle of letters. Esmie was ashamed that she had written so few over the four years of war. Her heart was hammering as she took them, resisting the urge to flick through and see if her final letter was among them. Perhaps it had never been delivered or if so it might have arrived after David was killed, so that he would never have known how his dreams had been dashed. If it was in the pile, she prayed that it was still unopened.

'Thank you, Mrs Drummond.' Esmie gave a nervous smile and pushed the letters in her jacket pocket.

They saw her to the door. William said, 'Please forgive me, Esmie, but I have to dash off and see to my exam pupils. You'll call again before you leave Ebbsmouth, won't you?'

Esmie said she would. With a distracted smile, William hurried off towards his study.

Esmie was stepping through the outer doorway when Maud stopped her with a firm hand on her arm.

'You won't find it in that bundle of letters.'

Esmie's heart lurched in fright. 'Find what?'

Maud's look bore into her. 'This,' she said, pulling a slim envelope from her dress pocket. Esmie instantly recognised her handwriting on one of Aunt Isobel's buff-coloured envelopes. Her last letter to David. The top edge had been neatly cut by a pen knife or letter opener. She felt sick.

'You've read it?' Esmie asked.

Maud's eyes blazed but her tone was icily calm. 'My poor boy,' she said, trembling. 'How could you write such cruel things? I never thought you could be so heartless. David adored you but you spurned him! How could you tell him that you never loved him? You played with his affections – with all our affections!'

Esmie gasped. 'You had no right to read my letter to David.'

'He was my son,' she hissed, 'so I had every right. You're contemptible! Coming here and pretending to be sorry our son is dead.'

'I am sorry,' Esmie protested, 'and I did care for David.'

Her eyes narrowed. 'Don't make it worse by lying. The only reason I allowed you to come and play out your little charade was for my husband's sake. He's a good man who has been devastated by David's loss. He's the one who insists on having the extra tea cup at every meal, and who had the portrait done. So I kept this nasty little letter from him – it would kill him if he knew what you'd written.'

Esmie's chest constricted as she tried to speak. 'I wish I hadn't sent the letter when I did, but it wasn't a cruel letter. It was affectionate but truthful. I wanted to have the chance to talk to him face-to-face but David demanded an answer from me and wouldn't wait. I never wanted to hurt David, just to make things clear between us.'

Maud shook with suppressed fury. 'Hurt him?' she cried. 'You killed him! Once he'd read it, he didn't want to go on – you gave him nothing to live for. He was reckless. His padre wrote and told us how he courageously went out looking for Germans in the enemy trenches to capture when it was all but over. Only a man with a death wish would do such a thing.'

Maud tore the letter in two and thrust it at Esmie. 'I will never forgive you! Your father would spin in his grave if he knew how you'd treated our son. That's how you repay our family's kindness to you all these years.' She shoved Esmie off the top step.

Esmie stumbled, almost losing her balance. 'I'm sorry,' she gasped.

Maud jabbed a trembling finger at her. 'I never want to see you again – so don't you ever come back here!'

Reeling from the woman's vitriolic outburst, Esmie fled down the path, gulping for air. She ran aimlessly, clattering into a steel hoop being bowled down the street by two boys. Ignoring the pain in her knee, she hobbled on, swallowing down the sobs that were choking her. But she couldn't outrun Maud's furious, grief-fuelled words that whirled in her head. '*You killed him! I never want to see you again – so don't you ever come back here!*'

In turmoil, Esmie did not know for how long she roamed the clifftops of Ebbsmouth, unheeding of those she passed in her hurry to escape the town. As the shadows lengthened, she found herself on the path leading away from the cliffs inland towards ancient St Ebba's church and its burial ground. The medieval building nestled in a sheltered glade under mature beech and oak trees. Esmie hurried into the cool of the churchyard and sought out her father's grave.

Crumpling onto the damp grass, she put her hand on the familiar gravestone and succumbed to the flood of tears she had held in check.

'Oh, Father!' she sobbed. 'I'm so sorry! I've let you down. I've caused so much grief. Poor David. Was I wrong to reject him? If I'd just pretended to love him then perhaps he'd be alive today . . . I can't forgive myself. If only you were here to tell me what to do. Mrs Drummond hates me but who can blame her? She's lost her only son and she'll never get over the pain. I know she won't – because I know what it's like to lose the person you love the most – I've never stopped grieving for you, dearest Father, *never*.'

Esmie buried her face in her hands and continued to weep. In her mind's eye, she could clearly see the father of her childhood: bald and smiling broadly under a yellowing moustache, smelling of pipe smoke; a slim-built man with a sinewy strength in his arms when he picked her up and swung her round. A man who made people smile the moment he walked into a room, who joked with passers-by about the weather and calmed squalling babies with Highland lullabies. A doctor who made others well but dropped down dead of a weak heart that no one knew he had. A widower who kept his grief private and never let it overshadow her growing-up. A father with a sense of fun who encouraged her to be adventurous but whose comforting hold was the safest place on earth.

As she felt his presence strongly, her sobbing began to ease. She became aware of birdsong and the soft trickle of the nearby stream. Her father would still have loved her no matter what mistakes she made in life; he would never have judged her.

A twig cracked nearby. Still on her knees, Esmie swung round, alarmed at the sound of footsteps. A tall figure dressed in tennis flannels loomed out of the trees.

'Sorry, I didn't mean to startle you. It's just I heard you . . .'

Esmie's pulse raced to see Tom Lomax standing before her. He was peering down at her in concern. What had he overheard? Only her anguish had made her speak her thoughts aloud. As he reached forward to help her up, she scrambled to her feet before he could touch her.

'I was just . . . This is my father's grave,' she explained.

'Yes, I see that,' he answered, stepping back. 'Sorry, I'm intruding.'

There was something vulnerable in his look that made Esmie say, 'No, you're not. Please don't go on my account.'

They eyed each other. 'I didn't expect to find anyone here this late in the day,' said Tom.

'Neither did I,' said Esmie, trying to calm her emotions. 'I thought you were playing tennis at Lydia's?'

Tom nodded. 'I was. Harold dropped me off – he's taking Tibby home.'

Then it struck Esmie what he was doing here; he had come from the direction of the Lomaxes' grave enclosure.

She made a guess. 'Have you been to see your mother's grave?'

Tom gave a sad smile. 'Yes.'

'But not with your sister?'

He shook his head. 'My sister thinks it's morbid. She doesn't understand why I still like coming here so long after Mama's death.'

Esmie glanced at her father's headstone. 'I understand,' she murmured. 'Do you talk to your mother here?'

'Not out loud,' he said, with the twitch of a smile.

Esmie coloured. 'I was upset.'

'Don't worry,' he said quickly, 'I didn't hear what you were saying. But I could tell you were distressed.'

'I'm all right.' She brushed at her damp cheeks.

'Why don't we sit for a minute,' he suggested, nodding at the bench by the church wall that was still in sunshine.

Esmie hesitated and then agreed. By the time they sat down, she had recovered her poise.

'Is it an anniversary for your mother?' she asked.

Tom shook his head. 'I just felt . . .' He slid her a glance, hesitating.

'Go on,' she encouraged.

'I felt the need to come and see her – tell her about my decision to buy the hotel. Not that I think the dead can hear . . .' He reddened. 'Now you'll think I'm like one of your mental cases.'

Esmie gave him a wry look. 'You're saying that to a woman you've just overheard talking to her dead father, remember?'

Tom smiled. 'That's true.'

They sat in stillness for a moment, though the silence between them didn't feel awkward. It surprised her that Tom would be the kind of man to come and commune beside his mother's grave; she liked him for it. His strong features were softened in the evening sun and his expression was reflective. Gone were the masculine bravado and teasing quips behind which he usually hid. She had a sudden urge to touch his face and smooth away the sad frown lines that etched his brow. To stop herself, she broke the silence.

'Your mother was a beautiful woman.'

Tom stared. 'How did you know that?'

'From the portrait of her that hangs in the dining room,' said Esmie. 'Or at least it did when I was nursing there. She was not just beautiful to look at but something shone out of her too. I used to think she was encouraging us nurses when things were really hectic. I'd look up and she'd be smiling right at me.'

Tom's eyes glistened. 'Yes, I always think that about her picture too – that she's smiling just for me.'

'And she cheered up the men,' Esmie added.

'Did she?' Tom looked pleased.

Esmie smiled. 'Yes, the patients nicknamed her their "Guardian Angel".'

He looked away, overcome. 'I'm glad to hear that,' he said, his voice husky. 'That's the way I think of her.' He sighed. 'Tibby believes that's unhealthy too. My sister always says, she was just a mother not a saint. But I think she must have been a saint to have put up with my father. Perhaps Tibby's right and I have this idealised memory of Mama – the memories of a ten-year-old after all.'

Esmie was taken aback by his candidness; it was as if in this quiet sanctuary they had both let down their guard.

'It sounds as if you were closer to your mother than Tibby was,' she said, 'so you have every right to remember her in a special way. You were lucky to have such memories. I hardly recall anything about my mother – she died when I was five – caught diphtheria from a child she was helping to nurse.'

'I'm sorry,' said Tom.

'There's no need to be,' said Esmie. 'My father filled her place ten-fold.'

Tom's blue eyes shone with compassion. 'How cruel that you lost him too. I liked your father – he was a kind doctor.'

Esmie gave a teary smile. 'Thank you.'

'So what has upset you so much that you've come here, Esmie?' he asked. 'Was it visiting the Drummonds? Lydia said you had gone to see them.'

Esmie tensed as she thought again of the upsetting visit. 'It was terrible.'

Tom nodded. 'You must all be so sad about David.' He reached out and covered her hand with his.

Esmie flinched at the unexpected contact. She withdrew her hand quickly and stood up, the intimacy broken.

'Please don't feel sorry for me,' she said. 'I don't deserve it. It's my fault that the Drummonds are grieving so badly.'

Tom frowned in confusion. 'How could you possibly be at fault?'

Esmie felt short of breath as he stood too and towered over her. She forced out her words.

'I refused David's proposal just before he died. Mrs Drummond found out. She will never forgive me. She blames me for his death – said he was reckless after I'd turned him down – and that he had nothing to live for.'

'That's hardly fair,' Tom protested.

Esmie looked at him unhappily. 'But it's true. When I wrote to tell David I couldn't marry him, I was relieved it was done. And just to make sure he wouldn't hold out any more hope for me, I told him that I'd never been in love with him so wouldn't change my mind in the future. I never for a moment thought David would try and harm himself. But I should have known, shouldn't I? David was always such a sensitive person. So his mother is right to hate me. I've robbed her of her boy.'

When Tom said nothing, Esmie felt weighed down with renewed guilt. His shocked face spoke of his disapproval. Without another word, she brushed past him.

He recovered himself and said, 'Esmie, let me walk you home.'

'Thank you,' she managed to say, 'but I'd rather be alone.'

He didn't insist. As she walked away, he didn't come after her. For a short while, in the graveyard, she had felt a bond forming between them that was more than just friendship; a closeness at the shared experience of having lost a beloved parent in childhood. And something else – like a physical spark igniting – that she shouldn't be feeling for the man her closest friend wanted to marry. She had said too much and been too emotional. This must never happen again.

Esmie quickened her pace and didn't look back.

Tom stood staring after Esmie's slim retreating figure, dumbfounded by what she had just told him. Not only had the upright nurse turned down David Drummond – a man who could have given her a comfortable life of leisure – but she had confided in Tom about her tortured heart. Still waters run deep, Tibby would say. Until this evening, Esmie had struck him as calmly in control and self-possessed. She joined in Lydia's banter and enjoyed herself but there was a reserve about her and at times her mind seemed far away.

Tom had found himself studying her in such moments; the way she rested her chin on her fist and tilted her face to the sky so that the light caught the attractive curve of her cheekbones and button nose. Sometimes she would sense his scrutiny and turn towards him, her eyelids fluttering wide in alarm, and then her large grey eyes would fix him with a quizzical look before she glanced away.

On first impressions, he had thought Esmie was content to live in the shadow of the pretty, vivacious Lydia. Until the day of their first swim together. It was then that Tom had realised Esmie did not see herself as living in anyone's shadow, or did not care if she did. She had run across the sand, lithe yet strong-limbed in her bathing suit, and plunged into the cold sea, revelling in the freedom of the moment. He still couldn't rid his mind of the image of Esmie, her shapely body dripping from the swim, pulling off her bathing cap to release a tumble of long wavy hair, and grinning with sheer joy. He'd felt a stirring of desire for her that day but he'd soon quelled it. Esmie McBride was not his type at all. She saw through flattery and looked upon men as if they all needed help, rather than bolster their egos and try and please them like Lydia did.

Then, half an hour ago, he had found Esmie distraught at her father's graveside. Gone was the poised, decisive nurse and in her place was a deeply emotional woman showing her vulnerability. He'd yearned to hold her and comfort her but she had recoiled from his touch.

Tom wandered back to James McBride's gravestone. On it was etched a tender inscription: *To a loving husband and father, and a true friend. Much beloved and greatly missed.*

His eyes prickled. It was how he felt about his mother, yet her grave was plain and unsentimental with nothing of comfort in the stark listing of her name and dates. He wondered who had commissioned the doctor's memorial stone: Dr Carruthers or William Drummond perhaps? Had Esmie been consulted about its wording? Probably not; yet whoever had had the stone made would have been in no doubt about the girl's deeply held love for her father.

As he turned away, he caught sight of a crumpled cotton handkerchief in the grass. Picking it up, he saw the embroidered initials: E.McB. It was damp with her tears and Tom felt again a pang of tenderness for Esmie. Pressing it to his nose he breathed in its lavender scent. What kind of man would stir the heart of such a woman? Tom had no idea. She was an enigma; like a sea creature that clammed up when you tried to touch it.

He stuffed the handkerchief in his pocket. He'd return it to her another day. Tom filled his lungs with scented air and turned to go.

Tibby was right; a churchyard full of ghosts was no place for a young man with a future ahead of him. He would press on with his plans for India and the Raj Hotel. The owner – a bachelor – seemed keen to sell quickly. It struck Tom more forcefully than ever how he didn't want to face such a future on his own. Was it finally time for him to fill the void left by Mary? He had loved brown-eyed Mary since they'd been eight years old and she'd shared her cake with him at a children's party. She'd been kind and warm-hearted and had grown into a woman of graceful beauty. He'd always known he would marry her. His guts twisted as he thought of her dying so suddenly . . . No, he must not think of her.

Yet these past couple of weeks in Lydia's company had made him realise how much he missed a woman's companionship. He doubted he could ever be as close to another woman as he had been with Mary – he didn't want to replace her – but there were aspects of marriage he was beginning to long for: sharing silly jokes and enjoying physical intimacy. He hated his empty bed. He wanted to lie again with a woman; one he could grow to love.

It annoyed him to think that his father might be right; perhaps the moment had come to get married again. A wife for the Raj Hotel. That's what he needed. Someone who wouldn't remind him in any way of his dark-haired Mary. He glanced across at the bench by the wall, now in shadow, and pondered his encounter with Esmie. She too had dark, graceful looks and a caring nature.

But he sensed a dangerous undercurrent to her personality; a woman who took risks and didn't care about her own safety. She was someone who kept her passions in check, but he had glimpsed today that sometimes she let her feelings overwhelm her. Esmie, with those disturbing, mesmerising eyes that made his pulse quicken, would be no good for him. Besides, she obviously didn't feel any attraction for him. When he'd touched her hand, she'd jerked away from him as if she'd been scalded.

The kind of wife he needed for his new life in Rawalpindi would be glamorous and outgoing. Attractive and fair Lydia would be more suited to such a role. She was uncomplicated and full of bonhomie and for some reason appeared to have taken a strong liking to him. Tibby, after her first trip to Templeton Hall, had startled him by saying Lydia was in love with him. '*She's like a boisterous, starry-eyed puppy around you,*' Tibby had said. '*Just longing for your attention.*'

Lydia also showed an aptitude for business which could be very useful and he could see her fitting in well to the busy social scene in Pindi. He wasn't in love with her yet, but he enjoyed her company greatly and found her physically very attractive. Was that enough to ask her to be his wife? Tom sighed. He wasn't sure. He would see how the summer – and his relationship with Lydia – progressed. Once the purchase of the hotel had been secured, he would decide.

Pushing thoughts of Esmie and Lydia to the back of his mind, Tom strode away from St Ebba's church with renewed determination.

Chapter 5

Esmie, still shaken by Maud's vitriolic accusations, tried to talk to Lydia about her disastrous visit to the Drummonds. 'It was even worse than I'd expected. Maud Drummond had read my letter to David and was furious with me. She as good as said that David took his own life because I'd rejected him.'

'What nonsense!' said Lydia dismissively.

'She told me never to visit again.'

'Well, what's done is done,' said Lydia. 'At least you don't have to bother with the tiresome woman again – I never did like her at school – always lecturing us on morals and spoiling our fun. Put it all behind you.'

Esmie could see that Lydia thought the whole Drummond affair was no longer of importance. Her friend didn't want to talk about such sad things and so Esmie didn't get the chance to tell her about the emotional meeting in the graveyard with Tom. Esmie was already regretting having unburdened her woes to the former captain. What had possessed her to tell him about her rejection of David? What must he think of her? She contemplated keeping out of his way but then chided herself for being a coward. Tom had been kind to her and was not to blame for any of the mess she had created.

Yet she needn't have worried. Tom never referred to their meeting in the churchyard either and kept his distance. He was polite and amiable towards her but there was no hint of the warmth of feeling she had experienced by St Ebba's Church. Perhaps in her overwrought state she had imagined it. Besides, after her confession about David, Tom appeared wary of her.

As May gave way to June, the friends continued to meet up, though less frequently as a foursome. Tom was increasingly attentive to Lydia, taking her to tea dances and to dinner parties around the county. Harold wasn't interested in attending the large formal balls that Lydia relished, as he confided in Esmie when they went on one of their frequent walks together.

'All that inane chit-chat – I'm no good at it. Tom's always been much better at the social graces than me. And I can't manage the vast amounts of drink like Tom either. I'm sorry to be a disappointment. I know Lydia is expecting me to partner you.'

'I don't mind in the least,' Esmie assured him. 'I prefer simpler pleasures too.'

Esmie thought there was another reason for Harold's reluctance to attend such social events: having to watch Lydia's growing infatuation with Tom. Harold hid his dismay well and Esmie only noticed because she too was alert to every gesture and look that passed between the handsome couple – the Templeton heiress and the war hero – who were becoming the talk of the county. It should have become easier to ignore her feelings since Tom had grown more reserved towards her but Esmie found herself thinking about him more and more.

His dark good looks preyed on her mind. When she caught his occasional glance, the startling blue of his eyes set her pulse thumping. Was it time for her to return to Vaullay to take up her work at the hospital again? She needed to be occupied. Her mixed-up feelings for Tom were doing her no good. But when she raised the idea with Lydia, her friend was aghast.

'Go to Vaullay? Whatever for? I thought you were enjoying being here with me?'

'I am,' said Esmie. 'I've had a marvellous time and your parents have been so kind. But I can't stay indefinitely and Aunt Isobel might need me.'

'I need you,' Lydia cried. 'Please stay. You're so good at keeping Harold company. He'll miss you if you go, I know he will.'

'I doubt it,' said Esmie.

'But he will. He'll be at a loose end and want to tag along with Tom and me – which is fine, of course. I'm very fond of Harold. But things are progressing so well with Tom, and you know how to talk to Harold better than I do. And don't suggest Tibby as a stand-in for you. She's hopeless. They have nothing in common – she's far too eccentric for dear Harold. So say you'll stay?'

Esmie gave in to her friend's pressure. She knew that Lydia was using her to keep Harold at bay but she owed the Templetons so much. When Esmie had been orphaned, theirs had been the most welcoming of households and Lydia had generously shared her parents and her home with her bereaved friend. Esmie promised to stay longer.

Lydia, wrapped up in her new love affair, was doing all she could to make friends with Tibby and to charm Colonel Lomax. Discovering that Tibby was a keen golfer, Lydia had arranged for them to play with her father. Sometimes Lydia would go over to The Anchorage and play on the rough pitch-and-putt course that had been created by the convalescing soldiers during the War. Tom, who thought he had outstayed his welcome with Harold's widowed mother and censorious maiden aunt, was back living at the castle but the colonel was still refusing to speak to him.

Tibby had taken Lydia to meet her father. At first he'd been frosty towards her but when she'd shown an interest in his toy soldiers and a capacity for drinking whisky, he'd been won over – or so Lydia told Esmie.

One time, when Esmie went with Lydia to hack around the course with Tibby, her friend brought up her concern over the rift between father and son.

'What can I do to bring them both together?' Lydia asked Tom's sister.

Tibby, pausing over a shot, was blunt. 'Marry Tommy and give my father an heir.'

Lydia blushed furiously and giggled. 'Goodness!'

Tibby putted successfully into the hole and picked up her ball.

'Well, you did ask,' she said. 'Lomaxes are terribly patriarchal – continuity of the line and all that. Papa can't bear Tommy but he longs for a grandson. If my brother gave The Anchorage a son and heir, Papa would stop all this nonsense about disinheriting him. Until then, you'll just have to accept Tommy won't get a penny from the old boy.'

'I'm not interested in his money,' Lydia insisted. 'I've got plenty of my own. I just don't want to see Tom estranged from his father.' She gave a sweeping gesture towards the towered mansion. 'Or cut off from all this. The Anchorage must mean so much to him.'

'Well, that's my advice,' said Tibby. 'A baby boy.'

Esmie and Lydia exchanged amused glances.

Esmie was taking her shot when a sudden call made her miss. Tom appeared through the belt of trees onto the lawn, his dark hair ruffled in the breeze and his handsome face smiling.

'Back luck,' said Tibby. 'Have another go.'

'Hello, you!' Lydia called over, abandoning the game to greet him.

'Don't let me stop you,' he said. 'I just brought some refreshment.' He held up a bottle of champagne. Behind him traipsed a kitchen maid with a tray of glasses.

'Ooh, bubbly, how lovely,' cried Lydia. 'What are we celebrating?'

Tom grinned as he popped the cork. 'I am now the proud owner of a hotel in Rawalpindi. I've just been with my lawyer and it's all signed and sealed.'

'Wonderful!' Lydia gasped. 'Oh, clever you.'

Tibby smiled. 'Well done, Tommy.'

'Congratulations,' said Esmie.

'Thank you, kind ladies,' said Tom as he poured from the bottle. The maid handed round the glasses.

'To Tom and the Raj Hotel!' Lydia raised her glass. The others chorused the same as they toasted him.

As the champagne frothed in her throat, Esmie felt instantly light-headed. Tom knocked his back and poured himself a second glass.

'Don't let me stop the game,' he insisted. 'Who is winning?'

'Your sister, of course,' said Lydia. 'I think we should retire gracefully from the game, don't you, Esmie? We're not nearly as good.'

'Fine by me,' said Esmie. 'This champagne has gone straight to my head and I'm not sure I can hit the ball.'

Tibby laughed. 'You haven't been doing much of that anyway.'

Esmie grinned. 'No, I haven't, have I?'

'Too much gossiping?' Tom teased.

The women exchanged knowing looks and laughed.

'Tibby was giving some wise advice,' Lydia said archly.

'About your game?' Tom asked.

'In a way, yes,' said Lydia and then burst into giggles.

Tom looked at them baffled. 'Am I allowed to hear what my sister has been saying?'

'Certainly not,' said Tibby. 'But something tells me you're going to find out in the fullness of time.'

A couple of days later, as Esmie was reading on the balcony, she overheard Lydia below in heated conversation with her father.

'All I'm asking you to do, Daddy, is to arrange a meeting – find out if he has any intentions towards me. You could invite him to your club or take him out for lunch.'

'Don't you think it's all a bit soon?' Jumbo asked. 'Five minutes ago you were keen on Colin Fleming and his vineyards. You hardly know Captain Lomax. He seems a nice enough young man but—'

'I love him, Daddy! And I think he cares for me. Please just ask him. You can find out more about his business venture. I told him you'd be happy to give him advice. That could be your excuse to have a chat.'

'Well, I don't mind having a talk about business,' he agreed. 'But as for marrying my baby girl . . .'

'I'm not your baby girl any longer!' Lydia cried. 'I'm a grown woman and I know what I want. I simply must know if I'm to be in his plans for India.'

'Has he hinted at such plans?' Jumbo asked.

'As good as,' said Lydia. 'He's told me such a lot about Pindi as if he expects me to go there. But I want this done properly with you asking him about his prospects and encouraging him to ask your permission to marry me.'

Jumbo gave a sudden laugh. 'My darling girl, you should have been a general rather than his driver – we would have won the War in half the time.'

'Is that a yes?' Lydia asked.

'If that's what you want,' he conceded.

'Oh, it is,' Lydia said, her voice animated. 'Thank you, Daddy. You're such a good sport.'

Esmie was disturbed at the exchange, wishing she hadn't overheard it. She shared Jumbo's concern that Lydia was rushing headlong into marriage with a man she had only known for a few weeks. Esmie was also uncomfortable with the idea that Tom was about to be manipulated into marrying her friend. She pushed away the thought. It was none of her business. Tom was a mature man and could make up his own mind on the matter.

Within a week, Tom had proposed to Lydia. They'd all been for a day out at the races in Newcastle with the Templetons; Tom, Tibby, Harold and Esmie. Tom was in high spirits and had been drinking all day. When they returned to Templeton Hall for a late supper, Tom seized Lydia by the hand, pulled her down the terrace steps and disappeared into the twilight.

Minutes later, they heard a shriek from near the ornamental pond. Minnie Templeton went to the French windows and peered out in alarm.

'Don't worry, dearest,' said Jumbo, smiling. 'It's just Lydia being excitable.'

Minutes later, Lydia was rushing into the house, squealing with joy.

'We're engaged! Tom's proposed and I've accepted. Golly, I'm so happy. Just look at my ring! Isn't it divine? It was Tom's mother's. It doesn't quite fit but we can have it altered.'

There were cries of delight from her parents and friends. Tom stood grinning foolishly as Jumbo and Harold shook him by the hand, and the women embraced Lydia.

'I know it's not a surprise for you, Daddy,' said Lydia. 'Tom said he'd asked your permission last week. I can't believe you kept it a secret from me!'

'I'm very pleased to have Tom in the family,' said Jumbo, winking at his daughter. He ordered Baxter to bring up a bottle of his best champagne from the cellar.

As they toasted the young couple, Minnie grew tearful. 'If only you didn't have to go to India, darling. It's so far away. Do you really have to run this hotel, Tom? I'm sure Jumbo could find you a business opportunity here.'

'Oh, Mummy, don't spoil it,' Lydia chided. 'India's going to be such an adventure but we won't be there forever. Once we've got things off the ground, we'll be able to hand over the day-to-day running to a manager. We'll have heaps of time to come back here and visit. And you can come out and stay.' She looked at everyone with shining eyes. 'You must all come and visit. We absolutely insist, don't we, darling?'

Lydia slipped a possessive arm through Tom's. Tom looked befuddled but nodded. 'Of course – all come – stay as long as you want.'

Esmie hardly slept that night. She felt a clash of emotions at the news of Lydia's engagement to Tom; great happiness for her friend, who was ecstatic to be betrothed, mixed with a twinge of envy that Lydia would be embarking on an adventure to a new exotic land with Tom. And something else – was it relief? – that Tom would be out of her reach. It baffled her to feel this way because at no point had he shown any romantic interest in her.

Yet, increasingly, she would feel her heart lift whenever she saw him. She would never ever admit such feelings to anyone but she couldn't deny them to herself; she was falling in love with Tom Lomax. Now that Tom was safely engaged, she must redouble her efforts to smother her attraction towards him.

As the rest of the household slept off their champagne celebration, Esmie rose early, pulled on her swimsuit, a pair of knee breeches she kept for cycling and an old jumper and crept out of the house. No one was stirring; not even the servants. With hot water on tap, no maid was expected to get up early and boil water in the kitchen. In one of the outhouses, she found the old bicycles that she and Lydia used to ride and pulled one out of its dusty corner. Checking that the chain and brakes still worked, she set off down the dew-soaked drive, revelling at the cool air and the sound of birdsong.

Twenty minutes later, Esmie was skirting the town and heading for the beach. Her favourite one nestled in a sheltered cove beneath steep cliffs. Leaving the bike propped against a hawthorn bush in full flower, she scrambled down the stony path, grabbing onto tufts of damp grass to stop herself falling. The tide was in so there was only a small rim of golden beach to walk on but Esmie unlaced her tennis shoes and plunged bare feet into the cold sand. She stood at the water's edge and let the ice-cold sea lap over her ankles. Seabirds soared overhead as the low morning sun sparkled on rippling waves. Esmie breathed in lungsful of salty air and then, stripping off, went for a swim.

Swimming always restored her vitality and optimism; it was the most joyous activity. One of her earliest memories was being taught to swim in Loch Vaullay by her father and lessons from Isobel Carruthers in the asylum bathing pool. '*Good for body, mind and soul*,' the doctor had declared. It was part of Isobel's treatment for the traumatised veterans in her care and Esmie saw how it helped in their recovery.

Emerging from the sea and rubbing herself vigorously with a towel, Esmie determined to return to Vaullay as soon as possible. She had been away for six weeks and was feeling the need to be working and useful again. Lydia and her parents would be preoccupied with plans for the hastily arranged wedding and she would just be in the way. Lydia wished to marry in Scotland before she and Tom embarked for India in late August. To Esmie, it would come as a relief to no longer have to skirt the town to avoid bumping into Maud Drummond or play along with Lydia's game of keeping Harold company and pretend to Tibby that she enjoyed games of golf.

Padding up the beach, her gaze was drawn to the top of the far cliff. Perched above the crumbling pink stone was The Anchorage. The ancient towered dwelling looked noble as its sandstone turrets and vaulted windows glowed in the early sunlight. For a moment, Esmie allowed herself to wonder in which room Tom Lomax slept and then she pushed the dangerous thought firmly from her mind. Shoes in hand, Esmie scrambled barefoot back up the slope. In the strengthening sea breeze, she cycled back to the shelter of Templeton Hall.

Later that day, Esmie told Lydia her intention to travel back to the Highlands. Lydia looked dismayed.

'But don't you want to stay and help me choose a wedding trousseau?' she asked. 'I thought we could have a trip to Paris to buy my dress. You can practise your French. It'll be such fun.'

'That's kind of you to offer – but it's something you should do with your mother,' Esmie said. 'And maybe Grace could join you from Switzerland?'

'And have my bossy older sister telling me what to wear?' Lydia retorted. 'No thank you!'

But her friend put up less resistance to Esmie going than previously.

'Well, as long as you promise to come back for the wedding at the end of July?' Lydia bargained. 'It would spoil the day if my best friend wasn't there.'

Esmie smiled. 'I promise. I wouldn't miss it for the world.'

With some relief, Esmie learnt that she would be gone from Ebbsmouth before the Templetons threw a lavish engagement party for the young couple. All the gentry of the county were being invited, along with the Templetons' business friends and acquaintances. Colin Fleming had gracefully accepted to attend and was showing no reproach at Lydia being so swiftly engaged to another in his absence. But Esmie was not surprised to hear that the diffident Harold had declined the invitation.

'He's gone on holiday,' said Lydia in annoyance. 'Just taken off with hardly a word to anyone.'

'Where to?' Esmie asked.

'Some missionary friends in Wales, Tom said. He thinks he's gone hiking.' Lydia gave a shrug. 'Strange man. But as long as he's back for the wedding it doesn't really matter. Tom wants him as his best man, so he'd better jolly well turn up.'

Esmie thought there was nothing to be gained by pointing out to Lydia that it might be Harold's way of dealing with his disappointment that Lydia was marrying his oldest friend and not him. Yet Lydia would never have entertained marriage to Harold – and had given him no encouragement – and Harold had never asked. However, Esmie felt sympathy for the kind doctor, who kept his feelings so private, and hoped that walking in the Welsh hills would bring him peace of mind.

Two days later, Lydia was dropping Esmie off at the railway station on her way to meeting Tom and Tibby for lunch. They kissed cheeks and Esmie thanked her again for her holiday at Templeton Hall.

'You will always have a home with us,' said Lydia. 'You're more like a sister to me than my own sister. You do know that, don't you?'

'Yes, I do,' said Esmie, her eyes smarting with tears. 'And I love all you Templetons like family too. I can never repay your kindness.'

'You don't have to,' said Lydia, smiling. 'Just make sure you come and see me married at the end of July.'

Chapter 6

As she travelled north, Esmie's spirits lifted at the sight of mountains and tumbling waterfalls. She turned her mind to her work at the hospital and was eager to discover how her patients had fared in her absence. She was in awe of her guardian, whose underlying philosophy for the inmates was to let them lead as useful and unrestricted a life as possible. Bathing, fresh air, exercise and keeping them occupied were the therapeutic remedies she employed at the asylum; resorting to opiates and restraint to subdue only the most violent or dangerously manic.

'Activity gives them a purpose and a sense of worth,' Isobel would say. 'Even the feeble-minded can get joy out of growing flowers or sewing handkerchiefs.'

Only the very ill were confined to bed, while the majority were encouraged into the gardens or to help at the asylum farm. There was a theatre for entertainments and dances – since the War there was a patients' band – and a library for reading and writing. The asylum had a church for Sunday worship and a heated swimming pool for regular bathing.

Esmie was particularly keen to see what progress her favourite patient, Tommy Grey, had made. Some of the more recent patients had been physically disabled by war as well as mentally shell-shocked and had been admitted because their families could not cope or they had no family to care for them. Tommy, a farm labourer from Perthshire who had served with the Highland Light Infantry, was one such man. A piper for his regiment, he had lost both legs in a grenade attack on his trench and when admitted to the asylum had been put in a separate room because his nightly screaming kept the others awake.

'Tommy has negative symptoms of psychosis,' Isobel had told Esmie when the wounded soldier had arrived the previous year. 'He's withdrawn, makes little eye contact and has lost the ability to speak.'

Esmie would push him around the grounds in his wheelchair and chat to him. Tommy never spoke back but he liked being out in the open air and would cock his head to listen to the birds and sometimes hummed snatches of pipe tunes. Then one spring afternoon, she'd detoured back via the hospital farm to see the first lambs of the year.

'Aren't they just the sweetest creatures?' she'd said, pausing by a gate to peer into the field.

'Aye, lambs. Spring's here.'

Esmie had looked round, wondering who had spoken. Tommy had looked her in the eye for a second and nodded, before dropping his gaze.

Esmie had hidden her astonishment and smiled. 'Yes, Tommy; spring is here at last.'

He'd said nothing more but Esmie's throat had tightened as she'd pushed him back, hardly able to contain her excitement at his attempt to speak again. After that, at Isobel's suggestion, the trips to the farm had become more regular and Tommy would sit in the barn and fix broken implements and sharpen tools for the farmer. Before Esmie left for her holiday to Ebbsmouth, Tommy had begun to talk about the recurring nightmares that disturbed his sleep: the enemy were breaching the trench and piling in on top of him until he suffocated.

Esmie had lent him Isobel's gramophone and each evening would play him soothing classical music or traditional Scottish songs when getting him ready for bed. By the time she went south, he was no longer waking every night.

Tommy Grey was one of the patients that Isobel thought could be cured.

'The problem is,' she had sighed, 'that even if he recovers completely from his melancholia, there's no home for him except here.'

After a long day's travel, Esmie stepped onto the platform of the tiny station at Vaullay and breathed in the sweet air, scented with heather and myrtle.

Aunt Isobel was there to greet her. 'You look exhausted, dearie,' said her guardian in concern. 'Too much high living in Ebbsmouth, no doubt. You can tell me all about it over supper.'

Soon they were driving through the gateway of the asylum and up its tree-lined drive. She waved in greeting to a patient she recognised who was pushing a wheelbarrow. His face broke into a smile of recognition and he raised his cap as the car passed.

'They've missed you,' said her aunt.

Esmie felt suddenly good to be back. 'How is Tommy?'

'Teaching Willie pipe tunes on his chanter,' Isobel answered with a smile.

'That's wonderful!' Esmie said in delight, thinking of the delusional Willie who thought himself the Kaiser.

They pulled up outside a cottage beyond the main buildings. Isobel had spurned the large villa that went with the job of chief medical officer in favour of the modest one-storey dwelling with its small garden of wild flowers and apple trees. She was given a cheery welcome from Isobel's maid, Jeanie, and a sticky kiss from Jeanie's two-year-old son, Norrie, who'd been hampering his mother's attempt to bottle raspberry jam.

That night, when Jeanie and Norrie had gone to their attic bedroom, Esmie and Isobel sat up late talking.

'So Lydia is getting wed,' said Isobel. 'A reason for rejoicing. But you seem sad. You're not the type to be jealous of others' happiness, so what is preying on your mind?'

Esmie knew her guardian would probe with questions until she got to the root of her sorrow. Yet she hesitated. Isobel had been fond of David and – like everyone else – had expected Esmie to marry him. Esmie had kept from her aunt that David had proposed and that she had turned him down. Now she couldn't bear to keep the truth from her mentor and guardian any longer, even if it meant Isobel thinking less of her.

So Esmie confided in the older woman about her guilt over the fateful letter and the confrontation with Maud. The only secret she held on to was her growing feelings for Tom and that she had returned hastily to Vaullay because she feared them getting out of control.

Isobel listened and said little. Finally, when Esmie fell silent, she spoke.

'Every day I deal with patients who are eaten up with guilt that they survived the War while their friends didn't. You feel this about David but you also have the extra burden of Mrs Drummond's bitter accusations.' The doctor's brown eyes were full of compassion. 'But as a nurse, you know that she is lashing out at you in her grief. We can't possibly know what state of mind David was in before he died. You have to accept that. Allowing yourself to be plagued with guilt helps no one. At least you were truthful to him.'

'I don't deserve your kindness,' Esmie said, a lump forming in her throat. 'But thank you.'

The clock on the mantelpiece struck eleven and Isobel rose. She leaned over and kissed Esmie on the top of her head. 'Tomorrow I have taken the day off and we're going to Loch Vaullay for a picnic and a swim – whatever the weather. What do you say?'

Esmie gave a tearful smile. 'I say yes of course. Thank you, Aunt Isobel.'

That night, Esmie sank into the soft folds of her old bed and fell asleep to the sounds of an owl hooting and the distant bleat of sheep.

Over the next few days, Isobel refused to let Esmie work in the hospital and chased her out for long walks in the hills and swims in the fresh water of Loch Vaullay. Esmie began to regain her zest for life and tried to put thoughts of the grieving Drummonds and her feelings for Tom behind her. But by the end of the week she had had enough of solitude and introspection.

'I need to work,' she told her aunt. 'Let me go back on the wards.'

'Good,' said Isobel. 'I was hoping you would say that. But it had to be your choice not mine.'

Esmie threw herself into nursing with renewed vigour and was assigned to one of the locked male wards. Some of the men had syphilitic insanity while others were diagnosed with dementia praecox – premature madness – another degenerative psychosis from which there was no cure. The ward was often noisy with patients shouting and singing in states of manic euphoria, or irritable and arguing with themselves. Some, like Willie, had delusions, while others hid under their beds in fear that the nurses were going to poison them.

Esmie and Isobel had long conversations over supper about the latest theories in the treatment of the psychotically ill. They discussed the use of electric sparks to slow the degenerative nerve condition of those with syphilis, and music therapy to calm sufferers of hysteria and lift the mood of depressives.

'The most progressive ideas are coming from Switzerland and Germany,' said Isobel. 'There's a new term, "schizophrenia", which is being used to describe a narrow range of dementias that might not be terminal. I'm optimistic that some of these patients can be cured. I've noticed one or two whose condition has improved rather than deteriorated since being admitted.'

'That's so encouraging to hear,' Esmie enthused. 'It's exciting to think you can make a difference at Vaullay with these new breakthroughs in diagnosis.'

'When I first came here thirty years ago,' Isobel said, 'there were patients sleeping in iron cages and others strapped into chairs with hoods over their heads. Can you believe it?'

She was contemptuous of long-held attitudes that insanity and a defective character could be inherited from a wayward mother, and disapproved of unmarried mothers being separated from their babies.

'Drives the young lassies into melancholia and hysteric anorexia,' said Isobel, 'and the bairns grow up in institutions without knowing the love of a family.'

Since returning to the asylum after Serbia, Isobel had rescued one such hapless young woman from this fate. Jeanie, heavily pregnant, had been abandoned at the gates of the asylum by her irate father. Now she was Isobel's housemaid.

That July, Esmie resumed her walks with the men who took it in turns to push Tommy down to the farm. Boisterous in the summer sunshine, they sped him down the hill laughing and shouting and ignoring Esmie's orders to slow down. These spontaneous moments of camaraderie reminded Esmie of the soldiers she had nursed in Serbia and Romania, bonded together in adversity. Much as she enjoyed being back working at Vaullay with her aunt, surrounded by the beauty of the heather-clad mountains, Esmie began to hanker for something more challenging.

She knew how easy it would be to drift along, working indefinitely at the asylum and making life more bearable for the inmates. More and more she began to think about going abroad again. The idea of going to the North-West Frontier excited her interest. She'd been following the news about the conflict with Afghanistan and from the scant newspaper reports it appeared that order was being restored and the Afghans were suing for peace. She talked it over with her aunt.

'Harold Guthrie's mission work at Taha interests me,' said Esmie. 'Not the religious side of it but working among the Pathans. It sounds more like the nursing I was used to doing with the Women's Hospitals – dealing with the battle-wounded, saving lives.'

'Have you talked to Dr Guthrie about you joining the mission?' asked Isobel.

'Not as such,' said Esmie, 'though he knows I'm interested in his work and they are always short of trained nurses. He said the mission weren't keen on sending women out to such a remote and dangerous posting, so they had to rely on male orderlies from among the local tribesmen.'

'What about female patients?' Isobel asked. 'I can't imagine Mohammedan women being happy with male nurses. Aren't they strict on purdah in the North-West Frontier?'

Esmie nodded. 'Harold says the women get very little treatment – most of the men won't bring their womenfolk to the clinic – and the nearest purdah ward is sixty miles away in Kohat.'

'Why don't you write to him?' suggested Isobel.

'You don't mind me going?' Esmie asked.

'Of course I mind. I'd worry about you in such a place – and I'd hate to lose you from the hospital – but I won't stand in your way if that's what you feel called to do.' Her guardian's face softened in a smile. 'Dear lassie, I can tell when you get that determined look in your eyes that there's little will stop you. And it would be selfish of me to try. You remind me so much of your dear mother.'

'Do I?' Esmie's heart squeezed.

'Oh yes,' said Isobel. 'She had the same inner strength – and the same bonny eyes.'

'You're the one who taught me to be brave,' Esmie said affectionately. 'Especially in Serbia.'

Isobel gave a short laugh. 'I spent most of the time frightened out of my wits. I was glad to give up working in theatre.'

'But you were an excellent surgeon,' said Esmie. 'You saved the lives of countless men.'

'That's generous of you to say so,' Isobel said, 'but more and more I'm finding satisfaction in trying to heal the mind. Thirty years ago, lunatic asylums were some of the few places where women doctors could find work. That's why I came to Vaullay. Now I think it's an area of medicine that's at the forefront of new ideas and possible treatments. That's why I came back here.'

'I can see that,' said Esmie. 'But I want to see more of the world. That doesn't mean I wouldn't want to return to Vaullay at some stage in the future.'

'You're quite right to do so while you're young and fit,' Isobel encouraged. 'And there will always be a home for you here whenever you want it.'

Esmie smiled. 'Thank you, Auntie.'

'So will you write to Harold Guthrie?'

Esmie nodded. 'Though I'm not sure if he's in Ebbsmouth at the moment. He took off to Wales after Lydia's engagement. He always had a bit of a soft spot for her.'

'Talking of Lydia,' said Isobel, 'how are the wedding plans coming along?'

'The last I heard was that postcard from Paris,' said Esmie.

'I must say,' said Isobel, 'I was surprised to hear Captain Lomax had gone with her. Sounds like a honeymoon before the marriage.'

Esmie felt herself reddening. 'I'm sure the Templeton parents made sure it was all above board,' she said with an embarrassed laugh.

'Wouldn't have happened before the War,' Isobel retorted. 'But then Lydia is a modern young woman and the world is no doubt a more colourful place because of her.'

Esmie grinned. 'That's certainly true.'

Chapter 7

Ebbsmouth, July

It was spitting with rain and blustery but Tom persuaded Harold to go for a swim in the cove below The Anchorage. The sea was choppy as they dived among the white-crested waves.

'Make the most of it,' Tom called to his friend. 'We'll miss it when we're back in the Indian heat.'

Afterwards, towelling himself down, Tom felt a resurgence of optimism that always came with a bracing swim. He had enjoyed his trip to Paris with the Templetons more than he'd expected. He wasn't one for big cities but there had been an air of celebration about the French capital as people strolled in the sunshine and drank coffee and cognac at pavement cafés.

Jumbo and Minnie had been good company; warm and generous, insisting on paying for his accommodation and meals. Jumbo had taken him off to see the artists around Montmartre rather than trailing round dressmakers and department stores with the women.

'I dabble in a bit of painting myself,' Tom had admitted. 'Landscapes mostly.'

'You must show me,' Jumbo had said. 'If they're any good I might buy one as an investment.'

Tom had laughed. 'My father thinks they're only good for hiding damp stains on the wallpaper. But I'd be delighted to give you one as a thank you for this trip. As ever, you've been wonderful and generous hosts.'

'Don't need to thank me,' Jumbo had replied. 'Anyone who makes my darling daughter this happy is worth their weight in gold. Even if you are taking her so far away.'

'I'm sorry about that.'

Jumbo clapped him on the back. 'Lydia's excited to be going to Pindi and we're greatly looking forward to travelling out with you for a holiday. It'll be reassuring for Minnie to be able to see where Lydia will be living. You'll probably have a hard job getting rid of us!'

'It'll be an honour and pleasure to have you, sir.'

Jumbo beamed. 'Once you're married, Tom, you can call me Pa.'

As the rain increased, Tom hastily stripped off his swimming costume and pulled on his clothes. He liked the idea of the Templetons coming to stay at the hotel; they would be jolly company and it would make Lydia happy. Tom grinned at the thought of Lydia. They had managed to sneak away and be alone on several occasions – or perhaps her parents had engineered it – and enjoyed some moments of intimacy. In the romantic surroundings of Paris, they had walked hand in hand through the Tuileries Gardens and kissed in the moonlight on the Pont Alexandre III.

Each time he had embraced her, Tom had felt a kick of desire at the taste of her moist lips and the feel of her shapely body pressed against his. He had thought about making an assignation to go to her room in the night but thought better of it. Lydia wanted to be a virginal bride, though he'd been left in no doubt how much she was looking forward to the marriage bed. She had shocked him by producing a copy of that racy new relationship manual, *Married Love*, by some woman called Stopes, which was full of frank advice on sex and how to plan a family.

'It's about a husband and wife being equal in marriage,' Lydia had told him. 'And it's not just about having children. I don't want us to go straight into all that – we should enjoy just being married for a bit, don't you think?'

Tom had been speechless and nodded in agreement. He was becoming used to her questions as being rhetorical; if Lydia wanted something to happen it would happen. He had stopped reading the book in bed – it made him too aroused to think of him and Lydia together – but his impatience to be married was growing daily.

He'd been further thunderstruck when his fiancée had asked him if he'd ever slept with prostitutes and to reassure her he had no sexual disease.

'I know what soldiers are like,' Lydia had said, 'and Esmie tells me they have heaps of ex-soldiers in the asylum with syphilitic madness from the War. I just want to be sure I'm not getting faulty goods.'

Tom had tried not to show how offended he was by her blunt questioning. For years after Mary had died, he hadn't wanted to make love to another woman. Since meeting Lydia, his appetite for sex was returning and so he had assured her he was in rude good health.

The rain was now heavy. Tom pointed to the boathouse above the beach and said to Harold, 'Let's shelter in there till it eases off.'

The two friends sat on old fish boxes just inside the open doors and Tom lit up a cigarette. He was pleased that Harold had returned from Wales in better humour than when he went – he had missed his company and conversation – but this morning his friend had come over in a state of agitation. So far he hadn't said why. Tibby had been pestering Harold with medical questions about her father's health; Tom had suggested a swim to get Harold away from the castle and allow the doctor to confide in him.

'So what's bothering you, Guthrie?'

'Nothing really . . . Well, not exactly bothering me . . . just puzzling.'

'Spit it out,' Tom encouraged.

'I've had a letter from Esmie,' said Harold.

Tom felt punched in the chest at the unexpected mention of the nurse. His eyes widened in surprise.

'Esmie? What does she say?'

Harold paused. 'Well, it's quite forthright. She wants to know if she can join the mission clinic at Taha.'

'With you?' Tom asked, astonished.

'Not exactly with me.' Harold's fair face reddened. 'She wants to nurse among the Pathans and wonders if I can put in a word for her with the mission society.'

Tom's heart began a slow thudding. Esmie in Taha was an unsettling thought. It was a long day's journey from Rawalpindi, and Harold and he could go for months without seeing each other, but they were bound to bump into one another – more than that – Lydia would want her friend to stay from time to time. Tom took a drag of his cigarette, wondering why the idea disturbed him.

'So, will you help her?' Tom asked.

'Well, it's out of the question,' Harold answered. 'I'll tell her that the mission would never offer a position to a spinster. The tribesmen wouldn't accept a woman who wasn't under the protection of a man – they'd get quite the wrong impression. I'd be putting Esmie in danger.'

Tom squinted at his friend through cigarette smoke. 'But not if she went out as your wife?'

Harold turned beetroot red. 'I—I couldn't possibly ask her,' he stammered.

'Why not?'

Harold threw up his hands. 'For all the reasons I've said before. It wouldn't be fair to take a wife into such a place. It's a man's world. There'd be little society there for a British woman.'

Tom gave a grunt of amusement. 'I don't imagine that's what Esmie would be expecting or wanting. She'd be there to work, not keep house.'

Harold studied him with pensive hazel eyes. 'But she doesn't love me. She would most likely turn me down.'

Tom thought of the time in the churchyard when Esmie had opened up to him about David and her inability to love him. Would Esmie reject another marriage proposal because she wasn't head over heels in love with Harold? Possibly, but wasn't it worth Harold taking the risk?

Instinct told him that Harold secretly yearned to have a companion, despite his protestations that, to best do his work, he should remain a bachelor. Harold was a loving man and deserved to have a helpmate in his lonely posting. He knew Harold would do nothing about it without a bit of encouragement, yet, if Tom did so, there would be no way he could avoid Esmie in India. But what was so bad about that? He was besotted by his entrancing fiancée and had hardly thought of Esmie for the past three weeks. He stared out of the boathouse at the rain pounding on the sand and had an image of Esmie running into the sea, shrieking with joy. His stomach twisted in regret.

He ground out his cigarette. His feelings had been confused in the weeks after returning home from war. Seeing Esmie swimming here had triggered his loss for Mary – she had been a keen swimmer too – but Esmie was quite a different woman from his gentle deceased wife. She had a strength of character that would be able to cope in India's wild frontier. She'd be good for Harold and the mission. There was nothing to feel uneasy about. And Lydia would love having Esmie nearby. He felt a wave of protectiveness towards his wife-to-be and put his selfish thoughts aside.

'Ask her to marry you,' Tom advised. 'You'll never know her answer unless you do. What's the worst that could happen? She says no and you return to Taha just as you planned, without anyone else being the wiser.'

Harold cracked his knuckles, which he did when under stress. 'You really think I should?'

Tom nodded. 'She's worked at the battlefront – she'll have no fanciful ideas of what life will be like. She'd be ideal. You get a nurse and a wife all in one. You may not be in love with Esmie, but you get on with her, don't you?'

Harold hesitated, his expression hard to fathom. 'I hold her in high regard,' he admitted. 'And, I must say, it would be pleasant to have a companion.'

'And a pretty one too,' Tom chuckled. 'So there you are then!' He stood up. 'If you marry Esmie and bring her to India, you'll make Lydia ecstatic.'

Bashfully, Harold glanced away. 'I'll think it over. Pray about it.'

Tom nodded, leading the way. 'Come on, Guthrie; let's make a dash for it.'

Esmie couldn't settle to anything. She went for a long walk around Loch Vaullay, Harold's letter – which he'd sent almost by return – burning a hole in her jacket pocket. She'd read it several times and shown it to her aunt who had shaken her head in bemusement. Stopping to sit on a rock by the lapping water, she pulled it out and reread his diffident words.

> *'. . . I think your request to work at the mission might be an answer to my prayers. You are a brave and caring nurse with all the qualities needed to thrive in such a place as Taha – a sympathetic nature and a strong constitution. But the mission would not consider you in your spinster state because you might be a target for kidnap or worse.*
>
> *Therefore, I am suggesting marriage. I think we admire one another's work and enjoy each other's company.*

I can offer you companionship and protection – and a comfortable house in the cantonment. We get local leave twice a year and a longer furlough back to Scotland every three years, so you would be able to visit Dr Carruthers then.

We would have to marry before I'm back in post in late September, which doesn't give you much time to make a decision. I quite understand if you'd rather not. There are other places in India where I'm sure they would accept a nurse of your expertise – there are hospitals in Peshawar and Rawalpindi – if you have your heart set on that part of the world.

But if my offer is of interest, then please write back and let me know as soon as you can.

Yours sincerely,

Harold Guthrie

P.S. I do miss our conversations and walks.'

Esmie couldn't help a wry smile. She wondered how long Harold had laboured over the wording. It certainly wasn't romantic – it read like a business proposal – but in its awkwardness she detected his shy eagerness. He was offering marriage but was bracing himself for her turning him down. She felt a wave of affection for the red-haired doctor.

Yet Esmie's first reaction was to say no. She didn't want to be his wife – or anyone's wife – she had decided to dedicate herself to nursing. She valued her freedom more than she wanted a husband.

Reading the letter again, Esmie was struck by what was left unsaid but was still acknowledged; that neither of them loved each other in a romantic sense. To Harold that didn't seem to matter; they had enough in common to make a successful partnership as colleagues and companions. Was that enough for her?

Esmie sighed and gazed out across the water. Perhaps she wasn't suited to marriage? She had been hopeless with men so far. She had shied away from involvement with David, whom everyone else thought would be the perfect husband for her, and she had fallen for Tom knowing that he was out of her reach.

Was she afraid of falling in love or letting herself truly love a man because she feared losing him? She saw now how she kept men at arm's length emotionally. Was this why she had run away from Tom Lomax? He was a man she had found it all too easy to fall in love with and she hated the feeling of not being in control of her emotions. But surely her feelings towards him would dissipate now that he was safely engaged and about to become Lydia's husband?

But what about Harold? She liked and admired him; in time she might well grow fond of him. He spoke of his work with passion in the way that her Aunt Isobel did. Esmie knew she could work well with him because she respected him as a doctor. But was that enough? Marriage was for life. If she accepted him then they would be bound together forever. There was a certain attractiveness about him and the thought of being intimate with him didn't displease her. But he might want her to bear his children and that thought filled her with alarm. Her nightmares of dying children were a constant reminder of the fragility of young life and she was terrified at the thought of having babies who could so easily be snatched away by death.

Esmie sighed as she watched a heron take off with slow flapping wings across the loch. She was twenty-five and at a crossroads in her life. The one thing she was sure of was that she wished to go abroad again to work. Harold was offering her that opportunity. Then she was struck by a sudden thought. Was Harold only proposing to her to overcome his unhappiness at Lydia marrying Tom? She was catching him on the rebound from disappointment. He might think marrying her was a good idea at the moment but would he come to regret it once he'd got used to Lydia being Mrs Lomax?

Esmie wrestled with indecision all the way home. Only when Isobel brought up the subject at supper time did her mind become clearer.

'So, dearie, what are you going to say to Mr Guthrie? Yes or no?'

'Neither,' said Esmie. 'Not yet. It's not something that should ever be decided by letter – I'll not repeat the terrible mistake I made with David. I need to talk to Harold face-to-face. The wedding is next week, so I'll see him when I go back to Ebbsmouth. Then I'll decide.'

Isobel nodded. 'Good decision.'

Esmie smiled in relief. 'Thank you.'

After that, her aunt changed the subject and began discussing the forthcoming summer fete.

Chapter 8

Ebbsmouth, late July

A couple of days before the wedding, Esmie arrived back at Templeton Hall in the middle of a crisis. A distracted Lydia met her at the station. She drove back erratically as she fulminated about the wedding plans. Her sister Grace's third pregnancy was too advanced and the post-war trains still too chaotic for her to travel from Switzerland. Both her husband and her doctor had advised against it.

'And now Colonel Lomax is refusing to come to the wedding.' Lydia sounded the horn in frustration. A delivery boy jumped out of the way.

'Whatever for?' asked Esmie.

'Because he's a pig-headed old reactionary!' Lydia replied, her fair face red with indignation.

'Meaning?'

'He says it's because he's housebound but that's a load of tosh. He's a snob. He thinks Tom is marrying beneath him just because Daddy wasn't born with a silver spoon in his mouth and can't trace his ancestry back to Robert the Bruce – or some such nonsense. It's not as if he has to put his stingy hand in his pocket,' Lydia cried, accelerating down the lane. 'Daddy's paying for everything, of course. But "his highness" won't set foot in Templeton Hall because we're "trade". Mummy's terribly upset and so am I. I've been nice to him all summer – the wretched old fool.'

'What does Tom say?' asked Esmie.

Lydia huffed in exasperation. 'He couldn't care less. Says I shouldn't get so het up about it. But of course I do. The colonel's going to be my father-in-law. I'm going to be a Lomax and The Anchorage will be my home – even though it's just for a short time before India. Is he going to refuse to have my parents round to visit? Imagine the indignity!'

'I know it's upsetting,' said Esmie, 'but he's always been an old curmudgeon and he's not going to change now. Perhaps if you make less of a fuss, he'll come round to the idea of attending. He's probably enjoying the drama.'

Lydia shot her a look. 'You sound just like Tom.'

Esmie flushed. 'Well, you shouldn't worry about living at the castle. Tibby said her father was very taken with you personally. He's just being provocative about your parents but no one at the wedding will care if he's there or not. He's known to be a recluse so people will just think he's not well enough.' She touched Lydia's arm. 'It's your special day – don't let the colonel spoil it.'

Lydia flashed a smile. 'Oh, darling Esmie, I've missed you. I need you to keep me calm. You had no right to stay away so long.'

Esmie sat back and unpinned her hat, letting the sea breeze whip at her hair. She asked, 'Have you seen much of Harold recently?'

'Not much,' said Lydia. 'He's been away the past couple of days visiting relations in Dumfriesshire – doing the rounds before he heads back to India, I suppose.'

Esmie slid her a look. Harold had obviously said nothing about the proposal or Lydia would have been interrogating her about it by now. She wondered if he had discussed it with Tom. Her stomach curdled. Soon she would have to face them both and make up her mind about the future. She closed her eyes and breathed in the smell of salty air. Either way, she was going to enjoy spending these last two days with Lydia before her childhood friend got married.

On the spur of the moment, Tom decided to drive over to Dumfriesshire and join Harold for a day's fishing before the wedding. He'd heard from Lydia that Esmie had arrived and he decided to leave the two friends to enjoy their time together. It would be a relief to get away from the hectic preparations and heightened emotions at Templeton Hall. He booked into a guest house in Dumfries and went out that afternoon to fish with his friend.

'You would think they were preparing for a royal *durbar*,' Tom reported to Harold as they cast their lines out over the river. 'The place is done up like a maharajah's palace, with marquees and bunting and electric lights all over the garden. It's completely over the top.'

Harold smiled. 'So you've left them to it.'

'Thankfully! Esmie's arrived and I hope will steady the ship. Lydia's still up to high doh about my father refusing to attend. I should have whisked her off to India and got married out there. I didn't want all this fuss – I just wish to have Lydia as my wife.'

Harold gave a nod of understanding. After casting his line again, he asked, 'And did you see Esmie before you left?'

'No, she was out with Lydia's mother on some errand while Lydia was resting.' He eyed his friend. 'Are you any further forward with your own marriage plans?'

'There are no marriage plans,' said Harold glumly.

Tom gave him a sympathetic look. 'So she's said no?'

'Not in so many words. She wants to tell me in person – but that's probably because she's letting me down gently.'

'Harold!' Tom chided. 'Why do you always imagine the worst? Perhaps she just wants more time to think it over. If she'd meant no, she would have told you so before having to see you again.'

Harold looked heartened by this suggestion.

They fished in silence. Tom felt the tension of the past couple of weeks leave him as he emptied his mind of everything but the handling of his rod and reel. The sky was overcast and the tranquil river was the colour of pewter. Beyond the trees he glimpsed the industrious sights and sounds of farming; voices calling across the fields, the neighing of horses and swish of machines. He would like to paint this scene. He'd store away the memory.

Gradually, thoughts of Lydia and the wedding began to intrude. He had seen a new side of his fiancée in recent days. She had taken huge offence at being socially slighted by his father and latched onto it obsessively to the exclusion of all other conversation. Lydia had insisted she did so on behalf of her parents but Tom thought that she merely stoked up their agitation by not letting the matter drop.

When Colonel Lomax had turned down the wedding invitation, she had gone to see him but he had kept to his room and pleaded illness. Since then, Lydia had bombarded his father with daily letters imploring him to attend.

Tom had tried to convince her that it was the wrong approach.

'Just ignore him. He loves all the adverse attention. It's just his way of getting at me.'

'Well, you should have made more effort to get on with your father!' Lydia had accused. 'Tibby doesn't have a problem with him but you seem to delight in riling him. And now it's going to ruin my wedding day! It'll be the talk of the county.'

Hurt, Tom had left. Later that day, Lydia had sent round a message inviting him to supper.

'Sorry,' she'd apologised. 'It's just pre-wedding nerves. I didn't mean to snap at you. You do know how much I adore you, don't you?'

In relief, Tom had taken her in his arms and kissed her. 'I can't wait for us to be married, my darling,' he said. 'Soon it'll all be over and we can get on with our new life together.'

Her pretty blue eyes had shown surprise. 'Oh, I don't wish the day to be over – it's the most important one of my life – and I want it to be one we'll always remember.'

Tom felt a twist inside. Mary had said something similar to him eight years ago. It would be bitter-sweet being married again in St Ebba's. He'd tentatively suggested having the ceremony in a church in a neighbouring village but Lydia had been so dismayed that he'd let the matter drop. He wanted her to be happy. Her youthful enthusiasm was a tonic for his jaded outlook on life and her excitement infectious. By the time he returned to Ebbsmouth he was sure that the ill-tempered exchanges over his father's behaviour would be forgotten.

On the morning of the wedding, Esmie grew tearful at the sight of Lydia in her French wedding dress. Her beauty looked ethereal under the long veil and the soft layers of silk and lace that swathed her body. She needed no rouge to bring colour to her pink cheeks or lipstick to her cupid's mouth. Her look was radiant and her blue eyes shone with joy.

'You look utterly beautiful,' Esmie gasped.

Lydia gave a trembling smile. 'Stop it or you'll make me cry and my eyes will be all puffy and Tom will look at me in horror and call it all off.'

Esmie laughed. 'Don't be so dramatic. He loves you and he's going to be so proud.'

'Yes, I think he does love me,' said Lydia happily.

Esmie's chest tightened. Lydia and Tom were lucky to have found love with each other and she wished them nothing but happiness together. Her initial doubts over their suitability together had proved unfounded. She knew that Lydia craved to be loved and needed someone to adore her in the way that her parents always had. Tom, she suspected, needed someone to care for him too. He never talked about his dead wife but she knew from Harold that he had taken Mary's death extremely badly. Harold thought that's why Tom had been brave to the point of being reckless in Mesopotamia. Lydia, she was certain, would be the right person to heal his bereaved heart.

Esmie was sure that the nerves she felt at the day ahead were nothing to do with seeing Tom but at the thought of seeing Harold for the first time since his proposal of marriage. She still hadn't made up her mind one way or the other but hoped once the wedding was over – and she had time to talk to Harold – her thinking would become clearer.

Before leaving Vaullay, at Isobel's insistence, her aunt had taken her into Inverness for a day's shopping before travelling south. Ignoring Esmie's protest that she was perfectly capable of making her own dress on her sewing machine, Isobel had bought Esmie a sleek powder-blue ankle-length summer dress and a raffia hat with matching blue ribbon. Esmie had bought new stockings and a pair of lacy gloves but resisted a pair of cream court shoes. 'I'll never get any wear out of them,' she had told her aunt. 'My Sunday shoes will be fine with a good polish.'

Now she was wearing her new outfit and had used many hairpins to keep her hair tidy under the straw hat. The only jewellery she wore was a silver brooch that had belonged to her mother.

Lydia clutched Esmie's hands. 'You manage to look cool and calm whatever you wear. I'm so glad you're here with me. Mummy makes me so emotional.'

Esmie smiled. 'I have a handbag full of hankies should either of you need them.'

Lydia laughed. 'Good. Stay close.'

Tom heard Tibby early that morning chivvying their father out of his room.

'Yes, you are going, Papa. Harold will be here soon to pick us all up. Mrs Curry has come in specially to get you ready.'

'I don't want to,' he complained. 'And I'm too ill.'

'No you're not. You can at least come to the church. I need you to accompany me. Then afterwards, if you don't feel up to the wedding party and a day of flowing champagne then I shall bring you home.'

'They're all so vulgar,' the colonel muttered.

'The Templetons are delightful,' Tibby replied. 'And Jumbo has the biggest selection of whiskies I've ever seen. I'm sure he'd like nothing better than sharing them with you, Papa.'

'I'm feeling too liverish today,' he said. 'I think I'll just stay in bed.'

'What a pity,' said Tibby. 'I'll send Mrs Curry away then, shall I? And I'm afraid I'll have to confiscate that whisky until you're feeling better. I'll be away all day too, so you'll have to get your own lunch and supper. But if you're liverish you won't feel like eating . . .'

'You can't leave me here on my own,' he said, his voice querulous.

'I'm afraid so,' said Tibby. 'I'm going to get ready now. I'll see you tomorrow.'

Tom saw Tibby march out of the colonel's room with a whisky bottle in each hand. She winked at him. A minute later, Archibald started shouting.

'Very well, if I have to go to this tawdry wedding! Where's Mrs Curry? Bring back my whisky you wretched girl!'

Tibby waited outside a couple more minutes and then called out. 'Mrs Curry will get you dressed. You can have a dram when you're ready to leave.'

Tom gave his sister an admiring look. 'I don't know whether to thank you or not,' he said wryly. 'But Lydia will be eternally grateful.'

An hour later, Harold arrived and the two friends stood outside while Tom chain-smoked and they waited for Tibby and the colonel. It had started to drizzle.

'I feel ridiculously nervous,' Tom admitted. 'Am I doing the right thing, Guthrie?'

Harold looked at him in alarm. 'You're not seriously having doubts at this stage, are you?'

Tom ground out his third cigarette. 'No, of course not. It's just the waiting.' He turned towards the house and called, 'Hurry up, Tibby. I can't be late.'

Harold pulled out a hip flask and offered it to Tom. 'Have a swig; doctor's orders.'

Tom smiled and did so. As the whisky took effect, a sense of well-being spread through him. 'I don't know what I'd do without you, Guthrie. No one could ask for a better friend.'

Harold looked pleased but changed the subject. 'Does Lydia know about the honeymoon being in the Lake District yet?'

Tom let out an amused breath. 'Of course. Lydia chose the hotel. It's where her parents used to take her and Grace on holiday. She says we'll get better service there because they'll remember her father.'

'Should be a good place to do a spot of painting too,' Harold said.

Tom laughed. 'I don't think Lydia will take too kindly to me spending our honeymoon going off with my sketchbook.'

Harold blushed. 'No, I suppose not.'

'Though I'm keen to stop and see some of the Roman Wall on our way,' said Tom. 'I've booked our first night in a town called Hexham, which is close by. At least that is a surprise for Lydia.'

He took another swig from the flask and felt suddenly emotional. Putting a hand on his friend's shoulder, he said, 'Guthrie, I've never properly thanked you for what you did for me in Mesopotamia. I wouldn't be standing here now if it wasn't for you. Tibby put about this ridiculous idea that I was a war hero just to please Papa – and Lydia's latched onto it too. They have no idea how wrong they are. I feel such a fraud. It's you who is the hero, Harold; you're the one who stuck your neck out for me—'

'Enough,' Harold interrupted. 'That's all in the past. We don't need to talk of it again. But for what it's worth, I think what you did required a special kind of courage and I will always admire you for it.'

Tom's eyes stung as he saw Harold's compassionate look. He gripped his friend's shoulder harder and swallowed. 'To me, Guthrie, you are the epitome of the ideal man.'

Harold's eyes glistened as he shook his head with a self-deprecating laugh.

Their conversation was cut short by a triumphant Tibby appearing with the colonel leaning on her arm. She was wearing an orange dress, purple coat, winter boots and a vast old-fashioned hat decorated with ostrich feathers that he suspected she'd dug out of their old playroom cupboard that morning. Tom's heart swelled in affection for his twin sister. Archibald was dressed in his old mess kit with a row of medals on his chest. Tom exchanged surprised looks with Harold before hurrying forward to help.

His father shrugged him off. 'Perfectly capable of walking down my own steps.'

Tom kissed Tibby on the cheek. 'You look amazing.'

'Outlandish, isn't it?' Tibby said with a throaty laugh. 'But all eyes will be on the bride, so I don't think it matters what I wear.'

Shaking off raindrops from her hat, Esmie accompanied Minnie Templeton to the front of the packed church. It was chilly inside but the gloom was dispelled by flickering candles on large wrought-iron stands. The rain was coming on hard now and two ushers stood with umbrellas at the ready for the bride and her father when they arrived.

Glancing to her right, Esmie was astonished to see Colonel Lomax sitting next to Tibby in the second row, staring rigidly ahead. She grinned at Tibby, wondering what spell she had cast over her father to get him to attend.

Tom, turning round in the front row, caught her look. Esmie felt her whole body jolt. He was looking groomed and handsome in his morning coat, his strong chin freshly shaven and dark hair smoothed into place. There was a tinge of colour in his firm cheekbones and jaw that betrayed his excitement. For an instant their eyes held each other and then he gave a slight nod and turned away to talk to Harold.

Shivering, she rubbed her arms and sat back. Minnie was chattering under her breath and looked close to tears.

'I so wish Grace and her family were here. She and Lydia might not see each other again for years. I think Lydia should visit Zurich before she goes to India, don't you? Where have they got to? It feels like we've been sitting here for ages. Do you think she's having second thoughts?'

Esmie put a comforting hand on the older woman's. 'Of course not. She'll be here in a minute or two.'

'She can be very impulsive,' Minnie fretted.

Her anxious comments were cut short by the organ striking up the bridal march. Glancing round, Esmie saw Lydia and her father appear at the back of the church. Tom and Harold stood up. As the bride walked forward a smile spread across Tom's face at the sight of her. Esmie's throat constricted. They were so obviously in love and made such a handsome couple.

The rest of the service passed in a blur as Esmie fought to stem tears of emotion for her friend. She couldn't imagine her and Harold being so engrossed in each other. Would it be wrong to marry him and not feel love?

Then the moment came to file out of the small country church and Esmie found Harold waiting to accompany her down the aisle. He was ruggedly good-looking in a morning coat, the stiff collar of his shirt digging into his thick neck, his broad face ruddy and smiling with good humour. He looked more like a robust farmer than a missionary doctor. His hazel eyes lit up on seeing Esmie but his smile faltered.

'Hello, Esmie.' His look was uncertain as he waited.

'Hello, Harold.' She smiled and fell into step beside him.

Outside it was still raining and there was hardly time to exchange more than pleasantries before everyone was dashing to the shelter of cars or carriages. Harold excused himself; he was detailed to drive Tibby and the colonel to the reception. Esmie travelled back with Lydia's parents in one of the ribbon-bedecked cars and handed out a fresh handkerchief to Minnie.

'Isn't she the most beautiful bride you've ever seen?' sobbed Minnie.

Jumbo chuckled in delight. 'Yes, but don't tell Grace you said that.'

'She certainly is,' said Esmie. 'And how happy she looks.'

'Thank goodness the old colonel turned up,' said Jumbo.

'I hope he behaves himself at the reception,' Minnie said, suddenly anxious.

'Just put him in a corner with a large dram,' said Esmie, 'and he'll probably just fall asleep.'

Jumbo laughed. 'Sound medical advice, Nurse McBride! That's what we'll do.'

The rain did not let up all day, so the planned tea dance on the lawn was abandoned and the buffet of sandwiches and cakes was served in the dining room rather than the marquee. But Jumbo made sure that there was plenty of champagne and whisky for the guests and, after short speeches and toasts, the house reverberated to the sound of lively chatter and raucous laughter. The band, which should have performed outside, set up in the conservatory and played popular tunes. Wedding presents gifted to the couple were displayed on tables in the large entrance hall.

Together, Lydia and Tom circulated among their guests, looking flushed and happy. Esmie was chatting to Tibby when the newly married couple stopped for a word. Tom, a little inebriated, leaned towards Esmie and kissed her cheek, just missing her lips.

'Esmie,' Tom said, 'thank you for being such a support to Lydia in the run up to the wedding.'

Esmie felt a rush of heat to her face. 'It was a pleasure.'

Lydia giggled. 'No it wasn't. I was up to high doh about Tom's father.' She nodded towards the colonel, in animated conversation with a landowning friend of Jumbo's. 'Now, look at him behaving like a lamb.'

Tom snorted in amusement. 'I've never heard him called that before. Maybe a wolf in sheep's clothing.'

Lydia gave him a playful pat on the jaw. 'Now, now, husband. You're not going to spoil things by being beastly to your father.'

'Nothing can spoil this day,' he said, planting a robust kiss on her forehead.

'Careful of my hair,' she warned.

He laughed and held out his glass to a passing waitress to top up his champagne.

Abruptly, Tibby said, 'Come on, Esmie; let's go and kick off our shoes in the conservatory and dance to the band.'

'Great idea,' Esmie said, feeling awkward in Tom's presence. 'I love dancing.'

'And there are lots of eligible men,' Lydia said with a conspiratorial grin, 'so make the most of the opportunity.'

Tibby gave a dismissive wave. 'We refuse to be wallflowers waiting for men to ask us – we'll dance anyway.'

Linking her arm through Esmie's, the young women sauntered off towards the conservatory, laughing.

Tom watched them go, feeling light-headed. He'd drunk too much already but he liked the euphoria and pleasant numbness that the champagne brought. Perhaps he shouldn't have kissed Esmie – she had seemed embarrassed by it – but he'd done it before thinking. She was looking so fetching in her blue outfit that brought out the blue-grey of her large eyes. He felt full of bonhomie towards everyone, and a strange relief.

He had feared that the ceremony would remind him too painfully of Mary but he'd been detached, going through the motions as if he were observing the vow-taking from afar. Eight years ago, he had married in military uniform on a blustery spring day full of scudding clouds and bursts of sunshine. The Maxwells had laid on a luncheon at their country house for two dozen guests and then Harold had driven Tom and Mary to Leith, where they'd embarked on a ship to Holland. Mary had always wanted to see the tulip fields.

Today was a complete contrast: the belting rain and the scores of guests, the jaunty music and the lavish party with copious amounts of drink and tables laden with food. The gregarious Templetons were quite different from the reserved and elderly Maxwells, who had outlived their only daughter by a couple of years and died heartbroken within three months of each other.

Most of all, fair vivacious Lydia was the opposite of gentle dark-haired Mary. He had never seen Lydia look more stunningly beautiful or desirable as she did now, with her pretty face pink with excitement and the fine silk of her dress revealing the curves of her body. She too was watching Esmie and Tibby disappear arm in arm.

'I'm surprised how pally those two have become,' she commented. 'I hope Tibby doesn't spoil Esmie's chances of finding a man.'

'I'm not sure she's looking for one,' said Tom. He took a slug of champagne and fumbled one-handedly for his cigarette case.

'Why do you say that?' She gave him a sharp look.

'Well, she's showing no interest in Guthrie's proposal.'

Lydia seized on this. 'Harold's proposed to Esmie? Why didn't you tell me?'

Tom cursed his indiscretion. 'Don't say anything—'

'I knew he was sweet on her,' Lydia said animatedly. 'I've been trying to match-make all summer. I'll have a strong word with Esmie. I can't believe she hasn't confided in me about it. She must say yes to him, then we can all go to India together!'

Tom's head spun. The room was stuffy and he was suddenly keen to be gone – to be alone with his new bride. He pushed his cigarette case back in his pocket, slipped his arm around Lydia and whispered into her ear.

'Never mind about Harold and Esmie. When are we allowed to leave? I can't wait for the honeymoon to begin, Mrs Lomax.'

Lydia giggled. 'Not yet. I want to enjoy the party.' Her gaze swept the room. 'Look, there's Alexandra from school. I simply must introduce you. She'll be so jealous I've ended up marrying Captain Lomax of The Anchorage.'

Lydia took him by the arm and steered him across the room.

Breathless from a chaotic attempt to dance the tango with Tibby, Esmie escaped outside. The rain had finally eased and there were people milling around on the terrace so she slipped off into the garden and stood under a huge dripping chestnut tree. She had already discarded her hat and now raised her face to catch the plops of rain and breathe in the earthy smells of the wet garden. She knew she was avoiding Harold and felt bad about it but she didn't want to be drawn into a conversation about marriage on Lydia's wedding day. There would be time to talk once her friend had left on honeymoon. The Templetons had pressed her to stay until the end of the week. 'It'll cheer us up once our darling girl has gone,' Minnie had said tearfully.

Esmie glanced towards the house, wondering when the bridal couple would leave. They appeared in no hurry to go, though she knew from Lydia that they had a couple of hours drive ahead of them to some mystery destination for their first night. Esmie tried to stop herself imagining what it would be like to spend the night with Tom, who must already be an experienced lover from his first happy marriage. Her insides fluttered. She wished she could stop thinking about him. She had hoped that during the weeks apart her attraction towards Tom would have fizzled out. But one glance at him in the church that morning had set her heart racing; it distressed her to think that she was still in love with him.

Suddenly, she caught sight of Tom weaving his way from the terrace towards her. Supressing a gasp, she pressed up against the tree, hoping not to be seen. He stopped to pull out his cigarette case, lit up a cigarette and then continued forward. To her consternation, he looked right at her as if he were seeking her out – though she knew he must only be heading for the shelter of the tree.

She edged around the tree trunk, her pulse racing. She could smell the smoke from the tobacco as he arrived.

'Esmie,' he said, 'I know you're there.'

She blushed as she stepped back towards him, her heart thudding. He leaned against the tree and drew deeply on his cigarette.

'I'm trying to sober up before driving to Hexham,' he said. He shot her a look. 'Oh dear, don't say anything to Lydia about Hexham – it's supposed to be a surprise.'

'Of course I won't.'

'I've drunk too much. I keep letting out secrets,' he confessed. 'I'm afraid I let slip to Lydia about Harold proposing to you.'

Esmie went hot with embarrassment. 'So you know about that?'

He nodded. 'Harold's worried you're going to say no. And I feel a bit responsible as I encouraged him in the first place.'

Esmie was astounded. 'Did you?'

He gave her a sheepish look. 'Sorry, was that wrong of me? I thought you'd be good for my friend – just the sort of plucky woman he needs at the mission. But do I need to warn Guthrie that you're not in love with him?'

'No,' Esmie said quietly, 'I'd rather you didn't say anything. I haven't decided . . .' Tom must never know that the man she loved was him. 'I'm not sure what to do next, if I'm honest.'

'Ah.' Tom glanced at her sympathetically and carried on smoking. After a pause he asked, 'Is that why you're unhappy?'

This startled Esmie. 'I'm perfectly fine,' she protested.

He eyed her keenly. 'It seems to me that you haven't really settled since the War. It's the way you talk about your time with the Scottish Women's Hospitals as if you were happier then. Is it that you miss the excitement of living by your wits – of living a simple life – the challenge of the battlefront?'

She gaped at him. How could he possibly know all that?

'At times I've felt the same about active service in the army,' he admitted. 'That sort of life gets under your skin – the comradeship and knowing that every day counts because it might be your last.'

Esmie was shaken by his observations; she hadn't thought he could be such a perceptive man.

'But you've turned your back on all that,' she pointed out.

His jaw tensed. He dropped his cigarette and ground it out. 'Yes, I have.'

He seemed about to say something more, then changed his mind and glanced back at the house. 'I just wanted to warn you that I've been indiscreet to Lydia about you and Harold – she's bound to say something. I'm sorry.'

'I can fend off Lydia's questions, don't worry,' Esmie said dryly. 'I've had years of practice.'

'And what will you say to my friend, Guthrie?' he asked.

She gave him a sharp look. 'That's between me and Harold.'

'Sorry, that was none of my business. It's the drink making me speak before I think.'

'I'll forgive you on your wedding day,' she said with a smile.

She noticed how a droplet of rain was poised on the end of a slick of his hair that had fallen over his forehead. Esmie had a strong desire to flick it off and smooth the hair back in place. It felt wrong to be standing alone under the tree with Lydia's groom but she was reluctant to hurry back inside. She had been enjoying a moment of solitude; it was Tom who had approached her. She became aware that he was studying her with that intent look in his blue eyes.

'So why are you hiding out here?' he asked. 'Was Tibby making you dance the tango?'

Esmie gave an abrupt laugh. 'Yes, how did you guess? I'm fond of your sister but she's a hopeless dancer.'

Tom chuckled. 'She is. But she makes up for lack of finesse with bags of enthusiasm.'

Just then, Esmie saw Lydia appear on the terrace. She felt a guilty pang.

'Mrs Lomax is looking for you,' she said.

For a moment, she saw confusion in Tom's look and then he spotted his bride.

'Ah, Lydia.'

He stepped forward and waved. She beckoned to him. Tom turned to Esmie. 'Shall we go in? No doubt Lydia will want you to help her change out of her dress. I think it's finally time for us to leave.'

'Yes, of course.' Reluctantly, Esmie left the shelter of the tree and led the way across the sodden grass.

In the short time it took for Lydia to change from her wedding dress into her going-away outfit, she bombarded Esmie with questions about

Harold's proposal and advice about accepting it. To Esmie's embarrassment, Lydia spilled out the secret to her mother as soon as Minnie joined them in the bedroom.

'Harold's proposed to Esmie! Isn't that wonderful?'

Minnie rushed across the room and, for the umpteenth time that day, burst into tears.

'That's marvellous news,' she cried, clasping Esmie to her soft bosom.

'But I haven't given him an answer yet,' Esmie protested. 'I'm still thinking it over.'

Minnie drew back. 'But you'll say yes, surely? Harold's such a nice man.'

'Of course she will,' Lydia answered. 'They're perfect for each other.' She turned from adjusting her pink felt hat in the mirror. 'Dearest Esmie, it'll make going to India so much easier if I know you'll be there too.'

Minnie blew her nose and smiled fondly. 'You must be special to Harold – he's never courted anyone before, as far as I know. His mother and aunt will be thrilled. Agnes Guthrie despairs of ever being a grandmother.'

Esmie fought down the panic rising inside. 'Please don't say anything to Harold's mother. I must have time to talk to Harold first.'

'I won't say a word,' Minnie promised.

Looking at Minnie's flushed, excited face, Esmie doubted Lydia's mother would be able to contain such gossip. Esmie would have to make up her mind swiftly and speak to Harold before the news of his proposal spread. She couldn't bear the thought of Agnes Guthrie being bitterly disappointed in the way that Maud Drummond had been.

Esmie was suddenly furious with Tom. If he hadn't drunk so much and been indiscreet, she wouldn't be under the pressure that she now was to accept marriage to the doctor. She hid her dismay as she helped Lydia retie a silk scarf. Then the three women were hugging and saying tearful goodbyes.

For a moment, Lydia seemed overwhelmed by the momentous step she was taking and her chin started to wobble.

'I'm going to miss you and Daddy so much, Mummy. And this place. I love my home. I didn't think it would be so difficult to leave.'

Minnie clung to her daughter and they fought back tears. Esmie patted their shoulders.

'This will always be your home,' Esmie reassured her. 'You're more likely to stay here when you're on leave from India than you are at The Anchorage.'

Lydia pulled away and gave a tremulous smile. 'That's true.'

'Come on, Mrs Lomax,' Esmie encouraged, 'you've got a husband waiting outside who's impatient to be with you.'

Dabbing away her tears, Lydia composed herself. 'I'm impatient too,' she said, beaming.

Esmie and Minnie linked arms and followed Lydia downstairs.

Chapter 9

The day after the wedding was a Sunday and Esmie knew that Harold would be at church and then spending a quiet day with his mother and his formidable aunt, who didn't approve of outings on the Sabbath or even reading – unless it was the Bible.

Exhausted, Lydia's parents rose late and were content to spend the afternoon sitting in the summerhouse keeping out of the thundery showers. Knowing they would want to recount the events of the previous day and suspecting that Minnie would have told Jumbo about Harold's proposal, Esmie decided to leave them in peace. She didn't relish further questions. So she took herself off for a long walk along the cliffs.

Alone with her thoughts, Esmie pondered her encounter under the tree with Tom and the revelation that it was he who had encouraged Harold to propose to her. A plucky woman, he'd called her, and ideal for the mission as well as Harold. It brought home to Esmie how Tom – unlike her – was not the least bit troubled at the thought of having her living close by in the same region of India.

Her insides twisted with a feeling that must be relief. It would make it easier for her to accept a future with Harold in India.

Gazing out over a choppy greenish sea, Esmie sensed she was on the verge of making up her mind. Tom had been right; she hadn't completely settled back in Scotland. Vaullay had been a place of refuge and healing after the gruelling years on the Continent. But now she was ready for a new challenge and a new cause.

Turning inland, Esmie walked briskly towards Ebbsmouth.

The Guthries lived in a former mariner's house on the edge of the town, where Agnes had moved after her stationmaster husband had died ten years ago. Her husband's spinster sister, Edith, lived with her and ruled the household. The approach to the house was under an archway made from the jawbone of a whale.

Shadows were lengthening across the front garden as Esmie knocked at the front door under its rose-covered porch. No one answered. Perhaps they were still resting? She should have waited until tomorrow. She half-turned to go, her nerve failing her. Then Esmie realised that if she walked away now, she might have changed her mind by the morning. She should stick to her instinct and act at once. Turning back to the door, she knocked louder and waited with a drumming heart.

It seemed an age – but was probably no more than a minute – before the door opened. In bare feet and his thinning hair tousled, Harold peered out, looking groggy from sleep.

He stared at her in astonishment. Instantly his face reddened.

'Esmie? What . . .?'

'I'm sorry to disturb you on a Sunday,' she said.

'Is something wrong?' he asked in concern.

Esmie shook her head.

From inside, Edith's querulous voice called, 'Who is it? What do they want? Don't they know not to call on the Sabbath?'

Harold looked torn, glancing over his shoulder and then back at Esmie.

Esmie said hastily, 'I'll come back tomorrow. It can wait.'

As she stepped away, Harold reached out and stopped her. 'No, don't go. Just give me a minute.'

He left her on the doorstep and disappeared inside. She could hear him placating his indignant aunt. He returned moments later, pulling on a jacket, his feet thrust into unlaced shoes. He shut the door behind him and gestured for Esmie to walk ahead. They didn't speak until they had passed under the whalebone arch and were hidden from view by a thick beech hedge.

'Sorry, I can't invite you inside,' he said. 'Mother wouldn't mind but Aunt Edith . . .'

'No, it's my fault. I know I shouldn't have called but I can't put things off any longer. You've waited long enough for your answer.'

Harold's look turned to alarm. 'So you've made up your mind?'

Esmie nodded.

'It was good of you to wait till after the wedding,' said Harold. 'Not to cast a shadow over the happy day. I imagine you want to get back to Vaullay as soon as possible – to your work and Dr Carruthers – and that's why you've come on the Sabbath. I don't blame you. Aunt Edith's from a different generation and doesn't understand. But I do. I'm grateful that you've given my proposal such consideration and that you've come to tell me in person—'

'Harold,' Esmie interrupted, 'please let me speak.'

'Sorry,' he said, looking miserable.

'I've come to say yes,' she said. 'I accept your proposal.'

He gaped at her as if he'd misheard. 'What? You do?'

Esmie nodded.

'Are you sure?' he asked.

She was disarmed by his boyish uncertainty and smiled. 'Yes, I'm sure. As long as you are.'

He ran a hand over his uncombed hair. 'Well, yes . . . I wasn't expecting . . .' Abruptly he smiled. 'Goodness. Thank you.'

They stood regarding each other. Esmie could tell he felt as awkward as she did. She hadn't meant to blurt out her answer. She should have given him more time to talk it through and discover if he really wanted to marry her or was only proposing because his best friend Tom had pressured him into doing so.

'Harold,' Esmie said, placing a hand lightly on his arm, 'I know this isn't a love match for either of us but I agree with all you say in your letter. I think we will be good companions and I'm eager to work alongside you in Taha.'

'Yes, yes!' Harold said with sudden enthusiasm. 'We can do God's work together.'

Esmie had a momentary pang of doubt. He must have seen it in her expression.

'You do believe in the work of the mission, don't you? That's very important to me.'

'I'll do all I can to further its medical work,' Esmie answered. 'But when you talk about God's work . . . I'm concerned about what you might expect from our marriage . . . that you might feel that our main duty is to procreate.' Esmie's cheeks burned at her forwardness but she wanted to be truthful with him. 'I want to nurse and be your partner in life but I don't want children straight away. If I was to become a mother so soon I wouldn't be able to do my work – my life would be taken up with worrying about keeping a baby safe and alive.'

She held his look, wondering if she had offended him. His face was puce with embarrassment but his eyes shone with understanding – or was it relief?

He took her hands in his; both hers and Harold's were shaking.

'Esmie, I'm glad that you're being frank with me and I have exactly the same fears about bringing a child into such a harsh place. The British cemeteries in India are full of children who haven't survived infancy. I know the reason you want to go to India is to work among the Pathans – you were quite clear about that – but I was equally clear that what I'm offering is friendship. So we're in agreement; abstinence will be our sacrifice to the greater cause of caring wholeheartedly for the sick.'

Esmie faltered. 'I— I didn't mean . . .'

He let go of her hands. 'We don't need to speak of this to anyone but ourselves – or mention it again.'

Esmie thought she hadn't made herself clear; she wasn't asking for complete abstinence. She knew there were ways of enjoying intimacy yet avoiding conception; she and Lydia had discussed it. But Harold was already stepping away. Impulsively, she leaned forward and kissed him on the cheek. She didn't want him to think that she shunned physical contact with him.

He looked uncomfortable and glanced towards the house. 'Best wait until tomorrow before breaking the news to Mother and my aunt.'

Esmie had the distinct impression that Harold had been referring to the Guthrie women when he'd said they shouldn't ever mention to anyone else his suggestion of celibacy. Agnes Guthrie would be pained by Esmie's reluctance to have Harold's children and Edith would be shocked at such a topic.

Esmie hid her disappointment that he didn't want to share the news of their engagement straight away. Now that she had made up her mind, she was eager to tell everyone. But she nodded and curbed her impatience. She could tell from Harold's glances that he was anxious not to linger outside.

'You must go back to your mother and aunt,' Esmie said. 'I can walk back by myself.'

He looked relieved. 'Are you sure?'

'Of course.'

'I'll pick you up tomorrow at eleven,' he said with a bashful smile. 'Then we can announce our betrothal to Mother and Aunt Edith.'

She smiled too but didn't attempt to kiss him again. It must all seem so sudden to Harold – she had caught him off guard – and she shouldn't be surprised that he was a little flustered.

As Esmie made her way back to Templeton Hall, her heart lifted with optimism. She had found a man who was offering her exactly what she wanted; the security of marriage that would allow her to act freely in her work, as well as companionship without the emotional entanglements of love. Surely Harold was an answer to her prayers?

Yet she felt a niggle of worry over his eagerness for their relationship to be platonic. That's not what she had meant when she'd expressed her concern about having children. A marriage without any intimacy would not be a true marriage. But maybe she had misunderstood him. Harold might be meaning abstinence while they settled into the work of the mission and got to know each other better. That would be a sensible approach. Esmie was sure that once they became familiar with one another – and their fondness grew – that intimacy would follow naturally. With that thought, she quickened her pace. Minnie and Jumbo would be the first to hear her news.

Chapter 10

Vaullay, August

Esmie and Harold were to be married in the asylum chapel at Vaullay. It was to be a small affair, with just Dr Carruthers representing Esmie's family and Agnes and Edith on Harold's side. Although both bride and groom were keen on a swift and quiet wedding, Harold insisted that they waited for Tom and Lydia to return from honeymoon so that Tom could be his best man. Esmie invited Tibby as well.

Esmie wore the powder-blue dress that Isobel had bought her for Lydia's wedding, skilfully embellished with trimmings of white lace around the neckline and hem. When her aunt had remonstrated that she would buy her a wedding dress, Esmie had been adamant. 'I'm not wasting your money on a new dress that will never be worn again. The blue one is perfectly fine.' She did allow her guardian to pay for a white headdress and veil, thinking it would at least keep her wayward brown hair in place for a few hours.

On the morning of the wedding – a bright summer's day with a light dew making the lawns sparkle – Isobel's cheerful maid Jeanie helped Esmie get ready while Isobel kept the inquisitive Norrie out of the way. She kept the two-year-old occupied with helping her tie together a posy of flowers.

'Thank you, Norrie.' Esmie smiled and took the posy from the small boy, ruffling his hair with affection.

Abruptly, nervousness seized her at the thought of what she was doing. She would be stepping over the doorway for the final time as Esmie McBride. The next time she came to Isobel's home it would be as Mrs Harold Guthrie. She fought to control her rising panic as doubt seized her. She was about to marry a man she hardly knew. She had enjoyed his company while on holiday at Lydia's but what would Harold be like in India? Soon it would be too late to have second thoughts. She caught Isobel's look.

'Your parents would be so very proud of you,' Isobel said, her eyes glistening.

Esmie cleared the lump in her throat and said, 'I don't know how I would have coped without you these past eleven years since Father died. I can't thank you enough for all you've done for me, Auntie.'

Isobel patted her cheek. 'I've enjoyed every minute of your company, dearie.'

'And I yours.' Esmie smiled. 'It's not that I want to leave you or the hospital . . .' She struggled to find words adequate to express her restlessness of spirit.

Isobel's look was full of compassion. 'Esmie, you mustn't feel bad about going. It's a fine thing you are doing. Ever since you were a wee girl, I've been struck by your courage and sense of purpose.' She squeezed Esmie's shoulder. 'And you are marrying a man of principle. I know you will make a success of whatever you are called to do.'

The words steadied Esmie and strengthened her weakening resolve. She smiled at her guardian in gratitude and managed a tremulous, 'Thank you.'

'Now, come,' Isobel said more briskly, 'let's not keep the Guthries waiting.'

Emerging from Isobel's cottage beside her aunt, Esmie was overwhelmed to see the way to the chapel lined with well-wishers from among the patients. Workers from the farm had also come to wave and cheer her on. In the distance she could hear the blast of bagpipes playing and wondered whom her aunt had got to play for her.

As they rounded the corner to the chapel entrance, Esmie gasped in astonishment. Tommy Grey was sitting on a dining chair playing his pipes and wearing his old regimental trews over the stumps of his legs. Tears flooded her eyes to see the effort he was making for her.

Isobel leaned close to shout in her ear. 'He's been practising daily down in the byre.'

'Thank you, Tommy!' Esmie called and raised her posy of flowers in salute.

He managed a quick nod as he continued piping. Inside the chapel, the bride's side of the church was filled with members of staff and patients while on the groom's side there was just one row taken up by Lydia, the Guthrie women and Tibby, with the groom and his best man sitting in front of them. Esmie was overwhelmed that so many had come to see her married. She had wanted no fuss but she was touched by the warmth and goodwill shown by so many.

As Esmie walked down the aisle with her guardian and saw Harold and Tom standing at the end waiting for her, her insides somersaulted. She had to force herself not to look at Tom. Harold, dressed in his best Sunday suit, stepped into the aisle and gave her a nervous smile.

The service was over quickly. The minister's short address was drowned out by excited exclamations from some of the patients and enthusiastic clapping. The hushes of staff members did nothing to curb their noisy enthusiasm. Esmie was amused and pleased that they'd wanted to attend and by the twitching smile on Harold's face, she was glad to see that he didn't mind either.

Soon they were out in the mild sunshine again and heading for the staff dining hall where lunch was being laid on.

'Goodness,' Lydia said to Esmie with a wrinkle of her nose as they stepped inside, 'it smells like school meals, doesn't it?'

'Except the food's better,' said Esmie, smiling. 'And we won't make you sit until you finish your tapioca pudding.'

Tom appeared at their side. 'My wife has got too used to rich hotel food these past two weeks,' he said with a grin.

Esmie tried to control her hammering heart. He was looking so handsome and relaxed.

'Well, I've been gathering ideas for the Raj Hotel,' said Lydia. 'It's going to be the best place to dine in Rawalpindi. I think we should hire a French chef but Tom's not sure.'

'I'm a man of simple tastes. Give me plain fish and a boiled potato over meat with fancy sauces.'

'Well, I'm sorry but you'll be disappointed here,' Esmie quipped. 'You'll have to force yourself to enjoy our roast mutton, reared on the hospital farm, and roast potatoes – also grown by our patients.'

'Sounds delicious,' Tom said. 'I always make an exception for mutton.'

At that moment, Harold came to steer her away to sit beside his mother and aunt.

The lunch passed pleasantly and yet Esmie's stomach was too knotted to eat much. She was acutely aware of Tom and Lydia holding forth at the far end of the table about their honeymoon in the Lake District. Lydia was complaining that Tom had spent far too much time dragging her around Roman archaeological sites and old churches but Tom just laughed off her comments in amusement. Esmie could tell that Lydia was enjoying the banter and, from the flirtatious looks she was giving her husband, it was obvious that it was all said in jest. They had a loving, teasing relationship and she had a pang of envy.

Esmie studied Harold while he spoke earnestly to Isobel; they were deep in conversation about the hospital. Soon Esmie would be leaving with him and they'd be alone for the first time as husband and wife. Taking advice from Isobel, Harold had booked them into a house on the shores of Loch Vaullay where a widow, Mrs Macmillan, rented out her spare room. A forty-minute drive away along a single-track road, they would stay there for three nights and then return to Isobel's cottage for a couple of nights before heading down to Ebbsmouth to say farewell to Agnes and Edith. Their passage to India was booked for the beginning of September, sailing from Liverpool.

Lydia had been vexed that Harold had not been able to get them onto the same ship going east as she and Tom in late August. Harold had confided in Esmie that even if he had, they wouldn't be able to afford travelling in first class like the Lomaxes so it might have proved awkward. Harold had seemed embarrassed by this but Esmie had assured him that second class would be luxurious enough for her.

'I'm used to economising when travelling,' she said. 'And sailing to India will be like a first-class holiday anyway.'

Privately, she'd been relieved that Lydia and Tom would be leaving for India before them and that it would be a while before she saw them again.

Harold glanced up and caught her gazing at him. They swapped tentative smiles and Esmie felt herself blushing. Would Harold stick to his pronouncement that they would not seek intimacy in the bedroom? Suddenly she hoped not. Now that the ceremony was over and she was committed to being Harold's wife, Esmie wanted to get the first night over with – to consummate their marriage – and begin their life together. And she wanted to get away from Tom. Even listening to his deep voice and amused conversation made her chest constrict with longing.

Harold stood up. He must have sensed Esmie's desire for lunch to be over for he swiftly thanked everyone for coming and said it was time for him and his bride to leave.

They said their goodbyes. Lydia and Esmie kissed cheeks.

'Oh, darling Esmie! The next time we see each other will be in India. Isn't that the most exciting thought in the world?' Then she whispered in her ear. 'You're going to have so much fun, Mrs Guthrie. Marriage really is a bed of roses,' she grinned. 'At least it is for me.'

Esmie's stomach tensed as she thought how different her marriage to Harold was going to be. It would be a union of convenience and purpose, not one of easy pleasure like Lydia's obviously was.

She managed to smile and say, 'Have a safe journey and see you in India.'

When it came to saying goodbye to Tom, Esmie stuck out her hand so that there would be no repeat of the impetuous kiss Tom had given her at his own wedding. This occasion had been a much more sober affair – a glass of sherry to toast the couple – and Tom wasn't the least bit inebriated.

'Well, Mrs Guthrie,' he said, taking her hand, 'I wish you and Harold many years of happiness together.'

She allowed herself only a brief exchange of glances and a fleeting smile. 'Thank you,' she said, and pulled her hand out of his clasp.

Her pulse was still racing as she retreated to Harold's motor car. Some of the patients had attached old shoes on strings to the back of the car and they made a clattering noise as they drove off. Stopping briefly at the cottage for Esmie to discard her veil and fetch her small suitcase, they set off for the drive along Loch Vaullay.

Their landlady, Mrs Macmillan, recognised Esmie as the young nurse from the hospital who frequently went for hikes along the shore or up into the hills.

'Knew your parents too,' she said. 'Your mother was well-known for helping out the folk around here – brought food and medicines if she knew there was illness in the family. Aye, a good woman she was, right enough.'

Esmie was touched to hear how popular her mother had been. Yet she wondered if Harold should have chosen somewhere further from Vaullay for their honeymoon, where they wouldn't be known or talked about. But Isobel had told Harold that the fishing was good and he was keen to try his rod in the loch.

Taking their cases upstairs, Esmie was encouraged to see that most of the attic room was taken up with a double bed; Harold could hardly avoid lying with her. There was a washstand with a basin, water jug and mirror; a chest of drawers for their clothes and a single chair. One of them would have to climb in over the bed to reach the far side. There was a chamber pot under the washstand, otherwise they would have to trek downstairs and outside to the privy in the outhouse.

Esmie suggested a walk by the lochside, thinking to put Harold at his ease. There was a new self-consciousness between them and they had said little to each other since leaving the asylum. He agreed with alacrity and went downstairs while she changed out of her wedding dress and into a comfortable skirt, light jumper and walking shoes.

As they strolled in the hazy sunshine, Esmie slipped an arm through Harold's and encouraged him to talk about the mission.

'Tell me what to expect when we get to India. From the moment we land, I want to know everything.'

He brightened at her request. 'We'll disembark at Bombay,' he said, 'and spend a night or two at the mission house there. It'll give us enough time to buy essentials such as medical supplies and anything you might have forgotten. Then we'll catch the train north to Delhi and Lahore – and then on to the North-West Frontier and Taha. It'll be two and a half days on trains but they're comfortable enough. I'm afraid it'll be terribly hot though – temperature will still be in the nineties – and won't drop till the end of October.'

'Don't worry,' said Esmie, 'I can work in the heat.'

Harold smiled. 'The cold season can be very pleasant though; more like our Scottish summer weather with a few days of rain.'

The path narrowed and Harold disengaged his arm to let her walk ahead. He became animated as he talked about his home at Taha.

'It's a bungalow in its own compound – might need a bit of repair as it's been used as an overflow by the army in the recent troubles – but it's quite spacious. Large dining room and sitting room – and two bedrooms so you can have your own.'

He slid her a look. Esmie was dismayed. 'Surely that won't be necessary?'

'I'm a terribly restless sleeper,' said Harold. 'Get up at all times of the night. I wouldn't want to disturb you.'

Esmie decided not to argue about it but hoped that by the time they got to Taha, sleeping together wouldn't be an issue.

'And there's a garden?' she asked.

'Of sorts,' said Harold. 'Probably badly overgrown but it has apricot and walnut trees – and a mulberry.'

Esmie smiled. 'Sounds delightful.'

He told her about the people at the mission: the Pathan orderlies who worked at the hospital and Reverend Bannerman, a retired Scottish padre who helped dispense medicines, extracted teeth and in emergencies drove patients to hospital in Kohat. There was one other female medic, a widow called Rupa Desai.

'I thought you said single women weren't allowed at the mission?' Esmie queried.

'Mrs Desai is the exception to the rule. She was married to one of our mission doctors, so people knew her before as a married lady. She's a trained pharmacist in her own right – and an Indian.'

'So what happened to her husband?'

'Tragically, Dr Desai was shot dead at Kanki-Khel, our outpost clinic in the hills.'

'How awful!'

'Terrible,' Harold agreed. 'Mrs Desai was very courageous in agreeing to stay on at Taha.'

'She sounds remarkable,' said Esmie. 'I can't wait to meet her.'

'Of course, we won't let her anywhere near Kanki-Khel,' said Harold. 'And from what I hear, it came under attack in the recent war with the Afghans and the clinic got burnt down. I'm hoping for news from Bannerman that all is now well. I won't be taking you into a theatre of war, my dear.'

'Harold,' said Esmie, 'I'm not new to battlefronts. Wherever you go, I'm going too.'

They walked round to the far side of the loch and stayed out until the sun began to dip in the west. By the time they returned to the house, the first evening star was rising in an aquamarine sky, and Harold had lost his reticence. In the parlour, Mrs Macmillan gave them a simple supper of fish and boiled potatoes. Esmie couldn't help thinking how Tom would have welcomed such fare. She wondered who would win the battle over the menu at the Raj Hotel and thought it would most likely be Lydia. She forced such thoughts from her mind as the landlady cleared the plates and lit an oil lamp, bidding them to sit in more comfortable chairs. Then she left them alone.

Esmie waited for Harold to suggest that they retire upstairs but instead he went to fetch the exercise book he was using to teach her Pashto so that she could talk to the local staff at the mission. She had encouraged Harold to do so but hadn't envisaged spending their wedding night wrestling with the new language. For the next two hours he got her to practise sentences and learn vocabulary. Esmie's head ached with tiredness and she kept stifling yawns.

Finally, fearing that he might keep her up all night learning Pashto, she said, 'Harold, I can hardly keep my eyes open. Let's go up to bed.'

'Sorry, my dear,' he said, with an anxious look. 'Have I overdone it?'

She shook her head. 'It's fine but that's enough for one evening.'

Calling goodnight to their hostess who was dozing in the kitchen waiting for them to retire, they mounted the stairs to their bedroom in the eaves of the small house, Harold leading the way with the flickering lamp.

'I'll get ready in the corridor,' he said, grabbing his pyjamas before Esmie could say anything.

Heart racing, she took off her clothes and pulled on her nightdress, brushed out her hair and crawled over the bed to the far side and under the covers. Any moment now, Harold – her husband! – would be getting into bed beside her. She wondered what it would be like to be encircled in his beefy arms and to feel his breath on her hair. He had a nice firm mouth; would he kiss her on the lips? Excitement fluttered in her belly.

When Harold returned, she watched him carefully fold his clothes over the chair. His pyjama top was buttoned to the neck, tucked into the trousers and tied securely with a cord. Studiously avoiding looking at her, he took a book out of his suitcase. Esmie's heart sank. Climbing into bed he glanced at her.

'Do you mind if I read for a bit? It helps me get to sleep.'

Esmie masked her disappointment. 'Not at all. What are you reading?'

He hesitated and, in the dim light, she thought he looked embarrassed. 'One of Walter Scott's novels, *Old Mortality*.'

Esmie gave a surprised laugh. 'I was expecting something much more worthy and religious. Does your aunt know you read romantic novels?'

Harold smiled. 'Yes. She doesn't approve but she can't complain because they were left to me by my father – her brother – and the only man who could do no wrong in her eyes. He had all of Scott's novels – and a large collection of other books of fiction.'

Esmie sat up, delighted. This was something they had in common that she hadn't expected.

'Will you read to me?' she asked.

He looked at her in surprise. 'But I'm halfway through the novel.'

'That doesn't matter,' said Esmie. 'I know the story anyway. My father had all of Scott's novels too and I've read every one of them. Sometimes he would read aloud to me.'

'If you'd really like me to?' Harold still looked unsure. Esmie nodded.

'Very well,' said Harold.

He turned up the flame on the lamp and started to read. He had a pleasant reading voice, not as deep or expressive as her father's, but with a calming rhythm.

In the cosy glow of the lamplight, Esmie relaxed back onto the pillow and listened. Soon the exhaustion of the day overcame her. She fell fast asleep to the soporific sound of Harold's voice.

Esmie woke before full light, wondering where she was. She peered around an unfamiliar room full of strange shadows. With a start she remembered she was lying in bed beside Harold. In the gloom she could see the outline of his bulky body and square face. He was lying on his back, snoring gently.

Esmie inched towards him and peered more closely. He had a strong weathered face but in repose he looked more youthful. The lines around his eyes were less noticeable and his sandy lashes looked soft as a child's. The buttons of his top strained as his broad chest rose and fell. A tuft of hair showed through a gap between the buttons. She had an urge to trace her finger across his brow and down his cheek, to touch the protruding hair. But would he be annoyed if she woke him?

Her fingers strayed to her own throat and her buttoned-up nightdress, recalling how Harold had read to her until she had fallen asleep. He had made no attempt to touch her. If she had stayed awake, would he at least have given her a goodnight kiss? Perhaps he had done so while she lay sleeping. Had he gazed at her in the lamplight and felt a stirring of desire as she did now? Or had he carried on reading, resolute in his vow of abstinence? She was restless and knew she couldn't stay there while he slept, and her frustration grew.

Esmie slipped from under the covers and crawled over the bed without disturbing Harold. Half-hoping he might wake and stop her going, she took her time unbuttoning and stepping out of her nightdress, folding it and putting on clothes. He slept on and so she crept from the room. Descending the stairs, she could hear Mrs Macmillan moving about in the kitchen and stoking up the range. Her first instinct was to go and help but she thought the widow might think it odd to find her there on the first day of her honeymoon and would probably chase her back upstairs to her husband.

Husband! Esmie's insides churned as she let herself out of the back door and across the yard to the outhouse. The air was chilly and the sky pink with the dawn. Minutes later, having used the privy, she left Mrs Macmillan's and headed down to the loch for a walk.

Leaving the path, she scrambled through a thicket of hazel bushes and reached the pebbly shore. The mountains in the east were dark against a sky that was rapidly turning golden. The still loch was mirroring the dawn light; not a soul was about. A heron took off from a nearby rock and soared across the glinting water. Esmie had never seen the loch look more beautiful and serene.

She had a sudden poignant memory of her father holding her hand by the lochside – she couldn't have been more than five or six – and coaxing her into the water. He had taught her to swim in this very loch and when they'd moved to Ebbsmouth they had gone sea bathing together. Esmie thought fleetingly of the day she had swum in the cove with Harold and Tom. She had struggled not to stare at Tom's tall athletic body and powerful limbs thrashing through the surf and had resisted the urge to trace her finger along the scar on his shoulder. She needed to expunge that memory. A cold swim would distract her fevered thoughts and dampen her desire.

Esmie discarded her clothes and waded naked into the shallows, sending out ripples across the calm surface. She gasped as she struck out into the loch and the deeper icy water. It took her breath away but filled her with exhilaration. This was the first day of her new life and she would embrace it with all her being. She would find a way to break through Harold's physical reserve. Like her, he was probably a virgin and feeling anxious about sex. That was why he had seized on the idea of abstinence to cover his embarrassment at her raising the issue of conceiving a child. It was her own fault for blurting out her fears when all she should have done was accept his proposal with enthusiasm.

As she swam back towards the beach and glimpsed the guest house on the hillside, with the daylight edging across it, she thought of the self-effacing man lying in the upstairs bed and felt a sudden affection for him. They just needed time to get used to each other; she mustn't be impatient with him. She was sure that she had done the right thing in marrying Harold. Together, they were going to do important work and – Esmie smiled to herself – probably read a lot of books.

Rubbing herself dry with a scarf, every inch of her body tingled as she fumbled back into her clothes. She wondered what adventures she would have and what places she would see before she next plunged into the waters of Loch Vaullay. Whatever the future with Harold had in store for her, Esmie knew that she was now ready for it.

Chapter 11

SS Galloway Castle, early September

Esmie spent the first week of the three-week voyage to India confined to their cramped second-class cabin being seasick. The bad weather that had dogged them through the Bay of Biscay had continued into the Mediterranean.

'I'd forgotten what a bad sailor I am,' she groaned as Harold hovered over her in worry. 'I'll be fine. Just leave me to sleep.'

'You'd feel better being up on deck,' he said. 'Get some fresh air. Take your mind off it by watching the waves.'

At the mention of waves, Esmie leaned over and heaved into a tin bowl by the bedside. She sank back and closed her eyes. 'I can't move that far,' she said weakly. 'Please don't feel you have to stay here. Go and enjoy yourself, Harold.'

He went, still muttering that fresh air would be the cure. Esmie couldn't bear to move. She tried to lie as still as possible and think of something else – something useful. In her head she went over the latest words of Pashto that Harold had been teaching her and which would be essential for living among the tribal people. She had also learnt that the name Pathan was just a general name used by the British for all Pashto-speaking people. There were, in fact, dozens of different tribes throughout the North-West Frontier, many linked through kinship but each jealously guarding their own territory.

'Sounds just like our Highland clans in days gone by,' Esmie had said as her husband had pointed out areas on a Victorian map he'd found among Aunt Edith's books.

'Exactly like,' Harold had agreed. 'They have chiefs called khans and the men are heavily armed at all times and use the same tactics of surprise in lightning raids on their enemies. A terrifying sight by all accounts – bearded and shrieking and brandishing weapons.'

'And will we be treating such men?' Esmie had asked, eyes widening.

'Of course,' Harold had said. 'If they come to the hospital we can't turn them away. Sometimes we have to make sure that feuding families are kept at opposite ends. But most of the time we are dealing with farmers and their families – with similar accidents and ailments as our own folk.'

Esmie had tried to memorise Harold's information about the different tribal areas. The mission hospital at Taha was in North Waziristan, which was populated with Waziris, while to the north of it, close to the Afghanistan border, they ran an outlying clinic in the mountainous Kurram Valley in the Kohat region. Here lived Gurbuz and Otmanzai.

'Both are tribes of the northern Waziris,' Harold had explained. 'But the Otmanzai are more powerful.'

When Esmie had looked perplexed, her husband had said, 'Think of the Waziris as a confederacy – like Clan MacDonald – with the Otmanzai as a senior branch.'

Esmie had nodded at this, so Harold had continued with enthusiasm.

'Of course there are other important tribes too; the Afridi to the north near Peshawar and the Mahsuds to the south who have their own sub-tribes such as the Manzai and Bahlolzai. The Mahsuds are the ones who have been causing so much trouble this summer in attacks on British soldiers. Then there are other smaller tribes; Bettanis and Bannuchis and Ormurs . . .'

'Stop!' Esmie had cried. 'I need to write all this down.'

She had done so and Harold had tested her each evening before he would read to her.

Now, as Esmie lay on her narrow bunk feeling ill, the names of the Pathans swam behind her closed lids like elusive fish. She wondered if Tom had fought against these tribes and if so which ones. He had belonged to the Peshawar Rifles so had probably seen action against the Afridis. What had his first wife Mary done while he'd been posted to outlying pickets in the Khyber Pass? Had she revelled in cantonment life or found time hanging heavily on her hands?

Had Tom's young bride been ill on board ship and apprehensive about the life she had chosen or had she stood at the deck rail with Tom and been impatient to get to India? She wanted to ask Harold these questions – to hear more about Mary – but didn't want to betray her feelings for Tom by bringing him up in conversation.

Lydia, by all accounts, was revelling in her new adventure. There had been letters from Marseilles and Port Said enthusing about life on board in First Class, with dinners, dances and deck games.

> *We're rubbing shoulders with the cream of British society in India. Do you know what the top civil officials call themselves? The Heaven-born! Isn't that priceless? And they certainly think they are too. I introduce myself as a captain's wife, otherwise they simply wouldn't speak to me. We're having such a marvellous time. Mummy and Daddy are enjoying every minute and have made heaps of friends – all the young officers love them – that's why my dance card is always full! And we're waited on hand and foot. India is going to be such fun!*

As the ship pitched in the sea swell, Esmie couldn't help a weak smile at her friend's excitement. Lydia was making the most of her new life. Esmie closed her eyes. Marriage to Harold was certainly not romantic, but then he had never promised that it would be. He was solicitous and brotherly but to her frustration he made no attempt to touch her and seemed embarrassed by her bedtime pecks on the cheek. The only time they had shared a double bed was in Mrs Macmillan's attic. When she had snuggled up to him and put an arm about his waist, he had tensed and then after a gentle pat on her hand had rolled onto his side and out of her reach.

Since then they had slept in single beds – neither Isobel nor the Guthries had double beds in their homes – and on board ship their cabin beds were hardly wider than luggage shelves. At least they were lucky not to be sharing their billet with anyone else.

She had the impression that Harold's fussing over her illness was masking a certain relief that she was too unwell to bestow night-time kisses. They hadn't even seen each other undress. Harold would always hurry to the bathroom when she began to disrobe, taking his pyjamas with him and waiting long enough for her to have got into bed before he returned. Not that she had any energy for intimacy in her present state, Esmie thought weakly.

It would be different once they got to India and became more accustomed to each other. Familiarity would bring greater warmth between them. It was just that they were both used to living single lives – particularly for Harold at thirty-three years old – and they needed time to adjust to being together. She sighed, willing the voyage to be over and for the day to come when she could bear to stand up and feel human again.

By the time they reached Suez Esmie was up and about and beginning to enjoy the journey. On the second-class deck, she joined in games of quoits and tennis and helped supervise activities for the children. Harold had made a new friend, Bernie Hudson, who was returning from furlough to Peshawar and worked for the Agriculture Department.

He was a likeable eccentric who stubbornly refused to replace his deer-stalker hat with the ubiquitous solar topee that everyone else was now wearing to protect their heads from the sun.

As they entered the Red Sea, the temperature rose and the breeze dropped. The crew changed into their light-weight white uniforms and passengers sought shade from the fierce sun. First-timers to India complained of the furnace-like conditions in the cabins with no sea breeze wafting through the ventilation pipes.

'I'm just thankful for the calm sea,' Esmie said to Harold and Bernie as they lounged in deck chairs. 'I don't mind the heat.'

'My dear girl, this is nothing,' said Bernie. 'Wait till you get to India.'

'I can't wait.' Esmie smiled, placing a hand on Harold's arm. She felt him stiffen and quickly withdrew her hold. She was beginning to realise that Harold was particularly uncomfortable in front of others with her small gestures of affection. She saw from Bernie's look that he had noticed this too but he carried on chatting as if it hadn't happened.

'Good job all that business with the Afghans is over,' Bernie said, reaching for his snuff box. 'I hear the RAF planes put the fear of God into them – they'd never seen them before. They scattered, leaving their guns behind.'

'Guns that our friends the Waziris and Mahsuds have got their hands on, unfortunately,' said Harold with a shake of the head. 'But I'm assured that all is now calm in Taha.'

'Well, if not,' said Bernie, taking a pinch of snuff, 'you are very welcome to stay with me in Peshawar until things are safer. The cantonment there is well fortified and I'm rattling around in a bungalow that's much too big for a bachelor.'

'That's very kind,' said Esmie. 'I'd be interested to visit Peshawar sometime.'

'Then you—' Bernie broke off to give a loud sneeze. He pulled out a brown-stained handkerchief, blew his bulbous nose and wiped his greying moustache. 'Must come and stay,' he said with a broad smile.

Chapter 12

The Raj Hotel, Rawalpindi, September

'Is that it?' Lydia stared in disbelief at the sprawling, low-lying building beyond a bald patch of grass and a dilapidated fence of flaking brown paint. 'It's falling to bits. Half the render – or whatever you call it – has come off.'

'It's superficial damage,' said Tom, hiding his own dismay and helping her down from the tonga that had brought them from the railway station. The hotel didn't look anything like the artistic drawings in the particulars of sale apart from the two palm trees shading the rusty iron-roofed portico and the glimpse of a veranda beyond.

Tom glanced round to see his servant, Bijal, supervising the unloading of their luggage. The sight of his calm, efficient bearer who had met them off the boat in Bombay gave Tom courage.

Tom said brightly, 'You'll have fun choosing a fresh colour scheme, darling.'

He saw Lydia's chin tremble. 'I wish Mummy and Daddy were here.'

'They will be soon,' Tom encouraged, squeezing her hand. 'It's only fair they should have a few days of sightseeing in Lahore – they're on holiday after all. And it gives us a chance to come on ahead and prepare things.'

He studied her warily. She had once again clamped her eau de cologne-soaked handkerchief to her nose. It was a mistake bringing her the short route through Saddar Bazaar past the noxious-smelling abattoir and the packed streets. Despite it being late afternoon, the heat was still intense and Lydia looked exhausted under her new solar topee.

'Can't we book into Flashman's?' Lydia asked. 'This place doesn't look habitable. Even the sign has fallen off its hinges.'

Tom couldn't help imagining what Esmie might say about the place with its covered-in veranda which someone had made an effort to decorate with brightly coloured pot plants. '*Charming – faded grandeur – but charming*.' Lydia was going to take a lot more convincing than her best friend. Harold and Esmie would be halfway to India by now . . . He banished the thought quickly.

'Dubois, the manager, is expecting us,' said Tom. 'I'm sure it'll be fine inside. Come on, Lomax Memsahib; let's go and inspect our new property.'

As he took his wife by the arm, a porter and a young boy came dashing down the hotel path. Reaching them, the plump dark-haired boy grinned and stuck out his hand.

'Hello, I'm Jimmy Dubois. You must be Captain and Mrs Lomax. I've been keeping an eye out for you. Sunil will take your cases. Have you had a good journey?'

Tom shook the boy by the hand and smiled. 'Hot and tiring,' he replied. 'But we're very happy to be here.'

Jimmy scrutinised Lydia. 'Are you feeling unwell, Mrs Lomax? Do you have a cold? My mother can get you a hot toddy.'

Lydia shook her head but kept the handkerchief in place. 'It's the smell and the dust. Just get me inside.'

'Please,' said Jimmy, 'follow me.'

To Tom's astonishment, they were met at the entrance by a large number of staff lined up under the portico out of the fierce sun. A short, plump dapper man in a suit with a purple cravat and matching handkerchief approached them, beaming.

'Captain Lomax! Madam! Welcome to the Raj Hotel.' He gave a courtly bow, ushering them into the shade. 'Charlie Dubois at your service.' He clicked his fingers and a servant stepped forward with a tray of drinks and dampened face flannels. 'Please,' said Charlie, 'avail yourself of refreshment and mopping of the brow.'

'Thank you,' said Tom, taking a flannel and wiping his sweat-stained face. He turned to Lydia who was looking askance at the flannels. Picking a glass off the tray he handed it to her. 'Looks like nimbu pani, darling.'

'Most reviving,' said Charlie, his round face creasing in a smile so broad his thin moustache almost disappeared.

Lydia took a tentative sip. Her face puckered in distaste. 'Smells of rotten eggs,' she muttered. She put it back on the tray. 'No thank you.'

Tom, embarrassed, seized another glass and downed the drink in one go. The lime flavour was tinged with sulphurous rock salt. It reminded him suddenly of Peshawar and his former home with Mary. Since arriving back in India he'd thought about Mary more than he had in years. The unexpected memory shook him and he quickly dismissed it.

Charlie began introducing the Lomaxes to his family and staff.

'Meet my good wife and better half, Myrtle Dubois – and this is our daughter, Stella.'

A diminutive, pretty woman with large dark eyes and a leggy girl with honey-blonde hair both bobbed in a curtsy. The girl spoke.

'Pleased to meet you, sir. I'm seven. Your frock is very pretty, Mrs Lomax.'

Lydia smiled for the first time. 'Thank you, Stella. So is yours.'

The girl grinned in pleasure but Myrtle pulled her daughter back with a look that told her not to interrupt her father's introductions. Charlie continued along the line of servants with a string of names that

Tom knew he wouldn't remember; there seemed an endless number of house and kitchen staff.

They were interrupted by a shout from inside.

'Charlie! Don't leave the poor Lomaxes to wilt in the heat. Bring them in, for goodness' sake!'

Charlie spun on his well-polished shoes. 'At once, Mr Ansom, sir! They are just partaking of a quick lime juice.'

'I'm sure they could do with something a lot stronger,' another male voice called out.

Charlie chuckled and swept his arm in an expansive gesture. 'Please, Captain and Mrs Lomax; come this way. The guests are most impatient to meet you.'

The line of servants parted as Charlie led them into the hotel lobby. Stepping from the dazzling sunshine outside, it took a moment for Tom to see anything in the gloom of the interior. It was instantly cooler under the whirr of ceiling fans. After a few moments he could make out dingy green walls, a clutter of cane chairs and tables, huge potted ferns and a large mahogany desk covered in ledgers which were propping up a sign saying, 'Reception.'

Standing in various poses among the rattan furniture were half a dozen elderly men and women already dressed for dinner and clutching drinks. He felt as if he'd stepped into an Oscar Wilde play.

A tall, craggy-faced man came forward and wrung Tom by the hand.

'Name's Ansom. Retired engineer. Railways. Good to meet our new owner.'

A more portly man, a tumbler of pink gin clenched in his thick fist, introduced himself next. 'Fritwell. Ex-army like you. Looking forward to having a good chinwag. You can call me Fritters – everyone else does.'

Ansom, who seemed to have assumed leadership of the guests, introduced Tom to several more. One lady waved an ear trumpet at him and smiled. 'Delighted to meet you, Captain Womack.'

'And this is retired Detective Inspector Hoffman,' said Ansom, ushering forward a man with an eyepatch and a lugubrious look. Hoffman tapped his patch and said, 'Blinded by a firecracker in Simla, not very heroic.'

'But you play the most divine waltzes on your violin, darling.'

Tom turned towards the voice and saw a tall elegant woman descending the staircase in a midnight-blue velvet evening gown and a headband of ostrich feathers. Stella, the Dubois' daughter, rushed to help her, holding up the train of the old-fashioned dress so the woman didn't trip as she descended.

Ansom exclaimed, 'Ah, there you are, baroness!'

'We have your drink ready,' Fritters called out, twiddling his moustache excitedly. 'Come and toast our new arrivals.'

Tom watched, entranced, as the slim woman made a regal entry down the remaining steps. Up close she looked much older, her porcelain features lined with tiny fissures around her eyes and mouth, and her neck was scrawny under a glinting emerald necklace.

'I am Baroness Hester Cussack,' she announced with a smile and a trace of a Middle-European accent. She proffered a bony bejewelled hand to be kissed.

With only a moment's hesitation, Tom raised her hand to his lips. He heard Lydia stifle a snort of amusement. The baroness turned and bestowed a smile on Lydia.

'What a beautiful wife you have, Captain Lomax,' she said. 'Madame Lomax, I can see you are a woman of style. Our hotel has been sadly lacking a woman's touch – the thankfully departed bachelor Littleton had no taste whatsoever. We look forward to seeing you enhance our home – I'm sure you and your handsome husband will return the Raj to its former glory.'

Tom, seeing Lydia quite lost for words, had to suppress his amusement. The baroness talked as if the hotel was hers and she was inviting them to stay. In fact, all the guests seemed completely at home. He wondered how long they had been living there. Littleton had indicated there were only one or two long-term residents. No doubt the amiable Charlie would brief him soon enough.

Ansom and Fritwell began fussing around the baroness, settling her into a chair at their table.

'Will you care to join us in a chota peg, captain?' asked Ansom.

'Umm, take away the taste of that god-awful nimbu pani,' added Fritwell.

Tom had a sudden craving for a strong drink but a quick glance at Lydia's tight expression made him resist.

'Perhaps after we've had time to wash and change,' he said.

At once Charlie snapped his fingers. 'Sunil, take the Lomaxes' luggage up to their flat.' He gave a deferential nod to Lydia. 'Please allow me to show you upstairs, Mrs Lomax. We have everything ready at your disposal. My good wife has chosen the linens and furnishings which I hope will meet with your approval and delight.' He waved her forward. 'Please, please; come.'

Tom followed Lydia and Charlie up the stairs and down a long dimly lit corridor, to a door at the far end. To Tom's relief, the room they were shown into was a large and airy sitting room with a veranda on either side. Through a further door he glimpsed a bedroom.

While Charlie supervised Sunil in placing their luggage onto racks in the bedroom, Tom studied the photograph of some ancient ruins hanging over the mantelpiece.

'Is that Taxila?' he asked the manager when he reappeared.

'It is indeed,' Charlie said with enthusiasm. 'I took the photograph myself. I am greatly interested in its history – I have a huge thirst for Indian archaeology.'

'I've never managed to visit Taxila,' said Tom, 'but I've always wanted to.'

'Then if you will permit me, sir,' said Charlie, 'I would be honoured to accompany you and Mrs Lomax and show you the jewel in Rawalpindi's crown.'

Lydia gave a short laugh. 'You can count me out. One set of fallen stones looks much the same to me as another whatever country it's in.'

Charlie looked crestfallen as he retreated to the door. 'Then I shall leave you in peace and tranquillity,' he said. 'Please ring the bell if you have any wants or requirements.'

'Thank you, Mr Dubois,' Tom answered. 'You've made us feel most welcome.'

'Please, call me Charlie.' He stood in the doorway, smiling tentatively and smoothing down his oiled hair.

'Charlie it is then,' said Tom.

Charlie continued to hover. 'Is there anything else I can do for you, sir?'

Tom glanced at Lydia. She shook her head. 'No thank you, Charlie.'

Charlie bowed. 'May I just take this opportunity, Captain Lomax, to say how very pleased we are that you have purchased the Raj. We hope that you and Mrs Lomax will have many happy years here. I speak on behalf of the Dubois family when I say that we are at your service, night and day.'

Tom was touched. He had a sudden feeling that everything was going to be all right and that he had done the right thing in buying the hotel. He thanked Charlie again and the manager bowed and left them alone.

Lydia flopped into a wooden armchair and winced. 'Goodness, this is uncomfortable! I thought the man was never going to leave. He's got the oddest way of speaking, hasn't he? I bet that timid little wife of his doesn't get a word in edgeways.' She pulled off her hat and sighed. 'And who are all those extraordinary people downstairs? Aren't there any normal guests? They look like part of the furniture. Do they live here permanently?'

'It would seem so,' said Tom with a rueful smile, discarding his jacket and pulling off his tie.

'Well, we'll have to see about that,' said Lydia. 'There's so much needs doing, it's overwhelming.'

'This room is nice,' Tom said.

She grimaced. 'The furniture's terrible. It'll all have to go. Mummy will need smelling salts when she sees the décor.'

'Well, that's something you can do together,' Tom suggested. 'I want you to decorate it exactly how you like.' He unbuttoned his shirt and grinned. 'Shall we go and inspect the bedroom, Madame Lomax?'

Lydia gave a huff of amusement. 'Madame Lomax indeed! Do you think that woman is really a baroness?'

'Why shouldn't she be?'

'I thought her accent a bit false and that grand entrance was so calculated – she'd been hovering in the shadows waiting for her moment to impress.'

Tom pulled Lydia to her feet and kissed her hand. 'Allow me to show you to your boudoir, madame.' He began planting kisses up her arm and nuzzling her neck.

'Oh, Tom, really,' she said, 'we don't have time for this.'

'We've plenty of time,' he murmured, nibbling her ear and beginning to undo the hooks at the back of her dress. 'I've been longing to get you alone for ages.'

'What does that mean?' Lydia stiffened. 'I thought you liked having my parents around.'

'I do,' Tom said. 'They're delightful company. But I want your company more.'

He couldn't tell her how much he craved the leisurely days of intimacy that they'd had on honeymoon and hadn't had since. On the long sea voyage every minute of the day had been taken up with socialising and keeping the Templetons entertained. That's why he had encouraged

Lydia's parents to spend a few days in Lahore before joining them in Rawalpindi. It had taken till now to get Lydia on her own.

Tom sensed her reluctance. He braced himself for her to push him away and say it wasn't the right time of day.

Abruptly she started to giggle. 'You should have seen your face when that baroness held out her hand to be kissed. Priceless! I thought you were going to drop on one knee!'

Lydia shook with laughter. Tom began to laugh with her.

'Put your arms around my neck, Madame Lomax,' he ordered.

In one swift movement, he pulled her off her feet and into his arms. Lydia squealed but wrapped her arms around him. Tom carried her into the bedroom and pushed the door closed with his foot. They collapsed onto the bed together with a squeak of springs.

Lydia laughed. 'That's something else that needs replacing.'

'Anything you want, my darling.'

As Tom began kissing her, he thought how lucky he was to have married such a beautiful woman.

Chapter 13

Three weeks after leaving a grey and wet Liverpool, the SS *Galloway Castle* was docking at the Ballard Pier in Bombay. Esmie stood at the rail transfixed by the teaming harbour as an army of stevedores ran up and down the gangplanks unloading luggage and carrying trunks that dwarfed them. The air rang with the clank of chains, blast of funnels and the general hubbub of disembarking passengers and cries of vendors. Beyond the chaos of the wharfs, shimmering in the morning heat, was the Gateway of India. Esmie was disappointed to see the triumphal archway was only half-built. She'd read about King George laying the foundation stone in 1911. War must have stalled the imperial project.

'Come on, my dear,' chivvied Harold. 'Time to set foot on Indian soil.'

Galvanised out of her reverie by the thrilling thought, Esmie followed her husband off the ship.

By the time they had claimed their luggage and Harold had completed the paperwork for their trunks to be sent on by train, Esmie was perspiring heavily in the humid heat. She longed to dive off the pier into the shimmering sea, though from the rank pervading smell of oil and effluent she would probably be ill if she did. Instead, she mopped her brow and climbed into a tonga beside Harold, waving farewell to Bernie who was going to stay at a friend's club.

Soon she forgot her discomfort as she took in the sights of tree-lined streets and dazzling buildings which reminded her of the Mediterranean, yet with the added vibrant colours of sari-clad women and men dressed in long white coats and tight-fitting trousers who thronged the pavements.

They passed the ornately decorated hotels close to the sea front and drew up outside a more modest three-storey building down a side street and next to a church. At the door of the mission house, their cases were taken by a skinny young man with a startlingly red-toothed smile, who staggered down a dark hallway with his load and disappeared up a flight of stairs. Esmie welcomed the cool interior. Upstairs, she wiped her face and neck with a damp flannel before they joined half a dozen other guests – all men – in the dining room for lunch.

Harold knew a couple of the other missionaries, one of them a headmaster and seasoned India-hand who had just seen his wife onto a boat home to visit family. Augustus Tolmie was a wiry balding man of middle-age who ran a mission school in Murree.

'Murree's near to Rawalpindi in the north Punjab, isn't it?' asked Esmie.

'It is,' said Mr Tolmie. 'We get a lot of British escaping the hot season in Pindi – especially the army-wallahs. The town doubles in size and becomes quite lively – too lively at times,' he said with a roll of the eyes.

'In what way?' asked Esmie.

He grunted. 'Well, I think some of the young officers think it is their duty to drink the Murree Brewery dry. Then they get up to all sorts of pranks like walking on bridge walls with sheer drops. Just this year, one drunken young subaltern fell to his death, poor misguided fellow. We try and keep them occupied with coming to church and playing sport but there are often too many temptations in the card rooms and dance halls of the cantonment.'

Before Esmie could ask him more about the hill station, the men were turning to talk of the recent unrest in the North-West Frontier.

'You show great pluck, Mrs Guthrie,' Tolmie said. 'I wouldn't be letting my wife go to such a place.'

Harold flushed. 'But I'm told that things are quiet again among the Waziris,' he said. 'My friend Bannerman said it was safe to return.'

'Are things ever safe among the Pathans?' the headmaster questioned. 'We heard some terrible tales from the garrison at Murree about attacks on the outlying British forts. The area is awash with weapons the Afghans left behind and the tribes are making the most of the Indian Army being weakened by our best troops still being overseas – or dead in the recent war.' He leaned forward and dropped his voice. 'I have it on good authority: this summer, some of the sepoys defected to the Afghans and took their firearms with them. Our frontier is being defended by inexperienced soldiers led by young officers who are just as green behind the ears. Those crafty Pathans sensed the upper hand and struck.'

Esmie remembered Tom saying something similar earlier in the summer.

'You may be right,' said Harold, looking anxious. 'But the danger has passed and the tribes have signed a treaty.'

Tolmie shook his head. 'The treaty signed last month was with Afghanistan, not the Frontier tribes. The Pathans are a law unto themselves.'

'I know these people,' said Harold stoutly, 'and they trust us at the mission.'

Tolmie looked sceptical. 'Be cautious in trusting *them*, dear chap. From what I heard, they showed no mercy in the raids – especially to their own kind. Mutilations and burnings. Some of the women—'

'Please, Augustus,' Harold cried, holding up his hands in horror. 'You are upsetting my wife.'

'Please forgive me,' Tolmie said at once. 'That was not my intention. I merely thought it best that you know what you and brave Mrs Guthrie are returning to.'

Esmie was alarmed by his words but she could see that it was Harold who was the more distressed. She jumped to his defence.

'We appreciate your concern for us, Mr Tolmie. But Harold and I are following our calling. We are doing God's work – just as you are in Murree – so nothing you say will put us off going to Taha. The good Lord will protect us.'

He looked surprised by her intervention but she knew that he couldn't argue against her uncharacteristically pious words. The headmaster bowed in acceptance.

'Harold, I see you have married a lady of spirit,' he said. 'I hope, when you next get leave, and Margaret returns from England, you will come and stay with us in Murree.'

Harold flashed Esmie a look of admiration and nodded in acceptance. Swiftly, he made their excuses and left. Yet for the rest of the day he was subdued.

Later, after they'd shopped for medical supplies and returned to their room, Esmie sat him down and asked, 'Are you worried about what Mr Tolmie was saying?'

'I suppose so, yes,' Harold admitted.

'He strikes me as the kind of man who rather likes to overdramatise events.'

'That's true,' he said with a ghost of a smile. 'But maybe I've been too ready to believe Bannerman that things are calm again and the danger is over.' He glanced at her anxiously. 'I'd never forgive myself if you came to harm because of my eagerness to get back to Taha.'

Esmie felt a surge of tenderness. 'I'm not going to come to any harm. I won't do anything rash, I promise.'

He shook his head. 'I'm thinking of leaving you in Rawalpindi with Lydia while I go and recce the situation at the mission.'

Esmie was alarmed by the suggestion. 'Certainly not,' she replied. 'You're not going to leave me behind anywhere. Besides, Lydia has her parents staying and any free time she has from the hotel she'll be wanting to do things with them. I mustn't encroach on their precious time together. And Tom will be busy setting things up at the Raj.'

She stood and went to look out of the window so he wouldn't see her cheeks reddening. The sun was already setting and the street was in shadow. She was momentarily distracted by how quickly night was falling in the tropics; so different from the long twilight in Scotland.

Harold was flustered. 'Esmie, you must do as I say. If I think it's too risky then you will have to stay with the Lomaxes.'

She turned to face him. 'Harold, I'm your wife, not your employee, and I have a say in this too. I haven't come all this way to be left twiddling my thumbs among the leisured classes of Pindi. I'm here to nurse and work alongside you, wherever I'm needed. If it's too dangerous for me then it's too dangerous for you. We either go together or not at all.'

He sat on the sagging bed, cracking his knuckles in agitation, floundering for a reply. She felt a lick of evening breeze and heard a call to prayer in the distance that reminded her vividly of Albania and the relief of surviving the retreat from Serbia. How very long ago that seemed now and yet, to Esmie, this arrival in India was somehow a continuation of that journey, a quest to find her real calling in life.

Finally, Harold said, 'We'll travel as far as Kohat on the train. I'll send a telegram to Bannerman to meet us there in two days' time. If he says it's safe, then you can continue with me to Taha.'

Esmie was triumphant that she had won this concession from Harold. She was discovering that he could be quite stubborn and she feared that once he had got the idea of leaving her behind in Rawalpindi he would not be shifted from it.

'Thank you, husband,' she said with a smile. He gave her a rueful smile back.

In the gathering dark, Esmie moved back across the room and sat on the bed beside him, sensing that now was the moment for intimacy. Harold, with his jacket and tie discarded and shirt open, was looking boyish and virile in the gloom. She was glowing from the heat of the day and felt desire curdle in the pit of her stomach.

'Why don't we . . . you know . . . before supper?' she whispered. Then leaning towards him she kissed him full on the mouth for the first time. His lips were firm and dry. She slipped her hands around his neck and continued to kiss him, her heart beginning to thud in excitement. But Harold sat rigid and didn't respond.

Esmie pulled away. 'Don't you want to?' she asked.

'It's not that,' he answered, looking away. 'But I thought I'd made it clear that I don't want to risk bringing a child into the world at such a time. Especially now I fear that the danger up north may not be past.'

Esmie put a hand to his hot cheek. 'We can take measures to avoid that, Dr Guthrie,' she said, gently teasing. 'We've both studied anatomy and know what to do to prevent conception.'

He glanced at her, his expression scandalised. Esmie burst out laughing.

'Harold,' she said in affection. 'I find you most attractive when you're blushing like a schoolboy.'

'I thought we were in agreement about not having children,' Harold reminded her. 'At least not yet.'

'We are,' she replied, 'but I didn't agree to take a vow of celibacy. I'm your wife and I want our marriage to be a loving one – physically as well as spiritually. Isn't that what you want – a loving relationship?'

His look was almost forlorn as he nodded.

Esmie grinned. 'Good. Then why don't we start before dinner? Work up an appetite?'

'Now?' he said, panic in his voice.

'Yes, now,' said Esmie, already beginning to unbutton her dress.

He stared at her as she discarded her clothes, unclipping her stockings and rolling them down her legs. With just her corset on, she leaned towards him and kissed him again, pulling at his shirt. He fumbled at his buttons while she covered his face with kisses. He tasted salty with sweat and his breathing was ragged.

Esmie felt excitement mount as Harold took off his shirt and she saw the thick growth of hair on his chest. She ran her hands over it and across his clammy shoulders. His body was pale and softer to the touch than she'd expected.

'Shall we get under the covers?' he asked, his voice husky.

Esmie wanted to lie naked on top. 'It's too hot,' she said.

'I'd rather,' said Harold, already reaching to turn down the bedclothes.

He climbed under the sheet and removed his trousers and drawers out of view.

Esmie pulled off her knickers and began to remove her corset when he stopped her.

'Please leave it on.'

'Why?'

'I find it more . . . alluring,' he said.

Baffled, Esmie did as he asked and climbed in beside him.

They lay on their sides facing each other and kissed; small darting kisses that left Esmie craving longer ones. But every time she opened her lips for a deeper kiss, Harold turned his mouth from hers and kissed her cheek.

She ran her hands up and down his body, her fingertips exploring his chest and thighs, the firmness of his buttocks.

'Touch me too,' she whispered, guiding his hands to where she wanted to be pleasured.

He fumbled with sweaty hands and she let out small sighs of delight. She waited for him to become aroused, impatient for the final consummation. Harold's breathing grew more rapid but nothing happened. Esmie tried to help excite him. He groaned and moved on top of her. Esmie closed her eyes in anticipation. Then abruptly, he was rolling away.

Esmie opened her eyes. She lay in confusion and almost certain that they hadn't made love. She felt choked with unsatisfied desire. Then she heard Harold let go a sob. Her disappointment turned quickly to pity. He was turned away from her. She leaned over him and rested her chin on his shoulder.

'I'm s-sorry,' he croaked.

'Don't be.'

'It's not you,' he said. 'I'm just overwrought about Taha and what we'll find.'

She kissed his shoulder. 'I know you are and I understand.' Swallowing her own frustration, she tried to reassure him. 'It doesn't matter. Next time it'll be better.'

Harold turned and faced her, his look hard to fathom in the near dark.

'Yes, God willing.'

Esmie thought it a strange thing to say but let it go. She felt abruptly drained and weary. Perhaps they could just stay in bed and skip the evening meal, fall asleep in each other's arms.

But Harold was already getting out of bed and pulling on his clothes.

'I wonder what's for dinner?' he said, brightening.

Esmie stifled a sigh. 'Smells like overcooked vegetables.'

Harold gave a grunt of amusement. 'Yes. Home from home.'

As she swung her legs out of bed, he turned and made for the door. 'I'll let you get dressed, my dear, and meet you downstairs.'

To the delight of them both, Esmie and Harold found themselves on the same train to Lahore as Bernie Hudson, still doggedly wearing his deer-stalker hat. He had a first-class ticket in a carriage next to theirs. When Esmie had queried why they were travelling first class, Harold had said, 'In second class we'd run the risk of having to share with Indians. I travel that way on my own but the mission wouldn't allow it for a British lady.'

Esmie wasn't sure if he was joking. It turned out that the train wasn't full – at least not the carriages for Europeans – as it was still the monsoon season and, months ago, the majority of British had decamped to the hill stations where the climate was more bearable. Despite the suffocating heat, Esmie pleaded with Harold to keep the slatted window shutters open so that she didn't miss any of the sights on her first journey in India.

Sitting with a handkerchief pressed to her mouth and nose to keep out the dust, she gazed for hours on end at the passing countryside as the train trundled across baked plains and scrubland. The mesmerising, monotonous miles were relieved by occasional villages of mud houses and shimmering oases of trees. She would disturb Harold from his reading or dozing with exclamations and questions.

'What are those long, thin chimneys for?' she asked. 'They're everywhere. Are they some sort of mill?'

'Brickworks,' Harold answered. 'Everything in village India is made from mud bricks – at least in this region.'

At stations, Esmie was agog at the sudden frantic activity and noise as families disembarked or scrambled for seats, carrying bed rolls and cooking pots, while vendors weaved through the throngs calling out their wares. Harold allowed them off to stretch their legs but cautioned her not to wander off on her own. At first she found the pungent aromas overpowering; wafts of oily cooking, human effluence and acrid dung fires. But soon her fascination with the lively commerce on the platform made her forget the noxious smells.

'What are those?' Esmie pointed at mounds of garish pink and green sweets. 'I've never seen such brightly coloured food.'

'Sweetmeats,' said Harold. 'Like fudge but even more sickly sweet.'

'Can we buy some?' she enthused.

'Certainly not! They're covered in flies.' Then he softened at her disappointed expression. 'I'll get Cook to make you some in Taha.'

Sometimes, when the train idled in a station, Bernie would join them from the next-door carriage, bringing his servant who would make them tea. In a vain attempt to keep the first-class passengers cool, menial servants – whom Harold called bhistis – came on to replace the melted blocks of ice with frozen ones in the centre of the compartments. At one stop, a waiter appeared and took their order for tiffin, which Harold explained was a light lunch. He suggested mutton chops. The order was sent ahead and at the next station another waiter appeared and led them to the first-class buffet where tiffin was served.

Electric fans whirred overhead and the high-ceilinged shaded room was deliciously cool compared to the oven-like temperature outside. Esmie, who thought the heat had robbed her of an appetite, polished off a bowl of chicken soup, a plateful of mutton, peas and potatoes, followed by banana and custard. Back on the train she fell asleep and didn't wake until it was dark and an attendant boarded to convert the seats into bunk beds.

As the train rattled on towards Lahore, she lay awake, lulled by its rhythm but too excited to sleep. Harold, in the bunk above, snored and babbled incomprehensible words. She knew he was still anxious about what they would find at the far end of the journey, even though he had received a telegram from Bannerman to confirm that he would meet them at Kohat. Esmie was encouraged by this and had told Harold so.

'If there was any danger he would be telling us not to come.'

Her mind raced ahead to their onward journey. The next train would take them north through the Punjab and would stop at Rawalpindi. But Harold had decided that they would not delay reaching Taha by breaking their journey with the Lomaxes. Esmie had quickly agreed. She regretted not seeing Lydia but wanted to be more established – both in India and as Harold's wife – before she was faced with Tom and Lydia's idyllic marriage.

Since the unsatisfactory attempt to consummate her own marriage, Esmie had hesitated in being demonstrative towards Harold. She waited for him to make the first gesture – a pat on the shoulder or her forehead brushed with his lips – before she gave him a tentative kiss on the cheek. She knew that what had passed between them in the mission guest house bedroom did not constitute consummation. She felt hot with embarrassment thinking about their failed attempt at love-making. What would she tell Lydia when they finally met up? Her friend was bound to demand details.

Suddenly Esmie was struck with a disturbing thought. Harold's haste to bypass Rawalpindi and head straight for Taha must be because he was as reluctant to see Lydia as she was to see Tom. Her chest constricted in panic. What if his lack of performance in bed had nothing to do with his anxiety over Taha and everything to do with still being in love with Lydia? He couldn't bring himself to make love to her, Esmie, because he felt no attraction towards her. Perhaps that was why he'd leapt at the idea of abstinence; it was just an excuse not to be intimate with her.

When Harold had said that Esmie was an answer to his prayers he had meant not as a wife, but as a nurse who could minister to the Pathan women where he could not. Harold might never like her enough to want to make love to her. The thought of years of barren marriage stretching ahead appalled her. But then whose fault was that? She had rushed into this marriage because it gave her the respectability she needed to live and work in a world of patriarchal men. She was using Harold as much as he was using her. She had known all this from the start; his letter of proposal had been little more than the offer of a job.

Yet, sometime in the last few weeks, Esmie's liking for Harold as a friend had grown into something stronger. She found him endearing – his thirst for literature, his eagerness to teach her Pashto and his touching concern for her welfare – but it was also more than that. By subtle degrees, she was finding him more and more physically attractive. He was solid, with a robust strength, lively hazel eyes and a diffident smile. She enjoyed waking up in the same bedroom as him and taking his arm when they walked in public. He was all the more attractive because he obviously thought that he wasn't.

Restless, Esmie crawled to the end of her bed and peered out of the slatted blind. It was pitch black. Then, as her eyes grew accustomed to the dark, she saw that the sky was littered with stars so bright they sparkled like diamonds. The thrill of being in India returned. She rebuked herself for her self-indulgent thoughts about her bodily yearnings. It was up to her to make the most of this marriage to Harold. Tomorrow they would reach Lahore and the day after that she would see the North-West Frontier for the first time.

Chapter 14

North-West Frontier Province

The Reverend Alec Bannerman was a tall, thin, white-haired man with a beaky nose and a booming laugh. He wore a clerical collar and an old-fashioned black suit that smelt of curry and mothballs. His only concession to the heat was a battered panama hat worn so low on his head that it made his ears stick out. Under a dazzling blue sky and on a dusty platform, he greeted Esmie with a crushing handshake, a broad smile and a welcome in Gaelic. Esmie liked him at once. Greeting Harold with the same firm handshake, he quickly assured his friend that Taha and the region was now quiet and that he would tell him in more detail on the car journey south.

'Motor car's at the entrance,' he said, leading the way out of the small station at Kohat. 'Malik is guarding it. Are you hungry? I've packed a tiffin basket but we can eat in the cantonment before leaving town if you like.'

'We seem to have done nothing but eat since we got on the train at Bombay,' said Esmie, her stomach twisting with nervous excitement. 'But Harold hasn't eaten much.'

Harold shook his head. 'I'm not hungry either. I want to hear all the news from Taha. You're absolutely sure it's safe for me to bring my wife there?'

'Taha is peaceful,' Alec assured him. 'I wouldn't have let you travel if it wasn't. There are more troops there than usual – which makes it safer for us . . .' He paused.

'But?' Harold queried.

'They've been taking up the lion's share of the hospital,' said Alec, 'which means that locals have been turned away.'

'They can't do that,' Harold protested. 'It's not supposed to be for the army – they have their own hospitals here in Kohat and up in Peshawar.'

'They do,' Alec agreed. 'But they've had need of us these past few months. The garrison at Taha has swelled to twice its normal size and there was an outbreak of cholera which the Brigadier blamed on Waziris from Kanki-Khel. It's all under control now but that's why the army aren't keen to have natives pouring in from the hills to be treated.'

'Cholera?' Harold said, aghast. 'And what of Kanki-Khel? Have you been able to visit since the peace treaty?'

Alec shook his head. 'I'm afraid not. We've had enough on our hands in Taha and we're not allowed to go into the hills without an armed escort. Up till now the army haven't been able to spare any troops but I'm sure that will change now the Afghans have been pacified.'

Esmie's insides twisted with nerves. Was the situation at Taha and the surrounding area very much worse than Harold had thought?

'You should have called me back sooner,' Harold said, his face creased in worry. 'I've been frittering away my time in Scotland when I should have been back here helping—'

'Nonsense,' Alec interrupted. 'As I said, it's all under control now. Besides, you deserved every minute of your furlough after your stint in Mesopotamia – not to mention the years of work you put in here beforehand without taking home leave.' He clapped a hand on Harold's shoulder. 'But I must say I'm glad to have you back, Harold. And' – he added, with a smile at Esmie – 'you have brought a delightful young wife.'

Harold's frown disappeared. 'Yes, I have,' he said. 'Esmie is going to be a marvellous addition to the mission.'

Alec laughed. 'Mrs Guthrie, I hope you realise that Harold is a tiger for work. But I shall do my best to make sure he spends some of his time with you.'

Esmie, trying to hide her anxiety, smiled. 'That's kind – but I too can't wait to begin work at the mission.'

'Excellent!'

As they passed from the shade of the station archways into the compound, Esmie had to shade her eyes from the glare. Beyond the town, a range of jagged grey mountains shimmered in the midday heat.

'That way lies Afghanistan,' Alec said. 'But there's no need to be nervous. We've signed a peace treaty and they've no wish to have our RAF boys flying over them again.'

As if to illustrate his point, she became aware of a low buzzing noise growing louder as a plane came into view and passed overhead.

Alec waved to the pilot and then pointed out to Esmie. 'He's heading for the aerodrome over there.'

At the car, Harold greeted a young man standing guard with a rifle at the ready, whose slim face was swamped by a large white turban.

'This is Malik, he's one of our orderlies,' he told Esmie. Then switching back to Pashto, he said, 'Malik, this is Guthrie Memsahib, my wife.'

Esmie was touched by the pride in Harold's voice. She greeted the young guard in Pashto and his stern face broke into a smile as he saluted her. She thought how his baggy olive-green shirt and pantaloons looked cool and comfortable. Her dress was already damp and clinging to her.

'Are you sure you don't want lunch at the club before we travel on?' asked Alec.

'I'd rather get to Taha as soon as possible,' Harold said, glancing at Esmie. 'If that's all right with you, my dear?'

Dismissing the tempting thought of a cool interior and one of those thirst-quenching lime drinks, nimbu-pani, that she was developing a taste for, Esmie nodded. She too was keen to get to her new home. It was only sixty miles away but Harold had told her it was a four-hour drive over bumpy terrain.

Esmie sat in the back of the mission's open-topped Ford with Malik, while Alec drove and Harold sat in front, peppering his colleague with questions about the current situation at the mission. Despite Alec's previous assurances, he admitted that wards were full and the locum doctor who had been filling in for Harold had succumbed to enteric fever and been sent to Murree to recuperate. Esmie wondered if the loss of Harold's replacement was the reason Alec Bannerman was so keen to encourage Harold back. She hoped he wasn't down-playing the risks at Taha. She had seen cases of cholera when working for the Scottish Women's Hospitals – acute diarrhoea leading to dehydration and death within hours – and it could rage through an army. Cleanliness had been the key and Dr Inglis had been rigorous about hygiene on the wards.

As they swung away from the narrow-gauge railway line and drove through the cantonment, Alec broke off his conversation with an anxious Harold to give Esmie information.

'That's the Governor of Kohat's residence,' he said, pointing at a large two-storey building with an arched veranda and high windows set in immaculately lawned gardens. On either side of the Mall were neat bungalows and the low-lying buildings of the barracks.

'This is an important army outpost,' he said over his shoulder. 'Railway was laid at the turn of the century to help transport troops more quickly to the unsettled tribal areas – but it's made it a lot easier for missionaries too, hasn't it, Harold?'

Harold nodded. 'Apparently, it was a four-day ride from Rawalpindi when the mission first came to Taha.'

'Was Kohat built by the army?' Esmie asked.

'No,' said Alec. 'It's always been a trading town. They come from far and wide to its emporium – for cloth and grain and tobacco. Far busier than any market day you'll see at home.'

Soon they were leaving the cantonment and skirting the town. Through the rising dust, Esmie glimpsed a warren of sun-baked mud walls and open stalls. A simple unadorned mosque gleamed white against a cluster of palms and the vivid blue sky. Her excitement at being in India reignited.

As the car rattled onto unmetalled roads, Esmie had to cover her face with her scarf to stop her coughing in the dust. Through stinging eyes she saw the oasis of Kohat recede and the land grow more barren as they were jostled over stony tracks that twisted through low hills. Occasionally, she saw a splash of green in the distance where walled villages nestled beside streams.

At her side, Malik kept alert with his rifle at the ready. Esmie's trepidation returned as she gazed at every rocky outcrop, wondering if a gunman lurked behind it ready to pick them off. Here she was, finally travelling through the infamous North-West Frontier; she could hardly believe it. But the only people she saw were occasional small boys tending a handful of skinny cows or old men with sun-cracked faces riding mules. Apart from the distant lowing of cattle and the cawing of a large bird, the rugged landscape was ominously silent.

The conversation between the men had ceased as Alec concentrated on avoiding ruts and large stones. They stopped briefly for Alec to go and relieve himself behind a large rock. He urged them to eat from the tiffin basket but Esmie, feeling queasy from the gruelling drive and apprehensive about what they would find at Taha, couldn't face egg sandwiches. They didn't linger.

Esmie must have dozed for she woke with a jolt as Harold cried out, 'There it is! Taha at last!'

Her stomach lurched. Peering through gritty eyes, Esmie saw that they had entered a broad valley with a meandering, half-dried-up riverbed. They were still surrounded by scrub and rocky mounds with the chain of arid mountains to the north, but in the distance she could see patches of golden wheat fields and green trees clustered around a settlement.

She sat up as they skirted a wider stretch of riverbed.

'This is where I come to fish,' said Harold, excitement in his voice. 'Taha Khel.'

Esmie looked at the muddy grey sand and flat stony banks with sparse clumps of rushes and wondered how any fish could survive there.

'But there's hardly any water,' she said.

'Different in the cold season. We get torrents in January and decent fishing.'

As they drove closer to Taha, the indistinct blur of beige walls and rooftops became more defined and the land around more irrigated. Date palms and tall feathery trees shaded fields of crops that were being harvested by hand. Men in grubby white shirts were scything corn and bundling it into sheaves. The lush green of small orchards and vegetable gardens seemed all the more vivid in contrast to the last hours of bald rock and thorny bushes. Piles of thin, oblong pinkish bricks were drying in the sun.

Her pulse hammered in anticipation as they drove up to the walled and gated town and trundled under a large archway where Indian soldiers saluted them. All about them were narrow streets of one- and two-storeyed houses, some with prettily carved window screens and doors. They passed an arcaded market with open stalls selling bright cloth and mounds of spices.

'This is the native quarter,' Alec explained. 'Mostly Waziris but some Hindu traders too.'

The customers appeared to be mainly bearded men in the same baggy clothing that Malik wore, some with neat white caps instead of turbans. They stared at the motor car with its topee-wearing passengers, their expressions phlegmatic. Barefoot boys chased after them, giggling and waving.

Alec slowed down to inch his way around a flock of goats and a group of men in dispute over a split sack of yellow powder that had fallen off a trolley. Aromatic yellow dust was settling over them all. Minutes later, the streets opened up and they passed a sentry post to enter the white-washed compound of the cantonment. Here the streets were wider and planted with trees to give shade. Long, low buildings stretched down one side of a central road while one-storey square bungalows lined the other. While the native town had been busy with people, the cantonment was almost deserted, save for two officers exercising their horses and a listless tonga driver swatting at flies while he waited for custom. Esmie imagined the British stayed indoors until the strength of the fierce sun waned.

Alec nodded at the shed-like buildings. 'We usually just have a garrison of one mountain battery and a few native infantry,' he said. 'But since the troubles in May we've a cavalry regiment stationed here too. Probably won't stay long. Some of the young officers are new to all this and are feeling pretty homesick. We try and give them hospitality and get them to church too.'

'Where is the mission hospital?' Esmie asked.

Harold pointed south. 'Over there. We'll go and see it later.'

'Plenty of time for that tomorrow,' advised Alec. 'You need to settle your new bride into Number Ten, The Lines first.'

Esmie's insides knotted. She wondered if Harold was feeling the same mix of expectation and nervousness as they approached their new married quarters. Except it was different for Harold; this was already dearly familiar to him. But would he find it difficult sharing his home with her? He would be used to doing as he wanted.

'Do you live close by, Reverend Bannerman?' she asked, trying to sound nonchalant.

'Just down the street at Number Fifteen,' he answered. 'And you don't have to be so formal, my dear. People just call me Padre, even though I'm retired from the army.'

They drew up outside one of the box-like bungalows, set back from the street and enclosed by a low brick wall. Esmie was pleased to see that there was shade from a medium-sized mulberry tree.

'I sent my mali round to water your grass,' said Alec. 'And your luggage trunks turned up yesterday. Your bearer, Draman, should have everything under control in the house. But if there's anything you need, just shout.'

'Thank you, Alec,' said Harold. 'You've been very thoughtful.'

Harold climbed stiffly from the car and opened the door for Esmie. It was a relief to get out. Every bone in her body ached from the jarring car ride and her head was fuzzy from the constant glare and dust. As Malik unstrapped their travel bags from the car, a youth came running from the house to snatch the bags from him.

'Ali!' Harold greeted him. 'So good to see you.'

The boy grinned and heaved the cases onto his head.

'I'll see you tomorrow,' Alec said, tooting and waving as he drove off with Malik.

'Come, my dear, and see your new home,' said Harold, smiling broadly for the first time that day.

The house was smaller than Esmie had imagined, though its gloomy central room was high-ceilinged and kept relatively cool by damp grass matting at the windows that subdued the light. No pictures hung on the walls, the wooden floors were bare of rugs and the furniture looked functional rather than comfortable. But she was just thankful to be there at last. She still felt car sick and her legs were wobbly from the journey.

A small bearded man wearing a black waistcoat over his long shirt welcomed them in with a toothy smile and a bow.

'This is Draman, my bearer,' said Harold. 'He's been with me since I first came to India. He's from near Rawalpindi and speaks good English.'

'Pleased to meet you.' Esmie greeted him with a smile and a nod. 'Dr Guthrie has already told me how well you run his household.'

Draman gave a deprecating smile and began issuing rapid orders to Ali. Minutes later, Ali returned with a tray of refreshments: black tea with slices of lemon and small dry-looking cakes. Esmie perched on a hard chair and took sips of the strong hot tea, realising how parched she was.

Harold hovered behind her, wolfing down a cake and talking to Draman in words that Esmie didn't follow. Perhaps they were talking in Urdu or Hindustani. Esmie wondered why Harold didn't address him in English. Closing her eyes, she could still feel the sickening movement of the motor car, so she quickly opened them again. A few moments later, she saw Ali and another servant appear from an adjoining room, carrying her trunk.

'That will be your room, my dear,' said Harold, nodding towards the room where the young men were taking her possessions.

Reddening with embarrassment, Esmie realised that Harold had instructed her things to be transferred out of his bedroom to the spare one. They would not be sharing a room let alone a bed. Her husband was going to carry out his vow of avoiding sex with her. She was suddenly dejected.

Without protest she followed Ali into the room, trying not to show how upset she was. There was a single bed, a cupboard for storage, a table with a pedestal mirror and chair. Off the room was a dingy closet with a boxed privy and a tin bath. Two bedframes with canvas webbing stood propped against one wall, reminding Esmie that until recently this house had been an overflow for army personnel. She thought fleetingly of her time in Serbia and the crowded room she had shared with half a dozen other nurses. Loneliness engulfed her. How she wished for that camaraderie now.

She sat down on the narrow bed, its springs creaking as she did so. Harold glanced in.

'I'll leave you to get unpacked and settled. I'm just going to pop down to the hospital and see for myself what's going on.'

Esmie sprang up. 'Let me come too.'

Harold looked awkward. 'You look exhausted. I won't be long. Tomorrow I'll show you round properly.'

With that he dashed away. Esmie sat down again, fighting back tears and trying to stem the panic rising inside. She thought she might be sick. She lay back on the bed and closed her eyes. What on earth was she doing here? She took deep calming breaths. It was bound to be strange and unnerving to start with until she grew used to the place and the people – and once she started to work. She could understand why Harold was itching to get back to his job and see for himself how the mission had been coping without him.

Esmie forced herself up again. The last thing she should do was give in to self-pity that might lead to listlessness and melancholia. She was here to help others, not become ill and be a burden. She must keep busy. She would begin by arranging her room.

Esmie began unpacking and putting her clothes away. On the makeshift dressing table, she placed her hairbrush and comb, the box containing her hairpins and her mother's silver brooch, and her most treasured possession, a framed photograph. It showed her youthful parents sitting in a Highland garden next to a young Isobel Carruthers who was clasping an infant Esmie on her knee. Esmie smiled and kissed the photograph and felt a surge of courage.

'Your parents would be so very proud of you.' Isobel's tender words came back to her. *'You are marrying a man of principle. I know you will make a success of whatever you are called to do.'*

Chapter 15

The next day, Esmie stood open-mouthed at the chaotic scenes at the mission hospital. The long verandas outside the wards were crammed with beds for those who couldn't be accommodated inside. Waziris lay with old gunshot wounds going gangrenous from being bound in sheepskin dressings, waiting stoically to be seen.

'They've been brought in from the outlying hills now that things are calmer,' Harold explained. He looked tired but full of purpose and Esmie realised now why he'd come home so late their first night in Taha. It had been after curfew and she'd been pacing the steps looking out for him. He had silenced her fretting by telling her that he'd already done three operations to save the limbs of two men and a boy of six.

This morning, a new queue of men squatted in the dusty courtyard, smoking, or lay on filthy blankets, their eyes glassy with pain. On the other side of the yard, cordoned off by makeshift curtains, a line of women hidden in voluminous veiled cloaks waited too, some of them clutching sickly children or trying to pacify wailing babies. Esmie was aghast at the scene. She hadn't witnessed such suffering since her time in Southern Russia two years ago.

'Can't we get the families out of the sun?' Esmie asked.

'The women's ward has been commandeered by the army since July,' Harold said, his look apologetic. 'We've set up a temporary theatre in one of the storerooms but there's nowhere else for them to sit.'

'Harold!' Esmie looked at him in disbelief. 'They're sitting in the dirt trying to feed their babies – no wonder so many have dysentery.'

'I'll do what I can,' he said distractedly. 'But I'm needed in theatre. Can you help Malik this morning?'

'Of course,' Esmie agreed, curbing her impatience.

For the next few hours, she joined Malik and the other male orderlies helping to process the outpatients, deciding who should see a doctor, and then cleaning and dressing wounds. Esmie was impressed by how dextrous and efficient Malik was in his work, talking gently to the younger patients and respectfully to his elders. He was far more than a rifle-bearing guard.

A tall and willowy woman with a sallow complexion and a shrewd assessing look in her dark-brown eyes introduced herself as Rupa Desai.

Esmie shook her hand. 'I've been looking forward to meeting you, Mrs Desai,' she said.

This was the widow Harold had told her about, whose doctor husband had been shot in a raid three years previously dispensing medicines in the remote outpost of Kanki-Khel – the same mountain village where the clinic had been burnt to the ground earlier in the summer.

Rupa was trained as a pharmacist, ran the dispensary and had worked on the women's ward before the recent crisis. Now she helped out in the dressing station. Esmie was keen to know more about her but Rupa said little apart from questioning patients and issuing instructions to the orderlies.

As the day grew hotter and the stench of bodies became overbearing, Esmie thought she would faint. Rupa worked on calmly, her manner detached but professional.

'Go and get something to eat and drink,' she told Esmie. 'You'll be no use this afternoon if you don't.'

'I'm really not hungry,' Esmie said. 'And there's so much to do.'

At that moment, a woman tore into the dressing station cradling a bundle and shrieking incoherently. As Rupa steered her to the side and tried to calm her, Esmie took the bundle of rags. With a gasp she realised she was holding a baby. Its eyes were closed and it made no sound. Alarmed, she bent to the baby's mouth but felt no breath.

Rapidly, she placed it on a table and pulled frantically at the dirty swaddling clothes that stank of liquid excrement. Esmie hid her fear that this might be cholera. The baby was a girl. Behind her, she could hear the mother wailing and beseeching. Esmie felt for a pulse. Her hope leapt as she found a tiny beat.

'Tell her she's still alive,' she cried.

Bending over the infant, Esmie covered her tiny mouth and nose with her own mouth and gently breathed into her. She massaged the baby's chest. Moments later, the baby exhaled and her eyes opened. She took one look at Emsie bending over her in her white cap and let out a whimper.

Esmie's eyes stung with tears of relief. The woman began babbling her thanks. She snatched at the child and as she did so, her veil slipped from her face. Esmie stared in horror. She was young but horribly disfigured; below her pretty almond-shaped eyes, her nose had been partially mutilated as if someone had hacked at it with a sharp blade. The skin was raw and puckered.

Quickly, Rupa steered the woman away from the stares of the male orderlies to a corner of the veranda that was curtained off. Esmie followed, swallowing down the bile in her throat. Behind the curtain, there was just enough room for a bedroll and Esmie wondered if this was where Rupa snatched moments of rest during hectic working hours. The woman crumpled to the floor, weeping and cradling her baby who was now mewling constantly.

Rupa talked to her in a low reassuring voice and examined the wound. She called for Malik. He came bearing ointment and bandages, anticipating what she would need, and then withdrew. While Rupa dealt with her patient, Esmie went to fetch a bowl of water, soap and a clean cotton cloth in which to wrap the baby. She set about bathing the infant, whose cries lessened as Esmie gently washed her in the tepid water. The baby's dark eyes fixed on hers in trusting puzzlement and Esmie felt a surge of protectiveness. She thought of Jeanie at Vaullay and her determination that no one was going to part her from her precious son, Norrie, and wondered if this was how she had felt.

'Can we keep the woman here at the hospital?' Esmie asked. 'I'd like Harold to check the baby over and make sure she doesn't have some underlying problem. I worried it might be a fever but I think she is just malnourished.'

'We can let her sleep here,' said Rupa. 'I just use this as a private space during the day – but she probably won't stay.'

Esmie turned to the young woman and in faltering Pashto asked what her name was and the baby's.

She looked at Esmie warily but with a glint of defiance. 'I am Karo and my daughter is Gabina.'

Esmie smiled. 'Gabina – pretty name. It means honey?'

Karo nodded.

'Yes, Gabina is sweet as honey,' said Esmie. Turning to Rupa she said, 'Can you ask her to stay and let the doctor see the baby?'

Rupa spoke to Karo in fluent Pashto. The Waziri, looking anxious, answered her questions.

'She says she'll stay for the baby's sake but she's frightened. She's run away from her village,' Rupa explained. 'Her husband came back from the fighting and accused her of adultery – just because she gave him a daughter.'

Esmie was appalled. 'So was he the one who tried to cut off her nose?'

'Yes, it's a way of punishing women and keeping them cowed. I've seen a woman who had her breast severed for adultery. Karo must be very worried for her baby to have come here and risked the shame of people seeing her mutilated.'

Esmie was sickened. 'Tell her she can stay in here and feed her baby – it'll be safe,' she said.

As the sun was dipping, Harold came to seek her out. He looked as drained and exhausted as she felt. Earlier, Rupa had sent for food and made Esmie eat a simple bowl of rice and dahl, and share a flask of tea. But Esmie had hardly stopped working all day, except to dash along the veranda to make sure Karo was still there and that Gabina was breathing.

As they closed up the out-patients dressing station, Esmie knew that those they hadn't dealt with would have to find somewhere to curl up under a blanket and join the queue again in the morning.

'There's a backlog of cases,' Harold sighed. 'They come such a distance and are worse for all the travelling. We need to get the clinic in Kanki-Khel going again so they can be treated nearer home.'

'I quite agree,' said Esmie. She glanced at Rupa, who was on the point of leaving. 'Harold, there's this woman from beyond Kanki-Khel with a sickly baby that I want you to have a look at. The baby stopped breathing earlier in the day. The woman's been attacked by her husband and hounded out of her village. She's nowhere to go. Can we take her and the baby home tonight?'

She saw Rupa's eyes widen in surprise. Harold was swift to scotch the suggestion.

'I'm afraid we can't do that – it would be showing favour. There are scores of women and children in need – we can't take them all home. Besides, their menfolk wouldn't allow it.'

'I'm not saying we should,' said Esmie. 'Just this one mother and her daughter who have no one to protect them.'

'My dear, you don't understand the ways of these people,' Harold said. 'They are proud and take offence easily if they think you are interfering in their domestic affairs. We know nothing about this unfortunate woman—'

'We know that her husband hacked off half her nose!' Esmie retorted.

Harold looked shocked. Rupa spoke up.

'It's true, Dr Guthrie. She needed treatment too. Perhaps you could just check the baby over to put Mrs Guthrie's mind at rest.'

Harold reddened at her gentle reproof. 'Of course. Where are they?'

Esmie gave Rupa a grateful look and then led Harold to the hidden part of the veranda. Even though the baby's dirty clothing had been taken away and burnt, the space behind the curtain smelt rank. The baby was whimpering, which Esmie found oddly reassuring; at least she wasn't too listless to cry.

'This is Karo,' said Esmie.

Karo looked at Harold in alarm and quickly covered her bandaged face. Esmie tried to reassure her. Harold spoke to her gently in Pashto and after a moment's hesitation, Karo handed over her daughter.

'She's called Gabina,' Esmie told him. 'It means honey.'

Harold gave her a brief smile. 'Yes, I know that.'

After examining the girl, Harold confirmed what Esmie suspected.

'She's very underfed and dehydrated. Possibly the mother isn't producing enough milk. The baby might have a chest infection too.'

Esmie put a hand on her husband's arm. 'Harold,' she said quietly, 'what if it was Jeanie and wee Norrie? We'd do our best for them, wouldn't we? Let's look after this poor woman – even if it's just for a few days until her baby's life is out of danger. We can't save every child brought to us here but we can save this one. Karo has no one else to turn to.'

She saw him struggling with his conscience, his brow furrowed. Yet there was compassion in his hazel eyes. After a long pause, he nodded and said, 'Very well. We'll find a room in the servants' compound.'

Esmie smiled in relief. 'Thank you.'

'But we can't make a habit of this,' he added as if already regretting his decision.

Esmie ignored this. 'Can you explain to Karo what's happening?'

As Harold did so, Esmie determined she would redouble her efforts to learn Pashto fluently. After this incident, it felt more important than ever that she could speak to their patients in their native tongue.

Chapter 16

Taha, October

After a fortnight at the mission hospital, Esmie found it hard to believe that it had once felt strange and frightening. The time flew by and her admiration for Rupa and the orderlies grew daily. The widow was unflappable and the men did their work with a mixture of earnestness and cheerfulness. They bantered among themselves and from the amused looks they gave her, she suspected they often joked about her.

In the main hospital building, Harold strove to treat the myriad ailments, from resetting broken bones to removing burst appendixes. Beds were still being taken up by army troops who were recovering from war wounds, while the women's ward – being set apart from the main building – was housing fever patients among the military.

Esmie, concerned for the Waziri women, went to Alec for help. She persuaded the former army padre to galvanise the army into providing a makeshift shelter for the women. Within a couple of days, a working party of sepoys set about building a structure of mud bricks and sacking in a corner of the compound that was shaded by trees.

To Esmie's surprised delight, Brigadier McCabe, in charge of the garrison, came to oversee it. He was a dapper man with a dimpled chin and greying at the temples. According to Rupa, he had a timid wife who chose to stay at the regimental headquarters in Rawalpindi rather than accompany her husband on tour.

'You do a grand job here at the mission,' pronounced the brigadier, 'and we're grateful that you allow us to use your hospital. It won't be forever, I assure you. Your husband tells me the numbers of fever patients are already dropping.'

Esmie didn't like to point out that the mission had had little choice as the army had commandeered twenty of their thirty beds. Still, she liked him for his concern.

'You must come round and have a meal with us,' Esmie offered, thinking he might be lonely without his wife and missing home comforts.

'How kind,' he said, looking pleased. 'I would like that very much, Mrs Guthrie.'

She thought Harold might baulk at her issuing the invitation – he was always tired-out by the end of the working day – but he encouraged the idea.

'As a bachelor it was all too easy to fall into a solitary home life here,' he confessed. 'You must invite whoever you want, my dear. I want you to be happy and feel at home in Taha.'

'Then we must have a few more furnishings,' Esmie said. 'Number Ten is about as comfortable as a schoolroom.'

Harold looked concerned. 'As long as it doesn't require a lot of expense. My mission stipend isn't generous.'

'Then it's just as well you married someone as frugal as me who can magic up almost anything on my sewing machine.' Esmie smiled and almost added '*and not as extravagant as Lydia*' but stopped herself in time.

Esmie had received several letters from her old school friend; happy letters full of her new life in Rawalpindi and the joys of sharing it with her parents.

'. . . We Templetons are a definite hit at the Club! We're there practically every day – playing bridge or tennis (in the evenings when it cools off a bit) – and of course there are dinner-dances. The etiquette seems to be that you get invited round to someone's house for dinner first and then you go on with your dinner guests to the dance, where you either stay with that group or join up with another dinner party to make a larger group. Either way, it's huge fun and it means one is never short of dancing partners!

People are beginning to drift back from Murree and the hill stations now that the worst of the heat is over. I can't wait for the cold season and all the social events here once the army are back in full swing. Cold season! Listen to me, sounding like an old India-hand already!

Daddy took Mummy and me up to Murree for a few days when the heat was still bad – it gets so humid in Pindi! Obviously, Tom couldn't come as there was too much to do at the hotel. It needs heaps spending on it but I've told Tom to go ahead and use some of my allowance from Daddy. Old Colonel Lomax is being as stingy as ever to Tom and won't give him a penny towards his new business.

Goodness me; what a lot of flirting goes on in Murree – it's as much a summer sport as tennis or cricket as far as I can see!

Tom's been an absolute darling about having my parents here – Pa and Ma he calls them – isn't that sweet? He's agreed that they can stay on another month so that they can enjoy Pindi when it's not so horribly hot.'

Later, Lydia had written reproachfully about Esmie and Harold passing through Rawalpindi without stopping to see them.

> *'. . . I simply can't believe you swanned through Pindi station and didn't come to stay! I would never have done that to my best friend. Mummy and Daddy were very disappointed too. You simply mustn't let that happen again. When will you come and visit? Can you do so before my parents leave at the end of October? At the very least you MUST MUST come for Christmas and New Year. I'm told that they celebrate Hogmanay in Pindi as if they were in Scotland!'*

Esmie was glad that Lydia was settling so well into her new life in India, although it worried her how her friend would cope once her parents sailed for home. She sounded very dependent on them for her social life and general happiness. She wondered about Tom and the hotel – Lydia hardly mentioned the place – but it all seemed a world away from life in Taha. Esmie was glad she was kept busy every waking hour so that she didn't have time to dwell on her feelings for Tom Lomax. She knew from the twist she felt in her stomach from just seeing his name written that her hankering for him hadn't gone away.

Her own marriage had settled into a routine of sorts. She and Harold rose early and breakfasted together on the veranda, discussing the jobs for the day. They would be out at the hospital until late, having lunch brought to them, and return after dark for a simple supper. It was then that she would slip round to the side of the veranda that faced the servants' quarters and wait for Karo to appear with Gabina, so she could check up on their welfare and practise speaking Pashto. Despite her difficulties, Karo had retained a sense of humour and would sometimes let out a raucous laugh at Esmie's attempts to speak her language. The Waziri woman even joked darkly about her husband's attempts to disfigure her. 'He is just half a man – he manages to cut off only half my nose.'

Now that Karo was being fed regular meals, her milk had increased and the baby was suckling properly again. Gabina no longer whimpered feebly or produced watery faeces. She was growing in strength daily and her gurgles of contentment touched Esmie's heart. She was a pretty infant with soft curls of black hair, big brown eyes and a pink bud of a mouth that creased into a smile of recognition when Esmie appeared.

Karo's presence in the compound had caused consternation at first. Draman had gone to Harold and protested.

'Sahib, she is bad woman,' the bearer had declared. 'She brings bad fortune to Guthrie Sahib.'

'I don't believe that,' Harold had said. 'She is homeless and the baby is sick. It's our Christian duty to look after them until they are well again.'

'Sahib, she is from a bad tribe,' Draman had persisted. 'It will bring trouble. Ali and his parents are from rival tribe. They fear attack because you bring bad woman here.'

Esmie could see that the usually jocular bearer was fearful but she didn't want to interfere. It was up to Harold to deal with his old retainer. To her relief, her husband managed to calm Draman down.

'Karo will only stay as long as is necessary and no more,' Harold assured him. 'But while she is here, I expect all the staff to be kind to her. Perhaps she can help you. You could give her a job peeling onions or some such.'

Draman had looked aghast at this suggestion. Shaking his head, he had hurried away and never mentioned Karo again.

A month on, Karo and Gabina were still living in the compound. Draman's distaste for the Waziri interloper had lessened once Karo had proved herself to have a knack for getting the hens to lay twice as many eggs as usual. Without saying anything, Karo had quietly taken on the role of feeding the hens. With Gabina strapped to her back, she would sing to them while she fed them grain.

The baby grew more alert and would smile and giggle at anyone who showed her attention. Even Ali, who at first had kept well away from the Waziri woman, was charmed by the sunny-natured Gabina. Esmie sometimes noticed him pulling faces and making her laugh. By late October, no one was mentioning sending Karo and her daughter away. Esmie was thankful for this; she was growing so fond of mother and child that she knew it would be a wrench if they left.

Esmie started to teach Karo how to use her sewing machine – the young Waziri was fascinated by it and clapped her hands in glee at what it could do. Her slim dextrous fingers were quick and her work accurate. Esmie never had to show her anything twice and she wondered if, in time, she could set Karo up as a seamstress so that she could earn her own living. Would a woman be allowed to set up in business in this most conservative of places? All the Indian tailors – darzis – that Esmie had come across were men. Nevertheless, it was a skill that would be useful to Karo whatever she did next.

As the evenings grew cooler, Esmie and Harold took to sitting indoors at the table and, by the light of a kerosene lamp, he would read while she worked her sewing machine, making clothes for Gabina or comfortable loose-fitting dresses for herself.

One chilly evening, Esmie was making some half-veils for Karo to hide her face-wound out of soft silk that she'd asked Draman to buy from the bazaar. It had been a particularly tiring day. Esmie sat back and rubbed her eyes.

'Harold, will you read to me? I don't think I can concentrate on sewing another stitch tonight.'

'Of course, my dear.' Harold looked pleased to be asked. He picked up a volume of Scottish poetry that he knew she liked and began to read.

Esmie moved to a more comfortable chair beside him and relaxed back into the cushions. There was something very calming about her husband's voice.

She was full of admiration for his skills at the hospital; no one was more dedicated to his patients or amiable with his staff than Harold. The only thing that marred her contentment at being his wife was his absence from her bed. He had never once come seeking comfort with her or given her the slightest encouragement for her to slip into his room at night.

Looking at him now, his square face and expressive mouth lit by lamplight, Esmie felt a tug of longing. Despite feeling exhausted she was filled with a need for his physical touch. The long day at work had not rid her of such a hunger. Was it the same for Harold? Should she make her desire for him more apparent? He was so inhibited in his shows of affection; perhaps he just needed more encouragement from her.

Tonight she wanted to lie in his arms and fall asleep with the feel of his solid body beside her. When he got to the end of a fourth poem, he closed the book and glanced up, catching her looking at him.

'What are you thinking?' he asked.

Her heartbeat quickened. 'How much I admire you.'

Even in the soft light she could see him redden. 'And I, you,' he said.

'I adore your voice,' she said softly, reaching out for his hand and squeezing it.

He smiled but she could feel him tensing ever so slightly.

'Harold.' She held on to his hand. 'Will you kiss me tonight?'

He hesitated and then stood up, still holding her hand. Leaning over he gave her a chaste kiss on the forehead.

'Harold, that's not what I meant—'

He disengaged his hand and patted her shoulder.

'I can hardly keep my eyes open. I'll see you at breakfast. Sleep well, my dear.'

Esmie sat swallowing down her frustration. She was suddenly overwhelmingly tired and it was several minutes before she had the energy to haul herself to her feet. She retreated to her solitary room, determined that sometime soon she would find a way of seducing her husband.

On Sundays, their one day off work, Esmie would invite people for lunch after church. Brigadier McCabe, Alec Bannerman and Rupa all came. The brigadier was a witty man and Alec had a fund of stories from his time in the army and Esmie was pleased to see Rupa relax and enjoy their company too.

She remembered how Alec had been concerned about some young homesick officers, so she made an effort to invite them along to Sunday lunch too. Alec was delighted by this and told Esmie, 'Number Ten is gaining a reputation among the young single officers for its hospitality. I hear them talking about the welcoming Scottish doctor and his attractive young wife.'

Esmie laughed with embarrassment. 'Well, we like having their company.'

Her favourite was a fair-haired cavalry officer, Lieutenant Dickie Mason. He was charmingly polite and solicitous and seemed popular among his peers. She was surprised to hear from Alec that Dickie had been the most homesick of them all when he'd arrived in the North-West Frontier.

'He'd been quartered in Bombay before that,' said Alec, 'where life was far more sociable. Just before he was transferred here, he got word that his sister had died of influenza. Hit him hard, poor boy.'

'How terrible,' said Esmie. 'I'm so sorry to hear that.'

'I think perhaps he looks on you as a caring older sister,' said Alec.

She redoubled her efforts to be kind to the young lieutenant.

Sitting around a simple table sharing food and lively conversation reminded Esmie of the early years of the War when she and her fellow nurses had eaten with the Serbian soldiers. It made her think of Tom and wonder whether he ever missed his life in the Peshawar Rifles and the camaraderie that came with living together and serving alongside his fellow men. Was running a hotel dull in comparison, despite being the life he'd chosen?

Then she chided herself for thinking about him. Try as she did, she could not banish Tom from her thoughts completely. Whenever she received another letter from Lydia, her equilibrium was disturbed. She didn't encourage the correspondence – she hardly had time to write these days – but Lydia's letter writing was increasing. Her most recent letter sounded less fulsome.

> '. . . *you ask about the hotel. Well, to be frank it's not exactly the Ritz. It's far from the most glamorous in Pindi – not a patch on Flashman's which is where all the best people stay. But Tom is trying his hardest to bring it up to scratch. It's all a bit shabby still – the old boy who had it before hadn't spent a rupee on it in years as far as I can see. And we have the legacy of a rather erratic manager – he's Anglo-Indian (that means mixed blood, to you and me) and although perfectly charming, he seems to spend more time talking to Tom about archaeology than menus. Tom's far too soft on him – and won't hear of sacking him as Daddy suggested – and his wretched family live in the hotel compound so if we did tell him to go, then they'd all be out of a home too. It's all a bit embarrassing but Tom will have to sort it out sometime.*
>
> *We had a wonderful time at the brewery last Saturday. I don't mean literally at the brewery! (The main brewery is up in Murree, by the way, and the soldiers*

drink gallons of the stuff). But there's a very entertaining deputy manager, Hopkirk, who threw a fancy-dress party at the brewery house. There's a tank in the garden (a swimming pool, to you and me) and lots of us ended up going for a dip fully clothed – it was a riot!

I'm getting terribly sad thinking about Mummy and Daddy leaving soon. Please can't you come and stay for a few days? Surely you're not needed ALL the time? I'm going to need you once my dearest parents have gone. Even just writing about it sets me off crying . . .'

Esmie wrote back saying how busy she and Harold were, that she was sorry they wouldn't be able to visit Rawalpindi before the Templetons left but to send them her love and to have a safe journey home. With Harold's agreement, she added that they were very grateful for the invitation for Christmas and would try and come then.

By early November, all of the army patients had been discharged or transferred from the mission hospital and, to Esmie's joy, the female ward began functioning again for the benefit of the local women. Their workload was still heavy but the numbers of out-patients had dwindled and they were no longer dealing with casualties from the summer conflict.

Harold began making plans for travelling to Kanki-Khel to reopen the clinic in the hills. It was decided that this would only be possible under a police guard.

'I'll take Alec with me,' he said.

'Wouldn't he be more use here with Rupa?' asked Esmie.

Harold looked surprised. 'I'm sure she can cope with you here to help her.'

At once, Esmie said, 'I'm coming with you, Harold.'

'That's far too risky,' he replied.

'So who is going to treat the women up there?' she challenged. 'I imagine they are even more conservative about who gets to see them than they are in Taha. Besides, my Pashto is just as good as Alec's now.'

'But I would worry about you all the time,' he protested.

'And I'll worry about you all the time if you go without me. Please,' she appealed. 'We came out here as a husband and wife team, remember? Wherever you go, I go too.'

Abruptly, he laughed. 'Oh, Esmie, my dear; you are a remarkable woman. I still can't quite believe I'm married to you.'

'Does that mean we're going together?' she asked with a smile.

Harold nodded. 'If I can double our escort, then yes; we'll go to Kanki-Khel together.'

Esmie was beginning to love her home at Taha. Getting up early, she would pad barefoot onto the veranda and watch the sun steal up through the veil of mist that cloaked the valley, enjoying the chill of the November air. By midday, the sky would be bright blue – not as harsh as in September – and the temperature would be pleasant. Harold had warned her that it would be getting cold in the mountains and they would need to take warm clothing and blankets. She had almost forgotten what cold weather felt like.

Soon after she had persuaded Harold to let her accompany him to Kanki-Khel, they had heard that the cavalry unit would be pulling out and returning to their base in Rawalpindi. Esmie would miss the lively company of the young officers and it made her all the more impatient to get on with their mission into the hills to re-establish an outpost clinic.

Before leaving for Kanki-Khel, the Guthries had a final lunch party for the cavalry officers, along with the brigadier who was staying on in Taha.

'I'm so grateful for your kindness to me, Mrs Guthrie,' Dickie Mason said, with one of his disarming smiles that made his cheeks dimple. 'I can't thank you and the good doctor enough.'

'It's we who should be thanking you,' said Esmie, smiling back. 'You've enlivened our dinner table. It's been a pleasure having you here. Hasn't it, Harold?'

Her husband nodded. 'A pleasure,' he echoed. 'But I imagine you'll be pleased to get back to Pindi and a bit of civilisation.'

Dickie shook his head. 'I can't imagine we'll find a more hospitable home or better company than here, sir.'

'Well said!' cried the brigadier.

Esmie laughed. 'Oh, I can see that chivalry in the cavalry is still alive and well.'

'I'm most sincere,' Dickie insisted. 'Rawalpindi will be new territory for me and I don't know a soul there. I'm looking forward to the polo and racing though. Do you ever visit, Mrs Guthrie?'

'I'm afraid I haven't been there either yet,' Esmie confessed. 'Though we plan to visit friends there at Christmas.'

His face brightened. 'Then please be our guests at the mess when you do. It would be an honour to return your generous hospitality.'

'How kind,' said Esmie. She glanced at Harold, knowing his lack of enthusiasm for formal dinners.

'We'd certainly like to come and watch some polo,' her husband replied. 'The regiments in Pindi are second to none for horsemanship. But there's no need to make a fuss of us.'

Esmie saw Dickie's eager look falter. She detected an underlying vulnerability in the lieutenant – so outwardly self-assured – and knew he was still grieving for his beloved sister. He was searching for friendship and a sense of home, and her heart went out to him.

Dickie couldn't know how trying Harold found alcohol-fuelled banquets and, fearing the young man might be feeling rebuffed, she said, 'You must go and visit our good friends the Lomaxes – they run the Raj Hotel on Nichol Road. Captain Lomax is a dear friend of my husband's and Mrs Lomax is a friend of mine from schooldays. They are good company and I'm sure will introduce you to others in Pindi.'

'Yes,' Harold agreed. 'Tom Lomax was a very good polo player before he hung up his spurs – he was in the Peshawar Rifles.'

'The Rifles!' Dickie's eyes widened with admiration. 'They're legendary. I'd very much like to meet him. Thank you.'

Esmie had a moment of doubt. Should she warn the young officer of Tom's jaded views of the army? She decided not to. She didn't want to prejudice Dickie against Tom before he met him.

On the final morning in Taha, before embarking for Kanki-Khel, Esmie did her dawn ritual of standing on the veranda. She breathed in the smell of dewy earth and acrid smoke from the early fires lit in the servants' compound. She had asked Karo if she wished to return to the hills with them – perhaps to her own kin if she would be safe there from her husband's family. But Karo had been adamant she didn't want to go and Esmie didn't press her. Rupa had promised to keep an eye on Karo and Gabina while Esmie was away.

Her friendship with the widowed Rupa had deepened the more they had worked together and Esmie had broken down the woman's initial reserve towards her. A couple of times, when Harold had been working particularly late at the hospital, Esmie had gone round to Rupa's small bungalow in the hospital grounds and shared her supper. Rupa was an enthusiast for food and often got her cook to produce family recipes of fish steamed in chutney or spicy chicken curry.

'My family turned their back on us when my husband converted to Christianity,' Rupa had confided. 'We were Parsees – I still am, I suppose.'

'Is that why you've stayed on in Taha?' Esmie had asked her.

Her friend had looked reflective before answering. 'One reason, yes. But I also feel closer to my husband here – though I could never go up to Kanki-Khel where he was . . .' Her voice had tailed off, her expression harrowed. Then with urgency she said, 'You must take very good care of yourself up there. Promise me you won't take any risks.'

Esmie had promised.

Gazing out over the low rooftops of the cantonment, she watched the native quarter emerging from the mist and the slender spire of a minaret poking through date palms. As she heard the early call to prayer – a sound she loved – a conversation came back to her of Tom talking with enthusiasm about the old town in Rawalpindi. *'You can hear the singing from the temples right across town.'* Was he waking at this very moment to the cry of the muezzin? Did it still thrill him? She hoped that he was enjoying being a hotelier and wasn't regretting his decision to leave the Peshawar Rifles.

Esmie wondered whether there was some deeper reason for him turning his back on his old regiment and life on the Frontier and not just his cynicism about war. Perhaps it was too bound up with the death of his first wife – had Mary died in Peshawar? Esmie realised she didn't know where it had happened, just that her death had been sudden. Was she buried in Peshawar – that fortress town on the edge of the notoriously dangerous Khyber Pass that led to Afghanistan?

Esmie's stomach knotted. She was about to venture into the wild and lawless borderlands herself. Harold and Rupa both would rather she didn't go but Esmie was gripped by that old feeling she used to get on nursing service; half fear, half exhilaration. Somewhere deep in her past, her parents must have instilled in her the obligation to go and help people in need no matter how dire the circumstances or at what personal risk.

She felt keenly that she was doing this work for her parents – because their lives had been cruelly cut short and their vocation left unfinished.

Did Tom feel a similar sense of obligation to his long-dead mother? Was that why he had defied his father and chosen a peaceful profession because he was striving to live up to the gentler qualities of warm-heartedness and kindness that he remembered in his mother?

Esmie had no way of knowing. She just hoped that the troubled former captain was finding a new peace of mind at the Raj Hotel. Taking a deep breath, Esmie turned from the view. Enough of contemplation. She must get ready for the trip. The mountains beckoned.

Chapter 17

The Raj Hotel, Rawalpindi, November

Striding in to the cramped hotel foyer after an afternoon's riding, Tom was startled by a sudden loud eruption. Some of the residents were already lounging in cane chairs in the dimly lit hallway, sipping pre-dinner pink gins under the fronds of over-exuberant ferns. One or two paused in conversation as the noise came again.

'Achew!'

It was Charlie Dubois sneezing; a sound that was more like a bellow than a sneeze.

Greeting his guests as he weaved his way past chairs, tables and brass urns, Tom found his manager hanging on to the reception desk for support while blowing his nose on a large white handkerchief. His eyes were streaming and his usually round smiling face was pasty and sweating.

'You look terrible,' said Tom in concern.

'I'm fine, sir,' Charlie croaked and made an attempt to stand erect. He was as immaculate as ever in suit and bow tie but looked on the point of fainting.

'Sit down, Charlie,' Tom insisted, steering him onto a cane stool. The normally ebullient man didn't protest.

'Maybe just for a minute,' he conceded, wiping his brow.

'You must get yourself to bed,' ordered Tom.

Ansom, the cheerful retired railway engineer, called over. 'That's what we've been telling him, Lomax.'

Fritwell, his portly companion and a former army quartermaster, huffed. 'He's been sounding like a twenty-gun salute all afternoon. We'll all be dying of the same lurgy if he stays there much longer.'

Ansom gave a loud laugh. 'We'd all rather have Mrs Dubois looking after us, wouldn't we, Fritters?'

Tom knew how they liked to tease the manager about how lucky he was to have secured the attractive Myrtle as his wife. But they had a point; Myrtle was far more efficient than her talkative husband, kept a sharper eye on the staff and tried heroically to balance the books. She stayed in the background while her husband played the welcoming host but would sometimes come in after dinner and play piano for the guests.

Charlie looked at him with glassy eyes. 'My wife's been called over to help her sister – she thinks Rose's baby is coming. Shall I send for her, sir?'

'No, of course not – she's needed more there. I can stand in tonight,' said Tom, 'and Jimmy can help me.'

Fritwell snorted. 'Good luck with that, Lomax. Jimmy Dubois will be out playing cricket till the cows come home.'

Tom smiled. 'He's a good boy and he can man the desk.'

'There's no nee— Achew!' Charlie's protestation was drowned out by another enormous sneeze.

Just at that moment, Stella, the Dubois' seven-year-old daughter, appeared on the stairs accompanying Hester Cussack.

'Ah, the Baroness!' Ansom cried. 'Led by the star in our firmament; young Stella! Stella, you must persuade your father to go and lie down. He won't listen to us crusty old koi hais.'

The young girl grinned and nodded but kept at Hester's side, holding up the worn hem of her evening gown to prevent her tripping.

Punctuated by Charlie's sneezing, the tall widow made her stately way downstairs, one step at a time, her strings of pearls glinting in the lamplight. Her thick grey hair was coiled into a style that had been fashionable a generation ago and she clung onto Stella with slim arms that were hidden in long black evening gloves. Her aquiline features still looked regal and Tom could imagine how she had turned heads in her youth.

Ansom had told him she'd been married to an Austrian baron and gentleman explorer. Fritwell said he'd heard she'd been lady-in-waiting and confidante to the queen of Sikkim. Lydia, rather cattily, repeated the gossip from the Club that she was the daughter of an Irish navvy and had been a chorus girl who had deserted her soldier husband for an Armenian businessman. Liking her, Tom didn't care.

Tom hurried forward to help, winking at Stella in encouragement. With her pretty green eyes and honey-blonde hair, the girl looked like neither of her parents. Perhaps her fair looks were a throwback to some British forebear. But she had her father's engaging personality and her mother's quick thinking. At seven, she was mature beyond her years and a great favourite with the permanent guests.

'Good evening, Baroness,' said Tom, proffering an arm and taking over from Stella.

Fritwell beckoned and raised his voice. 'Over here, Baroness. We've saved you a seat.'

'Ah ha! Thank you, darlings,' said Hester with a gracious nod of the head.

Tom hid a smile. The chairs were only ever half filled. This area of the hotel had been commandeered years ago by the small clique of long-time residents, from where they could see all the comings and goings of the hotel as well as the street outside. Lydia's attempts to confine them to the residents' sitting room at the end of the corridor had so far failed. Like cats they padded back to their favourite seats and could be found at any time of the day snoozing under copies of the Civil and Military Gazette or sharing a convivial drink.

'Here we are, Baroness,' said Tom, helping her into a lumpy chair that was covered in chintz cloth and padded with mothball-smelling cushions. Stella rearranged Baroness Cussack's hem to hide her dilapidated slippers.

'Thank you, darlings,' said the baroness, reaching for the glass of sherry on the carved table between her and Fritwell. 'Santé!'

'Good health!' said Ansom.

'Bottoms up!' said Fritwell.

Tom turned to Stella. 'Can you run and find Jimmy for me? I want him to take over reception. We've four more booked in tonight, arriving on the evening train. I'm ordering your father to bed. I'll do the meet and greet tonight.'

Stella gave him a questioning look. 'But Mr Lomax, I thought . . .?'

'Thought what?'

'That you were going to the Brewery dance tonight with Mrs Lomax.'

Tom stifled an oath. He'd completely forgotten. He glanced at the clock above the desk. It was almost six o'clock and they were due for drinks at the Hopkirks' in an hour. Riding around Topi Park this afternoon with the pleasant young Lieutenant Mason had been a chance to forget the daily concerns. They had talked about their shared love of hunting and fishing and Tom had promised they would go on shikar in the Himalayan foothills during the cold season. He hadn't thought of his homesick wife all afternoon, let alone the dance. Tom felt engulfed in guilt.

'I better go and talk to Mrs Lomax,' Tom said hastily, 'and explain the situation.'

He glanced at Charlie who was mopping his feverish face with a damp handkerchief.

'Stella, you help your father,' said Tom.

She hesitated. 'I could go and see if Mummy is still needed at Auntie Rose's.'

Tom felt his jaw reddening. The girl might be young but she was well aware of Lydia's moods and how the boss's wife could dissolve into tears at the slightest upset these days. Would Lydia be more annoyed by Tom missing the dance or at Myrtle Dubois stepping into the role of hostess at the Raj? To him, Charlie's wife was a godsend, and yet Lydia had instantly taken against Myrtle for thwarting her attempts to modernise the hotel. The redecoration kept being delayed and old furniture thrown out would reappear days later disguised with different cushions or counterpanes with explanations such as it was the baroness's favourite chair or had belonged to Mr Ansom's mother. Tom found himself constantly caught in the middle of their skirmishing, trying not to show favouritism to the practical level-headed Myrtle while also placating his wife.

Tom shook his head. 'No, Stella; we can manage without your mother. The health of your aunt and her baby are more important than me missing a dance.'

'Darling,' said Hester, 'go to the ball. The children can look after us.'

'I'll go along later,' said Tom, seizing a piece of writing paper from the desk and scrawling a quick message. He handed it to Stella. 'Give this to Jimmy and tell him to take it at once to Lieutenant Mason at the Westridge Barracks. And, Charlie,' he said, pulling the manager to his feet, 'go home.'

Heading for the stairs and taking them in twos, he heard the jocular encouragement from the residents.

'Good luck, darling!'

'Into battle, Lomax,' called out Fritwell.

'If the delightful Mrs Lomax wants a partner,' said Ansom with a chortle, 'then Handsome Ansom is ready and willing.'

At the end of the corridor, Tom braced himself before entering their two-roomed apartment. He thought it was a charming home with its sloping ceiling and two verandas; one overlooking the internal courtyard and the other the garden and the Saddar Bazaar beyond.

Lydia had filled their home with stylish Oriental furnishings that her mother had helped her choose and had hung a semi-erotic painting of dancing nymphs over their new, large and comfortable bed. His own watercolour of the ruins of Hindu temples at Taxila had been consigned behind the wicker sofa, Lydia declaring it too big for either room, and would have to wait for when they moved into their own house. Lydia had been pressing for this to happen ever since her parents had left. She hated living alongside the guests and so near to the bazaar. 'All bells and smells,' she complained.

As Tom walked into the small sitting room he got a heady waft of Lydia's perfume from the adjoining bedroom.

'Is that you?' Lydia called.

'Yes, my sweet,' Tom answered.

'You better hurry and change. We can't be late. Geraldine says the colonel of that new cavalry regiment is coming and I want you to make a good impression. I don't like the way some of the army lot cold-shoulder us just because you're no longer in the Rifles.'

Tom heard the excitement in her voice. He felt terrible for letting her down. Walking into the bedroom he saw Lydia sitting at her dressing table applying rouge to her cheeks. She was wearing a shimmering red gown that showed off her décolletage. Its lack of modesty would raise eyebrows among the matrons of Rawalpindi. She stood and turned towards him and he was struck anew at her beauty. Since coming to India her figure had filled out and she was even more voluptuous than before.

'You look like a goddess,' said Tom, smiling.

'And you look and smell like a stable boy,' she replied, wrinkling her nose. 'Bijal filled you a bath an hour ago but you'll just have to have it cold. Chop, chop.'

'Dearest,' Tom said, 'you'll have to go on ahead without me. Charlie's ill and Myrtle is helping at Rose's confinement. I'll come as soon as I can but we've new arrivals tonight.'

Her face puckered in dismay. 'Oh, Tom! You know how much I've been looking forward to this. You simply must come. Charlie can manage – he looked fine to me earlier. Just a bit of a cold.'

'It looks more like a fever to me,' said Tom, 'and I don't want him sneezing all over the guests. Anyway, I've sent him home.'

'What is the point of paying these people if they won't work when you want them to?' Lydia said in exasperation.

'Darling, that's not fair—'

'I'll tell you what's not fair – leaving it to the last minute to tell me we can't go to the dance!' She looked on the verge of tears.

'But you can still go,' Tom insisted.

'I'm not walking in there on my own!'

'You won't have to,' said Tom hastily. 'I've sent a message to Dickie Mason. I know he'll be delighted to escort you.'

Lydia pouted. 'That boy lieutenant? He's hardly out of school trousers. I want Captain Lomax to be at my side. I want my husband!'

'I'm sorry,' said Tom, beginning to strip off his riding clothes. 'But the needs of the hotel must come first. I'm trying to make a go of this. I admit it's been harder than I thought it would be – more hands on – but once things are more prosperous, we'll have heaps of time for dances and parties.'

Lydia flashed him an accusing look. 'It will never be prosperous if you keep the sort of second-rate clientele we've inherited. They're a bunch of no-hopers. Nobody who's anybody wants to stay here – only box-wallahs and Eurasians.'

Tom paused, half-undressed, and stared at her in astonishment. She'd made teasing comments about their permanent guests before but never spoken of them with such disdain. He felt offended on their behalf.

'Darling, don't speak about our friends like that,' he chided.

'They're not our friends – they're spongers who live here at half the going rate and still never pay up on time.'

'Well, it's better than having the rooms standing empty,' Tom said defensively. 'Besides, they're good people. Your parents liked them – Pa got on splendidly with Ansom and Fritwell.'

'Daddy would make friends with the Kaiser given half a chance,' she said dismissively. 'But Mummy saw right through that so-called baroness. You can tell how she puts on that false Austrian accent. Geraldine says she's the laughing stock of the Club and it's obvious she's as common as they come.'

Tom was irritated. 'And what has Geraldine Hopkirk done in life apart from marry a brewer?' he snapped.

Lydia's mouth tightened. 'Now who's being a snob?'

Tom's chest was tight with anger but he curbed his temper.

'Lydia,' he appealed to her. 'Let's not argue. I'm sorry I can't take you to the brewery dance but I want you to still go and have a good time.'

She relented quickly. 'I suppose I will just have to make the best of it with that Mason boy in tow. Esmie claims he has a good sense of humour at least.'

'He certainly does,' Tom agreed.

He was unsettled by the sudden reference to Esmie. Lydia's friend had resisted all attempts to be lured to Rawalpindi before Christmas. Word had it that she and Harold had gone into the mountains to dispense medicines and care. He was in awe of Esmie's courage – Lydia would never endanger her life for Indians – yet he felt guilty for thinking of her and comparing her more favourably to his own wife. He shouldn't have to keep reminding himself that he had chosen the beautiful Lydia because he loved her.

Bare-chested, he crossed the room and stood next to Lydia. Tilting her chin, he smiled. 'And when you get back, I'll make it up to you.'

He bent and kissed her lips. For a moment, he felt her respond and then she was pushing him away.

'You stink of horse,' she complained. 'Go and bathe.'

It was late and most of the residents had long retired to bed when Tom went out to the courtyard to smoke a cigarette. The stars were hidden in a blanket of wood smoke that spread from the nearby Saddar Bazaar. He listened to the night sounds; a watchman calling out, a dog barking and the tinkle of tonga bells. A sense of calm washed through him. He had coped with all the new arrivals, chatted to the guests at dinner and played cards with the regulars by the fire in the sitting room. Mr Hoffman, the former policeman who years before had lost an eye from a stray firecracker, had played waltzes on his violin and made the baroness weep with nostalgia.

Tom knew he had enjoyed the evening far more than if he had been at the brewery dance – but knew he could never admit such a thing to Lydia. Thinking of his beautiful wife, he felt a quickening of excitement. Thankfully, young Mason had turned up promptly to escort her to the dance and Lydia had left in better humour, planting a kiss on Tom's cheek and whispering suggestively in his ear, 'I'll see you upstairs later.'

But he would have to rein in his impatience; these brewery dos could go on until the early hours. The old Tom – the pre-war officer who had relished riotous dinners and dances – would have gone along even at this late hour. But he had lost the appetite for largescale socialising after Mary had died. Back home in Scotland he had only made the effort to attend county balls for Lydia's sake. He would just be tempted to drink too much and make a fool of himself. Stubbing out his cigarette, Tom glanced towards the Dubois' bungalow. A light was still on in the parlour. He would go and see how Charlie was.

As he mounted the steps of their veranda, he caught a glimpse through the window and, to his surprise, saw that Myrtle was back from her sister's and all the family were still up. Charlie was sitting in a chair by the fire with a rug tucked round his knees and Jimmy sprawled at his feet. Myrtle was on the sofa with Stella curled under her arm and the girl's head on her lap. He felt a sudden tug of envy at the domesticated sight. This is what he wanted for him and Lydia one day; a happy family and a welcoming home.

Perhaps he should give in to Lydia's desire for a house in the civil cantonment. It would be less convenient for work but she could create the comfortable home for them that she desired away from the prying eyes of the residents. Tom sighed. He couldn't really afford it. The hotel was running at a loss and he had no other income. Lydia said her father would pay but Tom was too proud to go cap in hand to his father-in-law. Lydia still received an allowance from her parents but Tom insisted that she spent that on herself. If they moved into a civil bungalow they would have to start entertaining Lydia's new-found friends and that would put extra strain on their tight budget. Tom would have to resist her demands until after the expensive Christmas season was over.

A servant let Tom in. Jimmy sprang up as Tom entered the parlour, his plump face beaming. Stella stirred and sat up, yawning.

'I hope nothing's wrong, Mr Lomax?' Myrtle asked, rising.

'Please don't get up,' said Tom hastily. 'Nothing's wrong. I just came to see how Charlie is.'

'I'm fit as a fiddle,' said Charlie, wiping his streaming nose. 'Please sit, sir.' He pointed to the chair beside him.

'My husband's not fit at all,' said Myrtle in her soft sing-song voice. 'But he refused to go to bed until I got back.'

Charlie wagged a finger at her and blew his nose. 'I'm fine. Don't fuss.' He turned to Tom. 'Jimmy will pour you a nightcap. I'm partaking of a hot toddy to quench my cold. Johnny Walker. Kills germs and warms the blood. Please, sir, do sit.'

Tom did so. He'd hardly touched a drop of alcohol since the Templetons had left but now felt the familiar craving. 'I won't stay long but a dram would be nice.' To Myrtle he asked, 'How is your sister?'

Myrtle's round face lit up. With her wavy dark hair and doe-eyed beauty she reminded Tom of a film star.

'She is tired but well, thank you,' she replied.

Stella piped up. 'And I've got a new cousin – a baby boy. Mummy says I can go and visit him tomorrow after school.'

'That's wonderful news,' Tom cried.

Jimmy, handing over a generous tumbler of whisky to Tom, grinned and said, 'Finally a boy cousin who I can teach to play cricket.'

'That is why we are celebrating so late,' said Charlie, stifling a sneeze. 'There is a new son and heir for the Dixon family.'

'Does baby Dixon have a name yet?' Tom asked.

Myrtle smiled. 'Sigmund Francis.'

Tom raised his glass. 'To Sigmund Francis Dixon; good health, happiness and a long life!'

They echoed his words, though only he and Charlie drank a toast.

Myrtle put an affectionate hand on Stella's head and told her to go to bed. Stella resisted.

'Do as your mother says,' Charlie ordered. 'You have school in a few hours, young lady. You must be bright-eyed and bushy-tailed.'

Stella went reluctantly, still chattering about her new cousin. A yawning Jimmy followed. When they had gone, Tom said, 'Your children are a credit to you. They are such a help in the hotel. But I don't ever want it to interfere with their studies.'

Charlie rolled his eyes. 'If Jimmy put the same effort into his lessons as he does the cricket team, he would be top-class pupil.'

Tom laughed. 'I was a lot like that at his age.'

'Then, sir,' said Charlie, 'he will turn out to be a good penny in the end.'

They drank to Jimmy and his future. Then they drank to Stella and her father's hope that she would find a rich and kind husband. At this point, Myrtle got up. 'Stella has a good brain,' she said. 'Perhaps she will become a nurse or even a doctor.'

She winked and Charlie laughed as if she had made a huge joke. Tom thought suddenly of Esmie. Stella was already showing that mix of a sharp, practical mind and a caring attitude that made Esmie such a good nurse. Plus, a large dose of courage. Nursing was one of the few professions into which an Anglo-Indian like Stella could enter and thrive. Yet she was still so young and might have quite different ideas from her parents as to what she would be when she grew up.

Myrtle hovered by her husband but he told her to go to bed and he would follow shortly. Myrtle said goodnight to Tom with a look that implored him not to keep her husband up too late.

Tom tried to leave after one dram but Charlie was in full flow about the ruins at Taxila – his favourite topic – and poured them both another whisky. Tom felt guilty at keeping him up but noticed how Charlie's sneezing appeared to have been banished by the liquor. It was late and the bottle was nearly empty by the time Tom left and walked unsteadily towards the hotel. The chowkidar let him in. He steeled himself for a telling-off from Lydia for not being there on her return but he found their apartment empty. Disappointment gripped him. He fumbled out of his clothes and fell into bed.

The next thing he remembered was being woken by Lydia climbing in beside him. Groggily he was aware of her hair falling onto his face.

'You've been drinking,' she murmured, running a hand over his chest.

'So have you,' Tom said, smelling wine on her breath. 'Good party?'

'Umm, very,' she said with a slight giggle. 'I missed you though.'

She traced her fingers down his naked torso and onto his thigh. 'Ooh, naughty boy isn't wearing any pyjamas.'

Tom felt his ardour stirring. 'Couldn't be bothered.'

'Good,' said Lydia, beginning to kiss her way down his body.

He shifted onto his elbows, excited by her foreplay. They hadn't had sex for nearly two weeks and despite being half-comatose with whisky, he was suddenly aroused.

Lydia pushed him back and, swinging her leg over him, climbed on top. Tom let out a groan of anticipation. This was going to be like their honeymoon all over again. He gave into her caressing. Within minutes she had satisfied herself and pulled away just before he climaxed.

She sank back, panting. 'Don't want any little Lomaxes yet, do we?' she said with a drunken giggle.

Tom lay there, half sated and half frustrated. He wanted to take her in his arms and do it all again, except slowly, tenderly. He wanted them to lie together and create a new life. Suddenly, his yearning for a child almost choked him. His head spun. It was just the drink confusing and jumbling up his emotions – the news of Sigmund Francis's arrival and the celebrations at the warm-hearted Duboises'. Lydia was right that they should have some fun before embarking on a family. He put out a hand to stroke her breast but she was already lying on her front and snoring gently.

Chapter 18

Kanki-Khel

Esmie and Harold were driven north-east out of the Taha valley in a police truck, taking an armed Malik with them as orderly and extra protection. Crammed alongside them were all their medicines, clothes, bedding and fuel supply, as well as four policemen and a driver. All day Esmie perched tensely on the uncomfortable slatted seat, her stomach in knots, and tried to peer beyond the flapping canvas. The truck bumped and rolled along dusty tracks and then began a slow ascent, twisting around narrow corners hewn out of grey rock.

Somehow Harold managed to read as the motor vehicle bucked, shuddered and belched smoke. Esmie tried her best to keep down her breakfast.

After three hours they stopped briefly for tiffin by a makeshift bridge of roughly hewn timber. Stretching her legs, Esmie squinted in the harsh sunlight at the barren slopes and a scattering of goats, and marvelled that the nimble animals found anything to eat. A narrow river chuckled under the bridge. She'd never seen such emerald-green water. From nowhere, a turbaned boy appeared with a large watermelon and bartered with one of the policemen.

They shared it out but the officer in charge, Sergeant Azim Baz, a burly Pathan with a magnificent full beard and moustache, didn't want to linger and they were soon on their way again. Harold put his book away, perhaps aware of Esmie's nerves, and began to chat.

'We're entering the territory of the Gurbuz Waziris,' he told her.

'That's Karo's tribe, isn't it?' she asked.

'Yes,' Harold said. 'The Gurbuz live mainly around Kanki-Khel.'

'Was it wrong of me not to persuade her to come with us?' Esmie questioned. 'We might have been able to reunite her with her family.'

'They might not take her back,' said Harold. 'She's brought shame on them with her adultery.'

'But she was wrongly accused!' Esmie protested.

'I'm sure you are right,' said Harold. 'But such things can spark feuds between tribes that last for generations. Her father and brothers might wish to keep quiet. If Karo returns then they might be forced to take revenge.'

'So she might never be able to go back to her family?' Esmie asked.

Harold sighed. 'I fear not.'

'And meanwhile her hateful husband gets away with his savage attack,' said Esmie, full of indignation.

Harold put a hand on her arm. 'Dearest, it's best if you don't show your disapproval of her husband's people. The Otmanzai may well come to the clinic and you must treat them like the others. Most of them are good and brave and just want the best for their families. There are bad apples wherever you go.'

Esmie was chastened. 'Of course. I'm sorry. You know I'll do my job as well as I can. I've just grown so fond of Karo and Gabina that it's hard not to be protective of them.'

'I know,' Harold said with a tender look. 'That's why you are such a gifted nurse – because you care so deeply.'

After that they fell silent but Esmie leaned against her husband and dozed, drawing strength from his solid presence beside her.

Just as the sun was waning, they entered a valley with a thin fertile strip of crops and clumps of trees whose dying leaves shimmered golden in the soft light.

'Kanki-Khel!' Harold said in hushed excitement.

His gladness turned swiftly to apprehension when he saw the charred ruins of the former clinic. Its blackened stone and scorched timbers were a stark reminder that the village had come under attack just months ago by invading Afghans.

It was too hazardous for them to stay in the village and a billet had been found for them in a nearby fortified farmhouse which served as a police outpost. From its elevated position, the police guard could survey the whole valley and watch for raiders from the north – Otmanzai country – and beyond. The arid mountains of the borderland looked closer and more defined, their peaks already dusted with the first snow of winter.

The sleeping quarters were ranged around a small, high-walled courtyard. Harold and Esmie were given a room with an earthen floor, bare of furniture except for a charpoy – a simple wooden bedframe crisscrossed with string – on which to sleep. But it was cleanly swept and the walls had been washed in lime and someone had put two small handwoven rugs on either side of the bed.

They left their clothing packed – there was nowhere to put it – and Esmie unrolled both their bedrolls on the charpoy. Harold looked on in alarm.

'You're not sleeping on the floor,' she told him firmly. 'It's far too cold and I could do with your body heat beside me.'

He flushed but nodded in agreement.

With darkness, the temperature plummeted. Esmie wondered if they had left it too late in the year for such an expedition. What if they should get cut off by the snow? Once it came, the road back to Taha might become too hazardous for a motor vehicle, even a sturdy truck. She dismissed her fears. Harold was adamant they should re-establish the clinic before the year was out. He would have gone without her if necessary. She would rather be marooned here with her husband than left alone in Taha for weeks without him.

That evening they shared a simple meal of vegetable curry and flat nan breads with the Indian policemen. Sergeant Baz wiped his greying moustache, belched in appreciation and sat back to smoke. He had been reluctant to bring them but had volunteered when the army had refused. Harold had explained to Esmie, 'It would be seen as inflammatory for the army to send in a presence after the trouble with the Afghans. The Waziris already suspect that we British are intending handing over the border territory to the Afghans to keep the peace between us.'

'And are we?' Esmie had asked.

Harold hadn't known. 'It's possible. Brigadier McCabe says it's easier to deal with one strong power than a myriad of independent ones. Anyway, he's been ordered to keep a low profile in the hills for now. So we must be thankful for Baz and his men – they don't scare easily.'

Esmie sat and listened while Harold and the sergeant talked quietly about the current situation.

'Is there any truth in the rumour that there's been fresh unrest in southern Waziristan?' Harold asked. 'McCabe dismissed it as bazaar gossip.'

Esmie felt her pulse increase as she awaited the answer.

'Yesterday there was an unconfirmed report that a police post had been attacked at Razmak,' Baz confided.

'Does that alarm you, Sergeant?' Harold asked.

He shrugged. 'Probably a couple of excitable Waziri youths throwing firecrackers.'

'So you're not worried?' Esmie asked.

He glanced at her and shook his head. 'Even if it's true, it doesn't mean that the Waziris are taking up where the Afghans left off. You can sleep well tonight. We border police are more than a match for the local riff-raff.' He gave her a wide grin as he extinguished his aromatic cigarette with a pinch of his large thumb and forefinger.

After that, Malik and the men who were not on guard duty began to settle down to sleep around the fire. Rather reluctantly, Harold and Esmie retreated to their small chilly room with Harold bearing a candle and leading the way. They quickly changed into their night clothes – Harold turned away and didn't look – and then scrambled into their bedrolls which were already lined with sheets and pillows. Harold blew out the candle and the room filled with the smell of burnt tallow. It was pitch black but some small creature was scuttling around in the dark. The charpoy dipped in the middle and forced them together. Esmie snuggled against her husband, slipping an arm around his warm body. She could feel the rise and fall of his broad chest.

'Put your arms round me, please,' she whispered, 'and warm me up.'

After a moment's hesitation, Harold did so, pulling her closer and rubbing her back. Her cheek lay on his chest and she breathed in his male smell. Her heart began a slow thudding. Was he feeling any kindling of desire too? It was so hard to know what Harold was thinking. Perhaps now that they were lying so close he might take the opportunity to kiss her goodnight. It felt so right that they were in bed together; this was what they should have been doing all along.

Esmie waited a few minutes but Harold just seemed content to hold her. She reached up and kissed him on the lips. She felt him tense.

'Are you warm enough, my dear?' he asked.

'Umm, yes.'

'Good,' he said and kissed the top of her head.

Then he disengaged and turned away from her. Esmie's insides twisted in disappointment. She huddled against his back. At least she could feel his warmth in the night. Perhaps the following night, when he had grown used to the situation, Harold might become more demonstrative.

As she was drifting off to sleep, Esmie thought she heard someone cry out. She came wide awake again, listening. She could hear distant sobbing. A guard shouted and the crying stopped. It suddenly occurred to Esmie that there might be prisoners held here. It unnerved her to think they might be housed in the adjoining rooms. Perhaps this very bedroom might have been used as a cell too. Whoever it was had fallen silent for now. Esmie squeezed herself against Harold and fell asleep, comforted by his presence.

The next day, a makeshift clinic was set up in two surplus army tents outside the police post. Word soon went round and a steady stream of people trekked up from the village. All day, Harold diagnosed ailments and dispensed medicines while Esmie and Malik cleaned infected wounds and dressed them. One moment they were binding up a dislocated shoulder and the next would be dealing with a baby's conjunctivitis. Esmie was struck once again by the stoicism of these agrarian people, some of whom had walked miles to carry their children to be seen by the feringhi doctor and his wife.

The women, in particular, impressed her. They gathered together in the purdah tent, chattering, sharing scraps of bread and fussing over each other's children. They reminded her of Karo in their fierce, scolding protective love for their infants. Occasionally there would be a burst of raucous laughter and Esmie would look up to see a group of young women glancing in her direction. She suspected they were sharing ribald comments about her, for she overheard them speculating on whether she was with child.

For the first time she experienced a rush of envy for the women who cradled their babies. Their love for their children seemed so natural and uncomplicated. They lived tough, precarious lives and yet seldom complained, jollying one another along. She was reminded of the comradeship of the Scottish nurses who had learnt to live each day to the full because there was no knowing what the morrow would bring. Observing the Waziri women with their offspring, Esmie wondered why she had spent so much time worrying over having children in such an inhospitable place. These farmers' wives showed no such cowardliness.

Harold and Esmie worked until sundown and then hurriedly packed up and retreated to the fortified tower. Exhausted by the non-stop day's work, they fell into bed as soon as the evening meal was over. She was asleep almost instantly and heard no strange noises in the night.

The next few days were just as hectic. Word was spreading quickly that the mission clinic was open again and Waziris were travelling from further afield.

Malik told Esmie, 'They know about you giving refuge to Karo and Gabina. They think you have special powers to stop babies dying.'

'But saving Gabina was just pure luck,' Esmie exclaimed.

Malik looked at her in surprise. 'Surely you believe it was God's will?'

'Well, yes, I suppose so.'

Malik smiled. 'That is why so many are bringing their children here.'

Esmie was touched to hear this but also dismayed. If they believed she had some sort of divine power, then sooner or later they would be bitterly disappointed.

That night Esmie was once again woken by a man crying out. This time he kept up a wailing protest despite the shouts of the guard. Oblivious, Harold slept on. She was amazed at how deeply and untroubled he could be in sleep. Esmie left the warmth of her bedroll and, pulling a blanket around her shoulders, went out to see what was happening.

The guard was banging on a door across the courtyard and shouting at the inmate to be quiet. Esmie couldn't understand the babbling response from inside but she could hear the distress in the man's voice.

Baz appeared, turban-less, his hair shorn.

'What's happening?' she gasped.

'There is no need to worry,' said Baz. 'The man is mad but harmless. Please, Guthrie Memsahib, go back to bed.'

'Is he a prisoner?'

'Not exactly.'

'So why is he here?'

Baz rubbed a hand over tired eyes. 'He was found running around – he'd torn all his clothes off – and was cutting himself with a dagger. All we know is that he's an Otmanzai. The locals were afraid of him and wouldn't take him in. So he stays here until his family come to claim him.'

Esmie felt a flutter of nerves at the mention of the tribe who had rejected and abused Karo.

'Do his family know he is here?' asked Esmie.

Baz shrugged. 'The previous officer-in-charge sent word to the Otmanzai but no one has come to fetch him yet.'

'Can I see him? Perhaps I can help him,' Esmie suggested.

Baz shook his head. 'There is nothing you can do at this hour. Please, memsahib,' he appealed, 'go back to sleep.'

Esmie returned to her room and lay in distress listening to the deranged man. She was reminded of her former patient, Tommy Grey, whose nightly screaming used to keep the other inmates awake. After a while the shouting stopped. Esmie determined she would press to be allowed to see the man in the morning.

It was late the next day before Esmie had a chance to ask about the man in captivity, by which time she had talked to Harold about him. Harold persuaded Baz to let Esmie assess the man as she had dealt with the mentally ill.

Heart drumming at what she might find, Esmie, accompanied by Harold, was led into the darkened room by a guard holding up a lamp. The room stank of rotting food and excrement. Esmie was aghast to see how young the inmate was – his hair was long and straggly but his chin was smooth as a boy's. His hands and feet were shackled and chained to the wall. He stared back at them in terror.

When Esmie approached him, the youth shrank back and started whimpering. She tried to reassure him in faltering Pashto.

'Don't be afraid. I won't hurt you. I am Guthrie Memsahib, the doctor's wife. What's your name?'

The young man stared at her uncomprehendingly. The guard said, 'His name is Zakir. At least that's what he shouts out when he talks to himself.'

She crouched down. Zakir shook his chains in agitation. The guard warned, 'Don't get too close – he will lash out like a mule.'

Esmie ignored this and, trying not to gag at the smell of him, drew closer.

'Zakir,' she said gently, 'peace be with you.'

He went still. Something in his look altered; a spark of understanding in his wild eyes. She carried on talking to him in a soft voice. It didn't seem to matter what she said, just the sound of her words seemed to calm him. She turned to the guard.

'Please can you fetch me some water and a clean cloth? And a plate of food.'

'I can't leave you alone with him,' he replied.

'What can he do tied up like an animal?' Esmie chided.

Harold said swiftly, 'I'll protect my wife while you get what she asks.'

Reluctantly the guard went, returning minutes later.

Esmie asked Zakir, 'Will you let me wash you?'

The man said nothing so Esmie dipped the cloth in the water and tentatively began to wipe his face. As she did so, she hummed a Gaelic tune. Zakir stared back with pain-filled eyes but did not try and push her away.

'Please unlock the chains so he can eat,' she said.

The guard shook his head. 'Sorry, memsahib. My orders are to keep him tied up. It's for his own safety. He tries to cause harm to himself.'

'Just while he eats,' Esmie pleaded.

But the policeman would not be swayed. So Esmie broke off a piece of flat bread and, scooping food onto it, raised it to Zakir's lips. 'Eat this,' she encouraged. 'It's very tasty and will make you feel better.'

He found it hard to swallow and Esmie wondered how long he had been refusing to eat. In between small mouthfuls, she coaxed him to drink water. After a few minutes, he sank back exhausted from the effort. Soon afterwards, they left him, Esmie promising to come again in the morning. Later she heard him crying out and rattling his chains again.

'We must do something,' she urged Harold. 'Go and speak to Baz, man to man. He's more likely to listen to you than me. At least get the poor boy unchained. I can't bear another night of his crying.'

Harold went to find Baz in the guard room. Esmie followed him but held back and listened at the door.

'My wife thinks Zakir is suffering from shell shock. She's treated such cases before. The young man has obviously been affected by the violence of the Afghan war.'

'The boy is a lunatic,' said Baz. 'I don't want to keep him here but what else can I do? If I let him go he will kill himself or someone else.'

'Let us look after him while we are here,' Harold suggested.

Baz sounded unconvinced. 'Sahib, you have enough to do at the clinic without bothering about that wild boy.'

Esmie nearly cried out in frustration but bit back her words hoping that Harold would put her case to the Pathan officer.

'My wife thinks she can help him,' said Harold. 'And we can ask around our patients to see if he is known to anyone. If Mrs Guthrie manages to calm him down and we locate his family, then that solves your problem too.'

Baz scratched his beard. 'Very well. But he stays in his cell.'

'We agree to that as long as you unchain him from the wall,' Harold bargained.

The sergeant frowned. 'This is most irregular.'

'I'll take full responsibility for my wife and Zakir,' said Harold.

With a heavy sigh, Baz reluctantly agreed. Esmie felt a surge of triumph and slipped away before she was noticed.

That evening, after the clinic had closed, Malik and Harold helped Esmie bathe and dress Zakir in clean clothes while a servant sluiced out his cell. The emaciated Otmanzai had cuts and welts to his wrists and ankles where the chain cuffs had chaffed his skin. As the men tended to his wounds, Esmie combed out his matted black hair and talked soothingly to him. Zakir trembled and mumbled under his breath but did not resist their administrations.

At Esmie's request, Baz provided fresh straw for the youth to sleep on, a thick blanket and a bucket in which to relieve himself, even though Baz said Zakir wouldn't use it. Esmie and Harold took food into the cell and sat and ate with the prisoner. Zakir watched them suspiciously but after a few minutes he allowed Esmie to feed him a few mouthfuls like she'd done the night before.

'It's as if he's forgotten how to do the simplest things,' Esmie said to Harold as they settled into bed. 'But I sense intelligence behind all the fear, don't you?'

'Perhaps,' said Harold. 'He certainly seems to trust you, my dear.'

'Oh, Harold, the poor boy has no one else to care for him,' she fretted. 'What terrible things do you think he's witnessed?'

'We must try and find his kin,' said Harold.

'But what if he has no family left? Perhaps they were wiped out in the recent war? We can't just leave him here to rot.'

'Esmie,' Harold said wearily, 'we can't take in every waif and stray you come across.'

'I know . . .'

'We'll find someone to take him in before we leave,' Harold said. He kissed her on the forehead and turning, blew out the candle.

Esmie lay staring into the darkness, listening out for Zakir. She knew what it was like to lose those most dear and to carry around that leaden weight of loss in the pit of her stomach. The grief she had experienced in childhood had dulled to a faint ache when she thought of her parents but occasionally some incident caused it to flare up like an inflammation. Seeing Zakir in such a wretched condition and all alone made her remember the pain of bereavement anew. She would do everything she could for the youth.

Esmie thought of the brave women who came to the clinic and knew, despite the losses she had endured, how lucky she was to be living the life she had chosen. She must live every moment of her life to the full.

'Harold,' she whispered. 'Are you still awake?'

'Yes,' he replied.

She shuffled close and slipped an arm inside his bedroll. 'I want you to love me.'

She felt him tense yet he didn't pull away. 'I do love you, my dearest.'

'Not in the way I want,' she said. She couldn't see his expression but she put a hand to his face and rubbed her thumb across his lips. 'Please, Harold. I'm tired of feeling alone in our marriage. I want us to make love.'

'But we've discussed this,' he said. 'We don't want children – not yet.'

'I feel differently now. I think I do want a child.'

He fell silent and Esmie thought he would turn away from her and dismiss her plea. She braced herself for his rejection.

'What has made you change your mind?' he asked quietly.

'You have,' she admitted candidly. 'My admiration and affection for you has grown these past months. I want this to be a true marriage and for us to be more than simply partners in work. Harold, I want to have our child. I see how the Waziri women manage against all the odds, so being a mother no longer frightens me.'

'Are you sure?' he questioned.

'Yes. Yes, I am. But you must be sure too. Do you want to be a father, Harold?'

There was a tremble in his voice when he replied. 'To be a father would be a great blessing.'

Hope leapt inside her at his change of heart. Encouraged, Esmie leaned over and kissed his mouth. 'I'm so glad you feel the same way,' she said, smiling in the dark. 'Let tonight be a fresh beginning for us.'

After some hesitation, Harold began to fumble with her nightclothes.

'Kiss me first, darling,' she said, trying to rid her mind of their one other attempt at sex that had ended in such failure in a stuffy room in Bombay. This time the air was freezing and the night so black that they couldn't see each other. Perhaps the reticent Harold would find it easier to make love to her in the dark.

They kissed and Harold stroked her hair. She heard his breathing quicken and he reached down to pull up her nightdress. She was surprised to feel that he was aroused so quickly. Without removing his pyjamas, he moved on top of her and began vigorous intercourse. Esmie hardly had time to adjust to it before he let out a long groan and came to a juddering climax. The next moment he was rolling away and pulling his bedroll around him. She could hear his panting subside.

'Goodnight, dearest,' he sighed.

Esmie mumbled a goodnight. She lay, a little stunned and sore. Was she elated that they had finally consummated the marriage? Tears prickled her eyes. She felt very emotional but couldn't work out what emotion. It was like a mixture of disappointment and relief – and a twinge of frustration. He had given her no time to become sexually excited and the experience had been painful. Surely love-making should take longer and be more pleasurable than this?

In the dark, she cried silently. Tears leaked from her eyes down into her ears and dampened her hairline. She brushed them away brusquely, annoyed at her self-pity. The first time – she didn't count the fiasco in Bombay – was bound to be fraught with inexperience and lack of finesse. Harold would improve as a lover. At least they had overcome the barrier of sleeping apart.

Yet as she lay sleepless, treacherous thoughts of Tom came to mind. She knew from Lydia's indiscreet comments that he was an accomplished lover. It was inconceivable that Tom would have slept apart from his wife as long as Harold had his. How she longed to have the sort of intimate relationship where she could fall asleep in loving arms. Esmie curled up tightly in her bedroll, trying to warm herself and drive away unwanted thoughts of the man she could never have.

Chapter 19

More than ever, Esmie drove herself at work. December came with snow flurries around the lower slopes but Harold hung on, wishing to delay their return to Taha as long as possible. One day Baz came seeking them while they ate a hasty lunch. Esmie could see by his worried expression that he had bad news.

'The attacks on Razmak have been confirmed,' he told them. 'The southern Waziris and Mahsuds are in open revolt. My advice is that you should pack up and leave as soon as possible.'

Esmie was alarmed but Harold pointed out, 'Everything is peaceful here. And there is much work still to do. Surely we can hang on a bit longer?'

With reluctance, Baz agreed. 'One more week at the most,' he cautioned. 'If the Waziris don't cause problems then the snow will.'

After a full day at the clinic Esmie would return and spend hours with Zakir. She cut his hair shorter and gave him an embroidered cap to wear. With his appearance less unkempt, he looked no more than thirteen or fourteen, and the policemen began to treat him less warily.

Esmie felt a huge sense of achievement when finally, with Baz's permission, she was able to coax the youth out of his cell to sit by the open fire and eat with the other men. Zakir would squat, rocking back and forth, while talking under his breath. When no one was looking he would shovel food into his mouth as if fearing someone would snatch it away. Gradually, this frantic behaviour lessened and occasionally Esmie was rewarded with a fleeting smile. The first time she heard him sing – a high-pitched haunting song – she thought her heart would burst with affection for the boy.

Yet he never answered any of their questions and they could find out little about him, except what the villagers had reported. He had come from the north – his accent was that of the Otmanzai – and had been found naked and raving on the edge of the settlement with cuts to his arms and wielding a dagger.

When Harold found himself resetting the leg of a young mullah from among the Otmanzai who had fallen from a mule, he asked him if he knew Zakir. The mullah said he did not but would ask in the remoter homesteads.

On hearing from Harold that Mullah Mahmud was a gentle soul who seemed respected among his followers, Esmie sought him out before he left. She got Harold to help her communicate.

'If none of Zakir's family has survived the summer fighting,' she asked, 'would you be able to take him into your home? He needs a lot of care but in time I'm sure his mind will heal.'

The mullah avoided her look, perhaps uncomfortable at being approached by a feringhi woman, so she relied on Harold to interpret her request.

'Allah will look after him,' Mullah Mahmud replied.

'Yes,' Esmie agreed. 'But only with your help.'

She wasn't sure that her husband conveyed her words for the man left making no promises.

'Well, if his own kin won't look after him,' Esmie declared, 'then we'll take him back to Taha ourselves.'

Harold gave her an exasperated smile but said nothing.

A couple of days later, there was a commotion outside the clinic tents. Esmie looked out to see a thin, beaky-nosed man, his head swathed in a grubby turban, shouting at one of the police guards and pointing at the women's tent. Other men were trying to restrain him. Esmie was about to step outside when Malik blocked her way.

'Don't go, memsahib,' he warned.

'Why not? What if he's come about Zakir?'

Malik shook his head. 'He's a bad man. He wants to make trouble.'

'Who is he?' Esmie asked.

'Baram Wali – Karo's husband. He's heard you are here. Please, memsahib, stay out of sight.'

Esmie was winded. So this was Karo's terrible husband. He was older and less imposing than she had imagined, yet she felt his menace. What did the man want with her? He sounded very angry. She tensed with fear. Around her she saw the worried looks and murmurings of the women. Then she heard Harold outside trying to reason with the irate tribesman. It sounded like Baram Wali was cursing her husband and then the altercation died away as the man was persuaded to leave before the police took action.

Once it was safe, Esmie went to Harold. 'Are you all right?'

'Of course, my dear,' he assured her. 'Despite all the shouting I don't think he would do us any harm.'

'He was after me, wasn't he?' she asked. 'Was this all because I've been asking around on Zakir's behalf?'

Harold put a steadying hand on her shoulder. 'There are some who think that foreigners – missionaries – have no place here. But you know that. We didn't come here for an easy life, did we? So we mustn't show fear. We're here to help others. Will you allow one rogue Waziri to send you packing, my dearest?'

Shamed by her panic, Esmie shook her head. 'No, never,' she agreed.

The warm smile that he gave her lifted her spirits and she went back to work with renewed determination.

At night, Esmie looked forward to their getting into bed in the hopes of love-making. They did so another three times in the space of two weeks. Harold's love-making had improved a little and it felt less like he was performing a physical fitness exercise. It no longer left her sore but it was always too brief, leaving Esmie impatient for the next chance of intimacy.

Harold always insisted on blowing out the candle and seemed less inhibited in the dark. Esmie didn't object, although it left her feeling guilty. For in the pitch black, unable to see her husband moving over her, she couldn't stop herself imagining that it was Tom who made love to her.

She knew it was very wrong of her to do so but it relaxed her quickly for the short bouts of sex with Harold. Afterwards, she would wonder if Harold had the same fantasy about Lydia. Perhaps that was why he always insisted that they did the deed in the dark. Whatever the truth was, at least they were now properly husband and wife. She fell asleep each night with the thought that they might already have conceived. The idea was both nerve-racking and thrilling – by next summer they might be parents.

Abruptly, one day in mid-December while busy at the clinic, Esmie heard distant gunfire. She went outside to peer into the low, dazzling sun but seeing nothing returned to her nursing. Half an hour later, Baz came hurrying out of the police post and burst into the tent where Harold was operating.

'We're under attack!' he bawled. 'You must leave at once.'

Esmie hurried into the adjoining tent to hear Harold arguing back.

'I can't leave in the middle of a clinic.'

'You must,' Baz insisted. 'A patrol to the north was fired on this morning. There are dozens of fighters heading this way. I'm arming the local militia.'

Esmie saw the anger on Baz's face and knew he was not a man to alarm easily.

'Harold, we must do as the sergeant says,' she intervened.

Suddenly there was a volley of rifle fire, much closer than before, that reverberated around the rocky hills. Esmie dashed forward and clutched Harold's arm.

'Tell the people to go,' she gasped. 'No one is safe here now.'

Her urgency galvanised Harold out of his stunned disbelief. He began issuing orders to the local orderlies to pack up the equipment.

'No,' Baz commanded. 'You must leave all this and come at once.'

Esmie and Harold hurried from the tent, calling to Malik to follow. Esmie expected Baz to take them to the police post but he ushered them quickly towards a waiting truck.

'But our patients?' Harold said in distress.

Baz was blunt. 'Dr Guthrie, you are no use to them dead. Get in,' he ordered. 'Hasan will drive you straight to Taha – if the road is still open. No time to fetch your things. I'll have them sent on.'

'You're not coming with us?' Harold asked in concern.

Baz shook his head, his look grim. 'I'm needed here. Hasan will alert Brigadier McCabe to the situation.'

'But we can't leave without Zakir,' Esmie cried. 'He must come too.'

Baz ignored her as he bundled them into the back of the lorry. As Malik leapt up behind, Baz spoke to him so rapidly that Esmie didn't catch his meaning. The orderly nodded, taking the rifle that the sergeant thrust at him. As the truck began to lurch forward, Esmie could hear Baz issuing orders for the patients to disperse. She felt sick to be running away and leaving these people to their fate and knew that Harold felt the same. But the gunfire continued and fear gripped her too. She knew that as feringhi missionaries they would be more of a target to the warring tribesmen than fellow Waziris.

Malik pointed at a pile of cloaks under the canvas. 'Memsahib – Sahib,' he said with a nod. 'You must put those on.'

Esmie, heart pounding at the sound of shouting beyond, scrambled forward. Lifting up the top cloak, she realised it was an all-encompassing burka.

'Please, Guthrie Memsahib,' beseeched Malik, 'you must wear it. And the doctor too. Sergeant Baz said it might save you both.'

She handed one to Harold. He looked affronted.

'I refuse to put that on! I'm not going to cower like a girl from any Waziri fighters,' he protested.

Esmie's anger lit. 'What does a little loss of dignity matter when our lives are at stake? If you refuse to put it on and they search the lorry, then you endanger the lives of Hasan and Malik who are trying to help us.' She shook the burka at him. 'If they're prepared to risk their lives saving us, then the least you can do is put on one of these!'

Shocked at her verbal attack, Harold meekly pulled on the cloak. They sat hunched in the back of the vehicle, as Malik took up guard by the flapping canvas cover and Hasan accelerated down the hill.

Esmie could see little through the mesh of the hood. The blood pounded in her ears. What would happen to Zakir? He would believe she had deserted him just like everyone else he ever trusted. And he would be right. She was saving her own skin before his. Esmie swallowed down her fear and self-disgust. She clung to Harold and prayed for them all.

It was daybreak the following morning before they trundled into Taha, their limbs stiff and frozen and their bodies jarred from the traumatic escape. The sound of rifle fire had pursued them down the valley but Hasan had not stopped and no one had ambushed them. The biggest threat had been the icy hairpin bends. Twice they had been ordered out of the truck while the driver inched his way around treacherous corners, skilfully keeping his vehicle from pitching over the edge into the gorge below. Esmie relived the terror she had experienced on the retreat through the mountains of Montenegro, seeing fellow refugees slipping on ice and plunging to their deaths.

But now they were safe. They pulled off their burkas and Malik helped them climb from the lorry. Esmie broke down in tears at the sight of their tranquil bungalow, the wood smoke from its fires mingling with the dawn mist, and an anxious Draman coming out to greet them.

Her relief at getting back to Taha was mingled with guilt at the thought of the people they had left behind. When Harold came back from reporting the situation to McCabe, Esmie could not hide her distress.

'I can't stop thinking about Baz and his men,' she fretted. 'And poor Zakir; what on earth will become of him?'

Harold looked grey with exhaustion. 'The brigadier is sending troops to relieve them. They won't have to hold out much longer.'

Esmie's insides knotted with worry. 'We should have come back sooner,' she said. 'By delaying we put Baz and his men in greater danger.'

'Oh, for goodness' sake, Esmie! We're not the reason the Waziris are in revolt. It's a much wider issue than a couple of missionaries.'

His outburst shocked her. 'I realise that,' said Esmie, 'but why did they attack Kanki-Khel first? Was it because of us and the clinic? Or was it that man – Karo's husband – stirring things up and wanting revenge against us?'

He gave her a bleak look. 'I believe completely in the work we do at the mission and don't regret a single minute that we spent there. I would have stayed if it hadn't been for wanting to get you to safety. I care nothing for my own. I put my trust in God.' The look of disappointment in his hazel eyes made Esmie feel leaden inside. 'I pray that your faith will make you stronger too.'

He walked past her, calling for Ali to fetch hot water, and then walked into his bachelor's bedroom and closed the door behind him.

Esmie spent the next couple of days in limbo. It wasn't just the aching tiredness from weeks of relentless work and little sleep but the dislocation of suddenly being back in Taha and feeling she wasn't needed. Harold took up at the hospital as if he'd never been away but Esmie saw how Rupa, Bannerman and the local orderlies had been coping well without her. Rupa, full of concern at her ordeal, insisted she stayed at home and rested. Esmie had thought herself indispensable and now saw that she wasn't; it was a salutary lesson.

There was a tense atmosphere around the town as news spread of raids in the hills. Would Taha become a battlefront again as it had been during the recent Afghan incursions? A curfew was reimposed and the residents of the cantonment stayed away from the old town for fear of violent outbursts.

Karo and Gabina, though, seemed delighted to see Esmie again and the young mother took pride in showing off the clothes she had made on Esmie's sewing machine. While Esmie had been away, Gabina had begun to take her first faltering steps.

'What a clever lassie you are!' Esmie cried, holding out her arms for the infant and sweeping her up in a hug of congratulation. Gabina giggled and pressed her head into Esmie's neck in a brief sign of affection, before pushing to be let down. It stirred something in the very core of Esmie; her love for the girl deepened with every day.

There were several letters awaiting her from Lydia, reproaching her for her lack of correspondence but excited about seeing her for Christmas even though Esmie had never written to confirm.

> *'. . . It seems an eternity since we last saw each other. You won't recognise me. I've grown quite fat and matronly on all the mess dinners and garden party teas I've been attending. But I have to fill my time somehow, don't I?*

Tom hasn't shown the least bit of interest in socialising – I can't believe how different he is to when he was wooing me last spring – he only seems to care about the wretched hotel.

So you see how I need Harold and you to dig him out of his lair for Christmas Week – there is such a lot going on. I know Harold will be able to jolly him along where I have failed – I think he misses his oldest friend quite a lot.

Make sure you bring some pretty frocks to wear – and at least two evening gowns. I don't want to see a trace of nurse's uniform – and I'll arrange for my hairdresser to come and do your hair, because I know they are as rare as hen's teeth in the mofussil . . .'

Esmie smiled at her friend's use of the colonial term for the countryside; Lydia was adapting fast to life in British India. Suddenly, she couldn't wait to see her again and listen to her amusing acerbic observations. For a short while Esmie longed just to do frivolous things like sip gin cocktails and go dancing; she wanted to enjoy the company of people who had nothing to do with the mission.

It might also be good for her and Harold to take a holiday. Esmie determined to press her husband to take time off from his work and for them to go and stay at the Raj Hotel. They had been thrown together more than ever in the past month and the stress of their time in the hills and its abrupt ending was taking its toll. Harold had resumed his old habit of sleeping apart as if the intimacy they had shared in Kanki-Khel had never been.

He avoided her by dashing off to work early and returning late. He didn't criticise her for staying away from the hospital but she felt she had somehow let him down. She couldn't rid herself of the guilt that she had brought hostile attention to the mountain clinic by intervening in the lives of both Karo and Zakir. If she had stayed in Taha as Harold had originally wanted, would the clinic at Kanki-Khel still be open?

The one thing that eased her conscience was a visit from Sergeant Baz.

'I can't tell you how pleased I am to see you safely back in Taha,' Esmie said. 'I feel terrible about putting you and your men in danger but I am so grateful for your prompt action in saving us.'

The gruff sergeant would take no credit. 'I was only doing my job, Guthrie Mem'.'

'What news do you bring? Is Zakir safe?'

The bearded Pathan gave away no emotion but she thought she saw his look soften. 'The army is in control once more, memsahib. I set Zakir free. By the time the fighting was over, he had disappeared. I'm sorry, but I don't know what became of him.'

Esmie was upset to think of the troubled youth escaping through the gunfire. She could only hope and pray that he had been rescued and shown mercy by fellow Otmanzai. Baz's visit left her with a heavy heart and she couldn't help dwelling on what might have happened to Zakir.

When Harold came home that evening, he was more sanguine. 'At least he is no longer incarcerated in a prison cell like a criminal,' he said. 'You saved him from that fate, my dear. We must believe that God has taken care of him.'

It came as a surprise and a relief when Harold returned the following day, announcing that he had wired the Lomaxes, telling them they would arrive in Rawalpindi the day after tomorrow. Bannerman would drive them to the station at Kohat for the early train.

'But I never wrote to Lydia confirming we were coming for Christmas,' Esmie said. 'I wasn't sure you wanted to . . .'

'I wrote to Tom accepting,' said Harold. 'The brigadier thinks it's a good idea to spend the holidays in Pindi. Things are too uncertain here. It may be that I'll return alone after Christmas and you can stay on with Lydia. You'd like that, wouldn't you, my dear?'

Esmie felt too worn out to argue. She didn't want to think beyond the next few days and the prospect of having a change of scene. She was heartened that Harold thought the same without prompting from her. Rawalpindi would do them both good. The men needed each other's company as much as she needed Lydia's. The four friends would be together again and she looked forward to them recreating the camaraderie of the previous summer. Esmie tried to quell her nervousness at the prospect of seeing Tom. Excitement fluttered in her belly. She tried to convince herself that it was in anticipation at seeing Lydia and staying at the Raj Hotel.

Chapter 20

The Raj Hotel, Rawalpindi, 23rd December

The tonga carrying the Guthries from the station drew up outside a low, freshly white-washed building with a pale-blue balustrade marking it off from the busy road. A garish red sign with gold lettering hung on the blue gate, proclaiming the Raj Hotel and its proprietor, Captain T Lomax. Esmie's stomach curdled with nerves. Beyond, two palm trees shaded its attractively pillared entrance and a peacock strutted across a pocket of lawn, heralding their arrival. They had caught an earlier train than planned so no one had been there to meet them at the station.

As Harold paid off the tonga driver, a plump boy came dashing down the hotel steps, a young porter at his heels, and bowed at Esmie.

'I'm Jimmy,' he grinned. 'You're Mrs Guthrie; I've seen your photo in Mrs Lomax's rooms. We weren't expecting you until this evening. Pa wanted to fetch you in the car.'

'I'm sorry,' Esmie said. 'We made good time to Kohat and caught the earlier train.'

'No need to apologise. Can I take your case? Sunil will take the other one.'

'Thank you.' Esmie smiled. 'Are you one of the Duboises?'

'Yes, I'm the eldest. I'm twelve. My sister Stella is seven. We tossed a coin to see who'd come and meet you and I won. She's getting the baroness ready for afternoon tea. She has about four changes a day.' The boy chuckled. 'The baroness, not my sister.' As he picked up Esmie's small case he said, 'This isn't very heavy. Are you not staying long?'

'Well, I don't have a lot of clothes to choose from,' Esmie replied in amusement.

'Don't you?' Jimmy asked in surprise. 'Mrs Lomax has heaps of outfits. She has to put half of them in one of the spare bedrooms. I bet she'd lend you some – or my mother will. She's petite like you are, Mrs Guthrie.'

'Jimmy!' a male voice barked from inside the hotel entrance. 'Come on, lad! Don't leave the VIPs waiting in the street.'

Jimmy rolled his eyes. 'That's Fritters – Mr Fritwell – he's a bit bossy. But it's just because he can't wait to meet you. We all can't. Pa says you've been to the Frontier. Is it true you had to run for your lives and nearly got killed by Pathans?'

Esmie was taken aback that the boy and his family knew so much. Harold must have written to Tom about it. At that moment Harold joined them and Esmie was saved from further questions as a well-groomed Anglo-Indian in a suit and lilac cravat appeared and bowed them inside.

'Mr and Mrs Guthrie, we're honoured to have you at the Raj.' He beamed. 'I am Charlie Dubois, the manager of the hotel. You must make yourself utterly at home.'

As they entered the hallway, Esmie had the sensation of stepping into a green grotto that had been enthusiastically decorated for Christmas. From floor to ceiling it was painted sea-green, and sprouting between the rattan tables and chairs were massive ferns adorned with gaudy paper streamers. Several people stood up and others waved hello as if they had been expecting them. A tall man with a long craggy face and a smoker's pallor grinned at her and extended his hand.

'I'm Ansom,' he introduced himself, pumping her hand. 'Very pleased to meet you, Mrs Guthrie. We've heard all about your heroics – the War in Europe as well as nursing on the Frontier – yes, very pleased to meet you indeed.' He let go and ushered her towards his companion. 'Meet my good friend Fritters.' Ansom then moved on to greet Harold.

One after the other, the residents claimed Esmie's attention and welcomed her to the hotel. Presiding over them all was Charlie Dubois, like some impresario in a theatrical production. She was charmed and overwhelmed by their friendliness.

Charlie said, 'I shall go and alert Mr Lomax to your arrival. He is just returning from a ride.' He hurried away through open French doors that led onto a shaded courtyard.

Esmie, her heartbeat increasing at the mention of Tom, was distracted by someone tugging at her sleeve. She turned to see a pretty blonde girl beside an older woman in an old-fashioned plum-coloured tea dress.

'Mrs Guthrie, may I introduce you to Baroness Hester Cussack?' asked the girl.

Esmie was entranced at the regal figure with the delicate porcelain-pale features under a headband bearing a single lime-green ostrich feather. They shook hands and exchanged pleasantries. Esmie guessed that her young companion must be Stella Dubois though she looked nothing like her brother or father. Perhaps the mother was fair.

'And you must be Stella?' Esmie smiled at the girl.

The girl's face dimpled. 'Stella Maria Dubois,' she said and bobbed in a curtsey.

'Stella is a little angel,' said Hester. 'My lady-in-waiting. Aren't you, darling?' She fondled the girl's hair.

'Esmie.'

Esmie swung round at the familiar deep voice and saw Tom in riding clothes striding through the French doors towards her. Her insides fluttered at the sight of his handsome aristocratic face – perhaps a little more gaunt, but creased in a smile.

'Welcome to the Raj,' he said, taking her hands and kissing her cheek. 'I wanted to be here to meet you but you beat me to it. How was your journey?'

Her face burned from the unexpected kiss and she found it hard to catch her breath. 'Fine, thank you,' she managed to say.

He nodded. 'It's so good to see you again.'

For a moment he held her look. She had forgotten quite how startlingly blue his eyes were against their black lashes. His gaze was full of warmth and she was suddenly tearful, realising how much she had missed him.

'And you,' she said, embarrassed by how husky her voice sounded.

Briefly he squeezed her hands and then let go, turning to Harold. The men wrung each other's hands with enthusiasm. Esmie was touched to see their eyes glinting with emotion, testament to their long and deep friendship.

A scream from the staircase made them all look up.

'Esmie! Harold!' Lydia squealed. 'Why did nobody tell me you were here?' She hurried down the stairs, flinging her arms wide and rushing at them.

Esmie and Lydia embraced each other, setting off a chorus of cheers from the residents. Lydia pulled away and dabbed at her eyes, ignoring the offer of a lace handkerchief from the woman wielding an ear trumpet.

'You look wonderful,' said Esmie, admiring Lydia's modern beige dress and her glowing complexion under neatly coiffured hair. She didn't look matronly at all.

'And darling Harold!' Lydia greeted him with a peck on the cheek and hooked her arm through his. 'You don't know how happy I am to see you both.'

Harold blushed at the attention. 'And we've been looking forward to it too.'

'Did Dubois collect you in the car?'

'We arrived early so jumped in a tonga,' said Harold.

'A tonga! How dreadful. I would have come myself but I was resting before tonight.'

'A tonga was perfectly fine,' Esmie said in amusement. 'It gave us a chance to see a bit of Pindi at a leisurely pace.'

'Through that awful Saddar Bazaar, I bet,' said Lydia with a shudder.

Tom said teasingly, 'Well, they're here safe and sound, and haven't been sold into slavery on the way.' He touched Jimmy on the shoulder. 'Please take the cases upstairs and show our guests to the Curzon Room.'

He turned to Esmie and she thought his look softened. 'Once you've settled in we'll have afternoon tea in the courtyard.'

She smiled. 'That sounds lovely.'

'Goodness me, no,' Lydia contradicted. 'It's far too gloomy at this time of day. I'll have Dubois send tea up to our flat so we can have a proper catch up in private.' She threw a dismissive glance at the residents.

Tom faltered. 'Well, if you'd prefer . . .'

'I do,' Lydia said firmly.

'I'll go and tell Charlie,' Tom said and beat a retreat through the French doors.

'Come on, let's go upstairs,' Lydia said, leading the way with Harold while Esmie followed behind.

'See you at dinner!' Ansom called after them. Esmie waved and nodded.

'No, you won't,' Lydia called. 'We're going to the Club.'

'Ah, jolly good show,' Ansom replied, sinking back into his cane chair.

Out of earshot, Lydia said, 'I warn you now, they'll drive you potty.'

'They seem a cheerful lot,' said Esmie, 'and so friendly.'

'Nosey more like,' Lydia retorted. 'They're always trying to find out my business. I can't bear it. The sooner Tom agrees to us living in the civil lines, the better.'

Esmie was awkward at her blunt opinion being expressed in front of Jimmy Dubois and wondered what the boy thought of it .

'Do they all live here permanently?' Harold asked.

'That lot do, yes,' said Lydia. 'It's like living in a nursing home – smells like one too at times. That's where half of them should be, of course. But Tom won't do anything about it. You would think we were a charity not a hotel. Anyway, I don't want to talk about it. I've got you two here and that's all that matters. From what Tom tells me, you both deserve a good holiday. We're going to have such fun together.'

Near the end of a long corridor painted pale green, Jimmy stopped outside a brown door.

'The Curzon Room,' he announced, throwing open the door with a proud flourish.

Lydia rolled her eyes and gave a brittle laugh. 'It was Tom's idea to name the rooms after famous viceroys. But don't expect the luxury of the Viceregal Lodge – or the view!'

Tom stood under the jacaranda tree in the courtyard, smoking furiously. A bird kept up an incessant squawking above his head. It put him on edge when he was trying to calm his nerves before going up to the apartment for tea. Myrtle had made a Victoria sponge cake in honour of the Guthries' arrival. He knew he should be up there changing out of his riding clothes but he was reluctant to join them, even though he was eager to see Harold and hear all his news in detail.

But he was finding Lydia increasingly irritating. She found fault in everything he did. In her eyes, he spent too much time with the Duboises and the residents instead of with her yet she didn't want him at her card parties or trips to the Club. One minute she complained he didn't go out enough and the next that he went out riding too often. He suspected Lydia must have complained to Dickie Mason that he went riding too frequently with Tom, for the young lieutenant was always finding excuses not to join him in Topi Park these days. Perhaps Mason had begun to be influenced by the opinion of the other officers in the army cantonment that Tom was persona non grata for turning his back on the Peshawar Rifles. Or was it possible that the truth had leaked out about his army career ending under a cloud in Mesopotamia? There was no one in Rawalpindi who knew him from there, so he quickly banished the thought. Lydia must never hear of it or she would never live down the shame.

Lydia argued with him daily about the hotel. He was dismayed at how quickly his wife seemed to have adopted the prejudices of the British in India, looking down her nose at the mixed-race Duboises and speaking imperiously to the Indian servants in a tone she would never have used with the servants at Templeton Hall. He blamed it on her friendship with the waspish Geraldine Hopkirk, the brewery manager's wife, who was obsessive about social rank and critical of all things Indian.

Lydia endlessly badgered him about moving out of the hotel to live near other British civilians.

'I want to live with our own kind, not have to rub shoulders with natives and half-halfs. The smells from the bazaar turn my stomach and Geraldine says if I live here much longer I'll start speaking with a chee-chee accent like Myrtle Dubois. I know she's only teasing but it doesn't do our standing in Pindi any good to be mixing with their sort.'

If Tom defended the Duboises it only seemed to rile Lydia further and make her all the more determined to move to the civil cantonment. She was rude to the residents – except for Fritwell who was ex-army – and increasingly arranged to eat out with friends at the Club or at Geraldine's. Why had his wife chosen such a woman as her closest friend? The plump and garrulous Geraldine was the biggest gossip in the cantonment; the antithesis of Lydia's long-time friend, Esmie.

Oh, Esmie! Tom ground out his cigarette with a sigh. One look into her beautiful grey eyes and his stomach had knotted in familiar longing. She had looked tired and a little strained – who wouldn't after her recent ordeal? – and yet her face had shone with kindness and her rapport with the residents had been instant. In comparison, Lydia's prettiness seemed superficial and her bonhomie contrived. Would Esmie see a difference in her friend or was his jaundiced view a result of weeks of worry over the hotel and trying to keep his wife happy?

Even in bed he seemed to be failing to satisfy her. They hadn't had sex for over a month – not since their drunken love-making the night of the brewery dance – and Lydia had rebuffed all his attempts at intimacy since. That was why he went riding so often, to release his pent-up frustration, in the way he had learnt to do as a young subaltern on remote pickets on the Frontier.

He wondered if he could confide in Harold about his present unhappiness. Or would his oldest friend be embarrassed by such talk? Harold had always had a soft spot for Lydia and might feel disloyal discussing her behind her back. Maybe Esmie would be a good influence on Lydia. But how would he feel if Lydia unburdened herself to Esmie about her disappointment in their marriage? It would pique his pride if Esmie was to look upon him as a failure too.

Tom pulled back his shoulders. His problems were his own and he should be the one to deal with them. He and Lydia would find a way to rekindle their former passion for each other. He would just have to work harder at making her happy. Tom crossed the courtyard, his insides clenching as if he were about to go into battle.

Chapter 21

'Don't eat too much cake,' Lydia warned. 'Or you won't enjoy dinner at the Club.'

'It's delicious,' said Esmie, licking jam from her fingers and relaxing back onto the comfortable cream sofa.

'Old dragon Drummond would have slapped your hand for that.' Lydia laughed and mimicked their former headmistress. '"Use your napkin not your tongue, Miss McBride!"'

'It's too good to waste a single crumb,' grinned Esmie.

'Goodness, life really must be primitive in the mofussil if you get excited over Myrtle's sagging sponge cake.'

Esmie eyed her friend. She seemed on edge, her comments either falsely hearty or a little too biting. Lydia had hardly stopped talking about Rawalpindi society since they'd gathered in her airy sitting room. Her life seemed to consist of one long string of social engagements. Perhaps it had been the same at home but she didn't remember Lydia being quite so particular about people's social backgrounds. Lydia rattled off the names of all the most important people of the army town as if Esmie should know whom she meant. While Harold and Tom were deep in conversation about the situation on the Frontier, Lydia had yet to ask Esmie anything about her life in Taha.

'And Dickie Mason is a very sweet man,' said Lydia. 'I'm so glad you introduced us. Did you know that Dickie's mother is a friend of Nancy Astor's?'

'Dear Lieutenant Mason. How is he?' Esmie asked, latching onto a name she knew. 'He was missing home such a lot; I knew you'd be kind to him.'

'I think we've cured him of his homesickness,' Lydia said. 'He's the one who invites us to things these days. He's a bit of a favourite among the ladies of the cantonment. I can see him being in big demand with the fishing fleet girls this cold season.'

'Fishing fleet girls?'

'Esmie, where have you been?' Lydia cried. 'You must know it's the pet name for British girls who come out to India fishing for a husband.'

'Oh, I'd forgotten . . .'

'He's too young to marry though,' Lydia pronounced. 'His colonel would never allow it. Not before he's a captain at least. So he can carry on having fun for a while yet. Geraldine and I will pick out someone suitable when the time comes.'

'Still playing matchmaker?' Esmie teased.

Lydia patted her knee. 'Well, it worked for you and Harold, didn't it?'

Esmie glanced at her husband, talking animatedly to Tom about the various Waziri tribes. She felt a spark of optimism that this holiday would bring them closer together again.

She gave Lydia a smile of agreement. Now was not the time to hint to her friend that her unorthodox marriage to Harold was under strain. She suspected that if she did it might become a source of gossip for Lydia to discuss with her new confidante, Geraldine. Her problems with Harold were private.

'So when am I to meet your friend Mrs Hopkirk?' Esmie asked.

'Tonight of course,' said Lydia eagerly. 'We're dining as their guests at the Club at seven-thirty. And then on Christmas Eve we're invited to a dinner-dance at Flashman's Hotel as part of their party.'

Tom interrupted his conversation with Harold. 'Flashman's?' He frowned. 'You never said.'

'Darling, I'm sure I did,' said Lydia. 'You just never listen.'

'But we're organising a party here . . .'

'What party?'

'Charlie's making his whisky punch and Myrtle's doing cocktail food. They do it every year – it's a Raj Hotel tradition.'

'That's for the residents, not us,' Lydia said with a dismissive wave. 'Besides, the Hopkirks are dying to meet Esmie and Harold. I want to give our friends a good time in Pindi, don't you?'

'Of course,' said Tom, reddening. 'But I think they'll enjoy Christmas Eve here – and we're seeing the Hopkirks tonight.'

Esmie could see that Harold was embarrassed by their friends' wrangling but knew he wouldn't intervene. So she said, 'Perhaps we could do both? Start here with a cocktail and go on to the dinner-dance?'

'Well, yes, I suppose we could,' said Tom with a grateful look.

Lydia gave a theatrical sigh. 'If we must. As long as we're at Flashman's by eight o'clock. Geraldine hates her guests to be late.'

'Heaven forbid we incur the wrath of the burra-memsahib,' Tom said wryly.

'Don't be so snide,' Lydia chided. She turned to Esmie. 'Tom likes to think he's so liberal-minded but he's just as snooty as his father when it comes to people in trade. But it's misplaced with Geraldine. She's just as much gentry as Tom is – her people own land in Buckinghamshire.'

Esmie saw Tom's jaw clench in annoyance. Their bickering made her uncomfortable and she didn't want to be drawn into it. She stood up.

'Well, if we have to be ready for seven-thirty, I think I'll go for a lie down. What do you want to do, Harold?'

She saw the indecision cross his face, whether to stay with the Lomaxes or retreat to their bedroom with her.

'I'd quite like to stretch my legs before dinner,' he said.

'But it's getting dark,' said Lydia. 'You can't go wandering around here once the light goes.'

'I'll come with you,' Tom offered, getting quickly to his feet. 'We can take a turn around the block – walk as far as the Scots Kirk on the Mall – so you can see where to go on Christmas Day.'

Harold agreed with alacrity. While the two men set off down the corridor, Esmie retreated to the Curzon Room. French doors gave onto a covered common veranda that encircled the inner courtyard. She stood at the rail, peering out over the courtyard below and saw Tom and Harold cross it, Tom's hand resting on his friend's shoulder as they conversed. Their friendship appeared unchanged whereas she was struggling to find anything to say to Lydia – not that she'd been able to get much of a word in edgeways with her friend talking non-stop.

She was troubled by the deterioration in relations between the Lomaxes. Lydia had complained about Tom in her letters but her tone had still been affectionate. Yet seeing them together, it was plain that they found it hard to agree on anything. She was sorry for Tom being the focus of Lydia's caustic remarks – they seemed uncalled for. But if the root of Lydia's unhappiness was Tom's stubborn refusal to live away from the hotel, then perhaps he should be less intransigent.

Esmie gazed out over the low hotel rooftop at the vivid orange sky. She had a partial view into the servants' compound beyond. At a squat bungalow bedecked in streamers and strings of Christmas lights, a girl was dancing up and down the steps, a puppy jumping at her heels. Warm light flooded out of the windows onto the veranda. The excitable dog tripped her and they fell in a heap. Esmie could hear the girl giggling and a woman's voice calling her inside. The girl scooped up the puppy and went indoors. Only as she disappeared did Esmie realise it must be Stella, the Duboises' daughter.

Her heart missed a beat at the simple domestic scene of a girl playing and a mother beckoning her in for supper. Had her own mother called to her with such tenderness when she had been a child? If so, she had been too young to remember it. Esmie was glad that the engaging Stella had a loving home and parents to look after her. She thought Tom was right to keep the Duboises in a job and home, even if it meant less profit for the hotel. She had a sudden understanding of why Tom might not want to move out of the hotel. Here he had a ready-made family of kind-hearted people. Perhaps that's all he craved. If only Lydia could see that.

Esmie retreated inside and closed the glass doors against the chill air. She gazed around at the mismatched furniture: a walnut wardrobe, a pine dressing table and two sagging single beds that had been pushed together, flanked by black lacquered side tables supporting two dim electric lamps. The room smelt musty, as if it hadn't been used for months, but it was spotlessly clean and the bedlinen looked crisply laundered. There was a homely charm about the place but Esmie could imagine how its dowdy appearance might irritate Lydia and lead to arguments with Tom.

Yet, their marriage was none of her business. She would have to try and stay neutral between her friends if she wasn't to make matters worse.

The Club was like a fairy-tale palace of stuccoed crenellations and pillared arches, lighting up the night and spilling light onto the gigantic lawns and shimmering trees of the club grounds. A band was playing on the terrace and Esmie could hear the chatter of dinner guests as they arrived.

The dining room was filled with men in uniform and dinner suits, and women in evening gowns. Esmie was wearing her best dress – the blue one she had got married in with the wedding lace removed – and a simple silver headband to keep her hair in check. Lydia was wearing a sumptuous red dress that showed off her curvaceous body and drew admiring glances. Esmie thought perhaps her friend's figure had indeed filled out a little since the summer – her cleavage and hips were more noticeable and her face was a little fuller – but it gave her a voluptuous beauty.

Lydia was in her element, chatting and flirting and showing off her new friends to Esmie and Harold. Esmie was surprised to find that Geraldine Hopkirk was older than she'd expected, a rather dumpy woman with a large double chin and a piercing voice. But she greeted Esmie as if they were old friends and swept her into the midst of her group.

Harold was pleased to find that among them were Augustus Tolmie, the headmaster of the mission school in Murree, and his wife Margaret.

'I discovered that the Tolmies knew you,' said Geraldine, 'so I invited them down for Christmas. Augustus tells me that he hasn't seen you since Bombay in September. You must have such a lot of catching up to do.'

Geraldine leaned towards Esmie and said in a conspiratorial aside, 'Margaret Tolmie is just back from visiting her frail old mother in Wales – missing her terribly – thinks she might not see her again. But that's the cross we bear in India – separation from our loved ones in the line of duty. My two scamps are at school in England. Miss them like blazes. Wait till you and Lydia have children then you'll know what I mean. Mind you . . .'

She didn't finish her sentence as she began ordering where her guests should sit. Esmie wondered what observation the woman had decided to keep to herself. Geraldine steered Tom into the seat next to hers. Esmie caught his wry look as he arched his eyebrows and they shared a glance of amusement.

To her delight she saw Dickie Mason pushing through the throng to join them, along with two of the other young officers she'd shown hospitality to in Taha. They greeted her and Harold with enthusiasm. There was a confidence and swagger about Dickie that was new. He sat between Esmie and Lydia and regaled them with stories of his two-day shikar near Murree. Esmie would have happily chatted to Dickie throughout dinner but felt obliged to also talk to the earnest Augustus who was sitting on her other side.

'Terrible business at Kanki-Khel,' said the headmaster. 'I did warn your husband but Guthrie's known for his stubbornness.'

'I prefer to say fearlessness,' said Esmie, springing to Harold's defence. She wondered how news of their narrow escape was already common knowledge in Rawalpindi. But she shouldn't be surprised; gossip appeared to be the lifeblood of this army town.

As the evening wore on, the room became stuffy and the conversation more raucous. Esmie saw that Harold was growing puce-faced and sweating in his constricting evening clothes and tight collar. He was sandwiched between Margaret Tolmie and a shy younger woman who seemed to be a protégé of Geraldine's – perhaps one of Lydia's fishing fleet girls. She could see Harold struggling to keep up a conversation with her. Esmie flashed him a smile of understanding and went back to listening to Augustus's long monologue about teaching methods at his school in Murree.

As pudding was served, Esmie reached for her napkin, which had slipped from her knee. Raising the linen tablecloth a fraction, she saw it on the floor and leaned down to grab it. As she did so, she stifled a gasp. Under the tablecloth she could see Lydia's hand resting on Dickie's knee and his hand covering hers.

Esmie sat up quickly. She glanced at Lydia. Her friend's cheeks were flushed but she looked back at Esmie with composure.

'Everything all right?' Lydia asked her.

'Fine,' Esmie answered.

'I hope you're enjoying the evening,' said Lydia. 'We've been dying to have you here, haven't we, Dickie?'

'Very much so,' Dickie enthused, turning to Esmie with a disarming smile. 'I hope you and Dr Guthrie will come to our party at the Mess on Christmas night.'

'Of course they will,' said Lydia.

'The chaps and I want to thank you both for your generosity to us in Taha,' Dickie continued. 'You have no idea how much it meant to us to visit your home – we were made to feel like one of the family.'

Esmie smiled. 'That's kind of you to say so. But it was our pleasure. You and your fellow officers brightened up our quiet home. We missed you when you left.'

'Ooh, apple charlotte and custard,' Lydia said with enthusiasm as a pudding plate was placed before her. 'My favourite.'

Esmie noticed how Lydia's hand appeared from under the tablecloth so she could pick up both her fork and spoon. Was there a special glance between her friend and the lieutenant as she did so? Esmie couldn't be sure. She looked up the table towards Tom. He was drinking a lot of wine and talking loudly with Geraldine and one of Dickie's fellow officers. She felt a stab of pity for Tom, doing his best to entertain his hostess while his wife flirted and brazenly held hands with a handsome young officer just four seats away from him.

Suddenly, Esmie couldn't wait for the dinner to be over and for them to be back at the Raj. She would much rather that they had spent their first evening dining in the hotel and getting to know the permanent guests. They seemed an interesting lot and she suspected they would have tales to tell of their long lives in India – stories and experiences that went beyond the narrow confines of the barracks and clubs of Rawalpindi.

It was nearly another two hours before the dinner party broke up and they climbed into tongas for the short journey back to the hotel. Esmie leaned against Harold in exhaustion and gave a sigh of relief.

'I haven't eaten that much in ages,' she said. 'I'm fit to burst. I think you might have to carry me upstairs.'

Harold gave a grunt of amusement. 'Thank goodness that's over. Margaret Tolmie was on the verge of tears about her mother the whole time, poor lady. And Miss Timmins had no conversation at all except about her dog Trixie. I'm not sure I can bear a whole week of such dinners. And I never got to chat properly with Tolmie.'

'Perhaps you could invite him over to the hotel for afternoon tea,' suggested Esmie. 'You'll most likely see him at the Scots Kirk on Christmas Day, won't you?'

'Yes, that's a good idea,' said Harold, brightening.

Back at the hotel, Esmie and Lydia went straight to bed. Harold needed little persuasion from Tom to stay up for a nightcap in the residents' sitting room. Esmie was asleep in minutes.

She was woken by Harold stumbling in much later. She'd left the electric side lamp on so that he wouldn't bump into the furniture. It was a novelty to be somewhere with electricity again. Esmie sat up.

'Sorry, my dear,' Harold mumbled. 'Didn't mean to disturb you.'

'I don't mind,' she answered, stifling a yawn. 'Did you have a nice chat with Tom?'

'Umm, yes. And Ansom was still up. Decent man. Engineer. Worked on the blueprint for the narrow-gauge line to Simla. Family's been in India for three generations.'

'Interesting,' said Esmie, eyeing her husband as he began to discard his clothes.

This was the first night they had spent in the same bedroom since their flight from Kanki-Khel. She longed for them to be intimate again. She'd loosened the covers between the two beds so that they could reach out for each other.

'You can turn out the lamp, dearest,' said Harold. 'I don't need it.'

She did as he asked but continued to sit up and wait for him to climb in beside her. She held her breath as he did so. He lay on his back and gave out a heavy sigh and a waft of stale whisky. Would the alcohol have fuelled or blunted his ardour?

'Harold?' she murmured.

'Umm.' He sounded on the verge of dozing off.

'Will you hold me?'

He hesitated and then put out an arm. Encouraged, Esmie snuggled into his hold and waited. After a few minutes, when he hadn't pulled away, she said softly, 'I was worried you were still angry with me for us having to leave Kanki-Khel so quickly. Is that why you haven't come to my bed? I've missed being with you.'

He didn't reply.

'Harold?' She put a hand on his chest. His breathing was regular. He was already asleep.

Esmie sank back in disappointment. It had been unrealistic to imagine that Harold would have the energy for love-making after such a long and tiring day. It was hard to believe that they had left Taha in the early hours of that morning. In a few minutes' time it would be Christmas Eve. Esmie took heart from the thought that there would be plenty of time over the next few days for her and Harold to lie together and resume their former intimacy.

Half an hour later, Esmie was still wide awake. Her mind went restlessly over the evening. Was there something going on between Lydia and Dickie? Surely not? All she had seen was a second's glance at Lydia's hand touching Dickie's knee and his fingers on hers. It might have been a fleeting moment – a sisterly pat on a younger man's knee. At the most it was Lydia being flirtatious. She had always been demonstrative in her shows of affection. It didn't mean anything more serious.

Esmie got out of bed, wrapped a shawl around her shoulders and padded over to the French doors. Slipping past the long curtain, she opened the windows as quietly as possible and went out onto the veranda. She shivered in the chilly air, yet it was mild compared to a winter's evening at home in Scotland. The sky was littered with stars and there was a faint light coming from the next-door window – Hester

Cussack's room. Other than that, the hotel was in darkness and all was quiet.

Esmie breathed in the scent of wood smoke that hung in the air – and something else – cigarette smoke. She glanced along the veranda in the other direction and saw that it was blocked off by a bamboo screen and some sort of climbing plant. The end of the veranda was private. Suddenly she realised that beyond was the Lomaxes' flat. The Curzon Room was a buffer between the proprietors' bedroom and the rooms of the residents. That was why it smelt of neglect; it probably hadn't been used since Tom and Lydia took over the hotel.

Esmie's insides fluttered to think that Tom had been standing close by, on the other side of the bamboo screen, smoking and looking out on the same scene. Perhaps he too was sleepless while his wife was not. She rested her elbows on the railing and closed her eyes, trying not to think about him. It was then that she heard the muted noise. Steps on creaking floorboards? She stood up and moved towards the screen. Was Tom coming out onto the veranda again?

Then it struck her what the source of the noise was; the rhythmic squeak and creak of bed springs. Esmie's face went hot. She thought she heard a groan. Tom and Lydia were making love. In her haste to leave the veranda, Esmie stubbed her toe and stifled a cry. Back in her bedroom, she closed the long windows and scrambled under the covers. But now that she knew what was happening, she couldn't block out the muffled sound of the creaking bed from the other side of the wall. She buried her head under her pillow, trying to curb her envy at their intimacy. Their marriage was obviously not in as much trouble as she'd thought. Her suspicions of Lydia over Dickie were unfounded and she was ashamed for even thinking them.

The noise from the next-door room ceased shortly afterwards. But Esmie lay for a long time, turning away restlessly from the peacefully sleeping Harold and trying to blot out thoughts of Tom.

Chapter 22

Sometime in the early hours, just after Esmie had fallen asleep, Harold woke up and was sick into his chamber pot. After the sweeper had been summoned to dispose of the contents, Harold fell asleep again. In the morning, Esmie left him sleeping and went down to breakfast alone.

Tom was in the dining room chatting to his guests. He smiled and came across to greet her. Esmie felt herself colouring, unable to rid her mind of what she knew he'd been doing while she'd been sleepless and feeling very alone on the other side of the bedroom wall.

'Harold's been unwell in the night,' she said. 'Too many drams probably.'

Tom pulled an apologetic face. 'My fault for leading him astray.'

'No, I think he needed to let his hair down.'

'That's generous of you.'

'Where's Lydia?' Esmie asked, looking about for her friend.

'Sleeping it off too,' Tom said, his broad mouth twitching with amusement.

Esmie glanced away, unable to meet his look. The baroness waved her over.

'Come, darling, and sit with me. We haven't had a proper chat yet.'

Esmie did so with relief. As a breakfast of poached eggs and fish was served by a waiter called Maseed, Esmie was questioned by an inquisitive Hester. She knew some of the other guests were listening in too.

Before breakfast was over Esmie felt as if she had recounted her whole life to the older woman, including every detail of her time in Serbia. The Austrian widow appeared well travelled.

'I knew Belgrade,' she said. 'My husband had business interests there. And we spent a summer in Scutari in northern Albania. Have you heard of the virgins of Albania? They are like honorary men and don't have to marry. A daughter can dress and live as a man and be the head of their family where there is no son.' Hester laughed. 'Such a quaint idea, don't you think?'

'Sounds quite unnatural,' said Fritwell, looking scandalised.

'Sounds liberating,' said Esmie, with a wink at the baroness.

'Ah, Mrs Guthrie,' said Ansom, 'are you one of these emancipated young women who are flocking to the ballot box at home?'

'I would be,' said Esmie, 'except I have another five years to wait until I can vote at thirty.'

'Well, young women are known to be too flighty,' Fritwell declared.

'Is that so, Mr Fritwell?' said Esmie. 'But not too flighty to do war work? Strange, don't you think, that we women were told we'd been granted the vote for helping win the War – but the majority of women who did war work have yet to be allowed to vote?'

'Bravo, darling!' The baroness clapped her hands in glee. 'That serves you right for being so pompous, Fritters.'

Tom, who had been talking with Charlie, came over. 'Mrs Guthrie, are you sowing dissension in the ranks?'

Esmie said, 'I'm afraid so.'

'How about I take you for a tour of the town?' Tom suggested.

Esmie was unnerved by the idea but could think of no excuse to refuse.

'Perhaps I should see if Harold would like to come?'

'Let the poor man lie in for once,' said Tom. 'He works far too hard.'

'Go, darling,' said Hester. 'If the good doctor appears, we shall look after him.'

'Of course we will,' Ansom agreed. 'He's a capital fellow.'

Esmie smiled. 'Thank you. Then yes, I would like to see Rawalpindi.'

Twenty minutes later, Esmie was squeezed next to Tom in the front of a battered four-seater Clement-Talbot that Tom had inherited with the hotel. He eased the motor car out of unprepossessing Nichol Road into Dalhousie Road and turned south towards the Mall, leaving behind the commercial quarter of open markets, bakeries, factories and the pervading smell of a slaughterhouse.

They passed the general post office, an imposing brick building, with a tonga-stand in front manned by tonga-wallahs in smart red tunics.

'That's Dhanjibhoy's,' Tom explained. 'They run up to Murree and even as far as Srinagar in Kashmir. That's why they have two horses each instead of the usual one.'

On the corner was a general merchant's that was already doing a busy trade.

'Bux and Sons is where I buy my fishing tackle,' said Tom. 'Not that I've had much time for it yet.'

'I know Harold is keen to join you if you can manage a day's fishing while we're here.'

'Of course,' Tom replied, flashing a smile. 'I'd like that too.'

The Mall was wide and tree-lined, with extra paths on either side for promenading on horseback. Some officers were out enjoying a trot in the cool morning air. Frost still lingered on the shaded grass, sparkling in the mellow sunshine, yet the dirt road had already been sprinkled with water to keep down the dust. The roadway was immaculately swept and clean.

They passed the large red-brick Scots Kirk with its tapering spire and then an imposing statue of the late Queen Victoria. Tom pointed out the shops on Canning Road.

'No doubt Lydia will be taking you there, so I've no need to,' he said. 'And that's the famous Flashman's Hotel – the Arcadia of hotels that we must strive to copy.'

Esmie heard the self-mockery in his tone and felt sorry for him. The hotel was set back in lush gardens and half hidden by mature trees. It looked altogether grander than the Raj. Opposite was the Club where they had dined the previous night. In daylight, Esmie could see how extensive the recreation grounds for cricket and tennis were.

'And over there is where the army play hockey and football,' said Tom. 'And there's a track for athletics.'

'Where is the polo ground that Dickie Mason was talking about?' asked Esmie.

He slid her an enquiring look before answering and she immediately regretted mentioning the lieutenant.

'That's up on the race course beyond the railway station,' said Tom. 'It's close to the cavalry barracks at Westridge where Dickie is stationed. It's a bit bleak up there – and very hot in summer – but it's handy for exercising the horses. You seemed to be enjoying chatting with Dickie last night.'

Esmie was alarmed that Tom had been observing Dickie. 'Yes, he's very easy to chat to. He was full of his hunting trip near Murree.'

Tom grunted. 'I'd offered to take him on shikar – he seemed keen – but I think he's keeping out of my way.'

Esmie tensed. 'I'm sure you're mistaken.'

'He makes excuses not to come riding with me.'

'Why would he do that?' Esmie held her breath, hoping he wasn't about to voice suspicion over Lydia.

She saw his jaw clench. 'I suppose because of the gossip.'

'Gossip?' Esmie tried to sound calm.

'I'm surprised Geraldine hasn't already briefed you.' Tom shot her a look.

Esmie reddened. 'About what?'

'About me turning my back on the Peshawar Rifles,' said Tom. 'The army don't like criticism – or one of their own resigning their commission just to become a hotel-wallah. I've let the side down.'

Esmie breathed out. 'I'm sure Dickie doesn't feel that way.'

'Then why else is he avoiding me?'

Esmie could think of nothing to say. She didn't want to come out with some platitude about the lieutenant being busy. Nor did she want to voice her suspicion that Dickie might be spending his spare time meeting Lydia. But what if Tom was right and he was being cold-shouldered by some of the army fraternity for quitting his old regiment? It might become socially awkward in a garrison town like Rawalpindi. Lydia would hate that.

Tom turned the car onto Strathairn Road and into the heart of the military cantonment. Esmie was amazed at the endless rows of mud brick barrack buildings neatly arrayed amid mature trees and clipped borders. Tom pointed out the garrison church, Christ Church, and the medical corp officers' mess. Spreading as far as the eye could see was a grid of troop huts, guard rooms, stables, hospitals, churches and parade grounds; a city in itself.

They drove through a commercial area of substantial two-storey native houses and arcaded shops, already bustling with pre-Christmas shoppers.

'This is Lalkutri Bazaar,' said Tom. 'It serves the army cantonment. Myrtle Dubois's sister and her family live here. The Dixons run a bicycle shop.'

'So it's an Anglo-Indian area?' she queried.

Tom shot her a look. 'Yes, I suppose it is. You don't have a problem with Anglo-Indians, do you?'

'Of course not,' said Esmie. 'Why do you say that?'

Tom pulled a face. 'Lydia does. She thinks the Duboises should live down here with their own kind. She wants me to get a British manager who will attract in a different sort of clientele.'

Esmie studied him. She thought Lydia was wrong but she hesitated to interfere. 'And what do you want?' she asked.

Tom gripped the wheel harder. 'I like the Duboises very much. They work hard and Charlie gives such a welcome to all the guests. Perhaps he's not so good with money but Myrtle is prudent and keeps expenses to a minimum.' He glanced at Esmie. 'Sorry, I shouldn't be dragging you into our business.'

She gave him a look of understanding. 'From the little I've seen of your manager and his children, I think they're delightful. Perhaps it might be a mistake to try and compete with the likes of Flashman's. It seems to me that Rawalpindi is big enough to have a range of hotels catering for different incomes and tastes. Flashman's may be grand but I think the Raj is homely and charming.'

A grin spread across Tom's handsome face. 'Do you really think so?'

'Yes, I do.'

'Thank you, Esmie. That means a lot to me.'

The warm look he gave her made her melt inside. Perhaps she had said too much. But she thought that he needed encouragement in his enterprise and reassurance that he was doing the best he could. She certainly thought that the friendly Dubois family were an asset to the hotel and not the liability that Lydia believed they were.

Esmie leaned back and looked around her as Tom drove and they meandered around the cantonments and bazaars of the army town. They fell into silence but it wasn't an awkward one. Esmie felt more relaxed than she had in weeks, lulled by the rhythm of the motor car, entranced by the sights and sounds of the attractive Punjabi city and comfortable in Tom's company.

Eventually, they turned east again and he drove out past the half-wilderness of Topi Park and on to the Grand Trunk Road that led out of Rawalpindi across the wide Sohan River and its meandering tributary, the Leh. They drove across a metal bridge over the shallow wooded gorge of the Leh River and then Tom brought the car to a stop at a many-arched stone bridge that spanned the Sohan. On the far side were crumbling low cliffs and scrub, fringed in the distance by a mountain range capped in snow; the Himalayan foothills. They looked majestic against the azure blue of a cloudless sky. Tom pointed to the north.

'That's the way to Murree. Looks like the snow's already arrived.'

'I'd like to visit the mountains,' said Esmie. 'Lydia wrote enthusiastically of her trip to Murree with her parents in the autumn.'

'Yes, she enjoyed it tremendously,' said Tom. 'She's missing her parents now though.' He gave a rueful look. 'And so am I. They were such good company.'

'I'm sorry that I didn't get over to see them before they left,' Esmie said.

'You were busy with work – they understood.'

Esmie shook her head. 'The Templetons have been like family to me. I should have made the effort, but I couldn't . . .'

'Couldn't what?'

Esmie's insides knotted. She couldn't admit that it was a reluctance to face Tom that had kept her away – the fear of her attraction towards him. Sitting close to him under the car's canopy with the sound of raucous birdsong from the trees behind, her heart began to thud. She didn't dare look him in the eye in case he should see the longing in hers.

'I – I couldn't manage it,' Esmie answered evasively.

'Tell me about your life in Taha,' Tom said. 'Harold only talks about his work at the hospital, not about the people you've met or the places you've been.'

Esmie felt more at ease with this subject and was soon telling him all about her new home on the arid plain, her colleagues and neighbours, the house servants and especially of Karo and Gabina. She told him how she loved to stand on the veranda and watch the early morning mist lift and how she had delighted in seeing Gabina take her first tottering steps. With Tom's prompting, she told him about the challenging trip into the mountains to Kanki-Khel, their attempts to help Zakir and her guilt at putting Baz and his men in danger. She unburdened her fear that her insistence on sheltering Karo had provoked the attack by the Otmanzai tribesmen.

Tom was adamant she was not to blame. 'The attack was not your fault, Esmie, you must believe that. I've fought against the tribes of the Frontier and they think strategically in all they do. The Waziris and Mahsuds are acting now because they think the British are in disarray after the War and have no more appetite for fighting. We've made peace with the Afghans in the hopes that they don't forge an alliance with Bolshevik Russia. But the Frontier tribes don't trust that we'll leave their territory alone, so they are striking while they think we are weak.'

Tom's look was earnest. 'You were brave and kind to take Karo into your home, so don't feel bad about it. Her husband may feel slighted by what you've done and that's why he was angry at the clinic – but you said yourself that the other men chased him away. Don't confuse a domestic fight with a tribal one.'

'That's what Harold said,' Esmie admitted. 'But I think he still feels my rash actions have caused problems and that I should never have gone to Kanki-Kehl. He didn't want me to.'

Tom laid a hand on her arm. 'Esmie, Harold thinks the world of you. I can tell by the way he speaks of your work.'

Esmie felt her skin tingling where he touched it. She said in a husky voice, 'I know he values my work. I just wish he . . .'

'Wished what?' Tom pressed her.

'Sometimes, all I want is for him to love me as myself, not simply as a nurse.'

'Oh, Esmie, I'm sure he does.'

She shook her head and looked into his eyes. 'It's not his fault. We married in order that I could work at the mission. We had an understanding. Not very romantic, I know. But now I think I want more from our marriage than he does. Harold is such a good man – an honourable man – and I feel disloyal even speaking to you about him when I know he's your greatest friend.'

Tom held her look. 'Do you love him?'

Esmie felt her chest constrict, hardly able to bear his scrutiny. She evaded the question.

'I want to start a family,' she confided. 'But Harold would rather we didn't have a child yet.'

Tom dropped his hold and leaned back with a heavy sigh. 'It's the same for us.'

Esmie was startled. 'Lydia wants a baby?'

He gave her a sad smile. 'No, I do.'

Her insides twisted with pity. 'Oh, Tom, I'm sure she'll come round to the idea soon. Once she's more settled.'

His look was disbelieving. 'I know she writes to you a lot. Does she strike you as unhappy?'

Esmie hesitated. She didn't want to break Lydia's confidences or hurt Tom's pride.

'I think she's enjoying Pindi,' said Esmie. 'But there's one thing that might make her happier and that's to have her own home in the cantonment. Perhaps she doesn't want to bring up a baby in the hotel.'

For an instant, Tom's face tightened in annoyance. Then he nodded.

'You're probably right. You're a wise woman, Esmie. And Harold is a very lucky man.'

Esmie's heart began to hammer at the tender expression in his blue eyes. What did he mean by that? Did Tom feel the same attraction that she did? Suddenly she feared where the conversation was going. She had to break the spell of intimacy that was making them both say too much.

She looked away. 'You said that the Duboises sometimes come here to picnic and paddle in the river. Is there time for you to show me where?'

When she looked back, Tom was swinging his lanky legs over the side of the car. He came round and opened her door.

'There's a path down to the Leh through the trees over there,' he said, his manner more breezy. 'We better not stay long.'

In a couple of minutes, they'd emerged from the trees onto a sandy riverbank.

'The river's still low at the moment,' Tom said, 'but there'll be more rain in January and then the fishing will be better.'

The sight of the glinting tranquil water was too tempting for Esmie. Without hesitating, she kicked off her shoes, lifted the hem of her skirt and stepped into the shallows in her stockinged feet. The water was colder than she'd expected but she revelled in the feel of it.

She laughed and waded up to her knees. 'A Christmas Eve treat!'

Tom chuckled. 'I'd forgotten how you throw yourself into water at the slightest opportunity.'

In a moment, he was pulling off his shoes and socks, rolling up his trousers and following her in. They stood in the river as their feet grew numb, swapping news from home and talking of safer topics such as Tibby's new-found passion for gardening and Aunt Isobel's plans for the hospital.

All too soon they were squeezing wet feet into their shoes and heading back to the car. They said little as Tom drove them towards town. But he didn't take her straight back to the hotel and Esmie wondered if he felt the same reluctance to end their time alone together. They might not have the chance again. She savoured each precious moment. Being with him and talking so frankly had stirred up the same feelings of attraction and empathy for Tom that she had first experienced when they had come across each other in the graveyard at Ebbsmouth. In different circumstances . . . Esmie swallowed down her yearning, making a supreme effort not to let her feelings for him show.

He detoured off the Mall, up Murree Road, so that she could catch a glimpse of the old city. The narrow streets and markets were thronged with turbaned traders and mules laden with produce. Amid the tall houses with latticed windows, Esmie saw the gleaming white domes of mosques and temples. It reminded Esmie of the bazaar at Taha but on a much grander scale.

Tom's attempt to weave further into the old quarter was thwarted by a camel train coming the other way. He turned and drove Esmie back to the ordered leafy streets around the Mall.

Esmie heard the large clock in the park chiming eleven o'clock as they headed along Edwardes Road and turned back up Dalhousie Road.

Lydia was standing on the steps of the hotel dressed in a smart green suit and matching hat, looking out for them.

'Why didn't you wake me?' she cried. 'I would have come with you. Good grief, Esmie, your skirt is wet. Where on earth have you been?'

'Paddling in the river,' said Esmie with a grin.

Lydia's eyes widened in disbelief. 'You really are the strangest girl. Tom, you shouldn't have let her. Goodness knows what horrible condition she might contract from that filthy water.'

'The water was clear and I'm fine,' said Esmie. 'But I'm ready for a strong tea or coffee.'

'Go and change,' Lydia ordered, 'and I'll have Dubois bring up coffee to our sitting room.'

'Is Harold up yet?' Esmie asked.

'No, he's not.' She turned to her husband. 'I don't know how much whisky you made him drink last night.'

Tom gave an apologetic shrug and followed the women inside.

Lydia monopolised Esmie for the rest of the day. While Harold stayed in bed resting, her friend took her out to the shops to buy last-minute gifts for the Dubois children.

'Jimmy and Stella are rather sweet,' said Lydia, 'even if their parents get on my nerves. And I love buying Christmas presents.' Suddenly her chin trembled. 'It's the first Christmas without Mummy and Daddy.

I wanted them to stay longer but they'd promised Grace they'd go to Switzerland to see their new grandchild. It's going to be hard. I'm so glad you and Harold are here.'

Esmie saw the tears welling in Lydia's eyes and grabbed her hand, squeezing it.

'I know how much you miss them – and they miss you. But we'll make the best of it,' Esmie encouraged. 'And maybe next year, they'll spend it here with you and Tom.'

Lydia's look was hard to fathom. 'I can't look that far ahead,' she said, pulling away from Esmie and quickly brushing away a stray tear.

After that, there was no more show of emotion as Lydia steered Esmie around the shops. They rummaged around a large store offering furniture for sale or rent.

'Lots of our people seem to rent things rather than buy,' said Lydia, 'as they get moved around to different postings at the drop of a hat. At least Geraldine, as the deputy manager's wife, should be staying put. The Hopkirks have a fabulous house off the Grand Trunk Road full of expensive teak tables and carved chairs. But Geraldine's got her eye on the manager's house – it's like a maharajah's palace in its own grounds. Even the governor of the Punjab doesn't have such a palatial residence. But that's brewery money for you,' said Lydia with envy, trailing her hand over an ivory-inlaid drinks' table. 'I want Tom to rent some better furniture for the hotel but he says we can't afford it. The place is so shabby, don't you think?'

'I think it has a certain charm,' Esmie replied.

Lydia gave an abrupt laugh. 'I don't know why I'm asking you – you've never been interested in that sort of thing. That's why you don't mind living like a nomad in God-forsaken places with Harold. I do admire you both but I couldn't live like that.'

Back out on the street, Lydia eyed Esmie and asked, 'You were out a jolly long time with Tom. What did he talk about?'

Esmie could feel herself blushing. 'Mainly about the town – pointing things out. And swapping family news.' She met Lydia's look. 'He asked me about life in Taha.'

Lydia clicked her tongue in disapproval. 'That was insensitive. Everyone knows what an awful time you've had there – having to run for your lives.'

'That was in Kanki-Khel,' said Esmie. 'Taha is different—'

'Well, still,' Lydia interrupted. 'You've come here to get away from all that and not have to think about it for a while.' She slipped her arm through Esmie's and began to walk. 'Did Tom say anything about me?'

Esmie hesitated and then decided to be frank. 'He asked me if I thought you were unhappy.'

Lydia stopped and scrutinised her. 'Did he? And what did you say?'

'That I thought you were enjoying Pindi but that moving out of the hotel might make you happier.'

Lydia gave a smile of triumph. 'Good for you! I hope he listened – 'cause he certainly doesn't to me.'

'Yes, he did listen,' Esmie replied. 'He wants you to be happy.'

'Sometimes I wonder,' said Lydia with a pout. 'Tom's so different from how he was back at home. There, he couldn't do enough to please me – quite swept me off my feet with his attention and promises of a grand future in India.'

'I seem to remember it was you who went after Tom and swept him off his feet,' Esmie reminded her.

Lydia gave an embarrassed laugh. 'Well, perhaps a bit of both,' she conceded. 'But here, he's turned into a dull boarding-house landlord who's forgotten how to have fun.'

'When you get a home of your own it'll be different,' said Esmie. 'You'll be able to do more together.' Glancing at Lydia, she added, 'Such as starting a family.'

Lydia laughed derisively. 'That's the last thing I want to do. I'm not going to turn into my boring older sister and churn out babies. They stop one having fun and ruin one's figure – and none of the young officers will look at me twice.'

Esmie was uncomfortable as she remembered Lydia's straying hand under the club dinner table. She was on the point of asking Lydia about Dickie when her friend changed the subject.

'So what are you going to wear for the dinner-dance at Flashman's tonight?'

'The same dress as last night,' Esmie answered.

Lydia was horrified. 'You simply can't. Don't tell me you've only brought one evening dress?'

'That's all I need in Taha,' said Esmie. 'Perhaps I could wear my Sunday dress with an evening shawl.'

'That's even worse!' Lydia exclaimed. 'No, I'll have to summon the darzi to shorten one of my dresses. One or two are too tight for me at the moment, so you might as well wear them.'

They curtailed their trip to the shops and Lydia hurried them back to the hotel to address Esmie's costume crisis. Her friend chose a low-cut beaded V-neck dress in emerald green and ordered the Indian tailor to alter the length and sew in a piece of black lace over the cleavage for modesty's sake. He worked away in the residents' sitting room, Lydia having chased out Mr Hoffman who had been dozing over a book. Esmie had never possessed such an expensive or luxurious evening gown and thought it too flamboyant, but didn't want to stop Lydia's obvious enjoyment in seeing her friend dressing up for the occasion.

The baroness and Stella, hearing about the darzi's visit, were not so easily banished.

'I've a beaded headband which will be a perfect match,' said Hester.

'We could put one of your feathers in it,' suggested Stella, full of glee. 'The bright-green one or the orange would be very pretty. Or maybe both together!'

Lydia rolled her eyes. 'Goodness, girl! We don't want Esmie looking like a vaudeville act.'

Esmie saw Stella's dashed expression and quickly said, 'I think I'd rather like to wear a feather. What do you think to a black one?'

'Perfect, darling,' said the baroness. 'Stella will fetch it for you – and the headband.'

The girl dashed away and returned with the sparkly headdress and luxurious black feather.

Lydia was still unsure. 'It's a bit showy.'

'I think Mrs Guthrie looks like a princess,' Stella said in admiration, holding up a hand mirror for Esmie to see.

Esmie laughed self-consciously. 'I'm not sure my Aunt Isobel would approve.'

Lydia smiled. 'Well, we won't tell her. Go on, wear it. After all, it's Christmas Eve and we're all going to have fun.'

Esmie was concerned about Harold. He'd stayed in bed all day and had hardly eaten anything. He looked pale and his eyes dark-ringed.

'I don't like to leave you,' said Esmie. 'I'll cry off tonight and stay here.'

Harold was insistent. 'Certainly not. You must go. Lydia will be very disappointed if you don't. I'm quite happy in bed reading and getting an early night. Then I'll be fresh for tomorrow. I'd hate to miss the Christmas Day service.'

Esmie knew Harold would find the formal evening an ordeal. Unlike her, he found no pleasure in dancing. Reluctantly, she agreed to go without him.

'I'll ask Jimmy and Stella to keep an eye on you while the Duboises are hosting their party downstairs. If you need me at all, they can send word. Flashman's is just minutes away in a tonga.'

'You mustn't worry about me, my dear. Go and enjoy yourself.'

Esmie indulged in a hot bath before putting on the fancy evening gown and headdress. Even Harold looked on in admiration.

'You look quite beautiful, dearest. I've never seen you so sophisticated.'

Esmie blushed and laughed. 'I just hope I can walk in it without tripping over the hem.'

As she descended the stairs, she could hear lively chatter and a gramophone playing Viennese waltzes in the dining room. Red and green streamers were strung between Chinese lanterns and looped across the top of the windows. Tables were laden with bite-size sandwiches, fried pakora, pastries and cakes. A jovial Charlie was mixing and dispensing his cocktail punch into blue-stemmed glasses. A glamorous dark-haired woman in a pink frock came towards her and held out her hand.

'I'm Myrtle Dubois,' she said with a gleaming smile. 'I'm very pleased to meet you, Mrs Guthrie. I do like your dress.'

'Thank you; it's lovely to meet you too.' Esmie smiled back. 'The gown is one of Lydia's.'

'I know. Stella told me about it. I must say it suits you better,' she said with a wink. 'But don't tell Mrs Lomax.'

'Darling!' cried Hester, catching sight of Esmie. 'You look divine. And my headdress has never looked better. Come and drink one of Charlie's whisky fizzes or whatever it is he puts in his punch. You'll float to the dance, I can assure you.'

Soon Esmie was clinking glasses with the others and joining in the general chatter. Jimmy was on duty at the gramophone, winding it up when it slowed and changing the records. The noise in the room was so raucous that Esmie didn't notice Tom and Lydia enter until they were almost beside her.

She turned and saw Tom regarding her. He was immaculately dressed in tails, with his thick dark hair groomed into place and his chin freshly shaven. Her heart thudded at his sudden appearance. Lydia was reaching for a cocktail, shimmering in a lacy cream dress encrusted with golden sequins and beads. She had a corsage of fresh flowers at her bosom and a matching one in her hair. She wore long cream evening gloves and a string of ivory beads, and her petite mouth was accentuated by a slash of red lipstick. The whole effect was startling.

'You both look wonderful,' said Esmie.

Tom was still eyeing her strangely and she wondered if her headband had slipped out of place, but Lydia gave a generous smile and leaning towards her whispered, 'So do you. If I were the jealous type, I'd be furious that the dress suits you better than me. But I'm not – so you must keep it. You can wear it back in Taha and make all the missionaries faint.'

'Thank you!' Esmie laughed and took a swig of her punch; it was already making her light-headed.

Lydia thrust a glass into Tom's hand and said, 'Ten minutes maximum then we go. We mustn't be late. I've already had to apologise for Harold not coming.' She moved away to talk to Fritwell, who grinned foolishly at her attention.

Esmie glanced up at Tom. He hadn't said a word since he'd arrived. 'Is everything all right?' she asked.

He cleared his throat. 'Yes, fine.' He gave a distracted smile and clinked his glass against hers. 'Happy Christmas Eve, Esmie.' He downed his almost in one gulp. Then he turned from her to speak to the baroness.

Esmie wondered what was preoccupying him. Was he annoyed with her? Perhaps Lydia had been badgering him again about buying a house and citing Esmie's support for the idea. Or maybe he was regretting taking her into his confidence earlier in the day and allowing himself to say things he hadn't meant to.

Charlie was just about to top up Esmie's glass when Lydia was at her elbow, steering her away.

'We have to go, I'm afraid,' she said. 'Enjoy your party. As long as the dining room is all ready for breakfast in the morning.'

'Thank you – and I promise you it will be, Mrs Lomax,' Charlie said with a slight bow.

'That's the best punch I've ever tasted, Mr Dubois,' said Esmie, wishing she could stay among the convivial guests. 'Perhaps Jimmy could take one up to Dr Guthrie. It might be the elixir he needs.'

'Of course.' Charlie nodded, looking pleased.

They were greeted with champagne at Flashman's before sitting down to a five-course dinner. Geraldine had rustled up a replacement for Harold; an American called Dempster who worked for an oil company. Geraldine seated him beside Esmie. He was amusing and Esmie felt caught up in the festive mood. After the meal, the Hopkirks and their guests went out into the garden to smoke and drink while tables were cleared and the room made ready for dancing.

When the band struck up and the dancing began, they were joined by a party of officers from the cavalry mess. Both Esmie and Lydia found their dance cards being quickly filled. Despite her disappointment that Tom hadn't been quick enough to mark her card, Esmie revelled in the dancing. The last time she had danced so energetically had been at Lydia and Tom's wedding, when she and Tibby had taken to the floor.

She noticed how often Dickie claimed Lydia as his partner. The young lieutenant did not try and hide his admiration for her and Lydia was enjoying being the centre of attention among the officers' party. If Tom minded, he didn't show it. She'd glimpsed him earlier talking to the American oilman but had hardly seen him since the dancing had started. Every time she'd cast about for him, there'd been no sign of Tom in the melee of dancers.

Now the evening was nearly over. Glancing down at her card, she saw that Dempster was her partner for the last waltz.

'I hope you don't mind but Mr Dempster asked me to take his place.' Esmie looked up, startled to see Tom holding out a hand to her. 'He's had to leave before the end.'

Her pulse quickened. 'No, I don't mind at all.'

Tom flashed her a smile as she put her hand into his. She could feel herself trembling and hoped he didn't notice. The floor was crowded with dancers, so Tom pulled her close. She was acutely aware of his warm hand on her back as he spun her around. Her throat was so tight with nerves, she couldn't speak. Every time she looked up at his face, he was regarding her with his vivid blue eyes. There was something feverish in his look. She wondered how much he'd been drinking. Her own head swam as they twirled around, heady from the champagne and the proximity to Tom.

'You look beautiful tonight, Esmie,' he murmured.

'Thank you,' she said, her breath catching as he gripped her more firmly.

'Did you enjoy our drive this morning?' he asked.

'Very much.'

'So did I. I'm wondering when we can do it again. Just the two of us.'

Esmie's heart pounded in her chest. This was dangerous talk. In that instant she felt reckless, her senses charged with desire for this man. She didn't trust herself. She thought that she might agree to anything he suggested. For the first time, she felt sure that Tom had feelings for her too. But he belonged to Lydia and she to Harold. Esmie would do nothing to betray or hurt either of them. She mustn't let Tom know how much she cared for him – thirsted for him with every fibre of her being. For a fleeting moment, she let herself imagine what it would be like to kiss his mouth and feel his heart next to hers. She went weak with longing.

Esmie looked away, overcome with shame at her thoughts.

'I don't think that would be a good idea,' she answered.

'Why not?' he demanded. 'I think we both feel something—'

'Please, Tom, don't say anything more.'

His jaw tightened as if he were biting back words he wanted to say. His hold on her slackened.

'Forgive me,' he said. 'I've drunk too much brandy with Dempster. Please forget what I said.'

Moments later the waltz ended and Tom, disengaging, took her back to her seat. Esmie was suddenly deflated. She looked around for Lydia but couldn't see her. Geraldine though, was making a bee-line for her.

'Have you enjoyed the evening, Mrs Guthrie?'

'Very much, thank you. I haven't danced this much in ages.'

'I'm so pleased,' she said, her fleshy chin creasing in a smile of satisfaction. 'I could see you were in great demand among the young men. What a shame your husband couldn't be here. I do hope he's feeling better soon.'

Esmie flushed at the mention of Harold. Was Geraldine rebuking her for enjoying herself too much without him? While he lay ill and alone, she had indulged in lustful thoughts about Tom. How ashamed she felt!

'Thank you for your concern, Mrs Hopkirk,' Esmie said. 'And for such a wonderful evening. I must go now and see how Harold is.'

'Quite right,' said Geraldine, with a steely look at Tom.

'I'll go and rustle up a tonga,' he said, leading the way to the entrance.

En route, they found Lydia with Dickie. Lydia, hearing how Esmie was keen to get back to check on Harold, waved at her and Tom to go ahead.

'Lieutenant Mason will see me safely home,' she said. 'Won't you, Dickie?'

Dickie grinned. 'I'd be honoured.'

Glancing at Tom, Esmie saw annoyance in his clenched expression. But he nodded and steered Esmie out of the building. In the sharp air, people were calling goodnight to each other as they climbed into tongas. Esmie wrapped a shawl about her shoulders and then Tom was helping her up into the seat of their hired vehicle and climbing in beside her. The driver cracked his whip and they moved off along the Mall. Esmie thought how magical it looked in the soft glow of the kerosene street lamps but kept the thought to herself. They sat in awkward silence. Esmie could not avoid jostling against Tom's arm as the tonga swayed.

'You're shivering?' Tom said.

'Just a bit.' Esmie gritted her teeth to stop them chattering. It was proximity to Tom that was making her shake. He pulled a rug from behind the seat and spread it over her knees.

'Thank you,' she said huskily.

They continued in silence. As the tonga turned up Dalhousie Road Tom asked in a low voice, 'Is there something going on between Lydia and Dickie?'

Esmie's pulse quickened. 'I don't . . . I think she's just being flirtatious. And so is Dickie – and half the officers in the cantonment, as far as I can see. It doesn't mean anything.'

Tom gave her a searching look. 'You're very loyal to your friend.'

It suddenly struck Esmie that Tom's ardour on the dance floor might have been to make Lydia jealous. Perhaps he didn't have the same strong feelings for her that she had for him after all? It gave her an odd feeling of disappointment and relief. She looked away, her eyes prickling with unwanted tears. It hurt to be caught in the middle of a jealous tussle between Tom and Lydia.

As if reading her mind, Tom said, 'I'm sorry. I shouldn't have asked such a question. The last thing you want on your holiday is to be dragged into our squabbles. Forgive me, Esmie.'

They didn't speak as they disembarked and walked into the hotel. All was quiet and the guests had gone to bed. Charlie was there to greet them with a tired smile.

'Did you have a splendid evening, Mrs Guthrie?' he asked.

'Yes, thank you.' She returned the smile. 'And did you?'

He nodded. 'All the guests seemed to partake of the punch with great gusto.'

'I'm not surprised,' said Esmie. 'It tasted delicious. Did Harold have some? Has he been any better this evening?'

'Stella took him up a glass of punch and some cake. He gobbled the lot. Dr Guthrie has been sleeping as soundly as a newborn baby since nine o'clock.'

'I'm so glad,' said Esmie. 'Please thank Stella for looking after him so well.'

He bowed. 'Certainly I will.'

Unexpectedly, Tom asked, 'Esmie, would you like a nightcap? I'm sure Charlie will join us.'

Unnerved, Esmie shook her head. 'Thank you but I'm ready for bed – and I want to make sure Harold is still sleeping comfortably.'

Did he look disappointed by her reply? Esmie no longer knew how to read his penetrating looks.

'Well, that just leaves me and you, Dubois,' Tom said, his voice sounding falsely jovial.

'Good night then,' she said and made for the stairs. As she turned on the landing, she saw that Tom was still watching her. She gave a self-conscious smile and hurried on. By the time she reached her bedroom door she could hear the murmur of the men's voices moving off.

By the light of the table lamp, Esmie could see that Harold was sleeping peacefully. He had a touch of colour back in his face and the lines of tension across his brow had vanished. It struck her how often, when awake, her husband wore a perpetual careworn expression. He carried the concerns of so many on his shoulders. She felt another rush of guilt for the desire she harboured for Tom. She had made solemn vows to Harold that now weighed heavily on her heart.

Esmie determined that, once and for all, she must rid her mind of feverish thoughts about Tom – and redouble her efforts to keep the promises she had made to her husband.

Chapter 23

Christmas morning passed pleasantly and more peacefully than Esmie had feared. In good spirits, Harold rose early and ate a hearty breakfast with the other guests. His sickness appeared over and Esmie suspected that the rich club dinner and too many drams with Tom had been to blame.

Tom and Lydia came down just in time to accompany their friends to the morning service at the Scots Kirk. To Esmie's relief, both of them seemed in good humour and Lydia hung on Tom's arm as they walked into church.

Esmie felt emotional as the building rang with the sound of hymn-singing and a padre from one of the Scottish regiments preached the sermon. Her eyes stung with tears as she thought of her dear Aunt Isobel and the patients gathering in the asylum chapel at Vaullay. When would she see them again? She exchanged looks with Harold and saw from his shining eyes that he was thinking of his loved ones at home too. She knew how much his mother and aunt would be missing him, even though they were used to him being away for years at a time. This was the biggest price that all those in service in India paid for working abroad: the long separation from family and home.

Afterwards, they stood in the sunshine as members of the congregation greeted each other. Being Presbyterian, the celebration of Christmas was low-key, yet there was a convivial air. No doubt the

Anglicans at the garrison church would be belting out carols – is that where Dickie Mason and his fellow officers were this morning? – and perhaps there would be sherry and mince pies in the hall afterwards.

But Esmie was content to slip her arm through Harold's and stroll back along the Mall. She needed time with her husband.

'We'll go ahead by tonga,' said Lydia. 'We have to play lord and lady bountiful to the staff. See you back at the hotel for a stiff gin afterwards.' She left, blowing them a kiss.

'Lydia seems on good form today,' commented Harold. 'They've obviously got over their tiff.'

'Tiff?' Esmie queried, hiding her disquiet.

'In the night,' he said. 'Heard them arguing. I suppose it woke me up.'

'I didn't hear anything,' Esmie admitted.

'No, you were sound asleep.'

'Could you hear what it was about?'

'No. Though I think I heard Tom shouting about Dickie.' Harold glanced at her. 'Did something happen last night at the dance?'

Esmie coloured. 'Lydia and Dickie spent a lot of time together. She was in high spirits – you know what Lydia's like – and Dickie is a bit of a flirt too. I think Tom read more into it than was really going on.'

'Oh dear,' sighed Harold. 'Lydia breaks hearts without even knowing it.'

Esmie was jolted by his words. Was that how he still felt about her? She decided to ignore the comment.

'I think there's something else that's upsetting Tom,' she confided. 'He seems to think he's being ostracised by some of Rawalpindi society for leaving the Peshawar Rifles.'

Harold seemed startled by this. 'He told you that?'

'Yes; when we went for a drive yesterday.'

'What did he say exactly?'

'That Dickie was avoiding riding with him because of it – and army people in particular thought he'd let them down.'

'Poor Lomax,' Harold said with feeling. 'Has anyone said anything to you about it? Has Lydia?'

'No, nothing.'

'Good,' said Harold.

'So you think there's something in it?' Esmie asked.

Harold gave an evasive shrug. 'Shouldn't listen to cantonment gossip. Tom left the Rifles for honourable reasons.'

Esmie glanced at him in surprise. She hadn't ever questioned that Tom would have left for reasons that weren't honourable. She had a suspicion that Harold was keeping something from her. But she didn't want to spoil the good mood between them, so didn't press him further.

By the time they'd meandered back to the hotel, Tom and Lydia had already distributed gifts to the Duboises and the other staff and servants. Up in the Lomaxes' sitting room, the tables and floor of the apartment were covered in baskets of fruit and bouquets of flowers which the Duboises and various hotel suppliers had given them.

'How generous!' Esmie exclaimed.

'It's nothing to the money and presents we've shelled out on the staff,' Lydia said caustically. 'And what are we going to do with all this fruit?'

'Stick it in the cocktails,' Tom said wryly.

'Even we couldn't get through that much,' Lydia laughed. 'No, it'll all get used in the hotel – and probably bought with the money we gave them.'

'Still,' said Esmie, 'you love flowers so that was kind of them.'

'Yes, I do.' Lydia was suddenly tearful. 'It reminds me so much of Mummy – especially the gardenias.'

Tom threw an arm around her and kissed her head. 'Come on; no tears on Christmas Day.' Quickly he handed round large glasses of gin and soda. 'Let's have a toast to the Templetons and all absent friends.'

They raised their glasses and echoed the toast. Esmie was glad to see Tom being solicitous towards Lydia and that she was being affectionate in return. Perhaps last night they had cleared the air between them. Their difficulties were just a proverbial storm in a teacup and nothing more. Esmie didn't think that her friends' marriage could be seriously put in jeopardy by a trivial flirtation with Dickie.

Esmie was painfully aware that she was a much greater threat to Lydia and Tom's relationship, should she let her feelings be known. For she was deeply in love with Tom and should never have allowed herself to be alone with him. It mustn't happen again.

So Esmie declined a second drink and excused herself to go and thank Stella in person for her actions the day before. 'She was so helpful to me over my outfit,' said Esmie, 'and then kindly looking after Harold.'

Harold seized on the opportunity to go too, agreeing they would meet up for lunch in an hour.

Esmie soon realised that all the Duboises were frantically busy making preparations for Christmas lunch and looking after the residents. She quickly handed over a present to Stella.

'Just a little something for you as a thank you for yesterday.'

Stella gaped at her in astonishment. 'But I didn't do anything.'

'Yes, you did,' Esmie said with a smile.

'You were my Florence Nightingale,' Harold reminded her.

Stella gave a bashful grin and tore at the wrapping paper.

'Don't rip it,' Myrtle cried. 'You can use it again.'

The adults laughed as Stella stopped to carefully unknot the string instead, her excitement palpable. Inside was an Indian rag doll exquisitely dressed in a crimson sari, miniature leather slippers, brass earrings and glass bangles. Esmie had spotted it when shopping with Lydia. She'd bought two: one for Stella and one to keep for Gabina for when she was older.

Stella couldn't hide her look of disappointment. Esmie wondered if the girl thought herself too old for dolls. She didn't really know what seven-year-olds played with these days.

'Thank you,' Stella said, trying to appear pleased.

'I can always exchange it if you'd rather choose another one – or something else.'

'No,' said Myrtle hastily, 'she'll love it. It's beautifully made – and so kind of you, Mrs Guthrie.'

Esmie went away baffled. 'She was probably just overwhelmed that you'd bought her a present. It was a kind thing to do,' Harold assured her.

At one o'clock, they all sat down for Christmas lunch in the dining room. Lydia chose Ansom and Fritwell to sit at their table with Esmie and Harold. It was a convivial affair and no one seemed to mind that the food was mediocre, the Bengali chef struggling to produce the traditional turkey luncheon that Myrtle had ordered. There was a rather watery but spicy chestnut soup followed by stringy roast fowl, boiled potatoes, cauliflower, cabbage and bread sauce that tasted of nutmeg. Tom made sure there was plenty of wine or beer for those who wanted it. The Dubois children proudly carried in two large Christmas puddings and handed them over to Tom, who poured brandy over the desserts and set them alight. The diners oohed and aahed as the blue flames flared and then died.

Stella said eagerly, 'There's a five-paise coin hidden in each pudding. I hope I win one!'

'The pudding's delicious,' Esmie said, glad that she could genuinely say so. It was a cross between fruit cake and ginger sponge, lighter than the traditional Christmas puddings she was used to, with a rich spicy treacle taste and served with sugary brandy butter.

'It's an old family recipe of my wife's,' said Charlie. The Duboises were sitting at the next table.

'Would you give it to me?' asked Esmie. 'Or is it a closely guarded secret?'

'I'd be happy to share it,' said Myrtle, looking pleased.

Tom leaned over and handed a spoonful to Stella. 'I'm too full. Can you finish this for me?'

The girl's eyes widened. She dropped the spoon onto her plate and fished out a piece of greaseproof paper. Unwrapping it, she squealed, 'Five paise! Thank you, Captain Lomax!'

Tom pretended to be shocked. 'Oh no! Have I given away the coin?'

Stella giggled. 'Yes, you have!'

'What a fool I am.' He dramatically buried his head in his hands.

For a moment, Stella's face fell, wondering if he was being serious. 'Would you like it back?' she asked, holding it out.

Tom looked up and laughed. 'No, no.'

Charlie put his arm around his daughter and chuckled. 'I think the coin is yours to keep, sweet pea.'

'Of course it is,' Tom reassured her as all the Duboises began to laugh. 'I was only teasing.'

Soon after, Lydia led her friends upstairs and ordered coffee to be brought to her sitting room.

'Tom, you shouldn't have teased Stella over that coin,' chided Lydia as she sat down on the sofa. 'She didn't understand you were joking. Eurasians don't have the same sense of humour as us.'

'She understood perfectly,' Tom replied.

'Stella was thrilled with it,' said Esmie. 'It's often the little things about Christmas that give the most pleasure, isn't it?'

Harold said ruefully, 'That's a good lesson for us all. Stella was happy with the surprise in the pudding rather than the expensive doll you gave her. I must mention it to Bannerman – it's good material for a sermon.'

'Didn't Stella like the doll?' Lydia asked.

'She wasn't very enthusiastic,' Esmie admitted.

'I told you so,' said Lydia. 'You should have given her something practical like the woolly hat and gloves that I gave her. She was pleased as punch with those.'

'Why did you think she wouldn't like the doll?' Harold asked.

Lydia was forthright. 'Well, it was too Indian. If you'd given her a British doll she would have loved it. That's the thing about Eurasians – they're always trying to be more British than we are.'

'Darling!' Tom exclaimed. 'You do talk nonsense sometimes.'

'Not nonsense,' Lydia said, bristling. 'I understand more about society here than you do, even though I've been here a fraction of the time. I listen and learn whereas you don't.'

Tom's jaw clenched but he didn't argue back. Lydia turned to Esmie.

'By giving her an Indian doll you're telling her you think she's still a native. Which in a way she is; though the Duboises are desperate not to be.'

'But I wasn't trying to tell her anything,' Esmie said, baffled. 'I just liked the doll and thought she would.'

Lydia shook her head. 'Darling Esmie, you've still got a lot to learn about India. It's just as well you've got me here to teach you what's what.'

Esmie wished Harold had never mentioned the doll and provoked further argument between Lydia and Tom about the Duboises, souring the cheery atmosphere. To try and regain his wife's good humour, Tom suggested that they all had a trip along the Mall to see if there was any cricket being played at the cricket club. Harold quickly agreed.

Esmie was glad to be out in the fresh air – it was another balmy winter's day of cloudless blue sky and mellow sunshine – and was relieved that there was cricket to watch. Lydia was soon chatting with the Hopkirks and other Pindi friends who had come to walk off their Christmas meals.

Taking Harold's arm, Esmie murmured, 'Let's take a stroll around the boundary and leave Lydia to it.'

Tom watched Esmie and Harold go. His head was fuzzy with too little sleep and too much alcohol. He would have to stop drinking so much once Christmas week was over – or perhaps after New Year – once the Guthries had gone back to Taha. For the moment, liquor numbed his feelings and helped him see life through a detached haze.

How else could he get through each day seeing so much of Esmie? Having her at the hotel was sweet torture. He craved the sight of her slim figure and attractive smile and yet could hardly bear the turmoil she stirred inside him. Whenever she regarded him with her mesmerising grey eyes he felt winded. He longed to touch her soft cheek and wrap tendrils of her wayward hair around his fingers. In his pocket, he ran his thumb over the lace of Esmie's handkerchief that he had failed to give back to her in Scotland. It gave him a strange comfort.

As they'd sat alone in his car the day before, Tom had found it almost impossible to resist kissing her button nose and full lips. Then, seeing her in the dazzling emerald gown, his longing for her had shaken him to the core. Apparently it had belonged to Lydia but he couldn't even remember his wife wearing it, yet on Emsie it showed off every curve of her lithe figure. At the dance, holding Esmie in his arms, he was sure that she had felt the same desire as he had. Why else did she tremble at his touch and gaze back at him with a similar look of longing? The memory of it set his pulse racing. Yet she had stopped him from declaring how he felt. And she had been right to.

Tom was gripped with guilt towards Harold. His friend was the most decent and principled of men; it wouldn't occur to him that Tom might covet his wife. How ironic that Tom had been the one to encourage Harold to propose to Esmie. Why had he done so? Was it possible that even before he married Lydia he was frightened of his feelings towards Esmie? Having her married off to Harold would keep her beyond his reach.

The nurse had unsettled him and at times made him angry. He had feared she had been assessing him as a mental casualty and so had belittled her radical ideas about treating shell-shocked men. But in the light of what Harold had told him about Esmie's work both at Vaullay and here in India, Tom saw how humane her methods were and he'd been ashamed at resorting to ridicule in his attempt to deflect her scrutiny.

If he was honest with himself, he realised that he had been attracted to Esmie from the very beginning; her simple beauty and dreamy self-sufficiency, her occasional outspokenness and her warm empathy. But Lydia had dazzled him with her voluptuous fair looks and her energetic drive. He had thought she was a far more suitable wife to take to India. With her sociability and gregarious nature, the Templeton daughter had been everything he thought he would need to start a new life in Rawalpindi and help him run the Raj Hotel.

Above all, Lydia was nothing like Mary. He could leave behind his old life in Peshawar – the army, the rigours of the Frontier and the grave of his beloved first wife – and reinvent himself as a hotelier and bon viveur with Lydia at his side. Now it appeared that Lydia had no real interest in the hotel or being a hotelier's wife. They had married far too hastily.

He had been deluded; it was impossible to shake off the past. The tragedy of losing Mary – the guilt he felt that he was away on patrol when she died so suddenly – and the traumas of the War would not go away just because he had changed occupations and remarried. He could drown his dark thoughts in drink and in trying to convince himself that he was in love with Lydia but neither gave him peace of mind. Back in Ebbsmouth, Esmie had told him as much when she'd gently cautioned him for drinking too much. No doubt she would tell him to talk about the things that haunted him – and to take regular exercise.

Tom stifled a sigh. The only person who came close to knowing about his demons was Harold. He had been the one man who had stood by him throughout the difficult years since Mary had died. But how could he talk to Harold when what now troubled his mind the most was his hopeless desire for Esmie?

He lit up a cigarette and tried not to keep glancing across the field at the Guthries who were making a leisurely circuit of the cricket pitch and in no hurry to return. At least he and Lydia had made up their differences last night. She'd finally returned to the hotel an hour after he had, to find him drinking with Charlie. He'd followed her swiftly upstairs to demand why she'd taken so long to come home but she'd immediately gone on the defensive.

'Because I knew you'd be having a nightcap with Dubois.'

'So are you having a fling with Dickie Mason?' he'd accused.

Lydia had laughed it off. 'Don't be ridiculous. He's far too young. You know how I like my men much more mature.'

She'd grabbed hold of his face and kissed him forcefully on the lips. Within minutes he was completely disarmed by her sudden appetite for sex. They had shed their clothes as fast as they could and made love on the Persian carpet. Lydia had given him a cat-like smile of satisfaction as she'd left him catching his breath while she pulled on her nightdress and climbed into bed. Their love-making had been brief but it had lanced the boil of resentment building between them.

Lydia's good mood had lasted all morning until their spat about the poor Duboises. Tom was pained by his wife's dismissive attitude towards the Anglo-Indian family; to him they were the closest he had to friends in Pindi. Now Tom's doubts about Lydia and Dickie were beginning to grow again. Tonight they were all invited to a party at the cavalry's mess and he would have to watch his wife flirting with the young officer again, while pretending that he wasn't persona non grata among the army elite. Perhaps he would make an excuse not to go. Then he chided himself for being a coward. A man who had faced attack by Afridis in the Khyber Pass shouldn't be afraid of a clique of standoffish sahibs and memsahibs in an army town.

The nausea came on abruptly. Before Esmie and Harold had completed their walk around the boundary, Esmie was rushing towards a bush and vomiting into it. Harold was full of consternation. Esmie was embarrassed but could do nothing to stop the retching. She felt dreadful. Harold rubbed her back and handed her a large handkerchief.

'Oh, my dear,' he said. 'That's just how I was yesterday. I hope I haven't passed something on to you.'

Esmie felt sick and dizzy. Harold said, 'I'll get a chair from the pavilion.'

Esmie stopped him. 'Can we just go back to the hotel?'

'Of course,' he agreed. Taking her arm, he steered her back towards their friends and explained why they were leaving.

Lydia looked dismayed. 'I bet it was Myrtle's Christmas pudding – far too rich. I hope you'll be all right for the party tonight.'

'Perhaps if I have a lie down . . .' said Esmie, fighting down another swell of nausea.

'I'll run you both back in the car,' Tom offered at once.

'Thank you, Lomax,' said Harold. 'Very decent of you.'

Esmie avoided Tom's look as Harold ushered her into the front passenger seat where she had so recently delighted in sitting next to Tom. They said little as they drove up the Mall, Esmie pressing Harold's handkerchief to her mouth in an attempt to stem her biliousness.

Back at the hotel, Esmie retreated to bed at once. 'Please don't stay,' she said to Harold. 'I just want to sleep.'

He nodded, stoking up the fire in the grate with logs of wood. 'I know just how you feel. You'll pull the bell if you need anything, won't you? I'll be downstairs reading.'

Esmie crawled under the covers, feeling clammy with sweat but shivering with cold. She couldn't believe how suddenly she'd fallen ill. Within minutes she was asleep.

It was dark when Esmie awoke. She heard a soft tapping at the door.

'Come in,' she croaked.

Stella appeared, concentrating on carrying a tea tray. 'Are you all right, Mrs Guthrie?'

'A little better, thanks,' said Esmie, switching on the lamp and attempting to sit up. She was less nauseous but her stomach was tender and she felt weak with lethargy. 'What time is it?'

'About nine o'clock. Dr Guthrie and the Lomaxes have gone to the party at the Mess. Dr Guthrie thought it best if you carried on sleeping.'

'Goodness, I didn't even hear him getting ready.'

'Mummy thought you should try some ginger tea,' said Stella, carefully placing the tray on the bedside table. 'Captain Lomax asked her what would help a sick tummy.'

'I'm not sure I could manage anything yet,' said Esmie. Even sitting upright had made her feel faint.

Stella ignored this and began to pour tea from the small china pot into a delicate cup. 'Just try a few sips, Mrs Guthrie,' she encouraged. 'Shall I stay and keep you company?'

Esmie was touched by the girl's concern. 'That's kind but you should be with your family on Christmas night.'

'We'll have our fun tomorrow,' said Stella. 'Captain Lomax has given us the day off so we can go and see our Dixon cousins. They always have a party on Boxing Day. Auntie Rose gives us lots to eat and we play games. My favourite is charades.'

'That's very grown-up,' Esmie said with a wan smile.

'I'm good at it.' Stella giggled. 'I love acting.'

'Tell me about your family,' said Esmie. 'Do you have many relations in Pindi?'

'Quite a lot,' said Stella. 'There's Auntie Rose and Uncle Toby and their two children – well, three now counting baby Sigmund. And Uncle Toby has a brother, my Uncle Ziggy, who helps in the bicycle shop and Auntie Lucinda and they've got three girls and two boys.' She counted them off on her fingers. 'So I've got eight Dixon cousins all together. Baby Sigmund is named after Uncle Ziggy. Then I've got relations on Daddy's side but they don't live in Pindi so we don't see them very much.'

'What a lovely big family you have,' said Esmie.

'Do you have lots of cousins too?' asked Stella.

Esmie shook her head. 'Sadly not. I don't really have any family left alive. I have a very special Aunt Isobel – she's not a blood relation but I love her like one. She's a doctor in Scotland.'

Her eyes prickled at the thought of how her kind guardian would have fussed over her had she been there.

'So you and Mrs Lomax aren't related?' queried Stella.

'No, we were friends at school. Her parents, the Templetons, were as kind to me as if I had been their daughter.'

Stella nodded. 'I liked them. They always said good morning at breakfast and Mr Templeton gave five rupees each to me and Jimmy when he left. Jimmy bought a cricket ball and I got a bell for my bicycle. We're saving the rest.'

Esmie smiled. 'That was kind of him.'

'Yes,' the girl agreed. She tilted her head in thought. 'I wish Mrs Lomax was more like that. She's all right with me and Jimmy but she's bossy to Mummy and sometimes shouts at Daddy.'

Esmie was dismayed. She'd heard Lydia's catty comments about the Duboises in private but was embarrassed to think her friend had been openly rude to the manager and his wife – enough that Stella had noticed.

'I'm sorry if she's been unkind to your parents,' said Esmie. 'She's not usually like that.'

Stella sighed. 'I wish it was you, Mrs Guthrie.'

'Wish what?' Esmie puzzled.

'I wish you lived here and ran the hotel with Captain Lomax instead of Mrs Lomax.'

Esmie was completely taken aback. 'You shouldn't say that.'

'Well, it's true,' Stella insisted. 'And Mummy thinks the same. I heard her say to Daddy after she met you. "The captain picked the wrong wife."'

Esmie flushed. 'You must never repeat such a thing, Stella. Especially not to the Lomaxes. Promise me?'

'Try the tea,' urged Stella, ignoring her plea. 'It won't be too hot now.'

Esmie took the cup in shaking hands and blew on the pale golden liquid. She braced herself to take a sip, thinking it might make her retch. Stella's frank words had set her pulse beating erratically. But the smell of ginger was calming and it tasted pleasant. When it didn't irritate her stomach, Esmie took further sips.

'That's nice,' she said. 'Please thank your mother for me.' She sank back from the effort and closed her eyes, wishing she hadn't been told about Myrtle's comment.

'Do you want me to go?' Stella asked.

'No,' said Esmie, not wanting to be left alone. Stella's chatter might distract her from thoughts about her and Tom. 'Tell me more about your family. I like to hear you talk about them. I'm still listening even though my eyes are closed.'

She felt Stella sitting down on the end of the bed as she began to talk animatedly about her relations in Lalkutri bazaar. Soon Esmie was asleep again.

She had no idea what time it was when Harold crept back into the bedroom. Stella had gone and so had the tea tray but the side lamp had been left on. Harold peered down at her.

'How are you feeling, my dear?' he whispered.

Esmie realised she no longer felt sick. 'A lot better, thanks. Stella gave me spicy tea which helped.'

'That's good.'

'How was the party?' Esmie asked.

Harold pulled a disapproving expression. 'Too much drinking.'

Esmie became aware of raised voices from the next room; Lydia's was querulous and Tom's angry.

Harold explained. 'Lydia spent most of the evening in the company of young Mason. I'm sad to say, Tom caught them kissing under some mistletoe.'

'Oh, Lydia.' Esmie sighed with impatience. 'Why can't she just be satisfied with what she has? Is Tom very hurt?'

Harold regarded her. 'Difficult to say. I got the impression he would have ignored the kiss if I hadn't witnessed it too. Mason looked embarrassed but Lydia just laughed it off as a little holiday silliness. They'd all had too many champagne cocktails.'

'The sooner they move into a home of their own, the better,' said Esmie.

'Well, I don't think they'll be getting any more invitations to the mess this holiday. He's told Mason to stay away from Lydia. That's probably what they're arguing about. For myself, I hope it's the last tedious party of the week. Tom and I are going fishing tomorrow.' He patted her hand. 'It will give you a chance to spend some time with Lydia and talk some sense into her – remind your friend of her wifely duty.'

Esmie's heart sank at the prospect. 'What makes you think Lydia will listen to me? She never has before.'

'Because you're a good woman,' said Harold. 'Lydia is too – but she's been too quick to adopt the loose morals of the shallow people she's mixing with here.'

Esmie felt her throat dry. If only her husband knew how much she struggled to be faithful to him – how in her thoughts she had failed to be.

'Harold, I'm no saint—'

'She chose to marry Tom,' Harold interrupted, 'and she must live with her choice. It pains me to see my old friend made a fool of. You must remind her of her vows to Lomax before she succumbs to further temptation.'

Esmie turned away, her cheeks burning with shame. Harold's words might just as well have been directed at her. She was no better than Lydia.

Chapter 24

The men left immediately after breakfast to go fishing. Before he went, Harold ordered Esmie breakfast in bed. She felt hungry but still weak and was content to stay in bed longer than usual. By the time she had washed, dressed and ventured downstairs, there were only the baroness and Mrs Shankley, the lady with the ear trumpet, sitting in cane chairs in the reception area.

'My little friend Stella has gone to Lalkutri with her family,' said Hester. 'Ansom and Fritters are out somewhere. I think they've gone to watch polo.' She turned to Mrs Shankley. 'What time did they go, Mrs S?'

Mrs Shankley pressed her brass trumpet to her ear. 'I haven't got a watch. But the clock says it's nearly eleven.'

The baroness gave an exasperated laugh. 'So it is. Thank you, Mrs S.'

Esmie sat down with them and began to chat. Minutes later, Lydia appeared on the stairs and joined them.

'Feeling better?' she asked.

'Much better, thanks,' Esmie replied. 'Even managed some kedgeree for breakfast.'

Lydia pulled a face. 'More than I did. Do you feel up to a game of tennis? I thought we could go to the Club. Have a bite of tiffin afterwards.'

Esmie would rather have sat quietly with the other women and leafed through the newspapers but she knew how much Lydia loved tennis. It would give them a chance to talk too.

'I'll give it a go,' she said, 'but I haven't played since leaving Ebbsmouth.'

'Not even at Taha?' Lydia cried.

Esmie shook her head.

'Well, we'll just have to find a couple of chaps to play doubles with, won't we?' She winked. 'Come on, Esmie.'

To Esmie's surprise, it was Lydia who tired more quickly on the tennis court. The sun was warm and she was soon out of breath.

'Sorry,' she panted, 'I need to sit down.'

Their fellow players – Dempster and a colleague from his oil company – made polite excuses for her.

'It's very warm today. Perhaps we could order you up some lemonade?'

A puce-faced Lydia accepted, fanning herself and going to sit in the shade.

'Are you all right?' Esmie asked in concern as she sat beside her on the bench.

'Absolutely fine,' Lydia said.

'Too much partying last night?' Esmie teased.

Lydia shot her a look. 'I suppose Harold told you about the mistletoe. Tom got it all quite out of proportion. Just a brotherly peck of a kiss, that's all.'

'Harold thought it was more than that,' Esmie said quietly.

'So I'm not allowed to have fun anymore?' Lydia was indignant.

'It's not about having fun – just not putting Tom in an awkward position.'

'Well, what am I to do if my own husband won't take me out and give me a good time? Dickie knows how to enjoy himself.'

'You have been spending a lot of time with him,' Esmie pointed out. 'Why don't you try and do more with Tom? Play tennis or golf or go riding together.'

'He wouldn't want to,' Lydia huffed. 'He never has time for me.'

'I'm sure he would if you suggested it. Even just go on a picnic.'

'And watch him fish or paint?' Lydia said dismissively. 'That's not my idea of a good day out.'

A waiter arrived with a jug of lemonade and poured it into glasses for them. Esmie sipped and watched the Americans carry on playing tennis together. She searched for a topic of conversation that wouldn't put Lydia on the defensive or make her homesick.

'Stella is a very sweet girl and so mature for a seven-year-old,' said Esmie. 'She brought me ginger tea last night and sat chattering till I fell asleep.'

'Umm, she's the best of that bunch,' Lydia conceded. 'But I don't know how much more I can bear being in the hotel. I'm not used to living like this – having to queue to use the bathroom and then finding deaf old Mrs Shankley's yellow dentures floating in a glass. It's enough to make the strongest constitution sick. And why should the Duboises have a house in the compound when we have to live in two rooms upstairs like a couple of travelling salesmen?'

'Would you want to live in the compound?' asked Esmie.

'No, of course not,' Lydia huffed. 'But that's not the point. The point is, why should they get a house at our expense when we, the owners, can't afford one? At least according to my scrooge of a husband, we can't.'

Esmie eyed her friend. She was flushed and frowning, her mouth pulled downwards in discontent. She'd hardly touched her lemonade. She looked a deeply unhappy woman. Lydia seemed to have forgotten how to enjoy the simple things in life: planning a picnic, chatting to a friend or the pleasure of a carbonated drink frothing in the mouth. Lydia complained of Tom being a different man in India; but since coming out here, Lydia was a changed woman. Was it homesickness? Or was she falling out of love with Tom? Was India just too much for Lydia or was it simply that she hated the Raj Hotel?

Esmie resisted placating her with anodyne responses about soon finding her feet or giving it more time to adjust to a new life. She knew her friend would dismiss them as unhelpful platitudes.

'Well, then,' said Esmie, 'if you really want to live away from the hotel, then do something about it.'

Lydia gave her a sharp look. 'What do you mean?'

'If you have money of your own to buy or rent a place, then start looking for one.' Esmie put a hand out and covered Lydia's puffy one. 'I can help you look – if you want me to.'

Lydia's eyes widened. 'Would you really?'

'Of course.' Esmie smiled. 'We could start looking around the agents' today if you like.'

'Even if it gets you into trouble with Tom and Harold?'

Esmie's heart skipped a beat. 'Why would they mind?'

Lydia gave a dry laugh. 'I know you've been told to talk some sense into me while they swan off fishing. They want me to be a good little wife who does her husband's bidding and doesn't cause a fuss. I'm right, aren't I? I can't wait to see Tom's face when he hears you've been actively helping me escape the hotel.'

Esmie was dismayed. 'Lydia, I want to help you find a home you're happy in – not to score points against Tom. You do want to share a home with him, don't you?'

Lydia's eyes slid away from Esmie's anxious look. 'Yes, of course. I want somewhere we can entertain our friends and not have to share the privy with incontinent old box-wallahs.'

Esmie couldn't help a wry laugh. 'Oh, Lydia, you are incorrigible.' She drained off her drink.

Lydia got to her feet. 'I'm ravenous. Let's go and have tiffin and celebrate the start of our mission to find me a house.'

As Esmie stood, there was something about Lydia that caught her eye. As her friend turned, dappled sunlight fell on her figure, accentuating the tightness of her tennis skirt and her thickening waistline. The pot-belly beneath the waistband. Lydia was scratching her right breast as if it itched against the tight fabric of her blouse. Esmie's heart thumped in shock. She let out a small gasp. Lydia caught her look.

'What is it?' she asked.

'Lydia . . .'

'Have my buttons come undone or something?'

Esmie moved closer and asked quietly, 'Are you . . .?'

'Am I what?'

Esmie glanced around; there was no one within earshot. She whispered, 'Are you pregnant?'

Lydia's mouth fell open in astonishment. 'Of course not. I can't be. Whatever makes you say that?'

'You look it.'

'What clap-trap!'

Esmie had a moment of doubt. Then she saw tears spring to Lydia's eyes. Her friend sat back down again as if she'd been winded. Her chin trembled.

'Oh, God! I've been praying that I'm not,' she whispered. 'I don't want to be.'

Esmie quickly sat beside her and grabbed her hands. 'But it's wonderful news. Tom will be over the moon.'

'How do you know that?' Lydia gave her a suspicious look.

Esmie blushed. 'Well, I'm sure he will be. He likes children.'

'But I don't,' Lydia said, her voice tearful. 'And I've been so careful to avoid . . .' Lydia bowed her head.

Esmie had a sudden appalling thought. What if Lydia had allowed Dickie to seduce her?

Gently Esmie asked, 'When did you last have your monthly bleed?'

Lydia began to shake. 'I thought it was just the travel that had put things out of kilter – coming to India – the heat and all that. You hear about your time of the month stopping because of such things, don't you?'

'So you haven't had one since you've been in India?'

Lydia shook her head. Esmie felt a stab of relief; the baby couldn't be Dickie's.

'So you could be four months gone?' Esmie calculated.

Lydia stifled a sob. 'Oh, how could we have been that stupid? That inept! Tom can be so careless.'

Esmie didn't like to think about Lydia and Tom being intimate. She put an arm around her friend. 'Come on, don't cry. You'll be happy about it once it's had time to sink in.' She squeezed Lydia's shoulder. 'And once Tom knows about it, he's not going to deny you a home of your own – not with a child on the way.'

Lydia looked up, her face brightening. 'Yes, that's true. At least it'll force him to be reasonable about a house. So it's not all a disaster, is it?'

When Tom returned with Harold after dark, he knew from Esmie's expression that something had happened.

Harold greeted her with a pat on the shoulder. 'You're looking much better, my dear. Have you had a good day?'

'Yes. We played tennis at the club and then went for a drive.'

Tom's insides clenched as she turned her gaze to him. 'Lydia's tired so she's resting. I've arranged for Maseed to bring supper up to your rooms when you get back.'

'Are you and Harold joining us?' Tom asked.

'No,' said Esmie. 'I've still not got my appetite back and I thought Harold could keep Mr Ansom company at dinner – Mr Fritwell is away for the night.'

'I'm sure Lydia would prefer it if you spent the evening with us,' he said, not wanting to be alone with his wife. She was less likely to harangue him in front of her friends.

Esmie shook her head. 'She just wants it with you, Tom.'

The way she spoke his name – was there tenderness and a little regret in her voice? – made his heart sink. Why did Lydia want to be alone with him? Was she going to confess about an affair with Dickie? Or perhaps she wanted to nag him again about moving out of the hotel. Tonight, he wouldn't have the excuse of slipping downstairs to talk arrangements with his manager and have a nightcap with Charlie. The Duboises had just returned from Lalkutri but were still off duty.

Tom swallowed. 'Well, if you're sure that's what she wants.'

'It is,' Esmie said. Her smile made his chest tighten in longing.

She turned and linked her arm through Harold's. 'Have you had fun? Did you catch any fish? Tell me everything.'

Tom watched her steer Harold towards the dining room. He felt engulfed in envy for his friend. For the umpteenth time, he wondered why he hadn't proposed to Esmie instead of Lydia or realised that the strong emotion she had provoked in him when they'd first met had been love.

With a heavy heart, Tom trudged upstairs.

Lydia was lounging on the chintz sofa in a silk dressing gown, her bare feet propped up on a cushion. Her hair was unbound and her face devoid of make-up. He hadn't seen her look so naturally pretty in months. Tom gave her a cautious look, wondering what it meant.

She held out a hand to him. 'You can come near me. I'm not going to bite.'

He gave a wry smile and approached the sofa, bending to kiss her on the head. She'd bathed and smelt of talcum powder.

'Esmie tells me you've had an enjoyable day,' he said, standing back.

'Yes,' she said, suppressing a yawn. 'She's been helping me pick out a house. I've found the perfect one on Buchanan Road.'

Tom tried to curb his irritation. 'You didn't have to drag Esmie into this.'

'I didn't,' Lydia said with a look of triumph. 'It was her idea. She thinks you're very selfish for not having done something sooner.'

He reddened. 'Lydia,' he said in exasperation, 'let's at least get the Christmas holidays over with first.'

'No, Tom,' she said firmly. 'I've waited long enough. I've arranged a viewing for tomorrow. You can come if you want but I'm going to rent it anyway.' She swung her legs over and stood up, arching her back. 'I want to be in there by the New Year.'

'That's impossible – we're too busy here.'

'I'm not. You can leave all the arrangements to me.' She padded to the sideboard and poured herself a sherry. 'Want to join me?'

'So your mind is made up?' Tom asked tensely.

'Yes. It's got everything we need.' She poured two glasses and handed one to Tom. 'A large garden and three bedrooms; one for us, one for guests and one for the baby.'

Tom thought he had misheard. 'For the what?'

'Our baby. I'm about four months pregnant.' Lydia knocked back her drink in one gulp.

Tom stared at her in disbelief. His heart knocked in his chest. 'Four months?'

She nodded, pouring herself another sherry. Tom began to shake. He clashed his glass down on the sideboard, spilling the liquor.

'Careful, darling,' Lydia admonished.

Tom's eyes stung. 'I'm going to be a father?' he rasped.

'You are.'

Tom felt pressure build in his chest and his throat constrict. Suddenly he let out a cry – half bellow, half sob – and stumbled towards her. He grabbed Lydia in a fierce hug.

'Our child,' he gasped, clinging on to his wife and kissing her hair.

'Don't, Tom,' she protested. 'You're squeezing me too tight and spilling my sherry.'

Tom let go. The next moment he was weeping – uncontrollable sobs from deep in his core. The discordant noise rang round the room.

'For goodness' sake,' said Lydia, glancing at the veranda windows which had been left ajar. 'Don't let the residents hear you.'

But Tom was helpless to stop it. He sank onto the sofa and gnawed his knuckles in an attempt to stem the tide of emotion. How was it possible to cry so hard at such happy welcome news? He gulped and spluttered and tried to say how pleased he was. Lydia looked on speechless, then turned away to top up her spilled drink.

Esmie was standing in the courtyard below. Stella had pulled her outside to look at the full moon. Its white light lit up the rooftops like an electric lamp. As they gazed upwards in wonderment, they heard a man's loud sobbing coming from the open veranda windows of the Lomaxes' flat. Esmie felt a surge of shock.

'Is Captain Lomax crying?' asked Stella in concern. 'It doesn't sound like Mrs Lomax. Do you think she's been shouting at him again?'

For a moment Esmie couldn't answer. She assumed Lydia had broken the news of her pregnancy by now. It seemed an extraordinary response from Tom. She'd expected to hear whoops of joy. But this emotion was altogether deeper – primeval. Her heart squeezed to hear him so overcome with feeling.

A few moments later, someone crossed to the windows and closed them, shutting in the noise.

'I'm sure he'll be all right,' Esmie said.

'He doesn't sound it,' Stella said. 'Should I go up and see?'

Esmie was astonished by the girl's bravery. 'You're a kind girl. But no, I think we should leave them alone.'

Stella glanced up at the closed windows, her expression still worried. Esmie steered her further across the courtyard.

'Can you keep a secret?' Esmie asked.

The girl nodded.

'I think Mrs Lomax was giving Captain Lomax some good news. They're going to have a baby. But it's still early days and they might not want people to know yet, so you must keep it to yourself.'

Stella stared at her in bewilderment. 'So why was Captain Lomax upset? Doesn't he want a baby?'

'Yes he does; very much. But sometimes grown-ups show how happy they are by crying.'

Stella nodded. 'That's true. Uncle Ziggy cried when he was told about baby Sigmund being named after him.'

Esmie smiled. 'There you are then.'

Stella's face lit up. 'A baby in the hotel – I can't wait! I'll help Mrs Lomax look after it. Do you think it's a girl or a boy? I hope it's a girl. Boys can be quite annoying.'

'Shush now; remember, it's a secret.'

'Sorry,' said Stella, clamping a hand over her mouth.

Now was not the time to disappoint the girl by telling her that the Lomax baby would not be living in the hotel. Esmie pulled Stella into a hug.

'It is exciting, isn't it?' Esmie whispered. 'And I know you'll be a great help to the Lomaxes once the baby is here.'

Chapter 25

The next day the doctor was summoned and after a brief examination confirmed that Lydia was at least four months pregnant. The tension between Tom and Lydia seemed to evaporate overnight. Esmie noticed the difference at once. Tom strode about the hotel with energy and purpose again, full of bonhomie towards all comers and proudly protective of his wife. He went around with a permanent grin of euphoria. He fussed over Lydia, ordering her to rest in the afternoons and summoning hot drinks and warm baths. Lydia, taking advantage of his newly besotted state, pressed ahead with securing the house in Buchanan Road and ordering new furniture and appointing servants.

It didn't take long for the residents to work out that Tom's new solicitousness towards his wife – and Lydia's delight in being pampered – was because of the forthcoming baby. Tom didn't deny it when Hester asked him outright.

'Are we to hear the patter of tiny feet sometime soon, Captain Lomax?'

Tom flushed with pride. 'Yes, Baroness. The doctor thinks it'll be born in May.'

'Darling, I'm so pleased! But May is terribly hot. Perhaps you should arrange for Mrs Lomax's confinement to be in Murree?'

Tom frowned. 'I hadn't thought of that. You're right. Murree would be far healthier. Thank you, dear lady.'

Once the idea was in his head, Tom became adamant that their child should be born in the hills, away from the heat and summer fevers of the plains around Rawalpindi. Lydia acquiesced quickly.

'I suppose the hot season will be unbearable here – and all my friends will be moving up to Murree by then.'

'So that's what I'll arrange,' said Tom. 'I'll come up as often as I can. In the car it's less than a couple of hours' drive.'

Harold, not wanting to get embroiled in picking furnishings for the Buchanan Road bungalow, made arrangements to meet up with the Tolmies and other missionary acquaintances who were in Rawalpindi over the holidays. Lydia reproached him.

'You can go and meet your virtuous friends if you must, Harold. But you can't take Esmie with you. I need her to help me with the house. I'm finding it so difficult to make up my mind – pregnancy seems to be addling my brain.'

Harold went puce at her frank words. Esmie knew how uncomfortable he was at any mention of the word pregnant, preferring to use the euphemism of Lydia's 'delicate condition'. Esmie hoped it might spark her husband's interest in their having a child too – or at least allow them to talk about it – but when Esmie raised the subject Harold was evasive.

'Do we have to talk about this now, my dear?'

'If not now, then when?' she pressed him.

'It's not the right time,' Harold said in agitation.

'When will it ever be the right time?' Esmie asked in exasperation. 'I thought we'd agreed in Kanki-Khel that we both wanted to become parents.'

'That was before the clinic was attacked again. I misjudged the situation. From what I was hearing at the mess the other night, the situation around Taha is going to get worse again. They're talking of sending Mason's regiment back to the Frontier.'

Esmie knew he would always use the turbulence in the borderlands as an excuse not to start a family. Once, she would have agreed with him. But she had seen how women like Karo coped with bringing up children despite the uncertainties of frontier life. To Esmie it was a risk worth taking. She turned from Harold in frustration, wondering what it would take for him to change his mind. Perhaps when the Lomax baby was born and he saw how happy his friends were, then he would be persuaded to become a father himself.

Esmie spent long hours helping Lydia with household arrangements and keeping out of Tom's way as much as she could. He seemed wary of her now – his manner cordial but distant – and she imagined how he regretted his show of feeling towards her. It was only a week since they had gone out in the car alone together but it seemed an age ago. It was as if they were both trying to pretend that the confidences they had shared had never been spoken – or that Tom's advances towards her at the dinner-dance had never happened. She knew he must be deeply embarrassed to think of it now. Esmie could not rid her mind of Tom's howls of emotion on hearing he was to be a father and knew there was nothing in the world that he wanted more than this baby with Lydia.

Esmie was astonished at the speed of change at the hotel. Lydia got her wish to be installed in her new home by the end of the year and took possession of the rented bungalow on New Year's Eve. The plans to attend the Hogmanay Ball at the Club and have dinner with the Hopkirks beforehand were abruptly dropped. Tom had sent a message to Geraldine to say Lydia was indisposed.

From being dismayed at the idea of having a baby, Lydia now appeared to be relishing her new role as a cherished mother-to-be who must be treated with the utmost delicacy. The Lomaxes planned instead to have a small dinner party with just Esmie and Harold. A van was hired to take their possessions from the hotel flat to Buchanan Road.

That morning Esmie and Lydia took breakfast together in the flat before the removal men arrived. Harold had yet to return from his morning walk and Tom was downstairs talking to the residents. Esmie had overheard him reassuring Hester that he would be constantly popping in from Buchanan Road to make sure everything was running smoothly.

'I can't tell you how relieved I am to be leaving the hotel,' Lydia said, tucking into a large helping of scrambled egg on toast. In the past few days she had bought a whole new wardrobe of looser-fitting dresses and was looking more comfortable. 'Dubois can bring your luggage over later.'

Esmie gave an awkward smile. 'There's no point us moving just for a couple of nights. We're quite comfortable here in the hotel.'

Lydia gave her a look of surprise. 'What do you mean just a couple of nights?'

'You knew we would be leaving after Hogmanay. Harold wants to get back to Taha as soon after New Year as possible. He's arranged for us to stay with Bernie Hudson in Peshawar on the way home.'

'Who on earth is Bernie Hudson?'

'Remember I told you about him? He's with the Agriculture Department. He and Harold became good friends on the ship out here. He's been pressing us to visit for months.'

Lydia looked put out. 'So Harold would rather spend his last days of leave with some man he met on a ship than with his oldest friends? And he's going to drag you with him. I didn't think he could be so selfish. I've finally got a house to entertain my dearest friends in and you don't even want to stay.'

Esmie could see Lydia becoming upset. She put a hand on her friend's arm. 'We're really looking forward to having dinner at the bungalow tonight and we've still got another couple of days together. So let's make the most of it.'

'I suppose I'll just have to,' Lydia said with a sniff. 'It's so hard when everyone I care about has to leave after such a short stay.'

Esmie smiled in encouragement. 'You've got Tom with you all the time – and in a few months you'll have baby Lomax. I bet your parents will want to rush back out when he or she is born. Nineteen twenty is going to be such a wonderful year for you both, I'm sure of it.'

Lydia let out a long sigh. 'If it brings Mummy and Daddy back out to India then I suppose having this baby will be worth the effort.' She pulled away and put her hands on her rounded stomach. 'Do you know, I think I've felt it moving in the past few days? Is that possible?'

Esmie gazed at Lydia's bump and experienced a strange curdling inside. Lydia was carrying another life within her. She felt a mixture of trepidation and excitement for her friend – and a twinge of envy.

'Yes, it's very possible,' Esmie said.

'Oh, Lor',' Lydia exclaimed, 'it's really happening, isn't it?'

That evening Esmie and Harold took the fifteen-minute tonga ride to the new bungalow. The sitting room was already luxuriously appointed with Lydia's beautiful maple furniture, richly coloured Persian rugs and Chinese vases filled with fresh flowers. A fire crackled brightly in the grate and brass ornaments reflected the warm glow.

Tom welcomed them and his bearer Bijal handed around gin cocktails.

Esmie saw a large watercolour hanging over the fireplace.

'Is that one of yours?' she asked, peering closer.

'Yes, it's of the ruins at Taxila,' Tom said, smiling diffidently. 'My wife has finally allowed it on display.'

'It's very striking,' she said in admiration. She liked the semi-abstract style and bold colours; the piles of stones were purplish and the sky almost green.

Tom looked pleased. 'Perhaps I could run you and Harold out there? It's well worth a visit.'

'Too late,' Lydia said, 'they're abandoning us the day after tomorrow.'

'Are you?' Tom asked, catching Esmie's eye.

She couldn't work out if he was relieved or disappointed at the news. She had assumed Harold would have told him.

Esmie nodded. 'You've been more than kind to us and we mustn't outstay our welcome or you won't ask us again.'

Harold explained. 'We're taking the train back via Peshawar. Esmie hasn't seen the city yet and I thought she'd find it interesting. Staying with a fascinating fellow called Hudson. He's translating Dickens into Pashto.'

Esmie saw Tom wince at the mention of Peshawar. Was it because it reminded him of his time with the army or was there a more personal reason? She now knew that Tom's first wife had died there.

After drinks they dined on the shuttered veranda at a candlelit table, the space warmed by two charcoal braziers. They reminisced about the previous summer in Scotland and the outings they'd enjoyed as a foursome. The mood was mellow and Lydia was back to her vivacious self, teasing each of them and making them laugh. Seeing how well they could all get along, Esmie felt a sudden rush of optimism for both their marriages. In different ways, each couple had had a shaky start but things were being resolved. Tom and Lydia were being brought together by the anticipation of their future son or daughter, while her and Harold's partnership would strengthen as they continued in their shared work. Esmie prayed that, in time, the marriage would include a baby of their own.

Sitting around the Lomaxes' table, avoiding Tom's look, Esmie could imagine that she was happy and that the future would bring fulfilment. They returned to the sitting room and played cards while Tom put records of Scottish songs on the gramophone. By the time they were seeing in the New Year with toasts of whisky and singing Auld Lang Syne, Esmie was impatient to escape back to Taha and for 1920 to begin.

Chapter 26

Peshawar, January 1920

Icy rain whipped around Esmie's face as she emerged from St John's Church with Harold and Bernie. It was bitterly cold and the bare trees of the churchyard bent and swayed in the wind. The snow-capped mountains of the Khyber Hills had disappeared under a blanket of cloud and for a moment, huddling outside the gothic stone building, Esmie could imagine she was back in Scotland. Inside the church, they had sat on carved wooden pews under hanging gas lamps and Esmie had gazed at glinting brass plaques honouring the dead – mainly senior army officers and their families – and wondered about Mary Lomax.

On which street in the cantonment had she and Tom lived? Perhaps Bernie's neat bungalow was near it. How had Mary filled her days? Had she been as curious as Esmie to venture into the back lanes of the fortress town to watch the coppersmiths at work and bargain for brightly coloured Bokhara silks to make into clothes for the summer?

Since arriving two days ago, the weather had been too inclement to do any sightseeing and Esmie had only managed a glimpse of the walled city on a brief tonga ride with Harold and his friend. In the rain, the low-lying buildings of the bazaars and caravanserais had looked drab and the sound of braying pack animals, forlorn. Esmie had been sorry for the marooned traders standing disconsolately in the narrow serai entrances, wrapped in damp blankets, waiting to continue their journeys with their restless mules and camels.

Tomorrow she and Harold would return to Taha. Esmie was keen to go home and she chafed at these few days' delay in Peshawar. She would rather have spent them at the Raj in the genial company of the Duboises and the residents but Harold had been eager to leave. The announcement of the Lomax baby and the subsequent disruption to their visit seemed to have unnerved her husband. He'd hoped to go fishing again with Tom but his friend had been too busy seeing to the needs of his pregnant wife.

Struggling to keep her umbrella from whipping inside-out in the squalls, Esmie glanced at Harold, who was in deep conversation with Bernie. He at least was enjoying their stay in Peshawar; long games of chess and discussing books with the erudite Bernie by a cosy fire. While time had hung heavily for Esmie, the men had stayed up late, talking about everything from Dickens to the origins of the game of polo. Esmie realised how much Harold must miss intellectual stimulation in their remote outpost. His mother and aunt had provided it at home and there were one or two in Taha, such as Bannerman, who could talk about religion and books. But with Bernie, he had found a kindred spirit and Esmie didn't want to drag him away from these precious days of relaxation before they returned to the fray.

She consoled herself with the thought that Harold was probably happier being married to her than if he had followed his heart and proposed to Lydia. Apart from sport, Harold and Lydia had nothing in common. But then there was no logic to whom one fell in love with, and the old adage that opposites attract was often true. How else could she explain the magnetism she felt towards Tom? He was impulsive, extrovert, charming, quickly riled and did not hide his emotions; whereas she was an observer who was slow to anger and held her emotions in check.

What had Mary been like? Harold remembered her in childhood as kind-hearted and a little shy, a daydreamer who could entertain herself for hours playing with a pet rabbit or drawing pictures. Tom, grieving for his mother and constantly belittled by his strict father, had grabbed on to Mary's friendship like a lifeline.

'It seemed natural that the two of them would marry,' Harold had said. 'Mary adored Tom. I always thought it would happen even though they were temperamentally very different.'

Even though Harold had been on furlough in Scotland when Mary had died, Esmie still found it astonishing that he had never found out where Mary had been buried. Tom had never spoken about it and Harold had thought it intrusive to ask.

Bernie appeared at her side, offering his larger umbrella for shelter.

'Did you find any inscriptions on the church walls of interest?' he asked.

Esmie dragged her thoughts back to the present.

'Interesting but sad,' she admitted. 'Each one tells a story of love and loss.'

Bernie nodded. 'But so much endeavour too.'

Esmie gave up on her own umbrella and allowed Bernie to steer her out of the church grounds under his.

'Of course,' he continued, 'if you really want to get a feel of our past history in Peshawar then a trip to the British cemetery will tell you more than a dozen history books. So many gravestones and monuments detailing lives cut short, as well as their profession or regiment.'

Esmie's pulse quickened. Mary's grave might be among them. 'Are there graves belonging to the Peshawar Rifles and their families?'

'The Rifles? Of course. They have an illustrious history in these parts.'

'Is the cemetery far from here?'

'No, not far at all. It's this side of the cantonment – out on the Khyber Road.'

'Do we have time to go there before lunch?' Esmie asked.

'In this weather?' Bernie laughed. 'Your dedication to historical research is very commendable, Mrs Guthrie, but perhaps we should leave it till after tiffin and see if the rain eases off.'

Curbing her frustration, Esmie agreed. She didn't know why she thought it so important to track down Mary's last resting place, except that it made her feel closer to Tom. For some reason she couldn't explain, she wanted to pay her respects to the woman who had shown a simple kindness and love to the young Tom, and had made him happy in their brief marriage. If she could find Mary's grave, she might be able to better understand Tom's troubled mind and do something to help him find peace.

Or perhaps she was being fanciful. Tom didn't need or want her help now that he was going to be a father. Lydia and her baby were his future. It would be months before she saw them again. She and Harold had promised to return and visit once the baby was born but Esmie was doubtful she would manage to get Harold to take another holiday so soon after their Christmas leave.

She went over the last moments with Tom in her mind. He had driven her and Harold to the station after a tearful parting with Lydia. Lydia had howled at her going and Esmie had been emotional too, urging her to take care of herself and her unborn baby. As Harold was overseeing their luggage being carried onto the train, Tom had taken Esmie's hands in his.

'You don't need to worry about your friend,' he'd said. 'I'm going to take excellent care of her.'

Esmie had tensed at his touch, trying not to shake, and nodded. 'I know you will.'

He'd given her one of his intent looks. 'Your turn will come, dear Esmie.'

She'd felt her eyes sting with tears. She was about to ask him what he meant, when Harold had returned and told her it was time to climb aboard. Briefly, Tom had brushed her cheek with a kiss and she had swallowed down a sob of longing as he'd turned away and grasped Harold in a firm handshake. On the train ride she'd puzzled over his words and come to the conclusion he had meant that, one day, her turn to become a mother would come.

Back at Bernie's bungalow, all through a heavy lunch of mulligatawny soup, mutton cutlets, watery vegetables and rice pudding, Esmie kept glancing out of the window, hoping that the rain was lessening. Afterwards, they retired to the parlour where a fire had been lit since early morning and the men began to settle into chairs to read. Esmie looked anxiously out of the window; the light was already fading in the gloomy sky.

'Perhaps now would be a good time to visit the cemetery,' she suggested. 'Before it gets dark. It seems to have stopped raining.'

Harold stifled a yawn. 'I thought I'd read my Bible for a bit. It's really not an afternoon for going out. Perhaps we could go there on the way to the station tomorrow.'

Esmie knew that if they didn't go now, they never would. They had to catch a morning train and Harold would be fussing about them missing it.

'It's not on the way to the station,' she pointed out. She gave a look of appeal to Bernie.

He roused himself from his comfortable chair by the fire. 'I did promise Mrs Guthrie we would go after lunch if the weather improved – and so it has. You can stay here, Harold, if you like. I can show your wife around the graves – I'm a bit of an expert after all these years.'

Harold quickly changed his mind. 'No, no, I'll come too.'

They entered the cemetery under a creeper-covered lychgate. Esmie was immediately struck by the serenity of the place, the orderly rows of well-tended graves under the bare dripping trees. The clouds were clearing and a pale golden light was spreading over the emerging hills to the west.

'To the left we have the oldest graves,' Bernie was explaining, as he ushered her down the muddy path. 'Some of these date back to the 1860s. Mostly young soldiers far from home. Many of the tombstones are erected by fellow brothers-in-arms – their surrogate families out here.'

Esmie was touched by the tender inscriptions and the beauty of the stones; many of them elaborately carved and decorated to make them unique to the loved one buried beneath. The most poignant were the graves of the cantonment's children; sons and daughters carried off in infancy, presumably by violence or sudden disease. It reminded her painfully of Harold's reason for them not embarking on parenthood.

They walked around the site, stopping to read memorials to various regiments and for Bernie to give explanations.

'See how many were buried in 1879? That was owing to an outbreak of cholera during the Afghan campaign.' Then pointing to the western end of the cemetery, he said, 'Sadly there's a crop of new headstones from the end of the recent war – influenza, I'm afraid.'

The light was leaching from the sky and darkness would soon be falling. Harold said, 'I think we should be back in the cantonment before dark.'

Esmie decided to ask the question that had been on her lips since arriving at the burial ground.

'Is there a particular corner for the Peshawar Rifles and their families? It's possible our good friend Captain Lomax's first wife is buried here.' She glanced at Harold. 'We'd like to pay our respects.'

Bernie nodded. 'The Rifles are scattered about. It rather depends on the date.'

Esmie said, 'Just before the War, wasn't it, Harold?'

'End of 1912 or beginning of 1913,' he replied, sadness clouding his face. 'I was on furlough and didn't get back until March so the funeral was long over. Poor old Lomax was away on picket when it happened. Still blames himself for not being there. Not that he could have done anything.'

'What did she die of?' asked Bernie.

Harold reddened. 'I don't actually know. Some fever, I imagine. Tom has never wanted to talk about it.'

They skirted a water tank as Bernie led them to the far corner behind a hedge and searched among the graves. The stones were still unweathered and their lettering clear. Abruptly, he stopped in front of a slender headstone of white marble shaped into a Celtic cross at the top.

'Could this be it?' Bernie asked.

Esmie's throat tightened as she surveyed the inscription.

> *In loving memory of Mary Maxwell Lomax, dearly beloved wife of Captain T. Lomax of The Peshawar Rifles, born 2nd January 1888, died 5th January 1913. Erected by her sorrowing husband.*
>
> *'O for the touch of a vanished hand, And the sound of a voice that is still.'*

Esmie bit her lip to stop her tears. Her heart was heavy with sorrow at the loving, desolate words. How Tom had loved his Mary! In that moment, she doubted whether he could ever love another as much – neither Lydia nor her.

'Oh, Harold, it's so sad,' she said, reaching out for her husband and wanting to feel his warm presence. But he wasn't looking at Mary's grave. He was staring at the one beside it. A smaller stone with an angel statue placed beside it. He turned to her, his face ashen. Esmie's heart thumped.

'What is it?' she asked, dread knotting her stomach.

'I don't understand,' he said in bewilderment. 'Tom never said anything about . . .'

Esmie went quickly to his side and read the second gravestone. She gasped in shock.

In memory of Amelia Mary, infant daughter of Captain T. Lomax. Born 5th January 1913, lived four days.

'My flesh shall rest in love. Safe in the arms of Jesus. Of such is the kingdom of heaven.'

Esmie grabbed on to Harold to steady herself. She gaped at him.

'Tom had a daughter?'

Harold's jaw was clenched; he could only nod. Esmie looked at the grave again; the words seared her heart. His baby girl – his own flesh – buried here next to his wife. Had he returned from duty in time to see his daughter alive? Had he ever held her in his arms? If not, who had looked after his child for the four days she had lived? She could hardly comprehend Tom's suffering in this double loss.

Bernie said gently, 'Your friend's wife must have died in childbirth – the date matches that of the child.'

Esmie looked again at Mary's stone. January the 5th. Her eyes welled with tears. Tomorrow would be the seventh anniversary of Mary's death – and her baby's birth.

She heard Harold swallow a sob. 'My poor dear friend!' His voice was hoarse with sorrow. 'I never knew. I never knew.'

Esmie clutched his hand and squeezed it. She was too overcome to speak. She thought of Tom's uncontrollable weeping on the night he had learnt that Lydia was pregnant. Now she understood. He had been crying with happiness at this second chance of being a father – and in grief for the daughter he had lost.

Chapter 27

Early the next morning, before leaving Peshawar, Esmie and Harold returned to the cemetery to lay flowers on the graves of Mary and Amelia. The clouds had broken to reveal a topaz sky. The snow-capped mountains of the Khyber Pass looked close enough to touch. To Esmie there was a raw beauty about this resting place.

She had hardly slept for thinking of Tom's young wife and daughter. Had Mary gone into labour early? Had she sent for Tom, frightened it was all happening too soon? Did she live long enough to know she had given birth to a daughter and to cradle her to her breast? Esmie's heart ached for this woman she had never known but felt a connection to; they had both grown up in Ebbsmouth, ventured out to India as young brides and both fallen in love with Tom Lomax.

But it was the infant grave that made her heartsore. Beneath the tiny plot lay Amelia – named after Tom's beloved mother – who had only drawn breath for four days. Had she been born with Tom's dark hair and startlingly blue eyes? Who had nursed her and comforted her cries? Had she been born too prematurely and weak to survive or had she succumbed to some sickness that was passing through the cramped and heavily populated cantonment?

It was fruitless to wonder, for the end result was the same; Amelia had followed her mother swiftly to the grave and left Tom stunned in grief. He had been so traumatised by the double tragedy that he had told none of his family or friends – not even his closest friend Harold – that he'd had a daughter. Harold had not even known that Mary had been with child.

Esmie, Harold and Bernie had sat up late talking about it the previous night. The last time Harold had seen Mary had been before embarking on leave to Scotland at the end of the hot season in 1912, four months before her death. Mary and Tom had been in good spirits – perhaps in retrospect she had seemed a little tired – but there had been no mention of a forthcoming baby. If Harold had noticed nothing then it was probably because the pregnancy was not far advanced – and therefore more likely that Mary had gone into labour prematurely.

Esmie pressed her fingers to her mouth and swallowed down tears as Harold said prayers over the two graves.

' . . . and commend them both into your loving care, Lord, until the day of resurrection when we will be reunited with the dearly departed – all the great company of saints that dwell with you in heaven and that we miss so much here on earth. And comfort our friend Tom. May he turn to you in times of darkness and doubt and know that you walk with him and that he is loved. May he know that you hold his precious Mary and Amelia in the palm of your hand – safe and at rest – until he meets with them again in the life ever after. For Jesus' sake, Amen.'

Esmie could not stop the tears rolling down her cheeks at Harold's tender, comforting prayer. Seeing his eyes swimming with tears too, she took his hand and held it tight.

'Thank you, Harold.'

Without further speech, they left the cemetery, the only sound a solitary bird trilling unseen in the trees.

Esmie was sad to say goodbye to Bernie; he had been a kind and attentive host and Harold had been relaxed in his company. After a long day's travel by train and motor car – Bannerman picking them up in Kohat again – they were back in Taha by nightfall.

Despite being tired and queasy from the car journey, Esmie went straight to the compound to see Karo and Gabina. On catching sight of Esmie, the girl threw out her arms in delight and toddled towards her. Esmie scooped her up and cuddled her tight.

'How I've missed you!' she cried.

She tried to banish thoughts of Amelia's grave as she clung to Gabina. The girl was even more precious to her in the light of her discovery of Tom's dead daughter. How fragile new life was in this place and how easily Gabina too could have died if Karo hadn't come to the clinic. Then it struck her that the Waziri girl was still vulnerable to disease; so many of the graves in Peshawar had been for children who had survived infancy only to succumb to sudden illness in early childhood. She felt her old fear of motherhood gripping her with renewed force.

That evening, after a late supper, she broached the subject with Harold.

'I've been thinking about my longing to have a child,' she said quietly.

He shot her an anxious look. 'Dear girl, I thought we'd—'

'Let me finish,' Esmie interrupted. He nodded for her to continue.

'Finding Mary's grave – and seeing Amelia's – has been a profound shock to me. And I think to you too, Harold.'

'Yes,' he agreed. 'A terrible shock.'

'It's made me realise that my desire for a child is a selfish one,' Esmie admitted. 'I came here to nurse and help serve the people of the Frontier. What good am I to them if I die in childbirth like Mary? My wish to be a mother is still as strong but I must accept that my path in life may be to care for other people's children and not my own.' She gave Harold a sad smile. 'And I know that you don't feel the same way about having a family as I do. It would be wrong to force fatherhood on you – even though I think you would make a loving father – so I won't bring up the subject again.'

She saw his eyes glinting with emotion, reflecting her own regret. And yet she also thought she saw relief in his expression. He reached across the table, took her hand and pressed it tenderly to his lips. With a pang of affection, she wished he could be as demonstrative as this more often.

After that, Harold rose and, bidding her goodnight, retreated to his bedroom. Heavy-hearted, Esmie went to her own room and bedded down between chilly sheets, alone but resigned to making the best of her platonic marriage to Harold.

Soon Esmie was once more immersed in the day-to-day running of the clinic, working long hours alongside Harold, Rupa, Alec Bannerman and the orderlies. Rumours flew around the bazaar and cantonment about tribal uprisings and raids against British outposts. But the violence was happening further south and west from Taha and the mission carried on working and trying to ignore the tension.

Esmie resumed Sunday lunches at their bungalow for their friends and while they shared meals, Brigadier McCabe kept Harold and Esmie abreast of developments on the Frontier.

'The Gurkhas took on the Mahsuds at Ahnai Tangi – Punjabis of the seventy-sixth fought their way through to support. A bloody eight days of battle, by all accounts. Mahsuds have taken heavy casualties.'

From the brigadier they learnt that Dickie Mason's regiment had been sent south to relieve the garrison at Razmak and help hold back the rebellious tribesmen. Esmie wondered how Lydia and Tom had taken the news of Dickie's departure. The fuss over the Christmas flirtation must surely seem of no consequence now that they were looking ahead to the birth of their child.

Esmie had wanted Harold to write to Tom and tell him that they had visited Mary's grave and laid flowers – and done the same for Amelia.

'It might comfort him to know that we know – and that we'd paid our respects to them both,' she'd reasoned.

'I really don't think we should intrude on his grief,' Harold had replied. 'If he'd wanted me to know, he would have told me.'

'Perhaps it was all too much at the time,' Esmie had said. 'But that was seven years ago and he might now be ready to have his daughter acknowledged by his most trusted friend.'

But Harold had been uncomfortable with the idea. 'He's got Lydia now as his helpmate and a new baby on the way. Best not to dwell on the past.'

Esmie didn't press him further; he knew his friend best. She looked out for the young lieutenant passing through Taha – she was sorry for Dickie having to cope with the death of his sister and thought his dalliance with Lydia had possibly been his way of cauterising his feelings. In war, she had seen people dealing with death in unpredictable ways and she would not judge the bereaved. But Dickie and his fellow officers never appeared.

It was on an early February morning, as Esmie and Harold were eating breakfast, that they heard a faint droning noise. By the time they had gone out onto the veranda to see what it was, the noise had grown to a loud buzzing. Looking up, they saw aeroplanes, engines throbbing, crossing the pale sky like giant birds.

Karo came tearing round the corner, her face a mask of terror, a wailing Gabina in her arms.

'It's all right,' Esmie called out, going swiftly to them. She put her arms around the petrified woman and the child. 'They're planes – British planes. They won't hurt you.'

But Karo would not be reassured. She babbled incoherently, her speech too fast for Esmie to understand. Harold came over.

'She doesn't understand what they are,' Esmie said. 'How can I explain?'

Harold gave her a harrowed look. 'She does understand. She's seen them before when they dropped bombs near her village.'

Esmie felt punched in the stomach. 'Oh, the poor woman,' she gasped. All she could do was hold on to Karo and Gabina until the planes had passed overhead and disappeared south-west into the mountains. She thought of last summer and Tom's angry cynical words about dropping bombs on Kabul. Tibby had told her that Tom had challenged his father about modern warfare and riled him with his riposte, 'What is honourable about bombing men on horseback from the air?'

A few days later, news came through about the success of the RAF air raid. Dozens of villages had been destroyed. The Mahsuds, however temporarily, had been subdued. Harold and Esmie couldn't share in the general relief and celebration in the cantonment. All they could think about were the scores of casualties that must have resulted from the bombing. The only way to deal with their leaden feelings was to redouble their efforts at the mission hospital and do what they could for their patients.

The cold crisp days and occasional fog of January and February gave way to unpredictable sudden storms in March as the temperatures began to climb and the southerly winds of winter switched to those from the north-east.

By April, the midday temperatures on Harold's glass thermometer were already showing over eighty degrees. Esmie knew they had a gruellingly hot season ahead in Taha. While spasmodic unrest among the border tribes continued, there was little chance of getting back to Kanki-Khel and the mountains. Baz refused, point-blank, to provide another escort for the missionaries and the army had more pressing priorities.

Her thoughts turned more and more to Lydia and the imminent birth of her baby. Her friend had written frequently about life in Rawalpindi. She was happy in the Buchanan Road house and hosted regular lunches, games of bridge and tea parties with her friends while Tom was at the hotel.

> '*I've no idea what he does there all day,*' Lydia had written in her most recent letter, '*but it keeps him from being under my feet. He's been very sweet but I must say, he can be a complete bore about me resting and not overexerting myself. He treats me like an invalid which I'm not – though I am finding it harder to move around. My legs have swollen and my bump is enormous. I look and feel like an elephant. It's already horribly hot here and I can't wait to get up to Murree. I go at the end of the month. Tom's renting a cottage on Pinnacle Point but wants the birth to be in hospital, which I think is ridiculous as I'm perfectly healthy and would rather have the whole thing done discreetly at home. We've employed an ayah for the baby. Geraldine recommended her – she's a younger sister of the ayah that the Hopkirks used – or maybe it's a daughter or cousin, I'm not altogether sure. But she seems capable and doesn't squabble with the other servants which is a relief.*
>
> *DO say you will come up to Murree after the baby comes. I'll need some company for those dreary weeks when I'm not allowed to go far or socialise too much. Come even if Harold can't.*
>
> *Mummy and Daddy continue to be thrilled about the imminent arrival of baby Lomax but as yet they*

haven't said when they'll be coming out again. Daddy has business to take care of – he never stops – and Grace is staying for the summer with her brood so Mummy will be busy too. I haven't given up on them coming out for Christmas though.

Tom says to tell you that Stella is missing you and wants to know when you'll be back. You certainly made an impression on the girl, though I've never seen her playing with that Indian doll you gave her! I don't go to the hotel much – just pop in once in a while for a sundowner with Fritters and to show my face – can't have Myrtle Dubois thinking she's got the rule of the roost!

Give my love to Harold as always – and to you of course.

Your best friend, Lydia xx'

In the evenings Esmie would read out Lydia's letters to Harold. He always blushed at the messages for him.

'Is it any surprise that Tom is fussing about Lydia being near a hospital?' said Esmie. 'He must be so anxious that everything goes right this time. Do you think I should tell Lydia about baby Amelia so that she'll be more patient with Tom?'

Harold was adamant. 'You mustn't do that without getting Tom's permission first.'

'No, I suppose not,' Esmie conceded. 'And I don't want to make Lydia alarmed about women dying in childbirth. No, you're right – best not to say anything.'

'All we can do is to keep them in our prayers,' said Harold. 'And if you'd like to visit Lydia in Murree then you must do that.'

Esmie's heart leapt. 'Of course I'd like to go. Would you come with me?'

He shook his head. 'It's you that Lydia wants, dearest. My time is better served here.'

'Well, as long as you can spare me?'

Harold gave her a tired smile. 'I'm sure we can manage for a couple of weeks. As long as you don't stay away forever.'

Esmie shot him a look. She knew he was teasing but his words startled her. Did he harbour doubts about her and her commitment to him and the mission? Did he fear she wouldn't come back to him?

She put out her hand and shook his arm gently. 'You know I won't leave you.'

'Good,' he said, patting her hand in affection.

Chapter 28

Rawalpindi, May

A telegram came for Tom at the hotel. Tom's stomach lurched and his hands shook as he tore at the brown envelope.

'Labour has started STOP Lydia at home STOP Come soon STOP Geraldine.'

Charlie, who was hovering at the reception desk, asked anxiously, 'What has happened, sir?'

Tom took a large breath. 'Lydia's gone into labour.'

Charlie's eyes widened. 'That is a cause for great excitement,' he beamed.

Tom stood there stunned. Lydia was in the throes of childbirth. He felt panic rather than excitement.

Charlie said, 'You must go hot-foot to Murree, sir. Leave everything here to us.'

Tom stared at him, trying to calm his palpitating heart. 'Yes, yes, I must.' Still he felt paralysed, unable to move.

Charlie came around the counter. 'Shall I drive you up to Murree, sir?'

His manager's concern galvanised Tom. 'No, no, I'll be fine.' He ran a hand across his sweating face.

Charlie said, 'I'll make all necessary arrangements. Bijal will pack you a case and I'll get Cook to make up a tiffin basket. I'll prepare the motor car. All will be shipshape and ready within the hour, Mr Lomax.'

Tom nodded. 'Thank you, Charlie.' Suddenly, he felt a surge of nervous excitement. 'It's happening, Charlie. It's really happening, isn't it?'

Charlie grinned. 'And if you get your skates on, you shall be there for the birth.'

Tom remembered little of the forty-mile drive up to the hills. Bijal sat in the back with a scarf tied over his mouth against the rising dust and nursing the tiffin basket. Tom chatted to him to take his mind off what lay ahead. Bijal, a Pathan from near Attock on the Indus River, had been in his employment since Tom had first come to India. Older than Tom – he was around forty but still fresh-faced – he said little but had a deep soft chuckle that had kept up Tom's spirits on many an occasion.

As they ascended the steep curving road towards the hill station, the scent of pines and the cooler air greeted them. The road was busy with tongas bringing visitors to Murree and dotted around the hillside were the bleached canvas tents of the summer camps that would soon fill up with army contingents. The population of the Himalayan town swelled from around two thousand in the cold season to nearer ten thousand in the monsoon season, as the British, bringing their servants with them, escaped the heat of the plains to Murree or travelled on to Kashmir. Shops and boarding houses, closed half the year, opened up to cater for the influx.

Tom, in a sweat of anticipation, hardly noticed the drop in temperature as they gained Pindi Point at one end of the saddle-shaped ridge and entered the town. Driving as carefully but swiftly as he could through the busy streets of the cantonment, they passed the hospital, manse and cricket ground and on to the Mall. Tom wondered if he should have stopped at the hospital to see if Lydia was there but Geraldine had said his wife was still at home.

Passing Trinity Church and the post office, Tom steeled himself to pass the Birchwood Hotel where long ago he had stayed with Mary on a late summer leave. They had stood on its elevated veranda and he had pointed out the snow-covered mountains of Kashmir where they were travelling on to. He told her she would never see a more heavenly place. '*I'm in heaven now, Tom, just being here with you.*'

Tom's gritty eyes stung as he remembered her tender words. How he had failed her! Forcing Mary from his mind, Tom took one of the meandering tracks that burrowed into the wooded hillside of Pinnacle Point, where the villas of the British nestled among the trees.

Arriving outside Linnet Cottage, Tom cut the engine, scrambled from the car and leapt up the veranda steps, calling to Bijal to take care of the luggage. To his surprise, Geraldine was sitting in a cane chair, smoking. He'd never seen her smoking before. She quickly stubbed out the cigarette and stood to greet him.

'Tom, dear. I didn't expect you this quickly. How was your journey?'

Distractedly, Tom bent to kiss her cheek. 'Fine thanks. How is Lydia?'

Geraldine gave a tentative smile. 'Bearing up well. It all started yesterday—'

'Yesterday?' Tom exclaimed. 'Why didn't you send for me sooner?'

'Don't worry,' she said, 'it was just a few twinges. Didn't really get going till this morning.'

'I see.' Tom moved towards the inner door but Geraldine put out a hand to stop him.

'Come and sit down. I'll order tea. You must be tired. Such a hot drive. Then you can wash and change.'

Tom curbed his irritation at her high-handed manner. Geraldine had obviously assumed control of his wife and bungalow since his last visit over a week ago.

'I want to see Lydia first,' Tom said.

She looked scandalised. 'Certainly not. Poor dear girl is in the middle of labour. She won't want you seeing her like that. No, the less fuss the better.' She waved him into a chair. 'Nurse Jones is with her – I sent for her myself – and Lydia's ayah is helping too.'

She clapped for a servant and ordered tea and cake. Catching sight of Bijal, she commanded him to take Tom's suitcase to the spare bedroom. 'Just for now.'

Tom refused to sit down. 'How long has the nurse been here?'

Geraldine gave a vague smile. 'Oh, sometime after breakfast.'

Tom's gut tightened. 'But that's hours ago. Shouldn't things have happened by now?'

'Oh, it can go on for ages. My first son, Roland Junior, took thirty-six hours. I was like a wrung-out dishcloth by the end, I can tell you. Now, stop worrying and put your feet up.' She took his arm in a pincer-like grip and steered him towards a long chair.

Tom shook her off. 'I just want to see for myself – to let her know I'm here if she wants me.'

'Now, Tom, don't be difficult. Lydia really won't want you there. But I'll go in and tell her you've arrived.' She gave a little laugh. 'Maybe that will spur her on.'

In frustration, Tom watched her retreat into the house. He punched the doorframe. He knew it was usual for men to be kept away from women during labour, but he wanted to know that Lydia was all right. His biggest fear was that she would not survive the ordeal – or that the baby would not. Fear clawed inside as he tried to hear what was happening in the house beyond.

A door opened and closed. There was a murmur of hushed voices in the corridor, and then the door opened again. He thought he heard moaning before the door closed once more. Tom felt nauseated, hardly able to bear the waiting. He fumbled for his cigarette case and fishing out a cigarette, tapped it hard on the case before lighting up. He took a long drag and inhaled deeply, feeling the welcome tingle and an instant sense of calm spread through him. This wasn't unusual; giving birth was a long process, wasn't it?

He clenched his jaw. How would he know? He hadn't been there when Mary had been fighting for her life . . . A wave of anxiety swept through him once more. He mustn't think of it; he mustn't tempt fate with his dark thoughts of the past.

For a moment he thought he heard a cry as a door opened again. Geraldine was saying something placating but in a brisk voice. Moments later, she re-emerged from inside the gloomy bungalow.

'All's well,' she said with a tight smile. 'Lydia is pleased to know you are here but she doesn't want you in the bedroom on any account.'

Tom's spirits plunged. He'd hoped his wife would have defied Geraldine and demanded to see him.

A servant appeared with tea and set about serving it to Tom and Geraldine. Reluctantly, Tom sat and half-listened to the garrulous brewery manager's wife talking about the new arrivals in town since his last visit. All the time, his thoughts were on Lydia and how the birth was progressing. Was she in great pain? Was the baby in danger? How he wished he knew what was happening! If only he could help in some way. Talk to her through the door, perhaps.

'Where are you going?' Geraldine demanded.

Tom was halfway across the veranda before he realised what he was doing.

'I just want to listen at the door,' he said. 'Say something encouraging.'

Geraldine was on her feet. 'You mustn't! She doesn't want you there. Tom, you must bear this like a man. Shall I get Roland to come over and take you to the club?'

Tom halted, grinding his teeth. Roland would be preferable to having to wait out here being bossed by Geraldine. He nodded.

'I'd appreciate Roland's company but I don't want to go to the club. He could come here.'

Geraldine considered this for a moment. 'Very well. Your servant can run over with a message. I'll tell Cook we'll have an extra one for dinner.'

Tom was relieved as Lydia's friend bustled off to make arrangements. He was tempted to stride into the house and barge into the bedroom where Lydia lay but his nerve failed him. She knew he was here but didn't want him anywhere near her while in labour. Tom sighed and lit another cigarette.

Roland arrived as the sun was setting over the trees. The men drank gin and limes as the sky turned green and then indigo. The stars came out. Dinner was served. The time crawled. The Hopkirks chattered. Tom kept glancing into the house. The waiting was pure torture.

'Go and see what's happening,' Tom begged Geraldine every twenty minutes.

She would disappear, leaving Tom on tenterhooks, and return with a little shrug. 'She's resting' or 'it won't be long now' or 'you really mustn't worry; these things take time.'

Tom couldn't sit still. He began pacing the veranda, smoking one cigarette after another while the Hopkirks finished their dinner. They made indulgent comments.

'You're bound to be anxious with the first one,' said Geraldine.

'You just have to leave it to the women,' Roland said, motioning the khidmatgar to pour Tom a brandy. 'They're the experts.'

By ten o'clock, with dinner over and no progress reported by Geraldine, Tom asked in agitation. 'Should we send for a doctor?'

He saw a look pass between the Hopkirks. Fear choked him.

'She should be in hospital, shouldn't she?' he cried. 'I knew it. I wanted her to have it there!'

Geraldine stood up. 'Now stop it, Tom. You're making yourself ill. We need you to be strong, not go to pieces. What good will it do Lydia if she hears you shouting?'

Tom ran his hands through his hair. 'I'm sorry,' he said, trying to calm down.

'Drink your brandy, Lomax,' Roland encouraged.

'That's better,' said Geraldine as Tom sat down again. 'I'll go and see what's what.'

As midnight approached, Tom could hear Lydia's cries ringing around the bungalow. The nurse must have opened the window to let in the night air, for Lydia's shrieks came louder now. He ground his teeth at the animal noise of distress. It was echoed by the constant screams of nocturnal birds and animals in the surrounding forests.

Two hours earlier, the middle-aged Nurse Jones had come out to reassure him that she'd delivered countless babies and that this one was just being lazy but would come soon.

'Mrs Lomax is a strong lady. There's no need for concern.'

For the past hour Geraldine had stayed in the room with Lydia while an inebriated Roland worked his way through the decanter of brandy. Tom's cigarette case was empty. His throat was raw with tobacco smoke.

'Not long now, Lomass,' Roland slurred.

Tom's head was fuzzy with drink and worry. He no longer knew what to do. Should he demand a doctor to attend his wife? He had a sudden desire for Harold and Esmie to be there with him. Only they could give him the reassurance he craved. They would not be fobbing him off with platitudes and treating him like a petulant child. They would be telling him exactly what was going on – and Esmie would be a soothing, encouraging presence for Lydia – not like the thin-faced Nurse Jones whom he could hear shouting at his exhausted wife to push, push.

All at once, there was a prolonged scream from the far bedroom. Tom's blood froze in his veins. He started for the door. A dozing Roland was roused by the cry.

'What— What?' he asked, sitting up groggily.

Abruptly, all went quiet. Tom stopped. His heart was hammering so hard that he thought it would burst out of him. He could hear nothing. Bile rose in his throat.

'Lydia?' His voice sounded a ragged whisper. *Please make a noise; let me know you're alive.* He could hear his own breathing; it sounded like he was running uphill.

Just then, he heard it. The tremulous cry of a baby. His heart missed a beat. He strained to hear, not trusting what he'd heard. It came again, louder this time.

Roland said. 'At last, Lomax.'

Tom lurched forward and clattered into the shadowed interior. The passageway was dimly lit by a kerosene lamp hanging overhead. He stood outside the closed bedroom door, breathing hard, his hand hovering over the handle. He could hear women's voices; the nurse being brusque, Geraldine's excited. The baby was bleating but he couldn't hear Lydia. Tom stood in indecision for several moments more, then threw open the door and barged in. It smelt sickly sweet, a stifling aroma of blood, sweat and long hours of exertion.

'Lydia?' he cried in concern.

'Mr Lomax!' the nurse cried.

'You can't be in here,' Geraldine gasped.

Tom ignored them both, rushing to the bedside and peering down at his wife. Her hair was stuck to her temples. Her eyes were closed.

'Lydia!' he shouted.

Suddenly her lids fluttered open. She stared at him in alarm, then her confusion vanished.

'Tom,' she said. She sounded relieved but looked utterly spent.

'My darling.' He took her limp, damp hand and pressed it to his lips. He gripped her warm fingers, proof that she was alive. His eyes prickled.

'Come now, Mr Lomax,' chivvied the nurse. 'Out of the lady's bedroom. Your wife needs to rest.'

Lydia had already closed her eyes again. Tom stood up straight, his legs still wobbly with relief. As he turned, the young ayah stepped forward and held a cloth bundle towards him. For a moment he was nonplussed. Then he saw the tiny crinkled face in the folds. Shock went through him. He was too overcome to move.

'You have a baby boy,' said Geraldine, looking pleased. 'Isn't that marvellous? I'll carry him outside if you like, so you can show him off to Roland.'

She stepped in front of the ayah but Tom reached out quickly. 'No, let me.'

The young nanny smiled up at him as she carefully pressed the swaddled baby into his arms. As Tom felt the weight of him – heavier than he'd expected – he felt a surge of possessive love. He had a son; a living, breathing baby in his arms. The newborn stared myopically as if searching for him in the lamplight. Tom was shaking so much he feared he might drop him. He held him closer and tentatively kissed his pinkish forehead. He smelt of the womb. The baby's mewling subsided.

'Lydia,' he said, turning back towards the bed with his precious bundle. 'We have a son.' As he said the words aloud, his throat constricted.

Lydia gave out a soft groan of acknowledgement but was too tired to open her eyes. Geraldine put a hand on his back and steered him away.

'Let's leave her be. You can have a celebratory nightcap with Roland.'

Tom, heart bursting with pride, returned to the veranda clutching his son. He stood in the night air, grinning foolishly.

'Lomax!' Roland cried, getting to his feet.

'Tell him the good news,' said Geraldine.

'I have a . . .'

All at once, Tom's chest and throat went tight. He couldn't get the words out. His eyes flooded with tears. He gripped the baby harder, clenching his teeth together to stop himself breaking down in front of the Hopkirks. But he couldn't control the emotion rising inside. It was just as he had experienced it when Lydia had first told him he was to be a father. Relief and joy. And pain.

Tom sank into a chair. Still clutching the infant, he bent over him and let out a howl. He wept and shook while the Hopkirks made futile attempts to chivvy him to stop.

Eventually Geraldine turned to the ayah. 'Take the baby from Lomax Sahib, will you? Give him a wipe down and put him in his cradle. There's a good girl.'

Tom allowed the ayah to prise his son from his arms. A moment later, Roland was thrusting a large whisky into his hand instead.

'Cheers, to you and baby Lomax! What's he to be called?'

'Andrew,' Tom said hoarsely as he wiped his eyes with his sleeve, mortified at his loss of control in front of Lydia's friends. Lydia would be very embarrassed when she heard about it – and he didn't doubt that Geraldine would tell her. By tomorrow, the whole of Murree would know about the former captain of the Peshawar Rifles who had wept like a girl over the birth of his first child.

Tom took a gulp of whisky. Except it wasn't his first. The image of the forlorn infant grave in Peshawar was seared on his mind. He had buried all thought of his dead baby daughter until Lydia's pregnancy, almost convincing himself that she had never existed. He'd told himself it no longer gave him pain to think of her – how could he grieve for a baby he had never held in his arms? She had been a slight weight in a tiny coffin.

But holding his new son, Tom's sense of loss for Mary's daughter – *his* daughter – had erupted inside again. His euphoria at the arrival of his son was mixed with the return of grief for baby Amelia.

Tom took another long slurp of his drink to try and staunch the pain.

Chapter 29

Taha, July

Esmie had never known heat like it. The sun beat down relentlessly, day after day. It hung overhead, a ball of fire in a dazzling sky, burning the lawns of the cantonment yellow and sending the glass thermometer soaring to over 100 degrees. By breakfast time, the bungalow was already too hot. The punkah-wallah's best attempts to pull on the large cloth fan merely wafted around the hot stifling air.

Harold said it was the hottest summer he had ever experienced in India. There was an outbreak of typhoid fever. Esmie was quick to spot the symptoms, having seen it rage through the armies in central Europe. She worked long hours on the isolation ward at the hospital. Remembering the lessons taught by Dr Inglis, she was strict on cleanliness and encouraged recovery with a soft diet of rice with curds, stewed apple and custard.

The fierce heat took its toll in the barracks too. After long months of fighting on the Frontier, the soldiers billeted in Taha were still being sent out on manoeuvres under the broiling sun.

The hospital filled up with men suffering from heat exhaustion; cramps, vomiting and severe headaches, their skin red and burning to the touch. Esmie and the orderlies fought to bring down their temperature, wrapping them in damp sheets and giving them fluids. But some were already delirious and lapsed into comas. By the end of July, ten men had died of heatstroke.

Harold took on the grim task of writing to their families, trying to convey some words of comfort about the bravery of their sons or husbands. Esmie, upset by such deaths, railed against the futility. As he sat at his desk late one evening, sweat dripping off his brow, Esmie let out her frustration.

'They shouldn't be sending the men out in such conditions. Even in the shade it's like an oven. They're being overexerted – and they're not drinking enough. By the time they get to us it's too late.'

Harold, sitting at his desk, looked up with tired eyes. 'They're soldiers doing their duty. It's not for us to interfere in army strategy.'

Esmie's eyes stung. 'But it's such a criminal waste of life. Imagine being a parent and hearing that your boy has died of sunstroke.'

Harold gave her a long sorrowful look. 'Esmie, whether they die on the battlefield or in the barracks, the grief will be just as acute.'

Esmie was shame-faced at his gentle rebuke. She had no right to harangue him. He was only trying to bring solace to the bereaved. Life was tough on the Frontier and was just as likely to be snatched away by disease or accident as through combat.

'I'm sorry, Harold,' Esmie said, her anger deflating. 'I know you're doing your best.'

She went out onto the veranda, hoping for a lick of breeze. The night sky pulsed with stars and the garden throbbed with the sound of insects. She envied the servants who lay out on the veranda at night and slept in the open. Karo, who had recently started working for her in the house, had chosen to bed down with Gabina on a curtained-off stretch of veranda leading to Esmie's room.

Esmie's solitary bedroom was like a hot tomb. She would go to bed late and get up before dawn to walk in the garden before the brief coolness evaporated with the rising sun. For the few hours of broken sleep, she would lie on top of the bedcovers, sweating under the mosquito net and fantasising about swimming in Loch Vaullay.

Esmie sat down and by the light of a kerosene lamp, she pulled out Lydia's latest letter that had come two days ago and reread it.

> '. . . *I'm back into the summer dresses I was wearing last year – what a joy it is that they fit me again! I still have a bit of a tummy but I've started playing tennis again so things are firming up nicely. Murree is absolutely jam-packed with visitors now. I hear it's been horribly hot on the plains. We have 'heaven-born' all the way from Delhi staying as well as many of the regiments. Did I tell you that Dickie's turned up on leave here? He's full of stories about the fighting around Razmak. I'm glad to hear it's all much safer now – I do worry about you so – being stuck down there with all those Pathans.*
>
> *When are you coming to stay? You promised you would come after the baby was born. Andrew is two months old already! You better come soon or we'll be packing him off to boarding school before you've had time to meet him.*
>
> *People say he's looking more like Tom with every passing day. I can't really see it. I suppose he has dark hair but his face is round and plump. Most of the time he either dribbles or cries. All the women pretend he's sweet but I've always thought babies are boring and having my own hasn't changed my opinion much. I wouldn't dare say so to Tom. He is completely besotted and comes up every four or five days to see us. I've told him he's spending far too much on fuel – and one of these days that old wreck of a motor car is going to fall to pieces on the mountain roads. But he won't be told.*

Anyway, when you come, I won't make you stay at home for hours cooing over Andrew. Ayah is very good with him and sees to all his needs. We'll be able to go out and about having fun. They say the monsoon is late this year but we've had a few thunderstorms which clear the air. It's beautifully fresh here and going for picnics is a joy.

You and Harold must come while I'm still here. Or come by yourself. Darling Esmie, I'm longing to see you.

Much love to you both,

Your best friend,

Lydia xx

P.S. the blanket you sent the baby is very useful already. When it's rained the evenings can be quite cool. He looks very snug in it, so thank you.

Esmie sat back, fanning herself with the letter. She was glad that her gift was proving practical. She and Karo had spent hours embroidering the soft wool blanket with birds, animals and Andrew's initials, all done in brightly coloured threads. But, oh, to experience the cool of evening again! She shut her eyes and tried to imagine the forested mountains and the dark shaded verandas of Murree. All she could feel was the prickly heat of her body in her sweat-soaked dress.

'That was a long sigh.'

She opened her eyes to see Harold standing over her. 'Sorry. I was just reading Lydia's letter again.'

'So I see.' Harold sat down. 'You must go and visit her. I know you're longing to see Lydia and Tom and the baby.'

Esmie felt fresh perspiration on her brow. Why had he mentioned Tom too? Did her husband have any inkling about her feelings for his best friend? She had redoubled her efforts to rid her mind of him these past seven months – or at least to try and think of him dispassionately. Since the news of Andrew's birth, she had found it easier to think of

Tom and Lydia bound together as a close-knit family. Lydia's latest letter might not describe domestic bliss but there was no doubt that Tom was a doting father. The only hesitation she felt in rushing to see the new baby was that she might have to cope with her strong feelings for Tom again.

'I can't go when there is so much to do at the hospital,' Esmie replied.

'We can manage. There are no new fever cases.' He gave her a look of concern. 'Besides, you are working yourself too hard. I worry about your own health in this infernal heat. The last thing I want is for you to collapse with exhaustion.'

Esmie gave him a quizzical look. 'Me collapse? What about my overworked husband?'

He smiled. 'I'm far more used to this climate than you, my dear.'

Esmie pondered the situation. 'Perhaps in August. I really want to see Andrew. But I don't want to leave you here.'

'Don't worry about me, dearest.' Harold yawned and stood up. 'I'll leave it up to you to decide. But be assured that you go with my blessing.'

Once the subject had been raised, Esmie could think of nothing else. Daily she craved the relief of sweet mountain air and rain on her face. Taha had become a fiery prison. It sapped all her energy. She wrote to Lydia accepting her invitation to stay at Linnet Cottage – even the name conjured up shade and mild weather – and made arrangements to travel.

Harold discovered that Brigadier McCabe was going to Rawalpindi in mid-August so asked him to accompany Esmie as far as the town. As the house in Buchanan Road had been shut up for the summer, Esmie would be staying at the hotel. From there, Tom would drive her up to Murree.

Esmie could hardly contain her excitement. Loath as she was to leave Karo and Gabina, or Harold and her mission friends, she would not miss the debilitating, relentless heat. By September the worst of the hot season would be over. She would return refreshed to her work and life at the Frontier.

The day came for departure. She ate an early breakfast of tea and toast with Harold as the call to prayer rang out across the old town. McCabe's driver would be coming for her in an hour. Gabina tottered out of the shadows and put her hands up to Esmie. She lifted the girl onto her knee and fed her a piece of toast. Gabina grinned, showing her new front teeth, and then munched. Karo hovered anxiously nearby ready to snatch her away if she misbehaved.

'She's all right here,' Esmie said. 'We're just having a last cuddle because I'm going to miss this wee lassie.'

Gabina waved her half-chewed toast and babbled happily. Esmie kissed her head of dark curls. She looked across at Harold and saw his eyes glinting.

Did he sometimes wonder, as she still did, how much a child would enrich their lives? Or was he thankful for Gabina, who filled the empty space in his wife's heart?

'We're going to miss you too,' Harold said quietly.

Esmie felt a pang of affection for him. 'And I, you.' She smiled. 'But it won't be for long. So take very good care of yourselves while I'm away, won't you?'

Esmie was touched by the greeting she received at the Raj Hotel the evening she arrived in Rawalpindi. Jimmy was looking out for her, ready to carry her case, and no sooner was she stepping through the doorway than Stella was rushing towards her with arms wide and hugging her around the waist. For the first time it occurred to Esmie that Tom's daughter, had she lived, would have been close to Stella in age. She wondered if Tom ever pondered that too and whether that was why he was so fond of the Dubois girl.

'Hello, Stella!' Esmie hugged her back. 'How's my favourite girl in all the world?'

'I thought Gabina was your favourite?' Stella asked, grinning up at her.

'She's my favourite baby,' Esmie said, laughing.

Stella gasped. 'You can't say that. Baby Andrew must be your favourite now.'

'Of course,' Esmie agreed. 'Have you seen him yet?'

'No,' Stella admitted. 'But Mr Lomax had a photo taken and I've seen that. It's on the mantelpiece in the sitting room. Shall I show you?'

Before Esmie could answer, Charlie came hurrying forward and greeted her with a bow. 'Good evening, Mrs Guthrie. I hope you had a good journey? Jimmy will take your case upstairs to your old room.'

Within seconds, she was being surrounded by residents shaking her hand and welcoming her in. After the heat of outdoors, the dim high-ceilinged hallway with its whirring overhead fans was blissfully cool.

'How was the drive from Taha?' asked Ansom.

'Military escort, we hear?' said Fritwell, twiddling his moustache. 'They know how to look after a VIP like Mrs Guthrie.'

'Quite right,' said Mrs Shankley, patting her arm, though Esmie was sure she hadn't heard a word.

'It's lovely to see you all again.' Esmie smiled. 'Where's the Baroness?'

'She's spending the summer in Kashmir,' explained Ansom. 'Always goes to a houseboat there. Belonged to some prince she knew. Can't cope with the heat.'

Esmie said, 'I can sympathise with her on that but I'm sorry to miss her.'

'Esmie!' Tom's voice from the stairs made her spin round, heart thumping. 'I wondered who could be making such a stir among the guests.'

She laughed, licking her dry lips. He jumped down the stairs two at a time and arrived in front of her, smiling. She leaned towards him, anticipating a kiss on the cheek but instead he took her hand and squeezed it.

'I've been doing tedious paperwork so I'm glad of the diversion,' he said, letting go his hold and thrusting his hands in his pockets. 'Once you've settled in, would you like a sherry before dinner? Then you can tell us all about your journey. And Harold – how is he? It was good of him to spare you but I'm very sorry he hasn't come too.'

'He's sorry not to see you as well,' said Esmie. 'He's working as hard as ever but seems to thrive on it.'

'Good, good.' Tom smiled and clinked the coins in his pocket.

She gave him a quizzical look. He seemed on edge, falsely hearty. She hoped she wasn't making him uncomfortable by being there. It suddenly occurred to her that, unlike Lydia, he might be reluctant to have her visit. Perhaps he was still remorseful at being too affectionate towards her the previous winter.

So, later, joining Tom and the residents in the hallway, she accepted a sherry and kept the conversation light, asking after Lydia and Andrew and then turning to chat to the others.

Tired from the long, dusty drive, Esmie didn't linger after dinner.

Tom said, 'We'll make an early start in the morning.'

She said her goodnights and retired upstairs.

When Esmie came down for breakfast at seven o'clock, Tom had already eaten and was smoking in the courtyard. The air was humid and thundery.

He ground out his cigarette and gave her a tight smile. 'Hope you slept well?'

'Better than for weeks,' she said. 'Taha's an inferno compared to here.'

Tom nodded. 'It's better here now the monsoon's arrived. More rain's on its way so we'll get going as soon as you've had chota hazri.'

An hour later, Esmie was saying goodbye to Stella and her friends at the hotel and climbing into the car beside Tom. Bijal sat in the cramped back seat with her luggage and provisions for the journey. As they trundled out of Rawalpindi along the Murree road and crossed the Sohan River, Esmie couldn't help thinking of the drive she had taken with Tom the previous December and wondered if he did too.

They spoke little – perhaps he felt inhibited by Bijal sitting close behind – or maybe it was having her next to him that made him unusually reticent. She spent the time gazing around at the emerald-green fields and pools of water that had appeared since the monsoon. It was such a relief after the arid, rocky landscape around Taha.

Unnerved by the lack of conversation, Esmie began to talk about Harold and their work in Taha, her sadness over the patients they had lost to fever and heatstroke and how little Gabina kept their spirits up with her sunny nature.

'It must be like that with Andrew,' Esmie said. 'A ray of sunshine in your lives.'

He flashed her a smile. 'Yes, it is. It's hard to believe there was a time when the wee lad wasn't here. I wish I could spend all my time in Murree but I suppose I'll just have to be patient and wait until Lydia brings him back to Pindi at the end of the monsoon.'

'I can't wait to meet him,' said Esmie. 'Tell me about him.'

Tom became animated. 'He has a lot of dark hair and amazingly long fingers – a very strong grip. He wraps his fist around my thumb and won't let go. He pulls funny expressions – sometimes he looks like a grumpy old man – and then he gives this huge smile and shows all his gums and I melt like butter.' He laughed. 'Geraldine says he looks like me but Lydia can't see it.'

Esmie felt a wave of tenderness towards him. After the terrible losses he'd had to endure, Tom was finding delight in his new son. He deserved it and she was glad for him.

'I bet your father is pleased to have a grandson and heir for The Anchorage too,' she said.

Tom gave a grunt. 'The old man sent a photograph of himself in uniform and told me to hang it in the nursery so that one day Andrew might be inspired to join the Rifles and redeem the family name.' He flashed her a wry look. 'No money has been forthcoming though. I'm not the least bit surprised but Lydia was hoping that her father-in-law would have been less miserly. She even took off the back of the picture frame thinking he might have hidden some bank notes for Andrew.'

Esmie gave a twitch of a smile. 'Maybe Andrew will inherit all the colonel's tin soldiers.'

Tom huffed in amusement and the subject was dropped.

As they left the plain and began to climb into the wooded foothills, the sky darkened and the wind whipped up in minutes, making the trees sway. Tom looked concerned.

'I think we'd better stop at the next dak bungalow – there's one belonging to the forest service in a couple of miles. We can have a second breakfast there.'

As they drove on, lightning streaked the sky and thunder rolled around the hills, the storm sounding nearer by the minute. When they drew up outside the squat bungalow, set back from the road, Esmie felt the first fat drops of rain. The sky overhead was black. By the time they were hurrying up the path, the rain was coming on hard. Tom took her by the arm and shouted, 'Run!'

Bijal ran behind them with the basket of provisions, calling for the chowkidar. An elderly man appeared from the house, struggling to put up an umbrella in the downpour. He held it ineffectually over Esmie and guided her up the steps. Under the shelter of the veranda, Esmie stood panting and laughing, her dress and shoes soaked. She pulled off her sunhat and shook the rain from her hair.

'I've been dreaming of this for months!' she cried. She caught Tom's look of surprise and blushed. 'The rain, I mean. It's wonderful. I never thought I'd miss it so much.'

Amusement flashed across his face. 'Yes, we Scots never appreciate our climate until we've experienced a hot season in India.'

He turned away to ask the chowkidar who was in residence and would they mind providing towels and brewing some tea. The old man explained that there was no one using the bungalow – the forester was in camp – but he would be happy to provide towels and tea. Tom sent Bijal with him to help and he quickly returned with towels and blankets. Esmie was shown into a musty-smelling bedroom where she changed out of her damp dress and wrapped a towel around her underclothes and then a blanket on top, securing it over her shoulders in the way she'd seen the Waziris do.

Padding back out to the veranda barefoot, she caught her breath at the sight of Tom, stripped to the waist and with a cigarette smouldering between his lips, rubbing his hair with a towel. On seeing her, he stopped. They both stared. Esmie's heart began to pound. She was reminded of the time they had swum together at the cove below The Anchorage; he was as leanly muscled as she'd remembered and the jagged scar on his left shoulder still noticeable. She was acutely aware of him looking at her bare legs and feet. The rain thundered on the iron roof and battered the garden below.

Esmie, trying to break the feeling of intimacy, raised her voice above the noise. 'Don't tell Geraldine about me dressing as a Pathan. She'll need smelling salts.'

He gave a distracted smile. Esmie moved to the back of the veranda and sat down, trembling. Tom turned away, dispensing with the towel. He flicked his cigarette into the storm and pulled on a coarse cotton shirt that looked as if it belonged to the chowkidar. She thought she had never seen him more handsome than in this slightly rumpled state wearing Indian cotton with his hair dishevelled.

Bijal and the old servant returned, carrying trays of tea and food. Esmie busied herself helping pour the tea, acutely aware of Tom lowering himself into the cane chair next to hers. She wrapped her hands around the warm cup to stop them shaking and sipped at the steaming tea.

For the next twenty minutes, Esmie and Tom sat, eating and drinking, hardly able to converse because of the noise of the downpour. Tom smoked and walked restlessly to the veranda steps, peering out as if willing the storm to pass.

Esmie knew how keen he was to get to Murree and his son. This delay must be a huge frustration to him. But she thought there was something else bothering him. Since meeting him again the previous day, Tom had seemed preoccupied and a little tense. She had never known him this stuck for words; he had always been able to make easy conversation. Perhaps he felt awkward to be caught in the storm with her; yet Esmie thought he was troubled by more than that.

Gradually the pounding on the roof lessened and then abruptly the rain stopped and the clouds broke. Sun streamed through the trees and steam rose from the sodden garden. Esmie went to fetch her dress and returned to hang it over the veranda railing.

'It shouldn't take too long to dry out – sun feels hot again.'

Tom, leaning on the veranda, shot her a look – was it one of irritation?

Esmie added quickly, 'Or I could change into another dress if Bijal brings my case in from the car. I don't want to hold you up.'

Tom shook his head. 'We can linger another half an hour. Allow the roads to dry out a bit too.'

Esmie sat down again. Bijal had refreshed the teapot, so she poured out another cup for them both. After a moment of hesitation, Tom stubbed out his cigarette and joined her. The quiet seemed accentuated following the noise of the storm. Water dripped from the roof and the trees; a bird cooed. All was peaceful.

Esmie eyed Tom in profile as he stared beyond the bungalow, his face rigid. His mind seemed far away.

'A penny for your thoughts?' she said quietly.

Tom started. He glanced at her and then away again. 'Sorry. I'm not being very good company. I'm just anxious to get to Murree.'

She saw a muscle working in his jaw and waited for him to say more. When he didn't, she asked, 'Is there something else troubling you, Tom?'

His look was wary. 'Why do you say that?'

'You seem faraway – not your usual self.'

He gave her a bleak smile. 'You're off duty, Nurse McBride. You don't need to worry about my mental health.'

She felt a strange tightening in her chest at his use of her maiden name. Had he realised he'd done so or was he thinking back to a time when they had both been unmarried?

'I'm never off duty for friends,' she said, with a wry smile. 'Talk about it if you want to.'

He sat back and sighed. Esmie waited. The old wooden veranda creaked in the warming sun.

In a low voice Tom said, 'Dickie Mason is in Murree.' When Esmie didn't say anything, he gave her a sharp look. 'You knew, didn't you?'

Esmie reddened. 'Lydia did mention he was on leave from Razmak.'

His expression hardened. 'I bet she did.'

'But she wrote about lots of visitors,' she replied. 'Dickie was just one of them.'

'She's seeing a lot of him again. Every time I go up there he seems to be around – playing tennis or having picnics. I wish I'd never introduced them.'

Esmie's stomach tensed; it was she who'd first suggested Dickie get in touch with the Lomaxes. But, gallantly, Tom wasn't blaming her. She was dismayed to hear that Lydia had taken up again with the young lieutenant but she couldn't believe it was serious.

Esmie defended her friend. 'You know how sociable Lydia is. She likes having attention paid to her. She's just enjoying hill station life – especially after the ordeal of a difficult birth.'

Tom ran a hand through his untidy hair. 'I suppose that's fair. It's just that I worry Lydia might . . .'

Esmie saw his brow furrow. 'Might what?'

'Go off with Mason and take Andrew with her.'

Esmie gaped at Tom. He couldn't really believe Lydia capable of that? But she saw from his agonised expression that he did.

'Oh, Tom,' she exclaimed. 'Lydia's not going to do that! She loves you too much. Why would she throw away all that she has with you for a junior officer who's stationed at the Frontier? It's unthinkable.'

His eyes looked haunted. 'She's not as enamoured of me as you think and Dickie's been promoted to captain during the recent campaign so he's not so junior.' He clenched his teeth and then added, 'But what I do know is that I couldn't live without my son.'

Esmie had a rush of pity. She knew why he felt that way.

'Has she given you any indication that she's planning such a thing?'

'No,' Tom admitted. 'But this thing with Mason . . .'

'I'm sure it means nothing,' Esmie tried to assure him.

Tom let go another long sigh. 'Sorry, Esmie. I have no right to burden you with my jealous suspicions. You're too easy to talk to.'

'I understand how precious Andrew is to you,' she said gently.

He gave her a harrowed look and shook his head. 'No, Esmie, you couldn't possibly.'

Hesitating for only a moment, Esmie put a hand on his arm. 'Tom, I want to tell you something. When Harold and I were in Peshawar we found Mary's grave in the cemetery.' Tom looked at her, stunned. Esmie ploughed on quickly. 'And we saw Amelia's grave next to it. We know you lost a daughter, Tom. I'm so very, very sorry. Harold had no idea Mary had died in childbirth.'

She saw him struggling to keep his emotions in check. 'I told no one – I couldn't speak of it.'

'I can understand that,' said Esmie. 'And I understand why Andrew is so special and how you must fear losing him.'

Tom's eyes welled with tears. She saw him swallowing hard.

Softly, she continued. 'We went back the next day and laid flowers – to show our respect – on Mary's grave and Amelia's. The inscriptions were beautiful. Such a peaceful place of rest too.'

Tom gave a deep groan. Suddenly he was reaching out to her, burying his head in her lap like a small boy and letting out a sob. Esmie's breath stopped. She was taken aback by the gesture and yet full of tenderness towards him. His grief was still palpable.

As he gripped her, she stroked his damp hair and murmured. 'It must have been terrible carrying the burden of that secret all this time – not even sharing it with your closest friend. I wanted to write and tell you we'd found out and laid flowers so you would know you didn't grieve alone. But Harold thought we shouldn't intrude and that you would have told him if you'd wanted him to know.'

Tom pulled away. He rubbed brusquely at his reddened eyes. 'Sorry.'

'Don't be,' she replied.

He stood up and went to the railing. She could see his shoulders tensing as he fought to bring his emotions back under control. He pulled out a cigarette and lit it. Esmie waited for him to take a couple of drags and then went to stand beside him. She was hot now in the blanket. She could still feel the imprint of where his head had lain against her thighs.

'You must think me a real no-hoper,' he said. 'Like one of your shell shock patients.'

'My patients aren't no-hopers,' she said.

He stared out at the view of the distant plain far below. She thought he would say something else flippant to hide his feelings and make light of what had just happened. But he surprised her.

Quietly he said, 'The only person who really knew about Amelia was a nurse who looked after her at the hospital. She was born two months too early and couldn't have survived. We hadn't told anyone Mary was expecting – she didn't want to jinx things by telling people before the baby came. She hadn't written to her parents either. I didn't get back to Peshawar until a week after the baby died – the message about Mary didn't reach me for days – we were cut off in the snow. I had to register the deaths and I had the gravestones done by a stonemason in Rawalpindi. Then I tried not to think about either of them.'

Tom took a long pull on his cigarette and inhaled deeply. Esmie, feeling he had more to say, kept silent. He ground out the cigarette and grasped the rail.

'I'd almost convinced myself that there'd never been a baby. It was Mary I grieved for – Mary that I missed. But then the War came and I was sent to Mesopotamia. There was this siege. We broke through. I saw this woman crying . . . her baby wrapped in a blood-stained blanket. After that I couldn't get the thought out of my head that the dead baby was Amelia.'

Esmie could see from his eyes he was reliving the horror. She put a hand over one of his.

'Oh, Tom, how terrible.'

She could see him gritting his teeth as he struggled to tell her more. 'That's when I knew I wasn't cut out to be a soldier. I was a mess. I started to disobey orders – should have been cashiered after a court-martial. It was thanks to Harold intervening that I wasn't. Saved me from disgrace – though some in the regiment never forgave me. Not that I cared for their opinion – all my close comrades were dead by then.'

Abruptly he stopped. He looked at Esmie intently. 'I'm telling you this in complete confidence. I don't want Lydia to know any of this. I don't want to give her any excuse to leave me and take Andrew. If she knew how weak I'd been . . .'

'Of course I won't tell her,' said Esmie. 'I won't tell anyone – not even Harold, if you don't want me to.'

Tom looked relieved. 'Harold guessed there was something that made me act the way I did – but he never asked me. I've always been grateful that he stood by me without question.'

Esmie had been about to ask him what he had done to risk a court martial – it must have been a grave offence – but this stopped her. He didn't want to tell her. He obviously thought he had said too much already.

'I'm glad you've spoken about Amelia,' Esmie said, 'and you can trust me to keep your confidence. I've seen what war does to men – it can push them beyond endurance – and I would never judge you. But, Tom, I don't think you're a weak man – far from it. Bravery comes in different forms and it must have taken great courage to tell me what you just have.'

Tom regarded her with keen blue eyes. To Esmie they seemed full of gratitude and warmth. For an instant, he squeezed her hand. 'Thank you, Esmie.'

She had never felt closer to him than in that moment. The feeling went much deeper than the physical attraction she had always experienced when in his presence. It made her heart swell with a fierce love that made her joyful and desolate at the same time.

Then he disengaged their hands and stood back. For a long time, as they gazed out at the rain-soaked view, neither of them spoke. Eventually, Tom cleared his throat.

'Perhaps you should get out of your Pathan disguise and put your dress back on.' His mouth twitched in a smile. 'Don't want to alarm the memsahibs of Murree.'

She smiled and nodded, not trusting herself to speak and betray her heightened emotion. Picking up her half-dried dress, Esmie retreated into the bungalow to change. Her heart was full. She was touched by the way Tom had opened up to her about his innermost thoughts and fears. She ached for him and the emotional scars he carried. She had wanted to wrap her arms about him and comfort him but knew that if she had it might have led to an outpouring of her own about how much she loved him.

The brutal truth was that she could only ever be a friend to Tom. The knowledge weighed heavily on her heart. Yet she would help him if she could, and if that meant talking to Lydia about not encouraging Dickie then she would try and do that.

Ten minutes later, Esmie was resuming the journey with Tom and Bijal. She waved at the hospitable chowkidar as the car splashed through puddles and birds flew up at the sound of the engine revving. Tom turned the car on to the mountain road and sped towards Murree.

Chapter 30

Murree

Esmie was entranced by the hill station, a hotchpotch of red-roofed villas and terraced hotels spreading out across the lush forested mountainside like a blossoming creeper. Gardens overflowed with the same blooms Esmie had seen growing in Minnie Templeton's flowerbeds: hollyhocks, gladioli, fuchsia, poppies and sweet pea. The mellow air was filled with the heady scent of pine and roses.

At Linnet Cottage it was almost possible to imagine she was back in Scotland. Beyond the dense ferns and fir trees that fringed the pretty garden, Esmie could see glimpses of shimmering blue mountains wreathed in mist. The cottage, with its latticed windows and green wooden porch smothered in roses, reminded Esmie of the Guthries' home in Ebbsmouth.

Yet she just had to promenade along the Mall to realise she was still very much in India. Cascading down the steep slope below the British cantonment like a pack of spilled cards was the native town, a ramshackle collection of tin roofs and trodden paths. Peering down from the ridge, Esmie could see Indians busily going about their business, while the oily, spicy smells of cooking and woodsmoke wafted up from the bazaar.

It made her think of Karo and Gabina, squatting around an open fire cooking their evening meal, and she realised how much she missed them. What would Karo have made of Murree? She would have delighted in the array of colourful shawls and blankets for sale from itinerant traders – and haggled fiercely on Esmie's behalf. But Esmie had shied away from bringing Karo as her personal servant, knowing how sensitive the young woman was to people seeing her disfigurement. The Waziri preferred to keep close to the bungalow and compound. Besides, Lydia would have balked at Esmie bringing Gabina too; her friend was baffled by her attachment to a native child.

Oh, Lydia! Esmie sighed as she thought about her friend. She had greeted Esmie with a tearful hug and squeals of delight and the first few days had been non-stop activity as Lydia showed off the town. There was never any time to get Lydia by herself as she constantly surrounded herself with other friends. There had been a series of tennis parties, picnics to nearby beauty spots, afternoon teas and dinner parties. The Hopkirks organised much of the socialising; Rawalpindi society had been transplanted to Murree for the hot season.

As Tom had warned her, Dickie Mason was always in attendance. But to Esmie he seemed to be just one of several young officers who courted Lydia's attention. Her friend was thriving on it. Three months after giving birth, she looked as trim and attractive as ever. But there was something manic in the way Lydia had to fill every minute of her waking day with socialising. On the couple of evenings they had dined at home, Esmie had retired to bed early to give Tom time alone with his wife. But through the thin walls she had heard Lydia berating Tom for something and he had eventually lost patience. Esmie had buried her head under the covers in an attempt not to overhear their arguing.

What pained Esmie more than Lydia's flirtatious behaviour was her lack of interest in Andrew. Esmie thought the baby delightful. He was plumply healthy and bright-eyed with a shock of dark hair that stood up in soft tufts. His large blue eyes – the same shape as Lydia's – would fix on Esmie whenever she leaned close.

Esmie loved to pick him up and cuddle him in the crook of her arm or balance him on her knee, supporting his back and head while she chattered nonsense to him. He would jam his fist in his mouth and gurgle back at her. Sometimes, if she tickled him, Andrew would respond with an infectious giggle that made her laugh too.

Tom would insist that Andrew was brought along on the picnics and the outings along the Mall. One afternoon, when Dickie joined them, Esmie tried to get Lydia to walk with Tom.

'You two go ahead and I'll push the pram,' she suggested, taking hold of the large black-hooded perambulator. 'Dickie can help me over the rough stones.'

'Goodness gracious, no!' Lydia cried. 'You mustn't do that. We can't have a cavalry captain being treated like a coolie! And you're not the baby's nursemaid. For heaven's sake, Esmie!'

Surprised by Lydia making such a fuss, Esmie quickly let go.

'That's Ayah's job,' Lydia chided. 'You mustn't put a servant's nose out of joint by interfering with their duties. Andrew is her responsibility.'

As the young ayah took over, Esmie glanced at Tom but he gave the faintest of shrugs and didn't interfere. He seemed nervous of upsetting Lydia. Instead, he took Lydia's arm and walked ahead with her as Esmie had suggested, pointedly ignoring Dickie and leaving him to step in behind with Esmie.

As they strolled down to the Mall, the captain was charming and attentive to Esmie, which made her think that Tom was probably worrying needlessly about Dickie's intentions. Nevertheless, she took the opportunity to raise the subject of his posting in Razmak.

'How much longer are you on leave?' she asked him.

'We'll return to the plains in September.'

'And then back to Razmak?'

He nodded. 'Most likely. After all the unrest this past year, they've decided to strengthen the outposts along the Frontier. Razmak will be fortified as a permanent barracks.'

Esmie didn't like to think of Dickie in danger but at least Tom would be reassured to hear that the young officer would be far from Rawalpindi in the coming cold season.

'Let's hope things are a lot more peaceful on the Frontier from now on,' Esmie said.

Dickie pulled a rueful expression. 'Perhaps with the army's might and the zeal of the missionaries, we British will eventually prevail over these wild tribes. But I'm not holding my breath. That's why we soldiers have to make the most of our leave. Murree is a slice of heaven after the desert mountains, don't you think?'

Esmie could only agree. 'It certainly is. I wish Harold could experience it too.'

Dickie gave her a smile of sympathy. 'I'm very grateful to both you and Dr Guthrie for introducing me to the Lomaxes. They're the most hospitable couple I know – more like family than acquaintances – and my fellow officers feel the same. Lydia has told us to treat Linnet Cottage like home.'

Esmie scrutinised his handsome fair face but he seemed without guile. She was sure that Dickie had no dishonourable intentions towards Lydia.

Later, when Dickie had gone and Lydia was dressing for dinner, she managed a snatched moment alone with Tom on the veranda and relayed the conversation she'd had with Dickie.

'I really don't think there's anything to worry about,' assured Esmie. 'He just sees you both as family and Linnet Cottage as home-from-home.'

Tom looked sceptical. 'His attentiveness to Lydia looks more than brotherly to me.'

'Dickie is just as charming to me and Geraldine so I think you're reading more into his flattery than you should. Like any soldier, he's just enjoying his time away from the Frontier.'

Tom brightened. 'I suppose so. And I can't blame him for that – I was just the same at his age.'

'There you are then,' she said with a smile.

'Thank you, Esmie,' he said, his expression softening into a look of relief.

Three days later, Tom returned to Rawalpindi and left Esmie and Lydia to enjoy their time together.

It was early September and Esmie had been in Murree just over a fortnight when, one evening, she finally got the opportunity of a heart-to-heart with Lydia. Their dinner guests were gone – Lydia had drunk a lot of wine – and the two friends were sitting out on the veranda listening to the screeches and rustlings in the dark forest beyond. Lydia was drinking whisky, saying it helped her sleep better. In a far room, Andrew woke up abruptly and began to wail.

After several minutes of listening to the baby howling, Esmie said, 'Shall I go and see if I can help?'

'No,' Lydia said, taking a glug of whisky. 'Let Ayah see to him.'

The crying continued. Esmie itched to go and pick him up and comfort him. Looking at Lydia's clenched face she could tell her friend was irritated by it. After several minutes more, Lydia suddenly got up.

'I can't bear it! It sets my teeth on edge. Why can't she stop him?'

She lurched into the house. Esmie went after her. Before she could stop her, Lydia went storming into the baby's room and started shouting at Andrew's nanny.

'Why can't you keep him quiet? It's your job, for goodness' sake!'

Ayah was clutching Andrew and rocking him vigorously. 'Sorry, Memsahib. I think he's teething.'

'Well, can't you give him something?' Lydia cried.

'Yes, I've rubbed his gums but still it is hurting him.'

Esmie saw the baby was puce-faced and the shouting was making him cry all the harder. She said, 'He looks rather hot. Let's cool him down a bit.' She held out her arms. 'May I?'

Ayah gave Lydia a wary look.

Lydia made a dismissive gesture. 'Do what you want – just make the noise stop,' she snapped and stormed out of the room.

Ayah handed Andrew to Esmie. She pulled the shawl away from his face and asked the nanny to fetch a cool cloth. While she did so, Esmie crooked her little finger and slipped it between the baby's gums. She felt Andrew bite down on it and marvelled at the strength in his jaw. He chewed and cried. Esmie bathed his hot face and neck and spoke to him soothingly. Still he howled. She put him on her shoulder and walked about the room, patting him, the way she'd seen Jeanie do with baby Norrie at Aunt Isobel's cottage in Vaullay. This seemed to pacify him. Gradually the crying subsided. Ayah gave her a smile of relief.

Esmie realised she knew little about the young woman, except that she came from near Rawalpindi.

'Do you have a child of your own?' she asked.

Ayah shook her head. 'No, Memsahib. But I've helped look after my sister's children. I like babies.' She brushed Andrew's cheek. 'He's closing his eyes.'

'Good.' Esmie smiled. 'Shall we risk trying to put him back in the cradle?'

Ayah nodded. 'I will rock him to sleep.'

Carefully, Esmie lowered Andrew into the cradle, which hung from a stand so that it could swing. His eyelids were heavy. As she put him down, his eyes fluttered open in alarm. Esmie kept her hand on his chest. 'There, there, wee man,' she said softly, 'close your eyes and dream a sweet dream.' She began to sing a Highland lullaby – 'Hush-a-by birdie, croon, croon' – it was about the only thing she remembered her mother doing for her when she was a little girl and couldn't get to sleep.

Andrew's eyes closed again. Her chest constricted at the sight of his dark lashes against his pink cheeks and his bud-like mouth parted. He looked so beautiful; vulnerable and trusting. He gave a small juddering sigh and then surrendered to sleep. Esmie touched the ayah on the shoulder and smiled.

'You do a very good job with Andrew. Lomax Mem' appreciates it even if she doesn't always say so.'

Ayah looked disbelieving but nodded her thanks.

Back out on the veranda, Esmie found Lydia sitting on the cane sofa nursing her whisky glass. In the unguarded moment, Lydia looked drawn-faced and weary. Esmie sat down beside her.

'He's asleep,' said Esmie.

'Thank God for that,' Lydia sighed. 'Did you drug him with something?'

'Nothing so drastic. He seems to like having his back patted – and a Highland lullaby. I could teach it to you.'

Lydia grunted. 'No thanks. I don't have the first clue about babies and I'm not that interested.' She downed the rest of her whisky.

'I'm sure motherhood will grow on you,' said Esmie. 'Not everyone feels attached to their baby from the start.'

'How would you know?' Lydia said. 'You haven't been through what I have.'

Esmie flushed. 'No, but I came across many new mothers when I was training in Edinburgh. Some of them were very young and frightened.'

Abruptly, Lydia's face crumpled. 'Sorry, Esmie. That was unkind of me.' She bowed her head. Her voice sounded teary. 'I don't feel the least bit motherly towards him. I don't feel anything very much at all. It's like he's someone else's baby – an intruder that I have to put up with. He just reminds me of how awful the birth was – I never ever want to go through that much pain again. I thought I was going to die. Sometimes I feel actual hatred.'

She looked up, her face streaked with silent tears. 'It's not natural to feel this way, is it?'

Esmie leaned over and put an arm around her shoulders. 'Your body's had a shock. It'll take time to adjust. But you're not the only young mother to have such feelings. For some it may come naturally but for others motherhood is something they have to learn – to practise at. Have you spoken to Tom about it?'

Lydia stiffened. 'Tom wouldn't begin to understand. He thinks the sun shines out of that baby. He's not interested in me anymore. He thinks I'm heartless for not spending every minute with the baby. But he has no idea what it's like – what I've been through. He just swans in for a couple of days and then goes back to his blessed hotel. I'm the one with all the responsibility – even though I never wanted a baby.'

Esmie was tempted to tell Lydia how Tom had suffered the loss of his first child; it might make her more tolerant towards him. But she had promised that she would keep his secret. It wasn't hers to tell.

'Things will improve once you're back in Pindi. Buchanan Road will be a proper family home.'

Lydia gave her a despairing look. 'How boringly domestic that sounds. I'm in no hurry to go back to Pindi – I prefer it here. Everyone is set on having a good time.'

Esmie leaned back and eyed her. 'You seem to be spending a lot of time with Dickie Mason.'

Lydia shot her a look. 'What's that supposed to mean?'

'It's an observation.'

'Has Tom been complaining to you? I bet he has.'

'He doesn't have to,' said Esmie. 'I can see how Dickie being constantly around you upsets him. You're not being very fair to Tom.'

Lydia was flustered. 'Why are you sticking up for Tom? You're supposed to be my friend. Can't you see how difficult life is for me being married to a man who cares only for his second-rate hotel? It's not the life he promised me. And I'm so far away from Mummy and Daddy – I miss them terribly. I feel so alone here. That's why I try and make friends with whoever I can. You can't blame me for that.'

'I'm sorry if you're unhappy in India, Lydia,' Esmie said gently. 'You've had a lot of change and upheaval in a short time. But you've only been married just over a year. Give it more time – and maybe a bit more effort.'

'Me make more effort?' Lydia exclaimed. 'What about Tom? He's the one who dragged me out here.'

Esmie held on to her temper. It was Lydia's unhappiness that was making her sound callous. 'All Tom wants is to live happily with you and Andrew.'

'Have you two been talking about me behind my back?' Lydia accused.

Esmie coloured. 'It's obvious what he wants. He hates being down in Pindi away from you both for days at a time.'

'Then he should leave the Duboises to manage the place,' Lydia retorted. 'It's what we pay them for. Tom doesn't have to stay there – he chooses to.'

Esmie gave up trying to reason with her friend or point out that Tom worried about the hotel's finances and her extravagance. Lydia had always been a little self-centred and didn't take kindly to criticism. But in her present frame of mind, Esmie could tell that nothing she said would get Lydia to see things from Tom's point of view.

Lydia muttered, 'I should have married Colin Fleming and all his vineyards.'

'You don't mean that,' Esmie chided.

'I half mean it!'

When Esmie didn't respond, Lydia sighed. 'Do you remember when we used to sit on the swing seat on the balcony at home and chat about school and boys and what we'd do when we grew up?'

'Yes,' Esmie said with a rueful smile.

'Wasn't life so much happier and straightforward then?' Lydia said, briefly resting her head on Esmie's shoulder.

Esmie thought how for much of that time she had been grieving for her beloved father and life had been difficult. She'd been grateful for Lydia's friendship and gregariousness; they'd been the antidote she'd needed to mend her sore heart. She must never forget how much Lydia had stood by her when she'd needed her.

'My holidays at Templeton Hall were some of the happiest times I remember,' Esmie answered.

'Oh, Esmie, I sometimes wish we could wind back the clock and be there again. Before I rushed into marriage and India and all this . . .'

It was the first time she had heard Lydia admit that she might have been partly to blame for her situation and having been too impatient to be married.

'But we're here, sitting on this seat,' Esmie reminded her. 'And I know you're going to make the best of your marriage and of India. Don't let a flirtation with Dickie come between you both.'

Lydia looked at her with eyes swimming with fresh tears. 'It's all right for you to say that. You and Harold love each other. Your marriage is a success.'

Esmie felt leaden. Her friend had no idea how wrong she was – or how much Esmie envied what she had. Yet she was prepared to make the most of her relationship with Harold and life on the North-West Frontier. She didn't expect things to be easy in the way that Lydia did. But it upset her to think that Lydia didn't love Tom. Surely their marriage could be repaired? For Andrew's sake it must be.

'I think you may be suffering from the baby blues,' said Esmie. 'It's not uncommon after birth. Why don't you speak to a doctor? They could prescribe something to give your spirits a lift.'

Lydia looked aghast. 'And risk having people spreading rumours that I'm mad? Certainly not. If the likes of Geraldine saw me going to the doctor's, they'd soon put two and two together.'

Esmie decided not to press the issue; she might mention it to Tom as a way forward. She stood up. 'I'm ready for bed. Come on, you must be too.' She held out her hand and pulled a reluctant Lydia to her feet.

Lydia held on to her for a moment. 'You're the only one I can talk to like this. I would never tell such things to Geraldine or the others. They gossip about me enough as it is. But I know you never would.'

Esmie was struck by how lonely Lydia must be, surrounded by superficial friendships, but with no one to confide in – not even her husband. As they said goodnight and went to their rooms, another thought occurred to Esmie. Perhaps that was what Dickie gave Lydia – a sympathetic manly shoulder to cry on?

Later that week, Esmie made arrangements for her departure. Tom would come and collect her in a week's time, take her back to Rawalpindi and put her on a train to Kohat. By then it would be two weeks since he had last visited. Esmie found it easier not having him around. It made her less tense and Lydia less moody.

Harold had written to say that all was well in Taha and that numbers were easing at the hospital, but that he was missing her and looking forward to her return. Esmie felt a mix of affection and guilt towards her husband. She had spent far too much time agonising over Tom and his problems while Harold worked hard, oblivious to how she felt for his good friend.

Knowing that he would want news of the Tolmies and their mission school, Esmie arranged to have lunch with Augustus and Margaret a couple of days before she was due to leave Murree.

'Do you want to come too?' Esmie asked Lydia.

'Good grief, no!' Lydia pulled a face of mock horror. 'Dickie says the Tolmies are always trying to stop the men from drinking and gambling – and they lie in wait for the officers on their way to the club and drag them off for hymn singing.'

Despite their late-night talk, Lydia had continued to see Dickie daily. Esmie was consoled by the thought that the officer's leave in Murree would also soon be coming to an end. Once he was gone and Lydia was back in Rawalpindi, Esmie hoped that the strained relations between Tom and Lydia would improve.

The day had started brightly but clouds were beginning to mass overhead. Lydia wanted her to order a tonga to take her across to Pindi Point but Esmie decided to walk.

'It's a chance to enjoy the fresh air,' she said. 'I'll be back in the heat and dust soon enough. And I want to do some shopping for presents on the way back.'

'But it'll take you an hour. What if it rains?'

'Then I'll get a tonga on the Mall.'

When she set off, Esmie was pleased to see Lydia in the garden with Andrew. She wasn't playing with the baby but at least she was watching Ayah entertaining the infant with a rattle. Her friend seemed in good spirits and waved her away.

'Be back in time for tea,' Lydia called. 'Geraldine's coming over to say goodbye.'

An hour later, Esmie was walking up the drive to the mission school, perspiring in the sultry atmosphere. She saw young children lined up and waving flags in welcome, their faces eager and full of curiosity. She waved back. Augustus was there to greet her with a young Anglo-Indian teacher, Miss Ratcliffe, who was in charge of the youngest children.

Standing beside them, the teacher led the children in a song. Esmie was touched by their warmth. When they'd finished, they excitedly gathered around her, grinning. Augustus allowed this for a couple of minutes and then told them to follow their teacher inside.

'I thought you might like to see round the school,' he said to Esmie. 'Then we can have lunch. I'm sorry to say that Margaret is not feeling very well. She won't be joining us. But we can eat with the children and staff.'

'I'm sorry to hear that,' said Esmie. 'I was hoping to see her before I go back to Taha.'

'Nothing serious,' Augustus said hastily. 'Just feeling a bit seedy.'

Esmie wondered if she was having a further bout of melancholia. Margaret's mother had died in February and she'd taken her death very hard. According to Harold, the headmaster's wife had not settled back in India after her visit to Wales the previous year.

Esmie was impressed with the school. Most of the pupils were orphaned but the teachers and house parents seemed kind – some were former pupils – and the children appeared happy. Yet she knew from her own experience of losing her parents young that it was possible to put on a cheerful face while internally feeling lost and upset.

But at least the Tolmies' school was providing a safe haven for girls and boys whose parents had died or abandoned them. They would get an education and a helping start in the world. Sitting among the friendly chattering children at lunchtime, Esmie remembered how she had longed for the love and protection of adults – Aunt Isobel, the Templetons and Drummonds – to fill the void left by her dead parents.

After lunch, Esmie asked if she could sit in on one of the classes. Augustus took her along to Miss Ratcliffe's classroom, where six- and seven-year-olds were doing reading and writing. They all stood to attention when the headmaster and Esmie entered.

'I'll come back for you in half an hour,' Augustus said and left.

Esmie, seeing the eager faces of the children, turned to their teacher and asked, 'May I read to one or two of them?'

'Of course,' said Miss Ratcliffe, smiling. She addressed her pupils. 'Now, who is sitting up straight and not fidgeting?'

The children sat bolt upright, several of them raising their hands high in the air.

'Please, miss, please, miss!'

'Choose me, please, miss!'

Their teacher beckoned to two small girls with neat pigtails to come to the front and sit with the visitor. They rushed forward, dragging their chairs beside Esmie while Miss Ratcliffe chose a book. Soon the girls were leaning on Esmie's lap and she was putting her arms about them as she began to read from *Alice's Adventures in Wonderland*, remembering how she used to love her father reading it to her.

It didn't take long before the other children were asking permission to be read to by the Scottish memsahib. Miss Ratcliffe abandoned her lesson and let the children gather round Esmie. They were full of questions. Esmie ended up telling them about Scotland and her home at Vaullay, her time nursing abroad during the War and her escape from Serbia over the mountains.

When Augustus came to fetch her, he found the children sitting at her feet, enthralled. He offered to give her tea but Esmie declined, sensing he was anxious to get back to his house and check on Margaret.

'I'm going to do some shopping on the Mall on the way home,' she said. 'Take some presents back to Taha. I've greatly enjoyed my visit, thank you. And please give my best wishes to Mrs Tolmie – I hope that she is better soon. If she feels up to me visiting in the next day or so, then do let me know.'

On the point of leaving, the rain that had been threatening all day started.

'You can't walk in this – I'll summon a tonga.' Augustus was adamant.

The rain was so heavy that Esmie agreed, asking to be taken straight back to Linnet Cottage. There was little point trying to shop in a monsoon shower. If it cleared quickly and Lydia could be persuaded, there would be plenty of time to push Andrew out in his pram for a walk before afternoon tea.

Esmie arrived back early at the villa and dashed from tonga to veranda as quickly as she could through the pelting rain. She shook her wet skirt and discarded her hat, remembering with a blush how she had done the same at the dak bungalow when she'd sought shelter with Tom. She would be seeing him again in two days' time. Her heart skipped a beat. But she was already steeling herself not to show her excitement at seeing him. Once he had put her on the train to Kohat, Esmie knew she must stay away from Rawalpindi and the Lomaxes – at least until they had overcome this rocky patch in their marriage.

All was quiet at the cottage and the veranda deserted. Esmie wondered if Lydia had gone out for lunch and been marooned by the downpour too. She wouldn't be expecting Esmie back until later. Walking through the house, Esmie decided to check if Ayah was in the baby's room, as it would still be Andrew's nap time. Quietly she tiptoed up the corridor and peered around the half-open door. The cradle and room were empty. Esmie was pleased to see that Lydia must have taken Andrew and his ayah with her on whatever outing she was on.

Esmie decided to change out of her damp dress before tea. As she turned back down the corridor she heard a noise from the next-door bedroom – Lydia and Tom's. She stopped. To her surprise, it was Lydia's voice; an indistinct comment and then a laugh. She was here after all.

'Lydia?' Esmie called out.

The murmuring stopped.

'Lydia, it's me. I'm back early. Margaret wasn't well.' Esmie tapped on the bedroom door. 'Are you resting or can I come in?'

'Wait!' Lydia called out. 'Don't come in. I'll be with you in a minute.'

Esmie, baffled that her friend hadn't called her straight in, replied, 'I'll just go and change – got caught in the rain.'

'Yes, you do that!'

Something made Esmie hesitate, uneasy. She was sure she heard a snort of laughter. Then Lydia was trying to hush someone. Esmie's stomach lurched. Lydia wasn't alone. Oh, please no! Esmie's pulse began to hammer. Don't let it be Dickie! Feeling queasy, Esmie retreated to her room and quickly changed her dress. She brushed out her hair with a shaking hand, hoping against all the odds that she had misheard. For one wild moment, she imagined that Tom had come early to Murree and that they were making up. But Tom would have shouted out a greeting.

Esmie went to wait on the veranda. Lydia must have planned this knowing Esmie would be out for hours. She had obviously sent Ayah out with Andrew and the servants away for an hour or so too. Esmie wished she was anywhere but there. If only it hadn't rained she would be shopping on the Mall. She didn't want to discover evidence of Lydia's affair. The rain was already easing. Esmie gripped the balustrade and swallowed down bile.

'Hello, Mrs Guthrie.'

Esmie turned to see Dickie, hair still a little messy, crossing the veranda. He smiled at her awkwardly. She nodded, unable to bring herself to speak to him. How could she have been so wrong about him? How foolish she felt for having assured Tom that there was nothing but a harmless flirtation between Lydia and the young lieutenant.

'Esmie, darling,' Lydia said brightly, following him out. She was dressed for afternoon tea but her loose hair betrayed the haste to get into her clothes. 'I didn't expect you back so soon.'

'Obviously,' Esmie said.

'My goodness, if looks could kill,' Lydia said with a nervous laugh. 'There's no need to play the head prefect with me.'

Esmie's anger suddenly ignited. 'So, what do you want me to say, Lydia, when I come back to find you in bed with him?' She threw Dickie a withering look.

'Let's all stay calm,' Lydia said. 'I didn't mean to put you in this embarrassing situation. Why don't we just pretend it never happened?'

'But it has happened!' Esmie retorted.

Dickie's fair face reddened. 'I think I better go. I'm sorry if I've caused upset.'

'Are you?' Esmie demanded. 'Because if so, it's not me you should be apologising to. It's Tom you've wronged.'

Dickie looked suddenly stricken. 'Yes . . . Sorry.' He made for the steps.

'Don't go,' Lydia cried, hurrying after him. 'This is my house and you're my guest.' She grabbed onto his arm.

'Sorry,' he said again, disengaging her hold. 'I really should go.'

'Please don't!' She pursued him down the steps. 'Please don't leave me.'

He marched swiftly down the steps and around the side of the house. It was only then that Esmie realised his pony was tied up beside one of the outhouses.

'Dickie!' Lydia shouted after him.

As he mounted his horse and trotted down the path, Lydia went after him, bawling his name. Appalled, Esmie ran after her. By the time she reached her, Lydia was weeping uncontrollably. Esmie had never seen her so distraught. She wrapped her arms around her but Lydia flung her off.

'Get away from me! I hate you!'

'Lydia, don't—'

'I l-love him and you've s-spoilt it all,' she sobbed. 'W-why did you have to interfere? You're supposed to be my friend . . . My *friend*!'

Esmie was dumbstruck by Lydia's outburst. Gone was the sophisticated, assured veneer of a Templeton and in its place was a howling, desperate woman. She hadn't seen Lydia behave like this since they had been adolescent girls and she used to lash out at her older sister Grace for some perceived slight or favouritism.

Esmie's anger turned quickly to concern. 'Lydia, I am your friend but it was a shock finding you with Dickie.'

Lydia, her face furious and tear-streaked, almost spat back, 'You're not my friend. I never want to speak to you again!' She pushed past Esmie and ran unsteadily back into the house.

Esmie stood for several minutes, shaking and trying to calm her breathing. All about her, birds chattered noisily in the trees like gossips. A dog barked from a neighbouring property. She wondered how far the sound of their argument had carried or who might have seen Dickie riding to and from Linnet Cottage, alone.

She felt miserable. Not only had she been caught in the middle of Lydia and Tom's unhappy marriage but she had failed to help either of them. Should she have been firmer with Lydia about keeping Dickie at arm's length or should she have warned Dickie off? Perhaps she should have told Lydia about Tom's baby daughter dying? Why had she dismissed Tom's fears about Lydia's unfaithfulness too readily? Was it because her greatest fear was the Lomaxes' marriage falling apart but her still being tied to Harold? Esmie felt ashamed of such selfish thoughts.

Her insides churning, Esmie returned to the house, wondering whether she should go to Lydia and comfort her. Standing outside Lydia's bedroom door, listening to her friend sobbing wretchedly, Esmie knocked.

'Lydia? Can I come in?'

But the crying didn't stop and Lydia didn't answer. Heavy-hearted, Esmie walked away.

Chapter 31

Esmie sent a chit over to Geraldine's cancelling the invitation to afternoon tea and making up an excuse that Lydia had been taken ill with a tummy upset. In the note, Esmie thanked her for entertaining her during her stay. She made no promise to see her before she left. Esmie couldn't face the thought of having to parry Geraldine's keen questions about Lydia or possible goings on at Linnet Cottage.

Soon afterwards, Ayah returned with Andrew, smiling and oblivious to the drama she had missed. Esmie eagerly plucked Andrew from his pram and gave him a cuddle. She breathed in his baby scent as he grabbed a handful of her hair and pulled in delight. Her eyes smarted with tears. He was the innocent in all this and yet she feared for his future. Kissing his soft cheek, Esmie prayed fervently that Andrew wouldn't be used as a pawn in his parents' wrangling.

Then she thought of Tom and her heart weighed like a stone. If he were to learn that his suspicions about Lydia's affair with Dickie were true, what would he do? He would be unable to bear being separated from Andrew; of that she was certain. How much would he be prepared to turn a blind eye to in order to keep his family together? A great deal, she imagined. Oh, Tom! How she wished she could save him from the pain of knowing. She longed to see him and yet dreaded it. Would it be best if she did what Lydia had wanted and pretend it never happened?

Carrying a burbling Andrew into the house, Esmie thought it probably was.

Lydia didn't come out of her room again until the following day. Esmie tried to have food sent in to her but she had locked her bedroom door. With little appetite and unable to bear dining alone on the veranda, Esmie took her meal into the nursery.

'Do you mind if I eat with you, Ayah?' she asked the young woman.

Ayah looked alarmed but agreed. They sat on durries on the floor and Esmie shared out her plate of fish, potatoes and cabbage. She learnt that the nanny was from an Indian Christian family – Episcopalians – and that her name was Sarah. Her father had worked in the army stables as a syce until he'd been crippled in an accident and so Sarah helped support the family now. She loved her job looking after Andrew.

Esmie helped give Andrew his bottle of milk, Lydia having given up feeding him herself soon after birth. Esmie felt a tug of tenderness as she held the baby in her arms and watched his look of concentration as he glugged the milk. A calm feeling of contentment spread through her. If only Lydia could experience a moment like this, Esmie was sure she would begin to love her son.

That night, Esmie hardly slept. She imagined Lydia lying awake and miserable too. Her crying had stopped but she had stayed locked in her room. As the dawn light crept through the cracks between the shutters, Esmie got up. Hearing Andrew grizzling, she padded along to the nursery and asked Sarah if she could feed the baby. She took Andrew onto the veranda and, wrapping them both in a blanket against the morning chill, she gave him his milk as the sky turned golden over the mountains of Kashmir.

Esmie knew she would never forget this peaceful moment – it was like an unexpected gift – the sunrise and the rose-coloured peaks of snow, the smell of damp earth and pines, the early twittering of birds and the warmth of Andrew's small body pressed against her. She imprinted it all in her mind to remember in the uncertain days ahead.

Lydia emerged from her room in the late morning, dressed smartly and with her hair pinned back and bound in a broad ribbon. Only her pasty face and puffy eyelids betrayed her distress from the previous day. Esmie, playing with Andrew on the veranda, watched her warily.

'How are you feeling?' Esmie asked.

Lydia ignored the question. 'I imagine you've had breakfast. I'll order some coffee. Would you like some?' Before Esmie could answer, Lydia was clapping her hands and issuing commands to her bearer. She skirted Esmie, the baby and Sarah and went to stand on the far side of the veranda. Scrabbling in her handbag, she pulled out cigarettes and a lighter and busied herself lighting up a cigarette.

'Lydia, come and sit down,' Esmie encouraged.

When she didn't, Esmie indicated to Sarah to take Andrew into the garden and then went and joined Lydia at the balustrade.

'Speak to me, Lydia,' Esmie entreated. 'I can't leave with this bad feeling between us.'

Lydia eyed her bleakly. 'Promise me you won't tell Tom what you saw yesterday?'

Esmie tensed. She hated the thought of keeping such a secret or having to lie to Tom but if Lydia was going to try and salvage her marriage then it was for the best.

'I won't talk about what happened, I promise. It's up to you what you tell Tom.'

Lydia's anguished look softened. 'I don't intend saying anything. I'm not going to make life difficult for Dickie.'

'For Dickie?' Esmie exclaimed. 'He's the one who's caused all this upset.'

'No, he isn't. He saw how unhappy I was and tried to comfort me.'

'Some would say take advantage of you,' said Esmie.

Lydia's eyes flashed. 'You still don't understand, do you? This isn't just some hill station summer fling. We love each other. I've been mad about Dickie since that night last year when he took me to the brewery ball – and he adores me.'

Esmie was horrified. 'Oh, Lydia!'

'I knew you wouldn't understand – you're too conventional – too like Harold. Everything has to be so moral and by the book. But some of us have a greater capacity for love – we have too much passion in our hearts just to love one person.'

Ignoring the slight, Esmie tried to comprehend. 'Are you saying that you love both Tom and Dickie at the same time?'

'I suppose I am,' said Lydia, stubbing out the cigarette she had hardly smoked. 'But since seeing Dickie again after the terrible time with the baby – well – I have deeper feelings for him than for Tom.'

Esmie put a hand on Lydia's arm. 'Yet you say you don't want Tom to find out? So you're not going to do anything foolish, are you?'

Lydia pulled her arm away. 'It's easier to stay with Tom, that's all.'

'Oh, Lydia, please don't hurt Tom. If you care anything for him and Andrew then you should give Dickie up.'

'Don't lecture me,' Lydia snapped. 'I can handle my own marriage. Tom doesn't need to know. The only way he'll get hurt is if you tell him.'

Esmie felt leaden at Lydia's cold words. Before she could say anything more, the khidmatgar arrived with coffee. The women sat together in tense silence, drinking and staring out at the garden. Esmie watched the ayah pushing Andrew up and down the neat paths and chattering to him. It pained her that Lydia could even think of jeopardising a life with Tom and Andrew for Dickie. But wasn't she being hypocritical? After all, Esmie also knew what it was like to love two men at the same time. She cared for Harold and yet yearned for Tom. The difference with Lydia was that she, Esmie, would never act on her impulses to satisfy her desire outside of marriage.

With her coffee half-drunk, Lydia announced she was going out and left shortly after in a tonga. She neither invited Esmie along nor told her where she was going. Esmie feared she had gone straight to seek out Dickie in his outlying camp but could do nothing about it. She spent the rest of the day feeling queasy with dread and trying to occupy herself by accompanying Sarah in taking Andrew out in his pram.

She avoided the Mall, where she might bump into Geraldine or others in Lydia's social circle, and went instead to the native bazaar to buy some last-minute presents: a new shaving razor and brush for Harold, a turquoise necklace for Karo and a wooden pull-along dog for Gabina. She was relieved at the thought of leaving Murree and escaping from Lydia's reproachful words and moodiness towards her.

Lydia didn't return until it was almost dark. Esmie, full of worry, had been keeping a look out for her. Lydia gave no explanation as to where she'd been and wouldn't look Esmie in the eye. She smelt of drink.

'I've got a headache,' Lydia complained. 'I can't face dinner. I'm going to bed early. I hope you don't mind?'

Esmie followed her. 'You must have something. Can I bring you a pot of tea? Or a nimbu pani?'

'No, thank you. I just want to be alone.'

In the night, Esmie heard Lydia crying again. She couldn't bear to hear her so unhappy. But when she went along and knocked on her door, hoping to comfort her, Lydia told her to go away. Later, just as Esmie was finally sinking into an uneasy sleep, she was startled awake by Lydia standing by her bedside. She looked pale and ghostly in her nightgown with her blonde hair hanging loose.

'Dickie's leaving.' Her voice sounded drained of emotion. 'He's going on shikar for the rest of his leave. No doubt you'll be pleased.'

Esmie struggled to sit up, befuddled by weariness. 'I think he's doing the right thing.'

Lydia's face looked taut. 'I want you to know that I blame you for his going – for making such a fuss. Affairs happen all the time in hill stations and no one bats an eyelid. But you made Dickie feel terrible and now I won't see him again.'

Esmie heard the desolation in Lydia's voice and knew that saying anything at all would just make things worse between them.

Lydia went to the door. 'I never thought I'd ever feel so resentful towards you, Esmie,' she said. 'It's time you went back to Harold and stopped interfering in other people's lives, don't you think?'

Esmie flushed at the accusation. Without waiting for an answer, Lydia left.

Through the rest of the sleepless night, Esmie's feeling of upset at Lydia's accusing words turned to anger. She was not responsible for Lydia's unhappiness. Lydia was the one who had selfishly embarked on an affair with Dickie without any thought of the damage it might do. Dickie, pricked by conscience at Esmie finding out, might have ended it earlier than he'd planned but Esmie was sure he saw it merely as a summer fling. If he had been as serious about Lydia as she claimed she was about him, Dickie would be standing by her and not escaping on shikar.

By morning, Esmie had her case packed. She'd contemplated hiring a tonga to get herself back to Rawalpindi so she wouldn't have to see any more of Lydia or face Tom. But as dawn broke, she knew such an action would be petty and cowardly. She would not run away. Perhaps Lydia might feel more contrite and they could at least part on speaking terms.

But Lydia took her breakfast in her room and didn't emerge until she heard the sound of Tom's car horn beeping to announce his arrival. Esmie, her stomach in knots, was waiting in the garden with Andrew and Sarah.

Tom caught his breath at the sight of Esmie in the garden, pushing Andrew in the swing he'd made out of a basket and rope for his son. She was pulling exaggerated smiles as the baby swung towards her and he could hear Andrew's delighted giggles. At the sound of the car, she turned and waved in greeting. His chest tightened.

All the way up the mountainside, he'd tried not to think too much about Esmie, and failed. He'd told himself that he'd set off at dawn in case it rained later but he knew he was spurred on by the thought of seeing her again. Passing the dak bungalow where they had sheltered from the storm and he had unburdened his innermost secrets, Tom had tried to suppress his hankering for her. Esmie, bare-legged and wrapped in a blanket, wet tendrils of hair falling across her grey eyes, had stirred passion inside him like no other woman ever had. Ever since she had arrived at the hotel, the previous day, Tom had tried to keep an emotional distance from her. But Esmie had been too perceptive and knew that something dwelled on his mind. Unable to confess to his inner turmoil about being in love with her, he'd told her instead about his fears over losing Andrew.

Tom took a deep breath, climbed out of the car and strode down the garden path. There was no sign of Lydia. Esmie scooped Andrew out of the basket and kissed his forehead.

'Here's Daddy,' she said and handed him over to Tom with a smile.

'Hello, Esmie,' Tom smiled back.

He gave Andrew a noisy kiss on the cheek and then lifted him high in the air. The baby's mouth opened in alarm, then Tom was pulling him back for another kiss and was rewarded with a gummy smile.

He eyed Esmie. 'You're looking well. The Murree air obviously suits you.'

He saw a blush spread to her cheeks. She turned towards the cottage. 'You've made good time. There's still some scrambled egg and toast if you're hungry.'

'Where's Lydia?' he asked.

'Having breakfast in bed.'

'On your last morning?'

She kept walking and didn't answer. As they reached the porch, Lydia appeared on the veranda and called down. 'Darling! You're early, how lovely!' She blew him a kiss. 'Come on up and we'll rustle up fresh tea and toast.'

'Splendid,' Tom answered.

Arriving on the veranda with Andrew still nestled in the crook of his arm, Lydia offered him her lips to be kissed.

'Let Ayah take the baby. You go and freshen up.'

When he returned to the veranda after a wash, he noticed that the women were sitting in silence and thought it odd. With disappointment he saw that Ayah had taken the baby to the nursery.

As he munched toast, Tom asked them about the past fortnight but Lydia waved away his questions.

'Tell us about Pindi. I'm beginning to miss it.'

Encouraged, Tom chatted about the hotel and some new business he was cultivating with the Chota Club on Edwardes Road as well as the Railway Institute. He expected a reproof from Lydia about pandering to the Anglo-Indians but none came. She seemed to be only half-listening. Esmie hardly said a word. She sat with her hands in her lap, her expression guarded. What was going on? He began to feel a growing unease. Had they argued over something?

'So what are the plans for the day?' Tom asked.

Lydia gave him a sharp look. 'You're taking Esmie back to Pindi, darling.'

'Yes, but we don't have to leave until late afternoon. I thought we could have a picnic with Andrew.'

'Tom,' Lydia laughed, 'the baby doesn't know about picnics. Besides, the barometer is indicating it's going to rain later so you better get on the road by lunchtime. Esmie doesn't want to get stuck here and miss her train in the morning.'

Esmie gave a tight smile and nodded. 'I'm ready to go whenever's convenient.'

The tension between the women was palpable.

'Is something the matter?' Tom asked.

'Nothing's the matter, darling,' Lydia replied. 'She's just longing to get back to Harold. Aren't you, Esmie? They've never been apart this long since they were married.'

Tom's stomach clenched at the mention of Harold, ashamed of his lustful thoughts about Esmie.

'Of course,' he agreed. 'We'll go after lunch. That still gives me a couple of hours with Andrew.'

He saw Esmie's look soften and her eyes glisten. She got up. 'I'll just go and finish packing.'

When she'd gone, Tom asked. 'Tell me what's going on between you two. You could cut the atmosphere with a knife.'

'Nothing's going on,' Lydia said, looking all innocence. 'She's just getting a bit tired of Murree.' She dropped her voice. 'To be honest, three weeks of Esmie is enough for me. She's become so earnest since her mission work, don't you think?'

Tom didn't think that at all. He was suddenly suspicious. Could it be that they had argued over Dickie Mason? There was no sign of the captain but it was only mid-morning.

'Have you had a falling-out over something in particular – or someone?'

'Of course not!'

'How is Dickie?' Tom said, watching her intently.

Her eyebrows shot up in surprise. 'Dickie Mason?'

'You know that's who I mean,' said Tom. 'The man who's been your shadow round Murree.'

'I don't know. I think he's gone on shikar.' Lydia gave a disarming laugh. 'Do I detect a little jealousy? Oh, Tom, how sweet!'

Tom was relieved. Perhaps his marriage wasn't in as dangerous a state as he'd thought.

'And, darling,' said Lydia, 'once you've taken Esmie to her train, I hope you'll be able to come back up for the weekend. I don't like being left here by myself so much. I'm tired of Murree.'

Esmie found it hard saying goodbye to Andrew. Sarah was about to take him for his afternoon nap.

'Would you let me put him down?' Esmie asked on impulse.

Sarah smiled and handed him over. Esmie carried him through to the nursery, whispering in his ear how much she would miss him. Reluctantly, she placed him in the cradle.

'You're nearly too big for this,' said Esmie. 'By the time I see you again, you'll be in a cot.'

She leaned in and kissed him. Andrew began to whimper at being let go. Esmie, crouching down, set the cradle gently swinging and started to sing the Highland lullaby that always seemed to calm the baby. By the time she'd finished, his eyelids were closing. Esmie stood up.

'I'll miss you, wee man,' she said, leaning in for one last kiss.

As she turned she gave a start. Tom was standing in the doorway watching her. His eyes shone.

'You sing beautifully,' he murmured.

Esmie gave an awkward smile, embarrassed at having been overheard. He walked across to gaze down at his son.

'I know I'm biased,' said Tom, 'but isn't he the most perfect baby you've ever seen?'

'I think he probably is,' Esmie agreed in amusement.

He held her look. 'Thank you for helping take care of Andrew. It means a lot to me that other people love him too.'

Esmie nodded, her throat constricting. She was growing too fond of the infant and knew how much she would miss him. The sooner she went the better. Without another word, Esmie hurried from the room.

Lydia gave her a stilted goodbye and proffered a cheek.

'Take care,' Esmie said with a kiss.

'Give my love to Harold,' said Lydia. Up close, there were dark rings around her blue eyes that her make-up did not hide. There was no warmth in her look.

'Of course,' Esmie said. She gave Lydia's hand a squeeze but felt her tense and pull away. Esmie was wretched that her long-time friend could be so cold towards her. In sadness, she turned to leave.

Minutes later, she was sitting in the Clement-Talbot being driven away by Tom. Esmie craned round to wave goodbye. Lydia was standing at the balustrade, a lone figure watching. At the very last moment, Lydia raised a hand in farewell.

Tom drove, acutely aware of Esmie so close that their arms touched when the car rattled over potholes and threw them together. There was no Bijal on the trip this time to inhibit their conversation but she seemed preoccupied and for half the journey hardly spoke.

As they passed the forestry dak bungalow, he noticed Esmie glance towards it. His gut tightened. He almost suggested that they stop there for refreshment but thought better of it and drove on. Dangerous to think where it might lead were they to be alone together in a place so emotionally charged – at least that's how he remembered it.

They descended out of the hills and the trees thinned. The plain was coming into view and the air was already considerably hotter and more humid. They would soon be approaching Rawalpindi and their time alone together would be over.

'Have you suddenly taken a vow of silence, Esmie?' he asked.

She shot him a look, followed by a self-conscious smile. 'Sorry, I was just enjoying the scenery – the last chance for a while to see hills that remind me of home.'

'So are you going to tell me why you and Lydia aren't speaking?'

He saw her cheeks redden. She glanced over. 'It's nothing . . .'

'It's something,' said Tom. 'I've never seen you two like that before.'

Esmie shrugged. 'Three weeks in a hill station is too long for me. I'm not good at being a lady of leisure – I need to be doing something. I'm afraid having me around wasn't as much fun as Lydia hoped.'

Tom was almost convinced. Lydia had implied much the same thing – that Esmie had grown too earnest. But Tom knew his wife's moods and didn't believe that Esmie would have created such a bad atmosphere. There was more to it.

'Was it to do with Dickie Mason?' he asked. From a quick glance he saw alarm on her face.

She answered evasively. 'Dickie's not around anymore.'

At once, Tom felt bad for putting her on the spot with his question.

'Sorry, that was unfair. Even if it was about Dickie I know you wouldn't say anything damning against Lydia.' She didn't respond. Tom added, 'I'm relieved to hear Mason's off the scene and if you had a hand in it, then I'm very grateful, Esmie. Now, if I promise not to talk about him or Lydia, do you think we can find another topic of conversation that we can both agree on?'

He was rewarded with one of her wry smiles and his spirits lifted.

'Tell me what Stella's been up to,' she asked. 'Is she still missing the Baroness?'

Tom gave a huff of amusement. 'Funny you should ask. Miss Dubois has gone on holiday to Kashmir to visit the Baroness.'

'Never!' Esmie exclaimed.

'Yes.' Tom grinned. 'She went last week with Mrs Shankley by tonga to Srinagar. I'm not sure who was in charge of who, to be honest.'

Esmie laughed. 'Good for them – what an adventure. I'd love to see Srinagar and Dal Lake.'

'You should go,' Tom encouraged. *If only I could take you.* He had to swallow the words he wanted to say. Instead he said, 'I can just imagine you swimming in the Lake.'

She shot him a look. Tom's heart thumped. He quickly clarified. 'You being such a keen swimmer.'

'Can you swim from the houseboats?' she asked.

'No, it's not safe – you can get tangled in the weeds and lilies. But if you take a boat out to the middle of the lake, the swimming is glorious. Surrounded by pleasure gardens and mountains.'

Esmie looked reflective. 'Sounds like heaven.'

He heard the yearning in her voice; he felt the same.

'Just like Loch Vaullay on a good summer's day,' he teased.

She gave a soft laugh. 'Then perhaps I'll persuade Harold to take me there one day.'

Tom felt familiar guilt. 'I got Guthrie there once on my first leave from the army – the fishing was good enough to lure him away from his work. But that was before I was married to Mary.'

To his surprise, he did not feel the familiar ache of loss at the mention of his dead wife's name. Since talking about her to Esmie the pain had lessened. But Esmie fell quiet again. Was it the mention of Harold? Perhaps her thoughts were already racing to be with her husband. Lydia had said Esmie was eager to get back to Harold.

All too soon they were driving into the bustling, dusty city and heading for the hotel. Jimmy was practising his batting moves on the scrap of lawn in front of the Raj. Esmie was quick to climb out of the car and rush forward to greet him.

Esmie had another broken night's sleep, plagued by doubts over whether she had mishandled the situation with Lydia. Her friend struck her as a deeply unhappy woman. Should she have insisted Lydia go to see a doctor about her melancholic feelings towards Andrew? Was that at the root of her problems and the reason why she had turned to Dickie for comfort? And yet Lydia claimed she had been in love with Dickie since last winter. Poor Tom! Esmie found a measure of solace in the fact that Dickie had broken off the liaison. If her friendship with Lydia was the main casualty – rather than Tom's marriage – then she would have to live with that.

Tom insisted on getting up before dawn to drive Esmie to the station for her train. The platform was already busy with porters balancing luggage on their heads and pedlars hawking their wares. Together they searched the manifests pasted onto the carriages that listed the passengers' names. Finding hers, Esmie steeled herself for the final goodbye to Tom. Her heart drummed as they watched the porter putting her suitcase on board, along with a tiffin basket that the hotel cook had prepared for her journey.

She had no idea when she would see Tom again. If the rift with Lydia wasn't mended, there would be no Christmas invitation to the hotel or any excuse to come to Rawalpindi. She felt a leaden weight on her chest at the thought of the months rolling on without seeing Tom and Andrew.

Dawn was breaking as they faced each other on the platform. People stepped around them but Esmie was aware only of Tom gazing down at her with those vital blue eyes that made her stomach somersault.

'Thank you for bringing me,' she managed to say.

Tom took hold of her hands. 'Oh, Esmie, it's I who must thank you. I'll always be grateful that you told me about visiting the graves in Peshawar – for the compassionate way you listened to me.'

Esmie began to shake with emotion. She tried to blink away the tears that welled in her eyes.

Before she knew it, she was blurting out, 'I don't know when I'll see you again.'

She saw the tension in his jaw as he struggled with some inner conflict. She held her breath, waiting for his answer. But none came. For an instant, Tom gripped her hands tightly in his. Leaning forward he kissed her on the lips.

'Goodbye, Esmie,' he said, his voice unsteady.

She was so shocked she couldn't speak. Stumbling away from him, Esmie clambered onto the train. She sat down quickly before her legs buckled. Peering out of the window, she saw Tom pushing his way through the crowd towards the station entrance. Her last glimpse of him was of a tall dark-haired figure, towering above those around him, caught in a shaft of light. Then he was gone.

Esmie sat trembling, the imprint of Tom's kiss still on her lips as the train jerked into motion and pulled out of the station. She shouldn't have allowed it. She hadn't expected it. Yet she had longed for it in countless daydreams. There was something very final in their parting; their exchange of words and the firm kiss. Tom would never have touched her lips if he'd thought they'd be seeing each other again.

Esmie struggled to make sense of it. There was no doubt in her mind now that Tom had feelings for her – the same strength of feeling that she had for him. It was as if the kiss acknowledged this and yet was a gesture of farewell. They both knew that they couldn't have each other. They had chosen to marry different people to whom they had made solemn promises. Tom was an honourable man and would not break his vows to Lydia however much she tested him – and he did not expect Esmie to break hers to Harold.

She was desolate at leaving him. Yet painful as that was, she knew that she was loved – that Tom loved her – and that brought a strange comfort to her sore heart.

Chapter 32

Taha, October

Esmie found that the best way to cope with the rift with Lydia and subduing her feelings for Tom was to work harder than ever. Like Harold, she spent long days at the hospital and returned after dark to eat a late supper and fall into bed too exhausted to think beyond the day. Harold asked her little about her time away in Murree and she decided not to tell him about Lydia's affair with Dickie. She knew how fond Harold was of Lydia and didn't want to lessen his regard for her. The affair was over and there was little to be gained by gossiping about it. She had written to Lydia twice since returning to Taha but had received no letter back.

Esmie did share her concern that Lydia appeared not to have any maternal feelings for Andrew.

'I suggested that she go to a doctor about it,' Esmie told Harold, 'but she was strongly against the idea. In fact, she told me to stop interfering. We didn't part on very good terms, I'm afraid.'

'I'm sorry to hear that,' said Harold. 'But I'm sure things will get better in time.'

'Not if she sinks further into melancholia. And he's such a sweet wee boy. Tom adores him but he needs his mother's attention too.'

Harold grew ill at ease at her enthusiastic descriptions of the baby so Esmie stopped mentioning him. Instead, she directed her own protective feelings towards Gabina, who was now running around the house after Karo and beginning to speak.

On Sundays, after Esmie and Harold had attended church and eaten lunch with Alec Bannerman, Harold would rest while Esmie spent the afternoon playing with the Waziri girl. They would build structures out of old cotton reels and storage tins for Gabina to knock down and Esmie taught her nursery rhymes. Gabina loved to sing and clap her hands. It also gave Esmie a chance to chat with Karo and they practised speaking in each other's language. Esmie grew fluent in Pashto. Only with Esmie was Karo confident enough to forgo wearing her face veil and reveal her disfigured face. Esmie determined that she would look after Karo and her daughter for as long as she was able.

Sunday evening was the one moment in the week when Esmie and Harold spent any length of time alone together. He would read to her while she sewed by lamplight and they would discuss any home news they had received. Sometimes, when talking about her Aunt Isobel and the asylum, Esmie would experience a sharp pang of homesickness. It was little more than a year since she had left Scotland, yet it felt like a lifetime. Perhaps next year she could persuade Harold to take her on home furlough.

An uneasy peace with the Frontier tribes appeared to be holding. There was talk of reconstituting local militias to help patrol the more lawless areas. Taha was quiet and any outbreaks of unrest were further to the south. Esmie wondered if Dickie Mason was back on duty on the Frontier; they had heard nothing of the young captain. Harold was encouraged by the situation enough to start talking about reopening the clinic at Kanki-Khel. But McCabe had ordered caution. They did not want to have to send troops into that area if they could help it, as it might be seen as a provocation. The new policy of the British Administration appeared to be containment rather than conquer and subdue. Such a tactic relied on the border tribes being left alone as much as possible, as well as being co-opted into policing the Frontier.

One day Esmie and Harold returned from a tiring day at the clinic to find a letter from Rawalpindi.

'It's Lydia's handwriting,' Esmie said, her heart racing with sudden nervousness. She opened it at once, as Harold looked on, bracing herself for further rebuke.

Esmie gaped in astonishment and reread it.

'Good news I hope?' Harold asked.

Esmie swallowed. 'Yes . . . I think so. She wants to come and visit.'

Harold's eyes widened. 'Lydia wants to come to Taha?'

'Yes. She's apologising for the way we parted and for not writing sooner.' Esmie felt a wave of relief. 'She sounds like the old Lydia. Oh, Harold, I'm so pleased. And she wants to bring Andrew too. You'll get to meet him at last.'

Harold look flustered. 'Is Tom bringing them?'

Esmie tried to hide her disappointment. 'No, apparently not. But according to Lydia, he's encouraging her to come. I think he was concerned that Lydia and I hadn't parted well.'

'I really don't think she should be attempting the journey alone and with such a young infant,' Harold protested.

'She's not travelling alone,' said Esmie, referring again to the letter. 'Brigadier McCabe's wife is visiting too. That's what's given Lydia the idea. She wants to come next week.'

Esmie saw the conflict in Harold's face. She knew he would want to see Lydia but the thought of her being in his place of work must be unsettling. He liked to keep his mission life quite separate from those he saw on leave. Having Lydia to stay might also stir up unwanted emotions in Harold in the same way as being near Tom did in her.

Esmie asked, 'Would you rather I put Lydia off coming? If you think it's going to interfere with your work . . .'

'No, don't do that,' Harold said quickly. 'Of course she must come. I know how much you want to see her and Andrew.'

Esmie's spirits lifted at the thought of seeing the baby again. 'Then I'll write back at once and say so.'

In the following days Esmie reread Lydia's short breezy letter many times, looking for clues as to how Tom was and what life was like back in Rawalpindi. They had opened up the house in Buchanan Road again soon after Esmie had left Murree. It seems Lydia's enthusiasm for hill station life had dwindled quickly. She made no mention of Dickie but Esmie knew that it must have largely been because he was no longer there.

Now that it was October, most of the other British on leave were also returning to Rawalpindi. There was mention of a card party with the Hopkirks and tennis with Dempster, the American engineer. Tom only got mentioned specifically in reference to some watercolour he'd done of Andrew.

> '*. . . we've hung it in the nursery. It's really not very good but I would never dare tell Tom that. I think he should stick to landscapes. Still, he seems pleased with it and no one's going to see it, so everyone is happy.*
>
> *I do hope you say yes to my visit. I've been feeling rather bad about the way we argued in Murree. I was beastly to you. I know I was upset but that was no excuse for the things I said. You know that I count you among the people I love the most, don't you? Dearest Esmie, please forgive me and say I can come and stay. I miss our chats and of course I'd love to see Harold too.*'

As a postscript to the letter, Lydia had written: *'I know you live in a small bungalow but I hope you can accommodate Baby and Ayah in their own room?'*

There had been no other mention of Andrew except in reference to the painting and to assure her that Tom was in favour of Lydia bringing the baby with her to Taha. Esmie wished that Tom was coming too. A small part of her hoped that he might turn up unexpectedly at the last minute.

The question of where Lydia and the baby would sleep preyed on her mind. With only two bedrooms in their small bungalow, Esmie saw it as an opportunity to move into Harold's room for the length of Lydia's visit – and perhaps beyond. But Harold must have been troubled by it too.

Three days before Lydia was due to arrive, Harold announced on their way to the clinic, 'I've been thinking of Lydia's request and she must have her own room. Bannerman's offered to put me up in his spare room while Lydia and the baby are here. No doubt you can find a place for the ayah and baby in the compound. I'll leave the details up to you, my dear.'

Esmie was so astonished by her husband's thwarting of her plan for them to sleep together that she could think of no rejoinder. Only later, over supper, did she challenge him.

'You didn't have to go involving Bannerman in our domestic arrangements,' Esmie chided. 'We can easily accommodate Lydia in my room if I move into yours.'

'I thought this would be more comfortable all round,' said Harold, not meeting her look. 'And Bannerman doesn't mind. He enjoys the company.'

In frustration, Esmie protested, 'Surely, Harold, you can put up with me in your bed for a week or so?'

He reddened. 'There's no need to raise your voice, dearest. The servants—'

'The servants know all about our strange marital relations,' Esmie retorted. 'Nothing I say will shock them.'

Harold looked at her in discomfort. 'I'm sorry; I thought we were agreed on this.'

'No, Harold, we were only in agreement on not having a baby yet,' said Esmie. 'You know that this sleeping apart is not what I want – I just have to accept it. But don't pretend that I'm as happy about our arrangement as you are – or that Lydia won't find it odd too.'

The subject wasn't mentioned again but there was a new tension between her and Harold which hadn't been there before. The next day, Bannerman's servant came round to fetch some of Harold's personal things and his room was made ready for Lydia. Esmie, embarrassed at the thought of Sarah and Andrew being banished to the compound, made arrangements with Draman that the baby and his ayah would share her room.

The night before Lydia arrived, Esmie lay sleepless in her bed, staring at the bedroll and cot ready for Sarah and Andrew, and wondered how she had got into such an unsatisfactory situation. Here she was, a married woman, lying alone and unfulfilled, waiting to share a room with the baby of the man she truly loved while her own husband went to lodge with a bachelor friend. She thought of the young and single Esmie – the headstrong nurse who thought nothing of volunteering for work on the battlefront – and knew how she would have laughed to be told she would accept such a situation. Not for any man would that Esmie McBride have put up with a marriage without physical love. But perhaps that's exactly what she had done. Was it because Esmie could not have the man she loved above all others that she had settled for this half-union with a man she could never love so deeply?

Esmie was shocked at how thin Lydia looked since she had last seen her seven weeks ago. Even rouge and red lipstick could not hide how drawn her face was, the cheekbones more prominent than ever and her eyes set in dark hollows. But her friend greeted her with her old warmth, a gush of words and a tight hug.

'It's so wonderful to see you!' Lydia exclaimed, her eyes moist with tears.

Esmie hugged her back, worried at how bony her friend felt yet thankful that there was no bitterness between them. 'And for me too. Did you have a good journey?'

'As good as could be expected, I suppose. God, you live in the back of beyond, don't you? The Brigadier's wife was a bag of nerves, gasping every time we rounded a corner and saw a native. She thinks every man she sees is a potential Pathan assassin. I have no idea why she bothers coming to Taha at all.'

'To see her husband, I expect,' Esmie answered wryly.

Lydia snorted. 'I'd get him to retire back to Eastbourne if I was her.'

Esmie showed her into the bungalow, telling Ali where to put the luggage and asking Draman to provide tea. She beckoned for Sarah to follow and couldn't resist lifting Andrew from his nurse's arms. She'd been itching to hold him since they'd arrived. He made no protest.

'My goodness, haven't you grown?' She kissed him on his soft, plump cheeks. Andrew thrust his fingers into her mouth and gurgled in delight. She was pleased to see that the baby appeared to be thriving.

'I think he remembers me!'

'Where's Harold?' Lydia asked.

'He's still at the hospital. He'll join us for dinner.' Catching Lydia's look of disappointment, Esmie said swiftly, 'He's really looking forward to seeing you and he's going to finish earlier than he usually does, so you're very honoured.'

Esmie noticed how Lydia hardly touched the afternoon tea of sandwiches and cake. She sipped at a cup of black tea well sweetened with sugar and lit up a cigarette. 'You don't mind if I do?'

Esmie shook her head, searching for conversation that wouldn't be one-sided. So far, Lydia had said nothing about Rawalpindi, while Esmie had talked a lot about Taha.

Esmie tried again. 'So how is life in Pindi?'

Lydia gave a characteristic dismissive wave of the hand. 'Oh, same as always. Tennis, bridge and all that.'

'The cold season will be starting soon, I suppose,' said Esmie, 'with all the socialising that brings.'

'Umm, I suppose so.' Lydia didn't sound enthusiastic.

'Which regiments are stationed there at the moment?' Esmie asked.

Her friend gave her a sharp look. 'Why do you ask?'

'Just wondered which mess would be vying to lay on the best ball this winter.'

Lydia blew out smoke. 'As a matter of fact, there's a contingent of the Peshawar Rifles in the Victoria Barracks.'

'Tom's old regiment?'

'Yes. I thought he'd be glad about it but he's not showing any interest in meeting up. Says they'll all be different from when he was with them and that all his friends are dead.' Lydia rolled her eyes. 'But that's my cheerful husband for you. So even if we get invited to their mess, I don't imagine Tom will go.'

Esmie thought uncomfortably of Tom's confiding in her about his disillusionment with his old regiment and army life – and he had alluded to some trouble that got him court- martialled – but it wasn't for her to break such a confidence.

'So how is Tom?' She tried to keep her voice as neutral as possible, though her heart was thumping.

Lydia shrugged. 'Same as ever.'

'So things are all right between you since . . .?' Esmie let the question hang.

'If you're referring to Dickie Mason,' she said in a tight voice, 'I haven't seen him since the day after you chased him away from Murree.'

'Lydia, I—' Esmie began.

'Let's not talk about it.' Lydia cut her off and stubbed out her cigarette. 'I don't want us to argue again.'

'No, of course not,' Esmie said, feeling contrite for having raised the subject.

Lydia put on a smile. 'Well, I don't know about you but I'm certainly ready for a chota peg. Let's celebrate us being together again.'

'Chota pegs it is then,' Esmie said, smiling.

Harold found them still on the veranda after dark, drinking whisky and soda and laughing over old school reminiscences. Esmie noticed how her husband blushed and became boyishly bashful at Lydia's teasing. As they sat having dinner together and chatting about home, Esmie could almost imagine that nothing had changed since the summer they had all spent together at Ebbsmouth – except for Tom's absence. She felt it acutely when they talked about The Anchorage and how Tibby was opening her home to impoverished artists.

'Tom says they have to work at least one day in the garden for their keep,' said Lydia.

'What does the colonel make of all these radicals taking over his castle?' Harold asked, amused.

'Oh, the old miser's very confused these days,' she answered. 'He thinks they're members of staff. If he catches sight of one, he shouts at them to smarten up their uniform or he'll sack them on the spot. They just humour him, according to Tibby.'

'Good for Tibby,' said Harold.

Lydia asked after his mother and aunt. Harold talked about them with affection. Esmie seized the moment to suggest, 'Wouldn't it be nice if we could go on furlough next year and see them?'

She thought Harold was about to pooh-pooh the idea when Lydia interjected, 'Oh, yes, do! We could all go back together for a visit. Summer time in Ebbsmouth, just think of it. You could stay at Templeton Hall and we'd go on picnics and theatre trips and have tennis parties, just like old times.'

'Perhaps the year after,' Harold said. 'I'm not due home leave until 1922.'

'Oh, Harold,' Lydia cried, 'it's not as if you work for the government or army and have to abide by their silly rules. The mission would let you take holiday if you asked them. I don't think Esmie can wait that long – I know I couldn't. I miss home so much. Mummy and Daddy . . .'

Suddenly Lydia's face crumpled like a child's. She put her face in her hands and started to sob. At once, Esmie was out of her seat and hurrying around the table to comfort her. Lydia's bony shoulders felt tense under her hold.

'I know how hard it is,' Esmie sympathised. 'I feel the same at times.'

'How can you know how I feel?' Lydia said, sniffling. 'You and Harold are only here while the mission needs you and then you'll go elsewhere. But I'm stuck in Pindi forever because of that wretched hotel.'

Harold looked shocked at her outburst. He pulled out a handkerchief and offered it with an embarrassed 'There, there, dear girl.'

Esmie was heavy-hearted. She was sorry for Lydia but her greatest sympathy lay with Tom, who was trying to make the best of his hotel business and provide for his new family. Yet it appeared that it wasn't enough for Lydia. She was too used to life at Templeton Hall, being pampered and adored by her parents; nowhere and no one else could live up to her expectations.

'Pindi's not so bad,' said Esmie. 'There's more social life going on there than there ever will be in Ebbsmouth. Why don't you encourage your parents to come out and visit again?'

Lydia pulled away and grabbed at the handkerchief that Harold offered across the table. 'Oh, don't mind me. It's those chota pegs of Draman's have made me maudlin. I'm perfectly fine really. Everything's perfectly fine.'

Shortly afterwards, Harold left for Bannerman's. Lydia gave him a baffled look as she kissed him on the cheek and said goodnight. When he'd gone, she said to Esmie, 'I hope I haven't caused too much disruption by staying. I don't see the need for Harold to go.'

'Don't worry. He'll come round for breakfast. He's keen to show you the hospital tomorrow too. And I've taken time off so we can spend it together – show you and Andrew the sights.'

It was as Esmie was retiring to her room and Lydia heard Andrew crying, that realisation dawned on her friend.

'Esmie,' she said, grabbing onto her arm unsteadily, 'you and Harold have separate rooms?'

Esmie went hot with embarrassment. 'Yes.'

'How very old-fashioned of you,' said Lydia. She gave an inebriated laugh. 'Mind you, it must be quite fun, having assignations in the night. Perhaps I should try that with Tom – spice up our marriage.'

'Goodnight and sleep well, Lydia.' Emsie turned away before her friend guessed the truth that there never had been any amorous visits from Harold – nor seemed likely to be in the future.

After four days, Lydia didn't hide the fact that she was bored. She had shown little interest in Harold and Esmie's work at the hospital – 'I hate the smell of antiseptic and seeing ill people' – and she was unimpressed by the old town. 'I can get all that native stuff in the Saddar Bazaar. Don't you have any decent shops here at all?'

Rupa gave them lunch one day. Lydia was intrigued to see inside her bungalow with its comfortable furnishings and pictures of Bombay but she hardly touched the food. 'It's delicious but my digestion can't really cope with spicy food since the baby was born.'

She thought the club house dull and the cantonment too small. Esmie invited Mrs McCabe round for tea but Lydia developed a sudden headache and went to lie down until the brigadier's wife had gone.

The one person whose company Lydia appeared to enjoy was Alec Bannerman's.

'He's such a jolly man,' she said in approval, 'and I bet he was handsome in his younger days. Strange he never married. I suppose being a Holy Joe might have put some women off. Not that I think he's the pious type myself.'

Alec arranged to take them for an outing to the local beauty spot at Taha Khel where he and Harold liked to fish. Esmie piled in the back of Alec's car with Andrew and his ayah while Lydia sat up front with the chaplain. When they arrived at the picnic spot, Esmie expected Lydia to make disparaging comments about the flat vista of sand and rock with its trickle of a river but she was fulsome.

'How delightful to get out of the town,' said Lydia, looking cool in a beige summer dress, a topee decorated with a paisley scarf and blue-lensed sunglasses.

Taking command of distributing the picnic and pouring iced lemonade from a vacuum flask, she encouraged Alec to tell stories about his escapades on the Frontier and in Afghanistan as a young army padre.

Lydia sat enthralled. 'Tom won't talk about his time in the Rifles – it's as if he's ashamed he was ever in the army. But I think it's all fascinating – so dashing and heroic, fighting the wild Pathans. It's why I married him – to be a captain's wife. Now he doesn't even want to use the title.'

Esmie was dismayed at her criticising Tom so openly in front of Alec.

'It wasn't a happy time for Tom,' Esmie pointed out. 'He only went into the Rifles because he was trying to please his father.'

'Tom's never tried to please his father,' Lydia retorted. 'If he had, the old boy wouldn't have disinherited him. Even giving him a grandson hasn't changed the colonel's mind.'

'From what Harold has told me about Colonel Lomax,' said Alec, 'no amount of pleasing would have made any difference. Some men make bad fathers.' He reached across and tickled Andrew under his chin. 'But it's not a hereditary disease,' he joked. 'I've met Tom – a few years ago in Peshawar – and I imagine he's a fine father to wee Andrew here.'

'I suppose he is,' Lydia conceded. 'He's certainly dotty about the baby.'

Esmie observed Lydia making a half-hearted attempt to pay her son some attention in front of Alec. She leaned over the baby and made a cooing noise. Andrew reached up and grabbed her glasses.

'Don't do that, you'll break them!' She prised his fingers off her tinted spectacles and sat back out of his reach.

That evening, Alec invited them round for supper, along with Rupa. Lydia drank a lot of wine and kept the conversation lively. She regaled them with her tales of driving generals in the War and dodging U-boats in the Atlantic to fundraise in America for the Scottish Women's Hospitals. Esmie and Harold had heard the stories many times but Alec and Rupa were held spellbound.

'What a brave young lady,' Alec said in admiration.

'Not really,' said Lydia, laughing. 'I was scared silly. But I wanted to do my bit just like Esmie was doing.' She caught Esmie's look. 'We've often talked about how life after the War was a bit of an anti-climax, haven't we? Obviously we were thankful it was all over and most of it was hideous but, because of the danger, we lived every day in the moment and you don't get that in peacetime – at least not as a woman.'

'Well, you do if you live on the North-West Frontier,' Alec said with a grimace. 'Isn't that so, Esmie?'

'I'm afraid all too often it is,' Esmie agreed. 'But I know what you mean, Lydia, about living in the moment – feeling all the more alive because life might be snatched away in an instant.'

Rupa said, 'I would much rather work in a peaceful Taha than live under the threat of violence.'

'Of course,' Harold agreed. 'And you know more than any of us how devastating the loss of a loved one can be because of it.'

Lydia gasped. 'I'm so sorry Mrs Desai; that was tactless of me. I didn't mean to remind you of your husband's cruel death.'

'No need to apologise,' said Rupa. 'He is always in my thoughts.'

'Well, I think you're so brave staying on here,' said Lydia.

'I'm close to him here,' Rupa said reflectively.

'You must have loved him very much,' Lydia said, her eyes filling with sudden tears.

'Yes,' Rupa said with a sad smile. 'And I still do.'

Shortly afterwards, Alec drove Rupa back to the hospital compound and Harold walked Esmie and Lydia back home along The Lines. Lydia's previous bonhomie had evaporated; talk of Rupa's murdered husband had turned her maudlin. Harold didn't linger, leaving Esmie to coax Lydia to bed. Her friend resisted, flopping into a veranda chair.

'Would you do that for Harold?' Lydia asked, trying with difficulty to light a cigarette. 'Stay on and work here if something happened to him?'

'Probably not,' Esmie admitted. 'But none of us know what we'd do in certain circumstances – not unless they actually happen. Anyway, I don't want to think of such a thing.'

'I know I wouldn't,' said Lydia, sucking at the half-lit cigarette. 'I'd marry again. But next time I'd marry for love.'

Esmie's insides clenched. 'But you did marry for love,' Esmie reminded her. 'You had your heart set on Tom from the moment he turned up last summer.'

'I had my heart set on marriage,' Lydia said, picking a tobacco fleck from her tongue. 'It's not the same thing.'

Esmie felt downcast. How had they all made the same mistake that summer in Ebbsmouth and married the wrong people? What a mess they had created.

'I wish . . .' Lydia began.

'Wish what?' Esmie asked.

Lydia sighed. 'That I hadn't said yes to the first man who asked me. I should have waited until . . .' She stubbed out her cigarette without saying what she should have waited for.

Esmie didn't press her – the subject made her agitated – and instead steered her friend into Harold's bedroom and helped her to bed.

Chapter 33

For the next couple of days Lydia spent most of the time visiting Alec, inviting herself in for drinks and chat and getting him to show her his army memorabilia. She left Andrew with Esmie.

'The Padre won't want a squalling baby in his house,' said Lydia, 'and you're so much better with baby than I am.'

Esmie didn't object. She was happy to have Andrew in her care and pushed him out in his pram around the cantonment. Sarah and Karo, although from quite different backgrounds, struck up a friendship over the children. Sarah, a Punjabi-speaker, had a few words of Pashto but they communicated mostly in English. Esmie returned from her perambulation with Andrew to find the women sitting in the shade of the back veranda, embroidering a shawl together and sharing sweetmeats, while Gabina played with her bobbins.

Neither servant showed any discomfort when Esmie sat beside them and joined in the sewing. However, Draman made his displeasure known by refusing to serve tea to the women and pointedly had afternoon tea for Esmie brought onto the memsahib's veranda.

Lydia didn't return for tea and it was dark when her friend finally appeared, just in time for dinner.

'Such an interesting man,' Lydia said, already inebriated. 'And so knowledgeable about the area. I could listen to him for hours.'

She chattered throughout dinner about the Frontier and repeated Alec's stories. There was something feverish about her speech and she seemed gripped by nervous excitement, exaggerating the tales she'd been told. For the first time Esmie worried that Lydia's previous melancholia might be tipping over into mania. Her friend quaffed wine that only she was drinking and pushed food onto her fork that she then didn't eat. From Harold's enquiring glances, Esmie knew her husband was concerned about Lydia too.

When the meal was over and Lydia paused to light a cigarette, Harold took the opportunity to ask, 'How long are you thinking of staying?'

Lydia looked so crestfallen that Harold quickly added, 'Not that we want you to go. It's just that Esmie is needed at the hospital and I don't want to outstay my welcome at Bannerman's.'

'Don't worry about me,' said Lydia. 'I can entertain myself. Esmie, you must go back to work. And I know Alec doesn't mind a bit. He enjoys having you, Harold. I think he's quite lonely. He loves having me round for a chin-wag.'

'I'm sure he does,' said Harold, 'but he's also a help to us at the hospital.'

'I'm not stopping him,' said Lydia, waving her cigarette at Harold.

'Won't Tom be missing you and the baby?' Harold persisted.

'The baby, yes,' Lydia answered with a curl of her lip.

Esmie intervened. 'Mrs McCabe is returning to Pindi in a week's time and I'm sure she would want you to accompany her again. That gives us another week together.'

She saw the look of panic on Lydia's face. Was she really so unhappy with Tom that she'd rather be in Taha, a town of which she was openly disparaging?

'But of course you can stay longer,' Esmie said. 'It's entirely up to you.'

Lydia gave her a grateful look. 'I promise I won't stay forever,' she said with a forced laugh. 'And you must go to the hospital, Esmie. Don't feel you have to chaperone me all day long. But I don't want to go just yet.'

The following day, when Lydia announced that Alec was taking her for a drive, Esmie decided to go into work for a few hours. Harold asked bemusedly, 'Has Bannerman fallen under the famous Lydia spell, I wonder? If he was half his age I'd worry but there can't be any harm in it, can there?'

'No, of course not,' said Esmie. 'I'm not concerned about Alec but I am about Lydia. She's behaving oddly – even manically.'

'She's drinking too much, that's all,' said Harold.

'That's not all,' Esmie insisted. 'It's just a symptom. I don't think Lydia's stable.'

'Lydia's just in high spirits.'

'You don't see her at night like I do,' Esmie pointed out. 'After you've gone she's either overwrought and wants to stay up half the night or she's maudlin and weeping.'

Harold looked concerned. 'Is there anything in particular preying on her mind that she's told you about?'

Esmie thought of Lydia's negative comments about Tom as well as the avoidance of talking about Dickie. She sighed. 'Not in so many words. But I think she's mentally fragile.'

'Well, if anyone can get her to talk about her problems then it's you, my dear.'

Lydia was effusive about her day out with Alec. 'And he let me drive his car on the way back through the old town – it was such a riot!'

When Esmie tried to get her to talk about anything more personal, Lydia refused.

'Why are you bringing up all that again?' Lydia accused. 'I don't want to think about the awful summer with the birth and I don't want to talk about Tom – or even Dickie – so you can't make me.'

Later, on the point of going to bed, Lydia was more conciliatory. 'I know you're well-meaning and you think I've got some sort of complex about the baby, but I'm fine. Really I am. I don't need your medical help, Esmie; I just need you as my friend. That's all I've ever wanted – for you to be my good friend.'

Lydia put it so simply. She wanted friendship; nothing more and nothing less. Was Esmie failing her, too obsessed about her mental state and the way she denigrated Tom? Esmie was too emotionally involved to treat Lydia's problems with a dispassionate and professional eye. She wished Aunt Isobel could be there to advise her.

Esmie pulled Lydia into a hug. Her friend felt diminished and fragile. 'Of course we're good friends. I'm sorry for fussing.' She kissed her on the forehead. 'I'll stop badgering you with questions if you promise that you'll ask for help if you need it.'

Lydia gave a teary laugh. 'Promise. Cross my heart and hope to die.'

Esmie laughed at her use of their schoolgirl phrase. 'Good. Then go to bed and sleep well, best friend.'

Lydia gave her one last hug and then did as she was told.

The next day at the hospital was a busy one and Esmie felt a certain relief to be working. It stopped her ruminating over Lydia, although she was keen to get back to see Andrew. She was about to leave when Harold appeared from the operating theatre, a towel wrapped around his left hand. She could see blood staining it.

'What's happened?' Esmie asked in alarm.

'Nothing much – just a silly slip of the knife – nothing serious.'

'Let me take a look,' Esmie insisted, guiding him towards the dressing station and sitting him down. He'd gone very pale.

But after closer inspection, she was relieved to see that the wound wasn't deep. She cleaned it and bandaged him up.

'Just as well I'm right-handed,' Harold said, making light of his injury. 'Thank you, my dear. Now I'll just go and finish off my list.'

'Harold! You'll do no such thing. You're coming home with me.'

'I can't,' he protested. 'There's too much to do.'

'There'll always be too much,' said Esmie, 'but you can't do it all. You're exhausted. That's probably why you cut yourself. Come home and rest – and see how you are in the morning.'

As they walked back home together, Harold confessed, 'Lydia's been on my mind. I was thinking of having a word with Bannerman about her – see what he thinks. He's a wise man and knows how people tick. Perhaps she's said something to him.'

Esmie slipped her arm through his. 'That's a good idea.'

There was no sign of Lydia at the house, though Esmie could hear Andrew wailing while Sarah bathed him.

'She must still be at Alec's,' said Harold.

'A shame she never takes Andrew with her,' Esmie sighed as she went to see the boy.

A little later, as she was giving Andrew his milk, she heard voices on the veranda.

'Esmie!' Harold called for her.

Handing Andrew over to Sarah, Esmie went out to see who had arrived.

'Hello, Padre.' Her smile died at the look of anxiety on both men's faces. 'What's wrong?'

'There seems to be some mix-up,' Harold said. 'Lydia hasn't been with Alec today.'

Alec's craggy face was frowning in confusion. 'She said she was going on a trip with you today – that's why she wanted to borrow the car. I said that was fine as I was spending the day with the McCabes.'

'The car?' Esmie queried. 'But I haven't seen her all day – I've been at the hospital.'

'So Harold's just told me.' Alec ran a hand over his face. 'I don't understand. I came round to see if you were safely back and to get the car.'

'So Lydia took your car?'

Alec nodded.

'When?'

'This morning.'

Harold looked ashen. 'She's been gone since this morning?'

Alec nodded. 'I presume so.'

Esmie felt queasy with panic. 'Did she say where she was going? Where she said *we* were supposed to be going?'

'No. I should have asked her. I offered to drive but she said she wanted to. A spin with her special friend, she said. She promised to take Malik with you both as protection.'

Harold gasped. 'Malik's been at the hospital all day too.'

Alec looked aghast. 'She won't have gone far on her own, surely? Perhaps she never left the cantonment – parked up somewhere and went visiting.'

Esmie shook her head. 'The only person she likes visiting is you, Padre.'

'Oh, dear Lord!' Alec cried. 'Then she must have broken down.'

'We must send out a search party,' Harold said at once.

Alec seized on the idea. 'Yes. I'll go and commandeer a motor car from the Mess.'

'I'm coming too,' Esmie insisted.

'No.' Harold was firm. 'You must stay here in case Lydia turns up while we're out. It's possible someone's found her car broken down and given her a lift back to town.'

'We'll try Taha Khel,' suggested Alec. 'Mrs Lomax was very taken with the riverside there.'

Then they were gone. Esmie was left, stomach churning, watching from the veranda as the shadows of the fruit trees grew rapidly across the lawn. Where could Lydia have got to? What had possessed her to take off in Alec's car alone? Assuming she was alone. A small niggling doubt began to worm its way into Esmie's thoughts. Only one thing – one man – might make her act so recklessly: Dickie Mason. What if she had come across him in the town or got word to him to meet her? She quashed the thought at once. Not even Lydia would be so foolish. Esmie also doubted that Dickie would take such risks for Lydia; it could finish his army career.

After a blaze of orange behind the mountains of Waziristan, darkness fell swiftly. Esmie went inside. Sarah was preparing Andrew for bed. When she explained to Sarah what had happened, the ayah burst into tears.

'I didn't know Lomax Mem' had gone,' she sobbed. 'She said she was spending the day with Bannerman Sahib.'

'No one's blaming you, Sarah,' Esmie tried to reassure her. 'I'm sure my husband will find her. Please don't worry.'

Esmie picked Andrew up and cuddled him to her for comfort.

'Mummy will come back soon,' she whispered in his ear. He smelt of newly washed skin and talcum powder. She kissed him and carried him back outside to look again in vain for any sign of Lydia.

Esmie was woken from dozing in a chair by Harold's return.

'Have you found her?' Esmie asked, heart jolting. 'Is she safe?'

'We've searched as far as Taha Khel and down the southern road too, but there's no trace of her.' Harold's expression was harrowed.

'We've alerted the police. They'll send out a search party as soon as it's light.'

'Can't you keep looking?'

'We've broken the curfew as it is,' he sighed. 'And we won't find anything in the pitch black.'

Esmie went to him. 'Oh, Harold. Where can she have got to? I can't bear to think of her out there on her own.'

'Neither can I.'

'How late is it?' Esmie asked.

'Gone midnight.'

'Let me get you something to eat.'

'No, thank you,' said Harold. 'Bannerman gave me a sandwich a few minutes ago.'

'How is he? I bet he feels terribly responsible but he couldn't have known that Lydia would trick him like this.'

Something in her husband's expression made Esmie ask, 'Is there something you're not telling me?'

'Alec checked to see if anything else was missing. Something had been bothering him. Lydia had shown a lot of interest in his maps of the Frontier.'

Esmie's skin prickled with anxiety. 'And was anything missing?'

Harold nodded. 'A map of Northern Waziristan.'

Esmie's pulse began to race. She felt bile in the back of her throat. The unease she had felt earlier returned with sickening strength. She forced herself to ask, 'Does – does the map show where Razmak is?'

Harold gave her a startled look. 'Yes, it does. Is that significant?'

Esmie swallowed. 'It could be. But I can't believe she would contemplate such a journey . . .'

'Why would Lydia go to Razmak?' Harold asked.

Before answering, Esmie hurried into Harold's bedroom and began to search it. Why hadn't she thought of doing so before? At first glance, it appeared that nothing was missing; there were still clothes hanging in the wardrobe and strewn over the back of a chair. But then Esmie noticed that Lydia's small portmanteau was gone, along with toiletries and her nightgown. Harold had followed her into the room.

'She's taken some overnight things,' said Esmie. 'So she's planned to go and stay somewhere.'

'Why on earth would she do that?' Harold questioned. 'And where? Esmie, why did you ask about Razmak?'

Esmie thought she would be sick. 'Because I think that's where Dickie might be stationed.'

'Dickie Mason?' Harold looked baffled.

'Yes,' Esmie said. Then she began to tell her husband all about the summer affair between Lydia and Dickie.

Chapter 34

Harold reproached her for not telling him about Lydia and Dickie.

'So that's the real reason you and Lydia had a falling out, is it?'

'Yes,' Esmie admitted.

'Why didn't you tell me?'

'Because I thought it was all over. And I didn't want you to think less of Lydia because of it. I know how dear she is to you.'

Harold looked deeply hurt. 'Is that the real reason she came here – as a way of meeting up with Dickie?'

'That's what I was wondering,' Esmie admitted. 'But we don't know yet that that's where she's definitely gone. She might have taken off on a whim and gone to Kohat for the night.'

Harold sighed heavily. 'My poor friend Lomax. He'll have to be told.'

Esmie's insides tensed. 'Tom doesn't know about me finding Dickie with Lydia – I promised Lydia I wouldn't tell him. He thinks Lydia's infatuation with Dickie is over. Let's not send word to Tom yet. If Lydia turns up, there's no point distressing Tom over the matter. I might be quite wrong in my suspicions.'

Esmie got no sleep that night. She dozed in a sitting-room chair, alert to any small sound that might be Lydia returning. She imagined her creeping in, drunk and a little contrite, explaining that she'd decided on a whim to drive to Kohat and drink gin slings at the club. But Lydia didn't come.

An exhausted Harold, at Esmie's insistence, had gone to lie on his bed to snatch some sleep before dawn. She could tell from the way he protected his left hand that the wound was causing him discomfort.

They were both up as early as the servants. In tense silence, they shared a pot of tea on the veranda, watching the sky lighten and the rooftops of the old town emerge out of a thin mist. The muezzin called.

'Let me come with you today,' Esmie entreated. 'I can't bear sitting around all day doing nothing.'

Harold's look softened. 'I know it's intolerable, but I don't think the police will thank us if they have to worry about another woman roaming the roads.' He stood up. 'I'll go and speak to Baz about our Razmak theory – and get the Brigadier to contact the barracks – and Dickie. See if he knows anything.'

Esmie nodded. These were all ideas that she had been turning over in her mind through the night. They were interrupted by the sound of Alec walking up the path. The padre waved in greeting. Esmie knew he would have had a sleepless night too.

Harold said to Esmie, 'You should go to the hospital – at least it will keep your mind occupied. And I feel bad that I won't be there today.'

Esmie watched him hurry away to join Alec. A lively twittering of birds was beginning in the trees and the acrid smoke from dung fires filled the air. It seemed the beginning to a normal day. But Esmie knew it wouldn't be. Wherever Lydia was, she had shattered the calm of the Taha community by her sudden disappearance.

Esmie spent the morning at the hospital, working through without stopping for a break. In the early afternoon, Rupa told her to go home.

'Rest and come back tomorrow. I know you want to be at home with baby Andrew. Perhaps there will be word soon.'

Esmie needed no further persuasion; despite driving herself at work, her mind was never far from anxious thoughts about Lydia. She joined Sarah and Karo with the children. There had been no word from the sahibs searching for Lomax Mem'.

The waiting was purgatory for Esmie. At one point, she walked round to Alec's house to see if there was any news but the padre had not yet returned. She called on Mrs McCabe but her husband was out and the brigadier's wife was lying down, incapacitated by a nervous headache. Esmie left a message to say she would send round a sedative to help her sleep.

It was almost dark when Harold returned to the bungalow, covered in a film of dust and his usually ruddy face looking drawn and anxious. Esmie's stomach knotted as she braced herself for bad news.

'Tell me,' she urged.

Harold sank into a chair. 'I've just come from McCabe's office. His aide-de-camp has returned from Razmak. Lydia's not there. You were right about Dickie being at the barracks though. He claims not to have seen Lydia since Murree and has made no attempt to contact her. He did admit that Lydia has written to him several times in recent weeks but says he's never encouraged her.'

'That doesn't mean she hasn't set off to try and see him,' Esmie said.

'That's true, but the police have combed the road to Razmak too and there's no sign of Alec's car.'

For an instant, Esmie's hopes lifted. 'Then perhaps she did go to Kohat?'

Harold shook his head. 'Baz has informed the police there. She's not at the club and no one has seen her.'

'She can't just disappear!' Esmie began to tremble. 'Oh, Harold! What's happened to her?'

He looked at her bleakly. 'Tomorrow we carry on searching – spread the net wider. In the meantime, Baz's men are gathering intelligence.'

'What do you mean by that?' Esmie asked in alarm.

'Putting their ear to the ground in the bazaar – picking up any rumours about a missing memsahib.'

Esmie gasped. 'Does Baz think there's something more sinister going on? That it's not simply that the car's broken down and she's taken shelter somewhere?'

'You know how thorough Baz is,' said Harold. 'He's just doing his job. It doesn't mean anything more than that.'

But Esmie could tell that her husband was deeply worried. He looked as if he had aged ten years in the past day and night. She knew he would do anything to get Lydia back safely. She tried to calm her jangling nerves; she must be strong for Harold.

'You must be tired out,' she said. 'I'll get Draman to arrange a hot bath and then we'll eat.'

Harold stared out at the dusk, his mind far away. Esmie doubted that he'd heard her.

'Tomorrow, Tom will have to be told,' he said quietly. 'He'll want to come and search too.'

Esmie's throat constricted. She could not stop shaking and all she could do was nod in agreement. She could hardly bear the thought of the anxiety this would inflict on Tom. She should have done more to get to the root of Lydia's unhappiness. How could she have let her friend go off like that, knowing that she was acting irrationally and increasingly manic? She hardly dared face Tom. As she went to instruct the bearer, Esmie made a silent plea: please let Lydia be alive!

The next day, Harold wired Tom and then went off with Alec to join the search. Esmie went to the hospital. It was mid-morning when Harold suddenly appeared. He steered her outside onto the veranda, his face a tight mask. Esmie's heart was hammering so hard she could barely breathe.

'Tell me,' she whispered.

'The police have found Alec's car,' he said, 'but not Lydia.'

Esmie felt like she'd been punched in the stomach. 'Where?'

'About five miles off the Razmak road – on the way to Kanki-Khel.'

'Kanki-Khel?' Esmie was dumbstruck. 'What? Why?'

She stared at her husband in incomprehension.

'Baz thinks it might be kidnap. He's informing the Superintendent of Police in Kohat.'

Esmie clenched her teeth. This could not be happening. 'Who would want to do such a thing?'

Something about Harold's harrowed look made Esmie feel dread in the pit of her stomach.

He didn't answer directly. 'Baz wants to speak to you – and to Karo.'

Esmie grabbed onto Harold to steady herself. 'Why? What does he think?'

Harold hesitated and glanced around before dropping his voice. 'From the rumours in the bazaar, he suspects the Otmanzai – especially if they've taken her to Kanki-Khel or beyond.'

Esmie's head reeled. 'Does he think it's Karo's husband, Baram Wali?'

'It's possible.' Harold's look was grim. 'If not him then some of his kin.'

Esmie felt faint as a terrible thought struck her. 'Did they mistake Lydia for me?' she gasped. 'Is that what Baz thinks?'

Harold said, 'It was opportunistic – they couldn't have known Lydia would be driving that way. But someone took advantage of her being alone and might have thought it was you. They might have recognised the car from the mission.'

Esmie stifled a sob. Harold took hold of her arms.

'Courage, dearest. At least if it is kidnap it means Lydia is alive. She is valuable to her kidnappers. If that's the case, Baz expects to hear of a ransom demand soon.'

Sergeant Baz came round later that day to question Karo about her husband's kin and garner anything useful she could tell them about the situation of the Otmanzai homesteads and fortifications. Esmie felt a stirring of hope that the burly, level-headed Pathan was in charge. He knew the area and people better than most and was encouraging.

'We will track down Lomax Memsahib,' he said stoutly, 'and return her to Taha.'

Before he went, he told Harold, 'Lomax Sahib is taking the train to Kohat. We shall escort him to Taha tomorrow morning. Shall we bring him here, sahib?'

'Yes, here,' said Harold at once. 'That would be very good of you.'

Esmie clenched her hands to stop them shaking. Tom had already left Rawalpindi. He must have dropped everything and caught the first train west. She felt a sickening mix of dread and longing at the thought of seeing him again.

That evening, Harold and Esmie sat up late on the veranda. At Harold's insistence, they had spent the afternoon working at the hospital and then Alec had come round for supper. They had all been subdued and he had left soon afterwards, saying, 'I'll not expect you, Harold – you'll want to be with your wife tonight.'

Esmie was grateful to the padre for his sensitivity. He looked as haggard and exhausted as Harold did. He'd also offered to put Tom up for a few days, so Harold would be moving back into his room permanently.

She observed her husband. His expression was so sad and reflective; the worry over Lydia had taken its toll. Esmie's heart went out to him.

How Harold must regret marrying her. His work was his life and anything else was a distraction, however genial he was in company. If she hadn't come here – or brought Lydia to their door – none of this upset would have happened. Esmie fretted over the decisions she had made – taking Karo into their home and interfering on behalf of the troubled Zakir – actions that might have provoked the Otmanzai to try and kidnap her but had led to her friend falling into enemy hands instead.

What would be the consequences for the mission clinic if trying to rescue Lydia provoked a backlash against the Otmanzai? Once word spread among the British of the kidnap of a British memsahib, there would be moral outrage. If the army or police went after the kidnappers with force, it might lead to greater unrest among the wider Waziri population. People's lives – not just Lydia's – would be at risk. Harold's hopes of reopening the clinic at Kanki-Khel might be dashed forever.

Deep down, Esmie knew that, put in the same position again, she would still try and help Karo and Zakir. She didn't regret doing so, but she felt a great burden of guilt towards Harold that she might have endangered his work at the mission. Would they ever be able to go back to working in close partnership again? As she gazed at him in pity, she knew that the greatest tension between them might never be resolved: her desire for a baby and his refusal to become a father.

Unexpectedly, Harold spoke. 'It's not your fault that Lydia is missing. I know you are blaming yourself – but I don't.'

Esmie was tearful. 'Thank you, Harold.'

He looked at her with sudden tenderness. 'You have been a good friend to Lydia – loyal and selfless – I don't think she appreciates how much you have always put her first.'

Esmie eyed him, trying not to blush. She thought immediately of how she had done nothing to stand in Lydia's way over marrying Tom. If she had told her friend that she was in love with Tom, would Lydia have still gone after him? Esmie suspected that she would have.

'Lydia needs more reassurance than most that she's loved,' said Esmie.

'Yes,' Harold agreed. 'I don't know why that should be. She's always had people to adore her yet she never seems to be satisfied with what she has.'

Esmie nodded. 'That's what's so sad. She has that beautiful baby boy and—' she broke off quickly.

Harold's eyes glinted with sadness. 'I know how much you care for Andrew. I'm so sorry, Esmie.'

Her heart skipped a beat. 'Sorry?'

'For not giving you what you want most of all – to be a mother.'

Esmie swallowed. 'There's plenty of time. Perhaps after all this is over – when Lydia's safely returned – we could go on local leave and have some time together. I know you'd make a wonderful father.'

Harold's expression turned desolate. He shook his head. 'I—I can't.'

Esmie's chest tightened. She had to ask him what had been preying on her mind since they'd married. 'Is it because of me – that you don't desire me enough physically?'

Harold didn't answer. She saw his jaw was clenched.

'I knew it,' said Esmie. 'Harold, I know you love another more than me but surely that doesn't mean we can't make the most of our marriage and eventually become parents.'

As she spoke he looked aghast. 'Another? How did you know?'

'Because it's always been obvious to me how you've cared for Lydia more,' said Esmie. 'I know how upset you were when she got engaged to Tom – why you suddenly took yourself off to Wales.'

Harold's expression changed. 'Oh, my dearest, you're quite wrong. It's not Lydia that I lo—' He clamped his mouth shut.

In confusion, Esmie searched his face. 'Then who?'

Harold's face turned puce. He had the desperate look of a man drowning. 'I've fought it – prayed about it.' His voice was husky, his expression guilt-ridden. 'I thought you must have guessed by now. We should never have married. It was very wrong of me to ask you, knowing that I couldn't truly be your husband. I'm so sorry, Esmie.' She heard a sob in his throat. 'I don't expect you to forgive me.'

Esmie's heart was banging in her chest as realisation began to dawn on her. He loved another but not Lydia. Was he one of those men who could only love another man? Was that why he found intimacy with her so impossible?

'But then you never loved me either, did you?' Harold said, full of regret.

'I care for you, Harold,' Esmie said, colouring.

'Care, yes. But not love. Neither of us loves each other.' He held her look. 'My dear, I know who you're in love with. I've seen how hard you've tried to suppress it but it's written all over your face every time you look at him.'

Esmie was nauseated. Surely he couldn't know? She put her hands to her burning cheeks.

'I'd never do anything to hurt you,' she whispered. 'Neither would he.'

Harold's eyes filled with compassion. 'I know that.'

Esmie's voice wavered as she asked, 'How did you know I felt like that about Tom?'

She thought she would cry at the mournful look on his face. 'Because I recognise your feelings, Esmie. I feel the same way too.'

Esmie felt winded. She searched his face but knew he was deadly serious. Harold loved Tom; his oldest friend. How had she not guessed? Yet, it made sense of everything. Perhaps deep down she had known, just hadn't wanted to face the truth.

'Oh, Harold,' Esmie said, reaching out and gently touching his bandaged hand. Tears stung her eyes.

He bowed his head. His shoulders began to shake. Esmie heard him quietly sob – and then she was weeping too.

Chapter 35

Early the next morning Baz came to tell them that police at the Kanki-Khel outpost had confirmed the rumour that a white memsahib had been seen on the road up to the border with a handful of Otmanzai. By now, they surmised, she would have been taken into the mountains beyond. They suspected Baram Wali's gang were responsible but no one would confirm it and no ransom demand had been issued.

Esmie felt numb. She had hardly slept a wink, her mind in turmoil about Harold's confession and his knowing about her feelings for Tom. Had Harold loved Tom since boyhood, or had it been a gradual falling in love in adulthood? Did Tom have any idea that his friend's feelings for him went deeper than comradeship? Esmie suspected not. How did she feel about her husband being in love with a man? And the same man as she was!

Esmie didn't know what to think. How could their marriage survive this? Harold was looking grey and his eyes glassy with lack of sleep. Yet, she forced such problems from her mind to try and concentrate on what Baz was telling them.

'So you definitely think Mrs Lomax is still alive?' Esmie asked in hope.

Baz said grimly, 'If they had wanted to shed blood, they would have left the memsahib for us to find.'

Esmie was nauseated by the thought of Lydia butchered and left for dead. Harold read her expression and said, 'Take courage, my dear.

Lydia is worth more to them alive than not. That's your opinion, isn't it, Sergeant?'

'Yes, sahib,' he agreed. 'We expect a ransom demand soon.'

'The not knowing is unbearable,' said Esmie.

'The police are doing their best,' Harold reminded her. 'All we can do is pray for safe delivery.'

Baz said encouragingly, 'You must not worry, Guthrie Mem'. The Superintendent is bringing Captain Lomax from Kohat. Then my superior will speak to the Brigadier and devise a plan for the rescue of Lomax Memsahib.'

Esmie was in awe of how many people were becoming involved in Lydia's plight. It would be the talk of every cantonment from here to Lahore before long. She feared the consequences of a large-scale rescue.

When Baz had gone, Harold said, 'One of us should be here to receive Tom. I think it best if I go to the hospital – I'm of more use there.'

Esmie's insides twisted with nerves. They had hardly spoken a word to each other since their midnight confessions. She wanted to say something to break the awkwardness between them – some reassurance that their marriage wasn't dead – but couldn't find the right words. He looked so miserable that her heart swelled with pity. Yet they couldn't deal with the implications of Harold's shock confession while Lydia remained in danger. She was their first priority.

'I'll come back at lunchtime,' he said. 'Or you can send for me if you need me.'

Esmie nodded. After her husband had gone, she could settle to nothing. Sensing anxiety in Sarah and Karo too, she organised them into a morning walk with the children to the cantonment maidan, an open stretch of yellowed grass fringed by trees that was sometimes used for games of cricket or military parades. The October sunshine was warm and the sky clear. Gabina relished tottering around the field, stopping to pick up a twig and present it to Esmie.

But the outing was only a temporary distraction from the constant nagging worry about what was happening to Lydia. Were her captors treating her well? Was she feeling very afraid and alone? Was she longing for Dickie or Tom to rescue her? At the thought of Tom, Esmie led them all home. She didn't want him to arrive to an empty house.

Harold came back for a snatched lunch but there was no sign of Tom. Esmie noticed that he was wearing a smaller bandage on his wounded hand. She felt bad for not thinking to redress his cut herself.

'Are you managing to operate all right?' she asked.

'It's fine, thank you,' Harold said over his shoulder as he hurried back to his work. 'Hardly aware of it at all now.'

It was mid-afternoon when a police motor car drew up outside the bungalow gate. Esmie went out onto the garden path, stomach churning. Tom climbed out of the back, followed by another man dressed in police uniform.

Esmie licked her dry lips and went forward to greet them. Tom, his blue eyes ringed with dark smudges, looked like he hadn't slept for two days.

They clutched each other by the hands and held on.

'Esmie!' His voice was croaky with dust.

Esmie could hardly speak for the lump in her throat. 'Tom, I'm so very sorry . . .'

She saw pain in his expression. He swallowed hard. 'We'll find her.'

He let go of her hands and stepped aside for his companion, a wiry man with a trim moustache and a crooked nose that must have been broken in some fight or sporting match.

'This is Mr Rennell, Superintendent of Police.'

Esmie shook his hand and invited them in. Rennell excused himself. 'Brigadier McCabe is waiting for me. We have much to discuss.'

'Of course,' Esmie said. 'You will keep us informed, won't you?'

'We'll be in touch very soon, Mrs Guthrie,' he promised.

She told Ali to bring in Tom's luggage and then to go and fetch Harold. As Rennell drove away, she led Tom inside.

'You'll want to see Andrew,' she said. She could tell Tom was finding it hard to speak. He nodded, his eyes glinting with emotion.

On the veranda, Esmie had fixed up a swinging basket like the one Tom had made at Linnet Cottage in Murree. Andrew was lying in it as Sarah pushed him. Tom went straight over, plucked his son from the swing and hugged him. Tears welled in Esmie's eyes to see the joy and relief on Tom's face. Andrew blew a raspberry and Tom blew one back. He kissed the boy's head and looked over at Esmie.

'Thank God she didn't take him,' he murmured. 'What on earth was she doing driving out there on her own?'

Esmie tensed. Had the police not shared her suspicion that Lydia was on her way to see Dickie? Perhaps they had thought it irrelevant once it was discovered that Lydia wasn't at Razmak and there was no proof that that was where she was heading.

'She was behaving out of character,' Esmie admitted. 'Or an exaggeration of her character – wildly exuberant one minute and deep in the doldrums the next. I couldn't get her to talk to me about what the problem was. I'm sorry; I should have kept a closer eye on her.'

Tom, still clutching Andrew, shook his head. 'She was the same in Pindi. I should never have let her travel here but she was so insistent on coming. To think how I could have put Andrew's life at risk. What if she'd decided to take him with her?'

'But she didn't,' said Esmie. She glanced across at the ayah, ever ready to see to the baby's needs. Esmie smiled at her fondly. 'I doubt if Sarah would have let her – she's very protective of him.'

Tom nodded at the nanny. 'Thank you, Sarah.'

'Why don't I take Andrew while you freshen up?' Esmie suggested. 'You can use Harold's room.'

He gave her a sharp look and Esmie flushed. She hid her embarrassment by hurrying to take the baby and going to order refreshments. By the time Tom had washed and changed, Harold had arrived.

Esmie watched the men grasp each other with firm handshakes but she could tell that Harold was being more reticent with Tom. As they took tea, Harold said little, letting Esmie answer Tom's questions. Esmie felt overwhelming pity for her husband. He must surely regret unburdening his secret to her because it lay between them, an invisible but widening gulf. It could never be unsaid and he would always now live with the fear that she might tell Tom of Harold's depth of love for him. She wanted to reassure Harold that she never would but that was for a future conversation. As it was, she also found it hard to be natural with Tom in front of Harold, for he knew the strength of her feelings too.

Their awkwardness was saved by the arrival of Sergeant Baz.

'I'm sorry to interrupt, sahib,' he said, 'but Superintendent Rennell and Brigadier McCabe wish for you to come to the Brigadier's house.'

'Now?' said Harold.

'Yes, sahib.'

Tom jumped up. 'Is there news?'

'A plan, sahib,' said Baz.

Tom looked eager as he grabbed his topee.

Harold turned to Esmie. 'I'll go with Tom. Will you be all right here on your own?'

Baz said, 'Sorry, sahib, but Guthrie Memsahib is to come too. The Brigadier was very insistent.'

They all exchanged looks. Esmie's insides tightened with nerves as she nodded and they followed Baz to his car.

They were shown into the brigadier's study, where McCabe and Rennell awaited them. They were seated around a table where a map was spread out. A bearer offered around glasses of sherry or whisky.

'Thought we might need a tipple to fortify us,' said the brigadier.

Esmie's stomach knotted as she reached for a sherry, trying to keep her hand steady. Tom took a whisky but Harold refused a drink. She could see the perspiration on his brow and knew her husband was as agitated as she was.

The brigadier took command of the briefing, Rennell nodding in agreement from time to time. In the last couple of hours they had received intelligence that a white woman had been seen inside Otmanzai country thirty miles north-west of Kanki-Khel and over the border. McCabe pointed it out on the map.

'Here at Gardan. It's a well-fortified place with the tomb of a holy man.'

Tom gasped. 'I served with an old subahdar from there – Tor Khan – a fine man. He talked proudly about the tomb of a Sufi saint.'

McCabe gave him an astonished look. 'Do you know if he's still alive?'

'I'm afraid I don't,' said Tom. 'He retired just before the War but he was as fit as a man half his age.'

Rennell said eagerly, 'We must make contact with him at once. A Pathan who has been loyal to the British could be invaluable to our cause. We'll need the permission of the Gardan headman, Mirza Ali, to enter his territory, so an ex-Peshawar Rifleman might help persuade him to cooperate. We'll send a message to Subahdar Khan on your behalf.'

'I'll take it myself,' Tom said stoutly. 'And I've brought money for a ransom too.' Esmie wondered if he had borrowed money on the value of the hotel, knowing he had no private income left.

McCabe shook his head. 'We know that if you show willingness to pay so easily that they will double or triple the amount. It also sets a precedent for kidnapping other British. Besides, we've received no ransom demand yet.'

'So what are you saying?' Tom demanded. 'That we leave Lydia to her fate? I would pay any amount to have her safe.'

'I'm sure you would, Captain Lomax,' said McCabe. 'But we can't encourage their lawlessness by doing so.'

'So what are you suggesting?' Harold asked. 'Rescuing her by force? Would that not put her life in greater jeopardy than paying a ransom?'

'It would,' McCabe conceded. 'That is why we are not planning a military intervention either. The situation in Waziristan is very volatile and the peace is paper-thin. If the army sent an expedition into independent tribal territory it would immediately provoke a hostile response and escalate tensions in the border region. The Otmanzai have tribal links across the border in Afghanistan and they would simply spirit Mrs Lomax further into the mountains. It would be nigh on impossible to rescue her from there.'

'So?' Tom prompted, his brow furrowed.

McCabe exchanged glances with Rennell and the Superintendent nodded.

McCabe continued, 'From our police sources, we think that the kidnap was a rash, unplanned action by Baram Wali and his henchmen without the knowledge of the mullahs or other Otmanzai leaders, such as Mirza Ali. We think—'

'Good God!' Tom exclaimed. 'Isn't Baram Wali that monster who hacked off his wife's nose? To think he might have Lydia in his clutches . . .'

Harold put a steadying hand on his friend's shoulder. 'We don't know for sure. Let's hear the brigadier out.'

Tom clenched his teeth and nodded.

McCabe continued. 'We think that if we get the mullahs on our side then they could put pressure on the kidnappers to release Mrs Lomax. That way, there would be no need for a ransom or violent intervention.'

'How would you do that?' Tom asked.

'By appealing to their conscience,' said McCabe, 'and reminding them that it is against their Muslim law to mistreat a woman by kidnapping her.'

Tom looked sceptical. 'I don't see how . . .?'

Rennell elaborated. 'Sergeant Baz says there is a very influential priest, Mullah Zada, who looks after the holy tomb in Gardan. He must be persuaded to negotiate with the kidnappers.'

'So you are planning a police expedition?' Harold asked.

'Of sorts,' said McCabe.

'Meaning?' Tom queried.

With a nod from the brigadier, Rennell explained. 'We are planning a low-key foray into the mountains – no more than three or four people with the help of local guides. This way we hope to attract as little attention as possible. Sergeant Baz will be in charge.' He paused. 'What we need is a British civilian – a person of courage and resourcefulness – to bargain on behalf of Mrs Lomax. Someone who speaks passable Pashto and won't be seen as a threat.'

'Non-military?' Harold asked.

Rennell nodded.

'Send me,' said Tom at once.

'You are ex-army,' said McCabe.

Again, McCabe and Rennell swapped glances. The superintendent said, 'We also think it would be invaluable if the envoy had medical experience in case Mrs Lomax is in need of treatment.'

'I will go then,' said Harold.

Rennell shook his head. 'You are too well known as a missionary, Dr Guthrie, and a Christian. The rescue party must be made up of Muslim Pathans – with the exception of the one person we have in mind.' He turned his assessing gaze on Esmie.

'Me?' She gaped at him in astonishment.

'Mrs Guthrie, if you put yourself into the hands of Mullah Zada he would be bound by his code of honour to protect you while you are under his roof.'

'You can't be serious?' Harold gasped.

'Certainly not!' Tom cried. 'What's to stop them taking Esmie too? You told me yourself that the brigands who took Lydia might have mistaken her for Esmie.'

Esmie, heart pounding, raised her hand to silence them. 'Let the superintendent explain.'

She saw Tom scowl as he bit back his words. Harold looked pale and sweating, his brow etched in anxiety.

Rennell addressed Esmie directly. 'Baz tells me that you and the good doctor treated a young mullah from the Otmanzai tribe and that you helped a lunatic boy from among his kin?'

Esmie said, 'Not lunatic. I think Zakir was suffering from shell shock. With care, I believe he would have recovered.'

Rennell nodded. 'The point being that, according to my sergeant, you made a good impression on Mullah Mahmud.'

Esmie said, 'I'm not sure about that. He was a gentle soul but shy in my presence. I wasn't able to persuade him to take care of Zakir.'

'But you showed your concern,' persisted Rennell, 'and Baz says that the mullah was overheard speaking about the feringhi nurse with admiration. That may be why he has been preaching in the village mosques condemning the kidnap.'

Esmie was surprised by this. She glanced at Harold, who gave her a fleeting smile.

The police chief continued. 'It's through Mullah Mahmud that we have heard about the sighting of Mrs Lomax in Gardan and he has agreed to accompany Baz to Gardan and seek a meeting with Mullah Zada. We think that the young mullah could be crucial to the negotiations, especially if he can influence the senior holy man.'

'It's far too risky,' Tom fretted.

McCabe answered, 'It certainly has its risks. Mrs Guthrie, you would have to face the possibility that they might exchange you for Lydia or they might keep you both. We can't force you to do this.' He looked at her with his steady gaze. 'But I know you are a brave and resilient woman – you wouldn't be working here in Taha if you weren't – and I've come to admire you greatly. I believe intervention by you offers the best chance of getting Mrs Lomax freed and brought back to Taha alive. Any British man venturing into the tribal territory might be seen as a provocation but a lady nurse with a reputation for treating Pathans would be given respect and, we hope, protection.'

Esmie was sick with fear at what he was asking. Yet, the thought of Lydia not being rescued filled her with a greater dread. She felt responsible. It was her duty to do all she could to help her friend – and those who loved her.

Rennell added, 'Of course, you must have time to think it over—'

Esmie cut him off. 'I'll do it. I'll go.'

'Esmie! We should discuss this first,' Harold exclaimed.

Esmie appealed to her husband. 'The longer we talk about it and delay doing anything, the worse the situation becomes for Lydia. It's already three days since she was taken. You must let me go.'

Harold looked desolate but nodded in acceptance.

'I'm coming with you,' Tom insisted. 'She's my wife and my responsibility.' He glared at the other men, defying them to argue back. 'I know the Frontier well and speak Pashto – I can help defend Mrs Guthrie and your officers. I can go in disguise and pass for a Pathan – I did it on occasion with the Rifles.'

The police chief frowned. Esmie realised she was holding her breath, willing Rennell to say yes.

'I can't allow it,' said Rennell. 'If you're discovered you would put Mrs Guthrie and my men in greater danger – and you would probably never see your wife again.'

Tom appealed to McCabe. 'But I could make contact with Subahdar Khan.'

McCabe wavered. 'You can go as far as the border with the rescue party. We'll try and arrange for this subahdar to be part of Mrs Guthrie's escort. But I can't allow you to go into Otmanzai territory. You mustn't jeopardise the mission, Lomax.'

Tom looked about to argue further when he caught Esmie's look. She shook her head. Tom sighed and nodded in agreement.

Esmie felt tension grip her forehead. She tried not to show her dismay that Tom would not be allowed to travel all the way to Gardan with her, but consoled herself with the thought that he would be with her as far as Kanki-Khel at the very least.

'When do we leave?' Esmie asked.

'As soon as possible,' said Rennell. 'Tomorrow or the day after if you need time to prepare. The whole operation depends on swift action so the kidnappers don't have time to disappear further into the mountains or become more emboldened.'

'In the meantime, Mrs Guthrie,' said McCabe, 'I assure you that we shall be recruiting a militia of Pathans in readiness for an attack should that become necessary.'

Esmie felt sick at the implication; the army would only send such a force if she should also become a prisoner – or worse.

'Let it be tomorrow,' said Esmie. 'Any more waiting would be unbearable.' She held Rennell's look. 'And, if he agrees to it, I'd like to take my assistant Malik with me. He's a competent orderly and has a cool head.'

Rennell nodded. 'I'll notify Sergeant Baz.'

'Bravo, Mrs Guthrie,' McCabe said with an expression of relief.

While Harold went to the hospital to fetch a saddle bag of medicines and dressings for Esmie to take, Karo helped her prepare a small bag of clothes and her bedroll. Sergeant Baz had suggested she take Pathan clothing to attract less attention. Karo talked about her husband's kin. She knew of Mullah Zada. The priest had no love for the British but

Karo thought he might be annoyed with Baram Wali for acting rashly and kidnapping a memsahib. It placed him in a tricky position.

'He won't want to appear weak among his fellow Otmanzai by giving into the demands of the feringhi,' said Karo, 'but neither will he wish to provoke the British authorities unnecessarily. No Waziri who has seen the steel birds dropping fire from the sky will ever forget it.'

Esmie, knowing how petrified Karo had been by the RAF bombing, hugged her. 'I know. But you are safe here – and so is Gabina.'

Karo looked sorrowful. 'My heart is heavy,' she said. 'If I hadn't stayed here, Lomax Mem' might be safe and you would not be putting your life in danger.' Her dark, almond-shaped eyes filled up with tears.

'None of this is your fault. It's the actions of bad men,' Esmie insisted.

At this, Karo grew agitated. 'You must beware of my husband's chief, Mirza Ali. Don't trust him. He will do what he thinks will give him advantage, even if it is the wrong thing. You must only deal with Mullah Zada, who is a man of honour.'

Esmie tried to smother her fear at her servant's words. 'I'll be careful. And I want you to stay strong and look after Dr Guthrie for me. Promise me you will?'

Karo nodded. 'And I shall pray to Allah for your safe return.'

Tom didn't linger long at the bungalow but left with Alec after an early supper, so that Esmie and Harold could be alone. Harold had been subdued since returning from the meeting at the brigadier's but once their friends had gone, he grew agitated.

'I should be coming with you,' he said unhappily.

'I know you want to,' said Esmie, 'but we have to accept what the police advise.'

'I'll worry about you the whole time you're away,' he said. 'You do know that, don't you?'

'Yes, of course I do.' She gave him a wistful smile.

His hazel eyes were glassy with tears. 'Esmie, do I disgust you? After what I told you last night . . .'

She was aghast. 'No, Harold; you mustn't think that!'

'But I've made you unhappy – tricked you into marrying me. I thought being married might help me overcome my – my feelings.'

Esmie put a hand on his arm. 'You didn't trick me into anything. I wanted to come to Taha and work here alongside you. That hasn't changed.' She squeezed his arm. 'Harold, I don't know what will happen in the long run – neither of us do – and freeing Lydia is all I can think of at the moment. If—' She checked herself. 'When I get back, we can talk about the future.'

He nodded in agreement but she could see how upset he was. Gently, she asked, 'Will you let me lie beside you tonight? I don't ask anything more than that. I just want to feel you next to me, Harold. It gives me such comfort.'

His eyes watered. 'Yes,' he said, his voice croaky. 'I'd like that too.'

That night, they lay together on top of Harold's bed, a blanket thrown over them and Esmie snuggled in under his arm.

She was terrified of what lay ahead. Her heart thumped anxiously in her chest. But she drew strength from Harold's warm body.

'Will you read to me?' she asked.

He gave a grunt of amusement. '*Old Mortality*?'

'Yes, please.' She smiled as he reached into his bedside drawer. It was the novel that they had returned to on several occasions since the first night of their marriage.

Harold began to read, in his deep, sonorous voice. Esmie rested her head on his chest. Her racing pulse slowed and calmness stilled her anxious mind. Her eyelids grew heavy. She would always love her husband's reading voice. It was the last thought she had before succumbing to sleep.

Chapter 36

Kanki-Khel

Esmie and Tom spoke little on the journey to Kanki-Khel as they took it in turns to sit in the front of the truck with Sergeant Baz and his driver, Hasan, or in the back with Malik and another guard. Swaying in the back of the truck, gripping on to a hard wooden bench, made Esmie travel sick – or that was her excuse for keeping her distance from Tom – and she spent most of the time up front staring rigidly out of the vehicle, trying to keep calm.

The journey was a painful reminder of her trip the previous year with Harold, when she had gone with such excitement and anticipation for the work that lay ahead. Now she was in dread of what was to come. What state would Lydia be in? What if they couldn't find her? What if the vengeful Otmanzai seized her too and had no intention of making a deal with the British? She might never make it back to Taha.

Then she looked at the stoical face of the Pathan police officer and was encouraged. Baz was a brave and wise man who was prepared to risk his own life for all their sakes. But he must also believe that they had a chance of success or he would not be undertaking such a hazardous task. Sitting beside him gave Esmie reassurance. She felt a renewed strength of purpose – and something else that reminded her of the times she had nursed in dangerous situations during the War – a surge of courage.

After a long tiring drive, in which Esmie felt every bone in her body had been jarred and jolted, they arrived in Kanki-Khel and disembarked inside the police outpost. Esmie was queasy and wondered if it was partly due to her being back in the place where she and Harold had lived for those short, intense but happy weeks before they had had to flee. Looking back, Esmie could see that relations between them had never been the same after Kanki-Khel; awkwardness had crept into their marriage and Harold had been more distant.

At the time she had thought Harold was disappointed in her for causing trouble over Zakir and not being as whole-hearted about the aims of the mission as he was. But now she knew how he must have been struggling with the physical side of their marriage – willing himself to love Esmie in the way she wanted but finding the whole act repugnant. While she had longed for bedtime and thought their intimacy was a sign that they were growing closer, Harold must have dreaded it. To him, the night time must only have brought upset and the realisation that he would never be able to love his wife. No wonder he had returned to separate rooms in Taha with such speed and relief.

Esmie thought of her parting from Harold that morning and her eyes stung with tears. They had said little, their words and assurances banal.

'Take good care, my dearest,' Harold had said, his hands resting lightly on her shoulders.

'Of course I will,' Esmie had replied. 'I'll be fine. I'll be back in a few days, I'm sure of it.'

'I've packed some chocolate and biscuits among the medicines – I know you and Lydia have a sweet tooth.'

'Thank you, Harold. What a kind thought.'

He'd looked glassy-eyed with emotion but she hadn't wanted to linger or draw out their goodbyes so she'd kissed him on the cheek and left swiftly to the awaiting truck.

Now she was being shown in to the same small room with the large charpoy that she had shared with Harold nearly a year ago. She plonked down her bedroll and went out into the arcaded courtyard, not wanting to linger in the gloomy interior.

Tom was waiting. He gave her an anxious smile. 'Are you all right, Esmie?'

She nodded. 'Just feel a little travel sick from the journey.'

'Can you manage some dal and chapatti? It smells good.'

Esmie shook her head and grimaced. 'Not just yet. Tea would be nice though.'

That evening, at Esmie's insistence, they ate with Malik and their police escorts. They were all in this together and it seemed absurd to keep to the rigid social code of the cantonment at such a time. They sat on bolsters under the courtyard arcade and Esmie forced herself to eat a small portion of the simple meal of curried potatoes, dal and chapattis. Then the men sat back and smoked and drank more tea.

Baz went over the plans. 'I've sent word to Mullah Mahmud and asked him to meet us here. I'm hopeful he will bring Subahdar Khan with him – I've asked him to. We'll have to wait until they come before our next move. It's too risky just to turn up at Mullah Zada's home in Gardan. And we need a guarantee of safe passage from Mirza Ali before we set off.'

Esmie felt a stirring of unease at the mention of the Otmanzai chief whom Karo had told her not to trust.

'And you think Gardan is where Lydia is being held?' Tom asked, not for the first time.

'It's most likely, sahib,' said Baz, 'but as I've said, we can't be certain.'

'Can't you find out where she is first?' Tom said. 'Rather than go off on a wild goose chase. We don't want Mrs Guthrie to be at any more risk than she already is.'

'Sahib, Mullah Zada will deal with any ransom demand or negotiation, so we must go through him. Getting the holy man's cooperation is of prime importance.'

Seeing how Tom was growing agitated, Esmie decided not to raise her doubts about trusting Mirza Ali. Instead she said, 'I'm sure Sergeant Baz is right about this. We just have to be patient.'

Tom sighed. 'Sorry, you're right of course. I'm just not good at sitting around and waiting.'

Esmie excused herself and went early to bed. She knew she wouldn't sleep but she found it even harder being near Tom and having to act normally. She didn't really know what he was thinking, yet she knew he was acutely worried over Lydia and would do anything to get her safely back. They were both feeling guilty at not having taken Lydia's increasingly volatile moods seriously.

She climbed into her bedroll and lay listening to the murmur of men's voices in the courtyard. Eventually they fell silent. Esmie imagined Tom lying down just yards away from her under the arcade where he had unrolled his bedding. Was he sleepless like she was? Was he thinking of Lydia and Andrew? That morning he had come early to the bungalow to see his son. Esmie had been tearful at the sight of Tom holding his son tightly in his arms and murmuring, 'I'll bring your mother back, I promise.' Then he'd kissed the baby goodbye and handed him over to Sarah. Perhaps at that moment, he had vowed to save his marriage to Lydia for his son's sake and that was why he was all the more determined to find his wife.

The next day, Esmie found the waiting almost as unbearable as Tom obviously did. No word came from Mullah Mahmud or any further news of Lydia's whereabouts.

That afternoon, Baz allowed them to take a walk outside the fort as long as Malik went as protection. He advised them not to wander far or attract too much attention. Esmie and Tom skirted the village and walked along the riverside. The poplar trees were turning golden and the air was sharp compared to Taha. A farmer went by on a mule and two grubby-faced children came up asking for matches. One carried a swaddled baby on her back. Tom fished out a box of matches and gave it to the boy. The children beamed and hurried away. Tom stared after them with a wistful look.

'Shall we sit for a bit?' Esmie suggested, reluctant to return to the fort.

Tom hesitated, as if movement was the only thing stilling his feverish thoughts. He nodded. They sat on flattish stones that Esmie presumed were used by dhobis for the scrubbing of clothes. Malik stood a discreet few paces away and kept guard.

Tom lit up a cigarette. Esmie watched the spiral of smoke rise into the still air. He regarded her.

'Before we left, Alec Bannerman let slip that Lydia had taken one of his maps as well as his car – that she'd quizzed him about the road to Razmak and the Frontier.'

Esmie's heart jolted but she said nothing.

'Do you think that's where she was going?' he pressed her.

'She wasn't thinking straight,' said Esmie.

'Or she was thinking of Dickie Mason,' Tom said with a bleak look. 'Why do I get the impression that everyone has been trying to keep me in the dark about where Lydia was going? Don't I have a right to know?'

Esmie avoided his look. 'We don't know where she was going – only that she was kidnapped. Lydia is the one to answer your questions when we find her.'

Tom nodded. 'Yes, you're right. I'm sorry – it's just going round in my head trying to work out what was going on.'

He carried on smoking, his expression tense. Esmie gazed at the way the sun sparkled on the tranquil river, feeling bad about not being open with Tom. But what use was it to feed his suspicions over Dickie when their focus should be on securing Lydia's release?

'You don't have to answer this,' Tom said, 'but how are things between you and Harold?'

Esmie felt her insides flutter. 'Why do you ask?'

'You both seemed . . . not yourselves.'

'The past couple of weeks have been a strain,' Esmie said.

'I understand about that – Lydia's visit turned into a nightmare for you both – but that's not what I mean.' He squinted at her through cigarette smoke. 'I see how you live at the bungalow, like brother and sister.'

Esmie's cheeks burned. 'Harold doesn't want us to have children.'

The stark words hung between them. Saying them aloud made the unhappy situation real, the decision final. She felt a wave of desolation to think she would never become a mother.

Swiftly, Tom ground out his cigarette and pulled out a handkerchief. Until he handed it to her, Esmie hadn't realised she was crying.

'I'm sorry,' he said, his look tender. 'I know how much you love children. I can't imagine why Harold should feel that way.'

Esmie wiped at her tears. Tom had obviously not guessed that his friend was homosexual. She wanted to protect her husband. Better that Tom thought Harold didn't want a family rather than admitting that he couldn't physically bring himself to have sex with her.

'The mission is his life,' she said. 'He would worry too much if we had a family here. I've come to accept it.'

She was about to hand the handkerchief back when something caught her eye; the initials E.McB. were embroidered on one corner. She looked at it in confusion. It was one of her old handkerchiefs from before she was married. Esmie looked at Tom. 'How . . .?'

His jaw had reddened. He stared back at her intently.

'You dropped it in the churchyard at St Ebba's. I picked it up, meaning to give it back to you but . . .'

Esmie's heartbeat began to quicken. 'But what?'

His look was almost fierce. 'I kept it so I had something to remind me of you. Wherever I was, I carried it with me so I would feel close to you, Esmie.'

She stared at him. The pulse in her throat made her breathless. She swallowed. 'You shouldn't have.'

'I know, I shouldn't.' Tom took her hand and gripped it. 'But I think even then, I knew deep down that I was in love with you.'

'Tom don't—'

'Let me finish,' he interrupted. 'We've both made our choice of partner in life and we can't change that. I would never do anything to betray my friend Guthrie. But you're in this dangerous situation and I might never get the chance to tell you this, if I don't do so now.' He ran his thumb over the back of her hand. 'I want you to know, Esmie, how much I love and admire you. I've never known a woman with more beauty and courage – not even my first wife, Mary, is dearer to me now. I'm filled with sorrow that you are married to a man who doesn't love you in the way you deserve – but full of admiration that you would put everything you have at risk to go and save your friend.'

The tender look he gave her made Esmie's heart ache. Her eyes were welling again with tears.

'My dearest Esmie,' Tom said. 'I wish I could undo time and go back to when we sat by the wall of St Ebba's Church. If I could, I would ask you to marry me.'

Esmie stifled a sob. She held his passionate look. This moment, however fleeting, was theirs alone. It might be the only chance she would get to be truthful to Tom about her feelings too. She was frightened of what was to come. Yet, sitting here under the autumnal trees beside the man she held dearest in the entire world, she felt brave. The thought of his love for her would sustain and support her through the ordeal. What happened after that – if they all survived – she would just have to accept.

She squeezed Tom's hand in return. 'And I would have said yes, Tom. I can't deny that I love you with all my heart too. I spent a long time trying to convince myself that I didn't, but it was like trying to turn back the tide – impossible to defeat. I married Harold so that I could do something worthwhile with my life and come to India to nurse where there was a great need for women medics. But I only said yes to him because I couldn't have the man I truly loved. That is why I have come to terms with the platonic marriage that I have. I don't want your pity, Tom. My life is enriched by other people's children – including wee Andrew. That's the life I've chosen.'

Esmie swallowed the tears in her throat. 'So when we go from here, we must never speak of this again or show our feelings for each other. It's enough for me to know that I'm loved by you, Tom. But you have Andrew's happiness to consider and he needs his mother. I accept that too.'

Tom's face was taut with sorrow. She saw him struggling to speak, yet his jaw clamped down on the words he wished to say. Better that he left them unsaid. Instead, he lifted her hand and pressed it to his lips, kissing it firmly and with sweet desperation. Esmie shook with emotion. For a long time, he simply held her hand and gazed at her with his handsome blue eyes. She wanted the moment to last forever, to never have to let go his hold. But she forced herself to do so.

'Keep this,' she said softly, pushing the handkerchief into his hand.

He gave her a wistful smile and a look of longing, before tucking the handkerchief back in his inner pocket. Then he helped her to her feet.

Her heart breaking, Esmie led the way back to the police outpost.

Chapter 37

Just before dusk, five riders appeared at the gates of the fort. Mullah Mahmud had arrived from over the border, bringing with him Subahdar Tor Khan from Gardan and three other Otmanzai.

Tom and his old comrade greeted each other with enthusiastic handshakes. Esmie was touched when the old white-bearded soldier extended his hand in welcome to her too and spoke in English.

'Guthrie Memsahib, you are a brave lady and it is an honour to meet you.'

'Thank you,' Esmie replied. 'And you are very kind to offer your help, subahdar.'

Mullah Mahmud was more reticent, obviously finding it awkward to have Esmie among their throng as they sat and ate together. But Esmie was not going to be parted from Tom any sooner than she had to be. Wary of the Otmanzai guards with their ragged beards and dark clothes, she sat close to Tom and listened while the men talked, hardly able to swallow her food for nervousness. The subahdar was explaining that they still didn't know exactly where Lydia was.

'But I believe she is alive. One of my servants is sure he saw a white woman leaving the homestead of Baram Wali's brother just before dawn two days ago.'

'So my wife could already be far from Gardan by now?' Tom asked in alarm.

'It is possible,' the old man admitted, 'but unlikely. The gang would need time to arrange for a new hiding place – asking favours of kin in Afghanistan, for example.'

'And you think it is Baram Wali behind this?'

Mullah Mahmud spoke. 'I believe it is him. He won't admit it to my face but he has been heard boasting about seizing a rich prize from Taha.'

Esmie's stomach turned to hear Lydia described in such terms.

The subahdar nodded in agreement. 'He and his kin are notorious for their wild behaviour – stealing and fighting are second nature to them. I would itch at the chance to send them packing.'

Tom gripped his shoulder. 'You are still a Rifles' man at heart, my friend.'

Esmie asked, 'So why haven't they made any demands for money yet?'

Tor Khan stroked his long white beard, a kindly look in his grey eyes. 'It might be a good sign that they haven't. Perhaps they never had a clear plan and don't know what to do next.'

Esmie didn't like to say that a criminal gang who couldn't agree among themselves might be a greater threat to Lydia than one who could. She wondered how much the Otmanzai warriors understood of the conversation which had been conducted in a mixture of English and Pashto. One was the subahdar's servant but the other two had been sent by Mirza Ali to look after the mullah. These two said little but their look was watchful. What if one of them was kin to Baram Wali and was already plotting how to capture her too?

It was agreed they would leave promptly in the morning. Gardan was a full day's ride away and over two passes.

'Mirza Ali is sending a larger armed guard to meet us at the border,' said the mullah.

Esmie saw the concern on Tom's face. 'I thought this was to be a small inconspicuous party. Does this escort have the blessing of Mullah Zada?'

The young mullah hesitated and then said with a fatalistic shrug, 'We cannot pass through Mirza Ali's land safely without it.'

After a moment, Tor Khan put his hand on Tom's arm. 'Help me up, sahib. My legs have grown stiff and I would be grateful if you would see me to my sleeping mat.'

Esmie saw the look of understanding pass between the two old comrades. There was nothing wrong with the subahdar's legs; he wanted a word in private with his former officer.

Esmie hardly slept. She tossed restlessly on her charpoy, falling into fitful sleep. She was woken at dawn by Malik bringing her a glass of tea with an encouraging nod. Groggily, she drank the sweetened tea and listened to the men saying their prayers in the courtyard beyond. Then Esmie got up and dressed in the loose pantaloons, long shift dress and thick woollen jacket that Karo had packed for her and tied a scarf around her head. Shivering in the cold, she was glad of her sturdy riding boots too.

Emerging from her room, she gasped in shock as a Pathan loomed out of the half-dark towards her.

'It's me!' the man said quickly.

'Tom? I hardly recognised you.'

He looked warrior-like in shalwar kameez, sheepskin waistcoat, turban and a belt bristling with cartridges. She heard the amusement in his voice as he answered, 'You hardly look like one of the sahib-log in your outfit either.'

She couldn't help but smile. 'No, I don't suppose I do.'

He steered her back into the shadows and lowered his voice.

'I'm coming with you over the border.'

Esmie's heart jolted. 'But you can't. Rennell and McCabe said—'

'They don't know the situation on the ground,' Tom interrupted. 'I don't trust Mirza Ali not to take advantage of another feringhi woman coming into his fiefdom. Tor Khan has appointed me his henchman and will vouch for me should I be challenged. Mullah Mahmud doesn't object to my coming – he told me he'd do the same if it was his wife in jeopardy.'

'What does Sergeant Baz say to this?'

'He's in agreement,' Tom answered. 'He won't say so, but I think he's contemptuous at his superiors for sending a British woman into tribal territory without any protection from her own kind.' Tom touched her on the shoulder. 'And so am I.'

Esmie's spirits soared. 'I can't pretend I'm not thankful. But you mustn't take any unnecessary risks, Tom. Promise me that?'

Tom gave her a wry look. 'No more than you will, Esmie.'

They rode on horseback for the border: Esmie, Tom, Baz, Malik, Mullah Mahmud, the subahdar and the three guards. Both Baz and Malik were also dressed in native clothes. There were no uniforms or topees to provide a target for snipers. Esmie's heart pounded as hard as the hooves of her pony – a stocky chestnut mare from the police stables – as the mountain tracks grew increasingly narrower and steeper. At the top of the pass a solitary mile post marked the border, which was overlooked by a fortified police picket. Waiting for them on the far side were a dozen more Otmanzai tribesmen.

Esmie took one last look back at distant Kanki-Khel, wondering if she would ever return to British India and Harold again. Turning back, she caught Tom's steady look of encouragement. She tried to convey without words how much she wanted him there. Then she kicked her horse forward and followed her escort down into Otmanzai country.

As the sun strengthened and the air warmed, they followed a river and entered a steep-sided gorge. Among the Otmanzai was a young, thin-faced man, who said he was a son of the chief. It troubled Esmie that the escort had been sent by Mirza Ali and not Mullah Zada. Although she had treated scores of men at the clinic in Kanki-Khel the previous year, she did not recognise any of the bearded and turbaned men, armed to the hilt with long knives, pistols and old-fashioned muzzle-loading jezails. The further they travelled into the mountains, the more her anxiety grew that they were being lured into a trap. Baz had left instructions that if they didn't return to Kanki-Khel within the week, then the army were to be called out.

Only the thought of Tom, riding close behind, stopped her from succumbing to fear and fleeing back to safety. How glad she was that he had defied orders and insisted on coming. The presence of the old subahdar was comforting too. Surely he must carry some authority over his fellow tribesmen? Or would it be held against him that he had soldiered for the despised feringhi?

After two hours, they stopped to rest the horses at a hut made of mud-baked bricks with a straw awning, where a toothless, weather-beaten man and a young boy served tea and slices of watermelon to the travellers. Baz paid them and tried to strike up a conversation with the old man, but he said little in response. Yet Esmie took heart from the fact that their escort had thought to provide them with refreshments. As they sat on a dusty carpet under the awning, she exchanged glances and encouraging smiles with Tom. Soon they were in the saddle again.

The path grew narrower and more precipitous. The midday sun dazzled the eye, glinting off buff-coloured rock and making Esmie perspire. Birds of prey wheeled in the air thermals above. Occasionally, she would see a cluster of low-lying houses nestled into the hillside, only distinguishable from the landscape by the splash of orange and yellow on their flat roofs from drying corn and gourds. Esmie thought of the women she had treated the previous November and wondered if any of them lived in these remote hamlets. What tough and isolated lives they must live, eking out a living in a harsh climate from a thin soil. Karo too must have come from such a place.

Esmie tried to imagine what it had been like for Lydia, forced along this route a few days earlier. How terrifying it must have been to be alone with her captors, perhaps trussed to a pony or mule, wondering when her ordeal would end and yet dreading where they might be going. Whatever Esmie felt, it would be nothing to the fear her friend must have experienced.

They trekked on. It occurred to Esmie that their escort might be taking them in a circuitous route so that they would not easily find their way back again without a guide. Baz had admitted that he had never ventured as far as Gardan before, though his mother's kin were distantly related to the Otmanzai and one or two had been on pilgrimage to the holy tomb. No British had been there since a border war over twenty years ago, when the army had sent troops in to subdue the tribesmen in revolt.

Eventually, the Otmanzai guards led them down a steep slope to a river crossing of uneven boulders around which the river swept. The first half a dozen Otmanzai plunged their horses into the shallows and got quickly across. Baz and Subahdar Khan followed. Tom brought his horse up beside Esmie's.

'Ready?' he asked. She nodded.

Esmie's pony whinnied nervously. She urged it on. It slipped and slithered between the rocks, nearly pitching Esmie into the rushing water. She cried out.

'Hold on!' Tom shouted. He was there instantly, grabbing the bridle and steadying the animal.

One of the Otmanzai, surprised at Tom's cry in English and mistaking his sudden movement as suspicious, turned, shouted and fired his gun in the air. Esmie's horse, spooked by the noise, bucked and scrambled for the far side, tipping Esmie from the saddle. She tumbled into the water, bashing her hip on a rock.

At once, Tom threw his reins for Malik to catch hold of and jumped down. Splashing through the water, he reached for Esmie and pulled her up. The guards began shouting and gesticulating at Tom. The subahdar barked at them in rapid Pashto.

'Are you all right?' Tom asked anxiously. 'Can you walk?'

Esmie clung on to him in shock. 'Yes,' she gasped.

As he helped her from the river, she winced at the pain in her hip. Her pantaloons were soaked but she was more concerned at the volatile mood of the tribesmen. Baz, who had dismounted on the far riverbank, hurried to help. Together, the two men supported her to a nearby rock and sat her down.

The guards began to protest but the subahdar answered back robustly that the memsahib should be allowed to rest. The chief's son had a heated exchange with Tor Khan, which Esmie couldn't fully understand but she knew it must be about Tom's identity. Mullah Mahmud arrived and intervened. His soft diffident words appeared to mollify the young chieftain and he accepted the subahdar's assurances that Tom was no threat to them. Calming his men down, the chief's son decreed that they would stop for a few minutes. He ordered them to hand around grapes and nuts from one of the saddle bags.

Esmie's hip throbbed and her head pounded.

Baz and Tom looked at her in concern.

'Guthrie Mem', can you ride any further?' Baz asked.

She was dizzy and sick at the prospect. 'I'll be fine. I just need to get my breath back,' she panted.

'You can ride with me,' Tom declared. 'My horse is strong enough for two and I'm not going to risk you having another fall.'

Esmie began to protest. 'I can manage—'

'I think that would be a good idea,' Baz said, agreeing with Tom.

Soon, the Otmanzai guards grew restless and ordered them to move on. The mullah offered to swap saddles so that Tom and Esmie could use his less rigid padded cloth saddle. With Malik's help, Esmie was lifted into the saddle in front of Tom. Luckily the horse did not buck at the extra weight. Malik took charge of Esmie's pony. As they moved off, she clung to the horse's mane while Tom gripped her around the waist with one arm and took hold of the reins with the other.

Esmie could feel the strong beat of his heart against her back, which matched the hammering of her own as they clung together. She could feel the warmth of his breath on her hair. It was sweet purgatory to be pressed so close to his body knowing that they would never be intimate. Yet she thought it was her fault that the guards had discovered so soon that Tom was not a Pathan. They muttered among themselves and threw glances at the feringhis.

Tom and Esmie could only ride at a walking pace and the sun was waning by the time they emerged onto a small plateau surrounded by almost vertical cliffs. Esmie's thighs had been rubbed raw by her damp clothes and she was light-headed with fatigue, yet she dreaded the moment she would have to leave Tom's safe hold and face the unknown.

A village of huts hugged the bottom of the far cliff, while the mountainsides were peppered with fortified houses that seemed to defy gravity. At the centre of the village was a simple domed structure that glowed dusty gold in the last rays of sun.

'The holy tomb,' Baz said with wonder in his voice.

'Gardan,' the subahdar confirmed with a note of pride. 'I will be honoured if you would stay at my home.'

But soon an argument broke out between the old soldier and the chief's son.

Tor Khan explained in agitation that Mirza Ali was insisting on Esmie being his guest instead.

'You will come to my father's homestead,' the young warrior decreed. 'My mother's zanana will be more comfortable than the house of a subahdar.'

Esmie could hardly refuse without insulting the chieftain. Besides, her party were completely outnumbered by Mirza Ali's men.

'That is very kind of you,' she answered as calmly as she could.

They skirted the plateau as the sun sank out of sight and the air instantly turned chilly. At the mouth of a narrow gorge, hemmed in by cliffs and a rushing river, lay a fortified farmhouse with high windowless walls and a towering gateway, reminding Esmie of the stark peel towers of the Scottish borders.

Although a strip of green irrigated fields and an orchard surrounded the homestead, it looked forbidding and impregnable. A place that, once inside, it would be impossible to leave without permission. Her stomach lurched in fear. Tom must have sensed her tensing. He squeezed her to him and murmured, 'Courage, Esmie. I won't leave you until this is over. You're a brave McBride and your father would be proud of you.'

How he filled her with courage!

'Thank you,' she said, more resolute, and she sat up taller.

Ten minutes later they were crossing the river by a wooden bridge. Ahead, the gates were being pulled open. The band of riders clattered into the compound. As swiftly as they were opened, the gates clanged shut behind them.

Chapter 38

That night, Esmie lodged with the women. She was taken to the women's courtyard and they dragged out a charpoy from the dark interior for her to sit on by an open fire. They crowded around her in fascination, never having seen a white woman before. Some children pointed and giggled.

Esmie's initial fear at being separated from the men was soon dispelled by the friendliness of the women. They dried off her woollen jacket, wrapped her in a thick black blanket and gave her a bowl of milk to drink, still warm from the goat. While the older women plied her with questions, a younger one was instructed to massage Esmie's legs, which Esmie knew to be a gesture of friendship.

'How far have you come?'

'Where is your husband?'

'Who is the memsahib who has been kidnapped? Is she your sister?'

Esmie was encouraged that they appeared to have heard about Lydia. She replied that she lived in Taha with her doctor husband. 'Lomax Memsahib is a friend – from . . .' Esmie searched for the word for school. 'Madrassa.'

They marvelled at her answers, amazed that memsahibs went to school.

'You must love her like a sister to seek her here,' said Mirza Ali's wife.

'I do,' said Esmie. 'Please can you tell me where she is being held?'

She shook her head. There were rapid words exchanged between the older women.

'None of us know,' she said. 'But we pray to Allah that she is safe.'

Esmie curbed her frustration. Did that mean that Mirza Ali didn't know either or just that he hadn't told his wife? These women were powerless to help in any rescue – it was only the men who would decide the fate of both Lydia and herself. She discovered that most of the zenana women had never even been beyond the fortress. The view from the roof was the limit of their world. These women were not poor enough to go out and work in the fields or rich enough to travel with their husbands to the towns.

They busied themselves keeping the bread ovens going and preparing an evening meal, their faces illuminated in the flickering light. Beyond the high mud walls of the narrow courtyard, stars pricked the night sky. The temperature had plummeted. Esmie guessed that Gardan must be at least a thousand feet higher than Kanki-Khel. In a week or so, the first snows of winter would come to the mountains. She shuddered at the thought of them being cut off here at the mercy of the elements as well as the Otmanzai.

Wishing that she could share a meal with Tom and her other companions, Esmie sat with the women and scooped food from a communal pot, a tasty dish of pilaf and spiced minced goat, raw red onions and rounds of thick brown unleavened bread. Afterwards, tiredness overwhelmed her.

Her charpoy was taken back inside where Esmie was to bed down for the night. The room was so dark that she could hardly see two feet in front of her. The floor was of beaten earth and it smelt of animals. Groping her way to the string bed, Esmie crawled into her bedroll fully clothed. She could hear dogs snuffling and a baby whimpering. She thought she would never fall asleep.

Esmie woke scratching, wondering where she was. The dark was oppressive. She sat up in alarm. From a tiny window high in the wall, a glimmer of daylight showed her she was in a room with three other charpoys. One was empty and the other two were occupied by young girls. A curtain hung over the doorway and a dog lay beside it, scratching at fleas. Esmie was reminded that she itched all over.

She climbed out of bed, wincing at the pain in her bruised hip, pulled on her boots and went outside. The air in the courtyard was so cold her breath billowed like smoke. Some women were already baking fresh bread. In the early light, Esmie could see that the courtyard doubled as a farmyard. Hens strutted and pecked at crumbs, hunting dogs yapped to be fed and her own pony was tethered in the corner alongside two mules munching hay.

Esmie made towards the heavy wooden door that led through into the main quarters. Mirza Ali's wife came after her in a hurry.

'You must stay here,' she ordered, shooing her away from the entrance.

'But I want to see my friends,' said Esmie.

She shook her head. 'Come; sit. Drink tea with me.'

Reluctantly, Esmie did as she was told. No doubt Mirza Ali would summon her later.

As the daylight grew stronger and shafts of sunlight penetrated the enclosed courtyard, Esmie noticed that the chief's wife had a weeping encrusted eye. She went and fetched her saddle-bag of medicine.

'Let me look at that,' she said, steering the woman onto the charpoy that had been carried out once more for Esmie to sit on. The others gathered round to stare and comment.

'You have conjunctivitis,' Esmie said. 'It looks sore.' She opened her bag and pulled out some ointment. 'First we must bathe your eye in warm water.' She took out a clean tin bowl from her bag and instructed one of the women to fill it with water from the well, then Esmie warmed it on the fire bricks.

After a few minutes, she dipped pieces of cotton wool into the dish and gently swabbed the woman's eye. After a short while, the chief's wife was able to open it but it was still bloodshot.

'This is going to sting,' said Esmie, trying to explain. 'Like a small bee. Buzz buzz.'

The women laughed and winced in sympathy but the chief's wife was stoical and didn't flinch as Esmie applied some lotion. To protect it from the dirt and germs, Esmie taped a piece of gauze over the infected eye. To her surprise, her patient almost preened, as if the bandage from the feringhi memsahib conveyed distinction.

Within minutes, others were coming to her with their ailments and Esmie was occupied all morning cleaning old wounds, applying dressings and administering ointments and tablets.

By the afternoon, she was restless and eager to know what was happening beyond the zenana. Were the men locked in a council of war over what to do? Had Mullah Zada been summoned? Perhaps Mullah Mahmud had taken Baz and Tom to see the senior mullah at his home by the saint's tomb. Surely word would come soon.

Esmie paced around the small courtyard almost bursting with pent-up energy. Doubts beset her once again over whether Mirza Ali could be trusted. She already felt like a captive confined to this dismal over-crowded yard. What if the Otmanzai chief had imprisoned the men of her party? How would she know? She clung to the belief that Subahdar Khan would not allow such a breach of hospitality. They were guests of the Otmanzai, not prisoners.

She occupied herself with teaching some of the children to play noughts and crosses using a stick on the dusty ground. When the light began to fade again, Esmie lost patience.

'You must allow me to see my friends,' she told Mirza Ali's wife. 'Please! I wish to be taken to see them now.'

This prompted lively discussion among the women. Eventually a boy was dispatched with a message. Almost an hour later, when Esmie was beginning to despair that anyone would come, Mirza Ali himself appeared. Esmie could tell by his swaggering gait and the way the women treated him with deference, that this was the headman of Gardan.

He looked of indeterminate age; his hair was hidden under a large white turban but his beard was grizzled. His skin was pitted with scars that showed he'd survived smallpox and he looked on her with shrewd dark eyes. He greeted her formally.

'I welcome you to my home, Guthrie Mem'. I trust you are being well looked after?'

'Very well, thank you. Your wife and daughters are being very kind.'

'And I see you have been giving out feringhi medicine to my women,' he said. 'I thank you for that.'

'I'm happy to do that, sir. But I have been here nearly a day and have been told nothing of the plans to rescue my friend, Lomax Memsahib. I hope you have come with news.'

He gave a non-committal shrug. 'These things are not easy to solve.'

She waited for him to elaborate. Instead he began fussing over one of the hounds.

Esmie persisted. 'I would like to be taken to see Mullah Zada. I'm told he has influence over the kidnappers.'

The headman shook his head. 'That is not possible. Mullah Zada has refused to meet with a feringhi woman.'

Esmie felt dashed. 'So who will he meet with? It's important to act quickly.'

Mirza Ali fixed her with a look. 'We don't know yet who these men are – if indeed your feringhi friend has been brought here at all.'

She fought to remain calm. 'Mrs Lomax has been seen in Gardan. It is openly acknowledged that Baram Wali is responsible for the kidnap.'

He feigned surprise. 'Is that so?'

Esmie was sure that Tom and the others would already have had this conversation. Perhaps he was belittling her because as a woman she shouldn't be challenging him. She changed tack.

'It's good of you, sir, to offer us hospitality and to help us in our search. In the meantime, are there others of your kin who have ailments that need treating?'

He looked pleased at her offer. 'My uncle has bad legs. He can hardly walk.'

'Then I shall speak to my orderly, Malik, and see if we can help him. I can come with you now.'

He considered this for a moment, as he fondled one of the dogs. 'Very well,' he agreed.

The conditions in the men's quarters were almost as uncomfortable as the women's, though they seemed a little less cramped and there were bolsters spread under an awning where the senior men sat and smoked. Esmie, clutching her medical bag, couldn't hide her relief at seeing Tom and Malik leaning against a wall sharing cigarettes.

Tom came rushing forward. 'Esmie! Are you all right?'

Esmie, aware of Mirza Ali's assessing gaze, nodded and gave a tense smile. 'The chief's uncle needs medical attention. Perhaps you and Malik could help me?'

'Of course,' Tom agreed at once.

Malik took the bag from Esmie as they were ushered over to an ancient-looking tribesman propped up by cushions. His face was as brown and wrinkled as a walnut under a vast white turban. He peered at Esmie with rheumy eyes, said something in a thin reedy voice that Esmie didn't catch and then began to chuckle.

'What did he say?' she asked.

Tom gave her a rueful look. 'He says your white face looks half-baked.'

Esmie gave a huff of amusement. 'I'll resist telling him he looks like a prune.'

Together with Malik they inspected the old man's legs. They were bent and stiff with rheumatism.

'He's never going to run again,' said Esmie, 'but we can rub on some embrocation and ease his joints.'

As they did so, Mirza Ali wandered off and Esmie was able to quietly ask Tom what, if anything, was happening to rescue Lydia.

'Baz has gone with Mullah Mahmud and the subahdar to speak to Mullah Zada – to try and persuade him to summon the kidnappers and confront them with what they've done.'

'When did they go?'

'Couple of hours ago. Mullah Zada wouldn't see them at first. He thought you might be with them and he's refusing to see a feringhi woman.'

This worried Esmie. 'So how am I to petition him on behalf of Lydia?'

'Mullah Mahmud might be able to win him round,' Tom encouraged.

'Were you not allowed to go either?'

'Baz thought it best if I kept out of the way too,' Tom admitted. 'Mirza Ali has been ridiculing me about having no control over my wife. Says if I'd kept her in purdah this would never have happened.'

'Imagine Lydia in purdah,' Esmie said wryly. 'You mustn't let him provoke you.'

'I feel so damn useless,' Tom said in exasperation.

'But you're not,' Esmie assured him. 'I feel safer having you here.' They exchanged quick smiles. Esmie murmured, 'I don't trust our host.

What if he's in league with the gang? He was pretending to have no knowledge of them and even implied that Lydia might never have been brought to the area at all. Yet the women of the zenana have heard about her.'

'I feel the same about him,' said Tom. 'I think he's an opportunist who's after something for himself. He's just waiting to see which way things go.'

Soon afterwards, Mirza Ali returned and told Esmie that his wife was expecting her back in the zenana.

'I would like to wait until Mullah Mahmud returns,' she said, 'and hear what he has to say.'

The headman spread his hands wide. 'Who knows when that might be? When these mullahs get together, they can talk for hours. Perhaps he will stay the night there.'

'Let the memsahib eat with us this evening,' Tom suggested.

The chief shook his head and laughed. 'And make my wife jealous? I cannot allow such a thing.'

Reluctantly, Esmie saw she had no option but to return to the women's quarters. As she left, she said firmly, 'I shall return tomorrow and treat your uncle's legs again.'

Unable to bear another night in the tomb-like flea-ridden bedroom, Esmie slept on her charpoy by the fire in the courtyard. Wrapped in blankets and with a scarf covering all but her eyes, she bedded down under the stars. One of the hounds came and lay down under her bed and she fell asleep to the comforting sound of mules munching hay.

The next day was similar to the first. During the hours of waiting, Esmie kept busy nursing the petty illnesses of Mirza Ali's household. In the brief time she was permitted into the men's courtyard to treat the old patriarch, Tom was able to tell her that the young mullah and Baz had returned once more to confer with Mullah Zada.

That night, lying sleepless in the courtyard, she could hear raised voices from the men's quarters. It sounded like they were holding a Jirga – a council of local men – judging by the volume and number of competing voices. She strained to hear but couldn't make sense of what they were saying. Overall, one voice dominated; a deep resonant voice that carried authority. Esmie felt hope flutter inside. Could this be Mullah Zada come with a plan to help them?

She could hardly bear the wait until morning and stayed awake long after the voices had ceased and the flicker of lamps had been extinguished.

On the third day, as Esmie was bathing the eye of the chief's wife and commenting on how it looked less inflamed, a boy appeared and summoned her next door. Her hope leapt as she hurried after him.

The tense expressions on the faces of Tom and Baz made her insides clench. They stood up as she came in but Mirza Ali, his son and henchmen continued to sit. Mullah Mahmud sat between the two sides. He greeted her without meeting her look. Esmie's heart thumped in her chest as she sat down on the cushion provided for her.

'What news?' she asked. 'I heard the meeting last night. Was Mullah Zada here?'

'Yes,' Tom said. 'He has spoken with the kidnappers.'

Esmie gasped. 'And they have Lydia?'

He nodded, his eyes glinting with suppressed emotion.

'That's good news, surely? Is she all right?'

'Yes, Guthrie Mem',' said Baz. 'They insist she is.'

'Oh, thank goodness!'

'But they won't release her,' Tom said angrily. 'They are demanding a small fortune – fifty-thousand rupees. And also for immunity from revenge attacks by the British.'

Mirza Ali raised his voice. 'That is enough feringhi talk. Speak Pashto so we all understand.'

Esmie took a steadying breath and said, 'My friends tell me that Mullah Zada has spoken to the kidnappers. Is it Baram Wali's gang?'

'Yes, yes,' the chief said with an impatient wave. 'As we suspected. I will send a force to smoke those rats out of their hole.'

'No,' Esmie said at once. 'We must do nothing to endanger Mrs Lomax's life. This must be settled peaceably.'

The young mullah spoke up. 'That is what Mullah Zada wishes too. Yesterday at the tomb, Baram Wali confessed to what he had done. He said it was in revenge for his wife and daughter being kidnapped by the feringhis.'

'That's nonsense,' Tom cried. 'He mutilated his wife and so she fled for her life!'

The young mullah held up a hand to quieten him. 'Mullah Zada has told Baram Wali that it is his duty as a Muslim to release the feringhi woman – it is against the laws of Islam to harm her.'

Esmie was alarmed. 'Has he harmed her?'

'He says not,' answered the mullah.

'So will he do as the mullah asks him?'

'He still wants money.'

'I must be allowed to see for myself that she is all right,' insisted Esmie. 'That is why I was sent – because I'm a nurse. Where are they holding her?'

'He won't say,' Tom said through gritted teeth.

'We think it must be near Gardan,' said Baz. 'It was noticed that Baram Wali's horse was hardly out of breath.'

'If I'd been there, I'd have followed the blackguard!' Tom fulminated.

Esmie turned to Mirza Ali. 'Can't you persuade Baram Wali to bring Mrs Lomax here? You must have influence over him. Then perhaps we can come to some arrangement to suit everyone. We just want my friend safely back with us. Please!'

Mirza Ali cracked his fingers. The gesture made Esmie think of Harold. Would it have been better if he had come in her place? She seemed to be making no difference here.

'Perhaps there is something else Baram Wali might accept in recompense for losing his wife,' said the chief.

'Such as?' asked Tom.

'The release of some of his kin,' he replied. 'There are three Otmanzai in prison in Taha.'

Tom and Esmie exchanged looks. So this was what Mirza Ali was really after. Tom turned to Baz. 'Do you know of these men?'

The sergeant nodded and murmured in English. 'Thieves and cattle rustlers.' Then he spoke to the chief. 'We might be able to negotiate their release if the memsahib was returned unharmed and allowed safe passage to the border.'

Mirza Ali nodded. 'I will see what I can do.'

Esmie gave Tom a smile of encouragement. For the first time since arriving in Gardan, she felt a surge of optimism. The worry on his face eased a fraction as he smiled back.

Esmie spent another night of fitful sleep in the courtyard of the zenana. In the morning she rose and splashed icy water on her face, stamped her feet and walked around to warm up her stiff limbs and aching hip. She wondered how Mirza Ali's negotiations had gone with Baram Wali the previous day. If all went to plan, today would be the one where Lydia was returned to them. Please let it be so! It had been ten days since her friend's disappearance and Esmie dreaded what effect such terror and loneliness might have had on her. Lydia was used to a life of leisure and people around her who looked after her needs. She hated dirt and discomfort, and she didn't speak Pashto. These past days must have been a living hell for her. Did she have any inkling that help was at hand and that there were people close by pressing for her release?

Soon after a breakfast of curds and raisins, Esmie was summoned to the main courtyard. She went with alacrity. Perhaps Lydia was already on her way. There was no sign of Mirza Ali or his son but as soon as she saw the eager expressions on the faces of Tom and Malik, her heart leapt.

'They've agreed a deal,' Tom said, his eyes shining. 'The prisoners in Taha in exchange for Lydia.'

Esmie put a hand to her thumping chest. 'And can we do that?'

'Baz has already left with the chief's son to take a message to the border post asking for the men's release.'

'That's wonderful!' Esmie exclaimed. She sat down quickly, feeling suddenly overwhelmed. The strain of the constant worry over Lydia had been relentless.

'Of course Rennell won't allow the Otmanzai to go free until he hears that Lydia is safe,' Tom cautioned.

Esmie's euphoria subsided. 'But won't the kidnappers want the same reassurances about the release of their kinsmen?'

Doubt flickered across Tom's face. 'It will depend on good faith on both sides. Baz is to organise a handing over at the border.'

'So when will Lydia be brought here?' Esmie asked.

'Soon, I hope.' Tom's anxious expression returned. 'Mirza Ali and Mullah Mahmud have gone to meet with the gang again. I can't help thinking that the chief has been pulling the strings all along. He won't let my old friend the subahdar be involved because he was in the Rifles. Says the gang resent the interference of a British loyalist.'

'But Mullah Mahmud is a good man,' Esmie reminded him, 'and has been a true friend in trying to find and rescue Lydia. He has helped us from the start.'

'Yes,' Tom agreed. 'The mullah is on our side thanks to you, Esmie. You are the one who impressed him.'

Esmie shook her head. 'He would probably have helped anyway. He's a man of principle and faith trying to do the right thing.' She sighed. 'I wish I knew what had happened to poor Zakir. The mullah doesn't know what became of him after the raid on Kanki-Khel last year.'

Tom gave her a tender look. 'Esmie, is there anyone in the world you don't care for or worry about?'

Esmie gave a bashful smile and turned away to speak to her orderly. 'Malik, let's give the old uncle his daily massage.'

It was late morning before the chief and the mullah returned. Lydia was not with them. Esmie, who had insisted on staying with Tom and Malik, felt queasy with apprehension.

'Why haven't you brought Mrs Lomax?' Tom demanded.

Mirza Ali gave him a disparaging look. 'My kinsman doesn't trust the feringhi,' he said. 'He will not allow your wife out of his sight until he hears the prisoners are on their way from Taha.'

'Are those his terms or yours?' Tom accused him in frustration.

'Tom, don't,' Esmie warned.

The chief snapped, 'Is it any surprise that Baram Wali is suspicious? Feringhi soldiers come here for only one reason and that is to kill.'

'I'm here to rescue my wife,' Tom protested. 'I intend no harm to anyone. I have given up my life as a soldier.'

'So you would not attempt to slay your wife's kidnapper if you had the chance?' he mocked. When Tom said nothing, the chief gave a grunt. 'I thought not.'

'Sirdar,' Esmie addressed the angry Otmanzai respectfully, 'we have come in peace and put ourselves in your hands. We want no harm to come to any of your people. All we ask is that Lomax Mem' is returned to us. If this happens then there will be no need for any vengeance on behalf of the British.'

Mirza Ali nodded, looking mollified. 'On that we can agree.' He exchanged looks with the mullah.

For the first time Mullah Mahmud looked Esmie in the eye as he spoke. 'Baram Wali has said he will allow you to see Lomax Memsahib – to prove that she has been well treated.'

Esmie's heart leapt. 'Will he? When?'

'Today if you wish.'

'Of course! Where?'

'At the house where she is being held.'

'No,' Tom said at once. 'It must be here or at a neutral place – Mullah Zada's home.'

Before the mullah could answer, Mirza Ali said, 'He could not be persuaded to bring her here because of your presence. And the women cannot be allowed near the holy site.'

Tom looked at Esmie beseechingly. 'Then you cannot go.'

Esmie's insides churned. 'I have to,' she answered. 'I can't bear the thought of her enduring another day of purgatory when there's a chance of me seeing her. Surely you want that too?'

Tom's face was harrowed. 'At least wait until Baz returns and can protect you.'

'No,' said Mirza Ali. 'He wants no feringhi lovers. Just the nurse.'

Tom glared. 'Then she won't go.'

'I will take Guthrie Mem',' the mullah said quietly. 'Allah will protect us both.'

Esmie marvelled at the young man's quiet bravery. When everyone else was at the end of their tethers with worry, he remained calm and reasoned. She saw the compassion in his dark brown eyes and knew she could trust him with her life.

'Thank you, sir,' she said. 'I accept your offer to go with me.' She ignored Tom's appalled look and turned to the chief. 'And I ask that my orderly comes with me too in case I have need of his medical help.'

After a moment's hesitation, Mirza Ali gave his agreement. Esmie knew her fate was now in his hands.

Within the hour, with her medical bag packed, she was riding out of the Gardan fortress beside Malik and the mullah, accompanied by three of Mirza Ali's men. Tom's helpless frustration was palpable. She could hardly bear to look at him in case her courage faltered. So she forced herself to look ahead and prayed that she would live to see him again.

Chapter 39

Avoiding passing the saint's tomb so as not to upset Mullah Zada, Esmie and her companions circumvented the village by riding on a steep path up the north-facing cliff. The ponies slipped on the icy ground and sent stones bouncing down to the valley below.

Esmie's whole body was tense with fear, her dread of coming face-to-face with Baram Wali again making her skin crawl. She remembered his venomous look and vitriolic outburst at Kanki-Khel. There would be little to stop him taking his revenge against her; her only protection was the words of a gentle mullah. Despite Mirza Ali's assurances, she didn't trust his men to favour her over their fellow Otmanzai if they had to choose. But she had known the risks from the start. McCabe had warned her that she might be taken prisoner too but what option did she have? She couldn't have lived with herself if she had shied away from the chance to save her friend – or at least bring her comfort and the hope of rescue.

Whatever Lydia's faults and however much their friendship had been tested in recent months, Esmie still cared deeply about her. Their friendship had been forged years ago in the pain and grief of her father's death. Lydia had stood by her then and she would stand up for Lydia now. The thought that she would be seeing her so very soon gave Esmie a renewed sense of purpose.

Esmie was surprised by how soon they arrived at the gang's hideout. It was half an hour's ride beyond Gardan. But soon she realised that this was not the place. A youth with a wispy beard appeared and approached the mullah, clasping his hand in deference. Esmie was reassured by the gesture. He told them to dismount and said they would be going the rest of the way on foot.

They toiled onwards and upwards, Esmie finding it hard to catch her breath in the thin air. The sun was at full strength and she was perspiring in her woollen jacket. Malik was carrying her medical bag as well as his rifle but she arrived exhausted outside a crumbling tower house near the top of the slope. Its walls were scorched from fire and looked half derelict. As they circled to the back, Esmie could see no doorway.

The youth whistled and shutters creaked open overhead. Another youth looked out, then disappeared again. A moment later, a rope ladder was thrown out of the window. Esmie watched in alarm. The youth nodded at them to climb.

'Is this the only way in?'

'It would seem so,' said Malik.

'Can you manage?' asked the mullah.

'Yes, thank you,' she said. She wasn't going to tell them of her fear of heights. It seemed insignificant to the terror she felt inside at the ordeal ahead. She didn't trust Baram Wali not to keep them captive too. So Esmie turned to one of Mirza Ali's guards and said, 'If we don't reappear by tomorrow, please send for your chief to have us released.'

The mullah went first. When he'd scrambled into the opening above, Esmie seized the rope and began to climb, thankful that she was wearing Pathan trousers and not a constricting dress. She swayed and gritted her teeth, forbidding herself to look down. In a couple of minutes she was at the window ledge and a youth with a squint was pulling her through.

With hammering heart, she looked around. They were standing in a tiny guardroom or lookout with hardly enough space for the three of them. Malik, his rifle taken from him, hauled himself in too. Neither the guide nor any of their escort followed and the boy in the tower pulled up the rope.

Esmie tried not to cry out when he pulled the shutters half-closed and they were plunged into semi-darkness. The cross-eyed boy opened a hatch in the floor and pointed down. In the gloom, Esmie could see rough steps of crumbling mud disappearing into the dark. The stoical mullah reached out and took her hand.

'Perhaps I can help you down?'

Esmie felt her throat tighten at the kind gesture. He sensed her fear and was putting aside his diffidence towards a feringhi woman to help her.

She smiled and they stepped cautiously onto the uneven stairs, feeling their way down. By the time Esmie reached the bottom, her heart was racing painfully. They appeared to be in almost pitch-blackness. Once Malik had joined them, the youth brushed past Esmie and she heard him lift a heavy latch. They were standing by a large wooden door. He pushed it open and bid them follow.

Esmie peered into a high-walled room like a large dungeon, except part of it was roofless and open to the elements. It was almost bare save for a low table and a couple of rugs on the earthen floor where three men were sitting and sharing a water-pipe around an open fire. They stared at the newcomers. A wiry fourth man with a prominent nose was standing waiting for them. Esmie tensed in recognition: Baram Wali.

Karo's husband gave her a sneering look but said nothing to her, turning instead to greet Mullah Mahmud. He beckoned for the mullah to sit with the others but Mullah Mahmud remained standing.

'First the lady-nurse must be allowed to see her friend,' he said. 'That is the purpose of our visit, brother.'

Baram Wali looked displeased. 'The feringhis can wait a little longer while you have tea and share a pipe.'

The mullah said, 'Do not forget your promise to me that the nurse be allowed to see the memsahib. This place is no longer secret and Mirza Ali's men stand waiting outside. It is important you keep to your side of the bargain so that your kinsmen in Taha go free. That is what you want, is it not?'

Argument broke out among the men on the floor. An older man gesticulated at Karo's husband and told him not to be weak, while a round-faced younger one tried to calm him. Esmie held her breath. Baram Wali scowled but gave a reluctant nod. He barked an order and a youth in rags and a filthy cap scrambled from the shadows.

'Bring the feringhi woman here,' he commanded. 'Then our guests can see how well we have been treating her.'

The youth pushed unkempt black hair out of his eyes. Esmie gasped in shock. 'Zakir?'

The young man stared at her in suspicion. Esmie pulled her shawl away from her head. 'I'm Guthrie Mem'. Don't you remember me?'

Recognition lit in his dark eyes. His mouth fell open in astonishment. The next moment he was throwing himself at her feet and clinging on to her.

'Get away from her!' bellowed Baram Wali. The other men stood and began to crowd around, demanding to know what was going on.

But Esmie crouched down and encircled Zakir in her arms. 'It's all right. Don't be frightened.' She stroked his head and murmured, 'I'm so happy to see you.'

The older gang member started remonstrating with Baram Wali. 'That boy should be whipped! He is too soft on the infidels.'

Baram Wali raised his hand to strike the boy. Esmie braced herself but didn't let go. Swiftly, Mullah Mahmud intervened.

'No, brother, don't hit him. He's one of Allah's children.'

'He's no better than a wild animal,' said the older kidnapper, spitting on the ground.

Baram Wali hesitated, not knowing who to please. He muttered, 'He has his uses.' Prodding Zakir with his foot, he said more forcefully, 'Get up and fetch the feringhi like I ordered. Go!'

The youth scrambled to his feet, shaking with terror. Esmie held on for a moment and said gently, 'Thank you, Zakir.'

Esmie's chest was tight with fear; the atmosphere was volatile. Mullah Mahmud was trying to calm the gang and get them to sit down with him. Baram Wali assumed control again and ordered the youth with the squint to bring tea and grapes. The mullah indicated for Esmie to join them but the aggressive man protested at this and she stayed standing with Malik at her side, staring at the door through which Zakir had gone. The wait seemed interminable but could only have been a couple of minutes.

Suddenly the door opened and Zakir was there with Lydia. She was still dressed in the clothes she had been wearing ten days ago and her hair was limp and straggling. Her face was pale and her expression anxious.

Esmie rushed to her. Lydia's eyes widened in alarm.

'Lydia; it's me, Esmie!' She held out her arms.

Lydia looked confused and then recognition dawned. She gaped at Esmie in disbelief. 'Esmie?'

'Yes.' Esmie smiled.

All at once, Lydia let out a sob and was groping towards her. They hugged each other tight. Lydia was crying so much she couldn't speak.

'We're going to get you out of here,' Esmie murmured, guessing that only Malik could understand what they were saying. 'There's a rescue party working for your release. Tom's here in Gardan too.'

'T-Tom?' Lydia stammered.

'Yes, he's a few miles away. They wouldn't let him come here in case it aggravates your gaolers but I'm allowed to see you – check that you're unharmed.'

Lydia shuddered and glanced around. 'These awful people. They're savages,' she hissed.

'That's enough feringhi talk!' Baram Wali cried. 'You can see that we have not hurt your friend. Now she must go back to her room.'

Esmie stood her ground. 'I need to check her over in private. I shall go with her. And I need my orderly too.'

'No,' Baram Wali said.

The mullah stood up and greeted Lydia politely and then turned to her captors. 'Brothers, there is no need to frighten the women. The lady-nurse must be allowed to examine the memsahib and she cannot do so in front of us.'

The four Otmanzai captors began to argue and gesticulate at each other.

Baram Wali looked annoyed but said to Esmie, 'You can go but not your servant.'

'Please let Malik stand at the door with the medicine bag in case I need him,' Esmie bargained.

'That sounds reasonable,' said the mullah. 'Don't you agree, brother?'

Baram Wali gave a dismissive wave of the hand. Quickly, before he changed his mind, Esmie steered Lydia towards the door, saying to Zakir, 'Please show us the memsahib's room.'

Zakir led them through a disused room and then another. There was a faint charred smell and some of the walls were blackened. It appeared that the place must have been burned in recent times – perhaps during the war with Afghanistan two years ago. They went down a short flight of spiral stone steps and through another empty room. Zakir pushed aside a makeshift curtain revealing a chamber whose walls had not been damaged by fire. Esmie was surprised to see it had a charpoy with a colourful blanket for sleeping, a rug on the floor and a high window that let in daylight. On a roughly hewn table was a bowl with the remains of some scrambled egg and bread. Her hopes lifted; Lydia had not been as badly treated as she'd feared.

Lydia caught her look. 'Not exactly the Savoy Hotel, is it?'

Esmie gave an astonished laugh, delighted at this spark of humour from her friend. Lydia's spirit had not been broken.

'Better than where I'm sleeping in the zenana,' Esmie replied.

'He brings me little comforts,' Lydia admitted.

'Baram Wali, your kidnapper?'

'No, that half-wit boy,' she replied. 'I don't think the others know he does it – they never come in here – but somehow he finds things.'

Esmie turned to Zakir who was hovering by the doorway with Malik.

'Zakir, thank you for being kind to my friend.' The youth gave a ghost of a smile. 'Can you stay beyond the curtain with Malik until I've had a few minutes with Lomax Memsahib?'

Zakir nodded and slipped out of the room. Esmie was encouraged to know that he understood her words.

As Malik handed over the medicine bag he said to Esmie, 'I'll have a quick look around. It seems to me this place is badly guarded by a couple of boys.'

'Be careful,' Esmie pleaded.

When they had both gone, Lydia said, incredulous, 'You sound like you know that savage boy?'

Esmie explained how she'd treated him in Kanki-Khel the previous year. Then she asked, 'Tell me how they have treated you. Do you have any injuries?'

'My feet are blistered,' Lydia complained, her eyes welling with tears again. 'They made me walk at night and hide during the day – I kept tripping in the dark. My ankle's sore and my shoes fell to bits. But the worst thing was not knowing where they were taking me or what they planned to do . . .' She clamped a hand over her mouth and stifled a sob.

Esmie was quick to put her arms around her in comfort. 'It must have been terrifying,' she sympathised. 'Have they hurt you physically?'

Lydia bristled. 'I'd have died fighting rather than allow them to touch me!'

Esmie squeezed her close. 'I knew you'd be strong.' She kissed her lank hair. Lydia pulled away.

'I must stink. I don't know how you can bear it.'

'I'm a nurse; I've smelt far worse.' She gave her a wry smile. 'I've brought a change of clothes for you.'

'I'll not put on native dress like you,' Lydia said stubbornly. 'The boy offered me pantaloons and a shirt but I refused to put them on.'

'It would just be until we get you out of here.'

'No.' Lydia was adamant. 'I'd rather stay in dirty clothes. At least in these I still feel like an Englishwoman.'

Esmie, deciding not to press her, delved inside her bag. 'Harold packed treats for us – chocolate and biscuits.'

Lydia's expression softened. 'Harold is here too?'

Esmie shook her head. 'He's stayed in Taha. The brigadier and police forbade any other British to be involved in trying to find you. It's thanks to the brave mullah I came with that I'm here at all. He's done everything in his power to track you down and negotiate with the kidnappers.'

Lydia looked dazed. 'A mullah? I don't understand.'

Esmie broke off a piece of chocolate that had melted and rehardened, and handed it to Lydia. 'Eat this and I'll explain.'

Lydia sat clutching the squares of chocolate, staring at Esmie as if she still couldn't believe she was sitting on the charpoy next to her. As briefly as she could, Esmie began to tell her everything from the time Lydia had disappeared up to the moment Esmie had arrived at the hideout less than an hour ago.

Lydia, chocolate melting between her fingers, blinked away tears.

'I've been so frightened. I hoped that the army or police were out looking for me, but I was beginning to think no one would ever find me here . . .' She swallowed down a sob. 'I didn't even know where I was – this place you call Gardan – or how far away I was from fellow British.'

'Tom knows an old soldier here; Subahdar Tor Khan. He's been helping us too.'

Lydia looked guilt-ridden. 'Tom has risked his life to come and rescue me?'

'Yes, he has. And he's defied the authorities to come here.' Esmie held her look. 'But he wants to know why you left Taha on your own – we all do.'

Lydia glanced away and began nibbling the chocolate. 'It was just a spur of the moment thing – I went for a drive on a whim. I know I should have told you but I didn't think I would be gone long.'

Esmie said quietly, 'You know that's not true. You were making for Razmak and Dickie, weren't you? You took clothes and the padre's map to help you get there.'

Lydia's shoulders sagged. After a long pause she said, 'I couldn't bear the thought of going back to Pindi and that bloody hotel.' She gave a despairing look. 'Yet for the past week I've been cursing myself for ever leaving Pindi in the first place.'

Esmie put a hand on her arm. 'You'll be back in Pindi soon, I'm sure of it.'

Lydia clutched at her hand, suddenly agitated. 'I don't know how you can bear it here at the Frontier. I hate it and the people are loathsome! You must get me out of here. Please, Esmie, you won't leave without me, will you?'

'Of course I won't leave you, I promise.' Esmie hid her own doubt that she would be allowed to go freely now that she was inside the gang's fortress. Or if she was, she could not be sure that she would be permitted to take Lydia with her. But she kept such fears to herself. 'Now, let's check your feet and ankle.'

Esmie noticed that despite Lydia's contempt for local costume, she had permitted Zakir to lend her woollen socks with leather soles to replace her ruined shoes. Hearing Malik return, she called him in.

'Did you find anything of interest?'

He shrugged. 'The house is mostly abandoned and you can see daylight through some of the walls – but it is too high up to jump to safety.'

Esmie nodded. 'Let's hope it won't come to that.' She beckoned him closer. 'You can help me bathe and treat Lomax Mem's lacerated feet and strap up her swollen left ankle.'

Lydia looked at him in suspicion.

'I don't want him near me,' she said, shrinking back.

'Malik is my most able orderly and I trust him with my life,' Esmie reassured her. 'He didn't have to come on our mission but he did so to help you. There are many Pathans who are risking their lives for you – don't forget that.'

Lydia looked contrite. 'Yes, I see that. I'm sorry if I was rude.'

They set about their task, Zakir bringing the fresh water that Esmie requested. He hovered near the door, humming under his breath. Esmie's heart went out to him. She suspected that Lydia would be in a far worse condition if it had not been for the young Otmanzai looking after her.

Esmie took her time, methodically checking Lydia over, taking her temperature and pulse, examining her eyes, ears and throat. One eye looked bloodshot and sore, so she gave her drops. All the while, she talked to her calmly, trying to distract her with small talk about life in the zenana and describing the weather.

Lydia responded to the welcome attention. 'I'll be fine once I've had a decent wash and can put on clean clothes. I've been dreaming of a warm bath. It gets freezing here at night.'

Half an hour later, Baram Wali was bellowing down the stairs for Zakir. Abruptly, the boy stopped singing and looked apprehensively at Esmie.

'I'll go with you,' she assured him.

Lydia gripped her. 'You can't leave me here. Don't go.'

'I'll come back,' Esmie promised. 'Malik will stay and protect you while I see what's happening.'

With a thumping heart, Esmie retraced her steps to the main room, Zakir at her heels. There was an even greater tension in the room than before, the men eyeing her with hostility.

'Why were you taking so long?' Baram Wali demanded.

'Lomax Memsahib needed treatment,' Esmie said calmly. She cast around the room. 'Where is Mullah Mahmud?'

The men shifted and muttered. Baram Wali said, 'He had to go.'

'Go?' Esmie asked, stunned. 'Where to?'

The leader gave an evasive wave. 'Mullah Zada summoned him.'

Esmie was suddenly suspicious. 'He wouldn't have gone without me and Malik – not without saying anything. Where is he?'

Baram Wali advanced on her, glaring. He thrust his face at hers, his sour breath overwhelming. 'Don't speak to me like that, feringhi whore! You should never have come here. We won't rest until every last one of you British is chased off our land back to India!'

Argument broke out among the men behind. Baram Wali swung round and shouted them down.

'It is decided! The feringhi nurse stays here until they give us the money we want. If they were stupid enough to send her to us, then they are stupid enough to pay what we ask.'

The younger round-faced man protested, 'But the mullah?'

'He'll do as he's told,' snapped Karo's husband.

'Is he still here?' Esmie demanded.

'Shut up!'

'What have you done to him?' Esmie was appalled to think that these men might have mistreated the holy man. If they had, then how much worse might they be towards her and Lydia?

'Please tell me you haven't harmed Mullah Mahmud?' Esmie cried. 'I demand to see him.'

'You will demand nothing,' the older gang member shouted, his look venomous.

'You will have to let us go,' Esmie persisted. 'You are just a handful of men against many. Most of the Otmanzai are on our side. Imagine what they will do when they hear you have imprisoned the mullah too?'

'She's right,' said the plump-faced younger man. 'We must let the mullah go.'

'Be quiet!' hissed the old man. 'That mullah has no authority here. He consorts with the infidel.'

Esmie, heart pounding, appealed to the wavering captor. 'If we don't return to Mirza Ali's tonight, he will send out a force against you. I have told his guard to go for help—'

'They have gone,' Baram Wali cut her off. 'No one is watching out for you. Mirza Ali is as keen to get money out of the feringhi as we are.'

Esmie felt nauseated. 'I don't believe you. He wants those prisoners released.'

'Prisoners and money,' Baram Wali said with a grim smile. 'Now you are our guest until we get what we want.' He cuffed Zakir. 'Don't give me that look. Take the feringhi back to the cell and make sure both of them stay there.'

Zakir reached out and took Esmie by the sleeve, his eyes beseeching. She stumbled after him, too shocked to make a fuss.

Malik took the news of their captivity with his usual phlegmatic calm but Lydia broke down weeping.

'I don't believe Mirza Ali is part of this plot over money,' Esmie said. 'He thinks he can control this gang to get his prisoner exchange but he's wrong.'

'I agree,' said Malik. 'His men might still be out there for all we know. We can't trust anything Baram Wali says.'

'The wicked man will do anything to get money,' Esmie said in disgust. 'Even keep the mullah prisoner.'

Lydia was distraught. 'I don't care about the mullah! What about us? I've got money – I'll pay anything to get out. If I'd understood a word they'd said I would have told them. You must tell them, Esmie. Say I have money!'

'McCabe wouldn't allow us to give in to ransom demands – even though Tom came with money. The brigadier was adamant the kidnappers would just keep asking for more and I think now he's right. These men have no scruples – they've lied to the mullahs and broken their promises.'

'Tom has money with him?' Lydia seized on this. 'Then why isn't he here offering it to these awful men?'

'Because our Pathan friends have been negotiating with them to accept a prisoner exchange instead,' said Esmie. 'We have to trust that this will still go ahead and that they'll put pressure on Baram Wali to agree.'

'And you trust them?' Lydia cried. 'I don't! They're dirty, greedy savages. Let them have their money.'

'Lydia,' Esmie said, trying to calm her, 'we must be patient. Mirza Ali and the others will come tomorrow if we haven't returned. Tom will insist on it.'

Lydia tore at her hair and let out a shrill scream. Esmie tried to hug her but her friend was too distressed and pushed her away. 'I can't bear it!' she wailed. 'I want to go home! I want Mummy!'

Esmie grabbed her and held her tight. Lydia's thin arms soon lost their strength to resist. She slumped against Esmie, sobbing. Esmie held her and stroked her hair until Lydia was too exhausted to cry any more.

The light was fading from the high window when Malik pulled back the curtain to let Zakir bring in a dish of chickpeas and coarse bread, along with goat's milk to drink. Something about Malik's expression alerted Esmie.

'What is it, Malik?'

Quietly, he said in broken English, 'Zakir he tell where they hold Mullah Mahmud.' He pointed at the floor. 'In room below – old stable, I think.'

'Is the mullah all right?' she asked anxiously.

'I haven't seen him but Zakir he says mullah is tied to post like mule.'

Esmie was indignant. 'How could they treat him like that? The poor man—' Abruptly, Esmie gasped. 'Did you say Zakir spoke to you?'

Malik shrugged. 'Mostly it is pointing, pointing. But he say few words too. I think he knows this place. I think he try tell me he live here before fire.'

Esmie turned and stared at Zakir who was trying to coax a listless Lydia to drink her milk. Was this Zakir's former home? It had obviously come under attack or been burnt. Perhaps it was here that his family had perished and that was how he had lost his sanity. If so, Baram Wali was using the situation to his advantage, forcing Zakir to work for him and provide a hideout where no one would come looking. Karo's husband must have captured Zakir after the attack on Kanki-Khel last December.

A thought struck Esmie. Softly she spoke to the youth. 'Is this your home, Zakir?'

At first she thought he was ignoring the question. He sat back on his haunches and began to hum. She waited and then asked him, 'Is this the place where you grew up? Is that why you know where everything is kept? The things you bring for Lomax Memsahib?'

Zakir stopped rocking and met her look. He nodded. Esmie stepped towards him. 'Zakir, do you know of any other way out of here, apart from climbing through the high window?'

Esmie looked at the boy intently, holding her breath. Again he nodded. She exchanged quick glances with Malik. Her heart began to drum.

'Where is it?'

The youth gestured with his hands, pointing at the floor.

'Below here where Mullah Mahmud is?'

Again Zakir nodded.

'Can you take us there tonight when the others are asleep?'

Zakir studied her with fearful eyes. She thought he would refuse and she would not blame him if he did.

'Yes,' he whispered in a hoarse voice.

Esmie's eyes smarted at his bravery. She took his hands and squeezed them. 'Thank you for your courage! You must come with us and escape too. I can't bear the thought of you being with these men any longer. We'll look after you.'

Esmie was rewarded with a rare smile.

Lydia said, 'What's happening? What are you saying?'

Esmie sat down on the charpoy and held her hand. 'We mustn't raise our hopes too much but there might be another way out of here.'

The wait was interminable. When dark came, Esmie and Lydia blew out the lamp and sat tensely, holding hands on the charpoy, straining to listen, while Malik lay across the doorway pretending to sleep. Occasional footsteps clattered in the distance and bursts of shouting echoed through the abandoned rooms. At one point, youthful voices grew loud and Esmie feared members of the gang were going to stay and guard them. But on hearing Malik's 'snoring', the youths didn't stay. They probably thought that two weak women and an unarmed servant would not try and escape.

Gradually the tower became silent. They were too far away from the main room of the kidnappers to hear if they had settled for the night but Esmie knew they just had to trust Zakir to come when he could.

She wondered what had been happening at the Gardan fortress once they realised that the mullah and nurse had not returned. Was Mirza Ali already sending out a rescue party or was he really in league with the kidnappers? Even if he tried to stall for time, Tom and the subahdar would be up in arms and once Mullah Zada heard how the gang had shown their duplicity, he too would be outraged. But how would the desperate warring men upstairs act if they were cornered? It would mean resorting to rescuing Lydia by force and violence – the one thing they had tried to avoid and the reason Esmie had agreed on the dangerous mission in the first place.

She closed her eyes and prayed silently that there would be another way out. Then further doubts beset her. Lydia was so weakened by months of not eating properly and now this ordeal that even if they broke free Esmie feared she would not be strong enough to walk back to Gardan. Would their ponies still be at the fortified house down the mountainside? Pushing negative thoughts from her mind, she concentrated on staying alert. She had decided she must leave behind the cumbersome medical bag and its contents, apart from her small electric torch. She grasped it now in her other hand. Despite the plunging temperature, Esmie's palms sweated and the torch felt slippery.

Esmie lost track of time. Her watch told her it was nearly one o'clock in the morning but it felt much later. Lydia leaned against her and dozed. Suddenly Malik was in the room and touching her shoulder. Esmie started. She must have dozed too.

'Guthrie Mem', Zakir is here,' he whispered.

She shook Lydia awake. It was pitch black. She turned on her torch and saw Zakir's anxious face in the doorway. He looked startled by the unusual light, so she handed him the torch and showed him how to use it.

Taking Lydia's trembling hand, Esmie followed Malik and Zakir. They crept back to the spiral staircase and began to descend. Lydia clung on, making it difficult for Esmie to keep her balance on the narrow steps. Inching down, they stopped for breath at the bottom. Zakir switched off the torch and listened. When no sound came, he turned it on again and they carried on along a low vaulted passageway, which must once have been a place of storage judging by some old mouldering sacks.

A noise startled them. Something scuttled past. Lydia stifled a scream, making Zakir drop the torch in alarm. The clatter of metal on stone echoed around them. Surely someone would hear it? Esmie's heart hammered as they stopped dead, waiting to see if anyone had been disturbed. She could feel Lydia shaking so she clutched her hand in comfort. No one came. Malik quietly picked up the torch and shone it for Zakir, nodding at the boy to continue. They crept forward once more.

After a few feet, Zakir pointed to a half-open door and they squeezed through the gap, one by one, so as not to make the door creak. Esmie could tell by the smell that they were in a former stable but in the torchlight there was no sign of any animals and an old entrance had been bricked up.

As Malik swept the room with the torch, Esmie gasped. Huddled against the bottom of a pillar, squinting up at them in alarm, was Mullah Mahmud. She went to him quickly.

'Are you all right?'

He gaped at her. 'Memsahib . . .'

'Shhh,' she said softly. 'We've come to get you out.'

Without further words, she helped Malik untie the cords from around his hands and feet and released the rope that kept him tethered to a ring set into the pillar. Esmie massaged his wrists and ankles to help the blood circulate so that he could stand and walk. She saw the look of gratitude in the mullah's brown eyes.

'Thank you, kind lady,' he said softly.

It was only then that Esmie wondered how they were to get out of this dark and dingy vault.

Zakir, taking the torch from Malik, shone it into the corner and beckoned them over. All Esmie could see was a large barrel and some putrid-smelling straw. Zakir put his shoulder to the barrel and began moving it sideways with surprising strength. Malik went to help. Under the barrel was a trap door no bigger than a coalhole. Prising it open, Zakir lowered himself in and nodded for them to follow.

He disappeared down it and the mullah followed. Lydia stood frozen. 'I can't bear confined spaces,' she hissed in terror.

'Take my hand,' urged Esmie. 'Remember how we used to hide in your dad's cellar and pretend it was our den? You can do this. I'll go first.'

Lydia took a deep breath and nodded. Crouching down, Esmie could see from the torchlight that there was a drop of about five feet into a dark pit. Her stomach knotted but she must show no fear in front of Lydia. Zakir and Mullah Mahmud held out their hands to help her down. She half-scrambled and half-jumped into the dark hole. With Esmie's encouragement, Lydia followed. Malik entered last, pulling the trap door shut as he went.

Esmie could feel rather than see that they were in a long dank passage, too narrow to walk side by side and too low to walk upright. Zakir led with the torch. But for the intermittent flicker of torchlight up ahead, they were in complete darkness.

Stooped, Esmie walked while gripping Lydia's hand behind her. She could hear Lydia's fast breathing as they groped forward. Esmie was disorientated in the confines of the dark never-ending tunnel but they appeared to be going deeper underground. The secret passage sloped downwards, getting ever steeper. She tried not to shudder at the thought of them being entombed below ground where no one would ever find them. Esmie swallowed down bile and pressed on, concentrating on the dancing torchlight ahead.

Abruptly, the passage ended and they were inside a barrel-roofed cellar. It smelt damp and musty and the walls dripped with water. But Esmie gulped with relief. Despite the dankness, the air tasted sharper, fresher and very cold.

'Where are we?' whispered Lydia. 'Please God, don't say we have to go back up that tunnel.'

'I think it's an old ice-house,' Esmie guessed.

Zakir crossed the cellar. Esmie could see no windows or openings but they all pressed on behind him. They rounded a corner and then ahead of them were half a dozen stone steps leading up to a small solid wooden door. Esmie's hopes leapt. Zakir went ahead, cautioning them with a hand to stay back. He jumped up the steps and felt with his hand along the top of the doorframe. After a moment, he found what he was looking for: a large rusty key.

She could hardly breathe as he fumbled with it in the lock. Please let it open! To have to return in defeat would be unbearable. Despite Zakir's warning, they all rushed towards the steps to help. Malik got there first, adding his strength to wrenching on the key. Finally, the lock turned. They scraped back two more bolts, pushed against the long unused door and heaved it open. From the bottom of the steps, Esmie felt a blast of icy air rush in.

'Please stay there, memsahibs,' said Malik. He and Zakir disappeared beyond.

Resisting the urge to rush after them, Esmie clung to her friend in the darkness and tried to control her ragged breathing. Where did the door lead to?

'Why are they taking so long?' Lydia hissed.

'To make sure it's safe,' Esmie whispered.

A minute – that felt like ten – passed and then Malik was returning with the torch.

'Please come,' he urged.

The steps were slimy and Lydia slipped, nearly toppling them both. But the mullah grabbed hold of her and stopped her falling. The next moment, they were all scrabbling through the doorway and into the night. They emerged amid a thicket of trees. Esmie could feel thorns catching at her clothes.

In a hushed voice she asked, 'Where are we?'

Zakir took her by the sleeve and pointed up the hill. There was enough light from the night sky for Esmie to see the forbidding outline of the old tower. They were about a hundred feet below it and on the far side from the window entrance.

Zakir gave her a look of triumph. He struggled to speak. 'No guard here.'

Esmie grabbed him in a hug of relief. 'You clever boy!'

When she let go he was grinning.

'We must hurry, memsahib,' Malik said. 'Zakir will show us the best way back to Gardan, avoiding Baram Wali's house.'

Together, they set off down the steep slope, skidding and slipping in the dark. It was too dangerous to use the torch for fear of attracting attention. Lydia managed the first downhill slope but when they began to follow the circuitous route of undulating tracks, she soon tired.

'I must sit down,' she panted. 'I can't walk a step further.'

Esmie took charge. 'We'll carry you between us.' She showed Zakir and Malik how to make a chair-lift with their arms to support Lydia. 'Go on, Lydia; put your arms around their necks.'

After a moment's hesitation, she did as she was told. They made slower progress and every so often, the men would stop to rest.

'I can help too,' offered Mullah Mahmud.

Esmie felt a wave of gratitude to the young man who was still risking his life for people that many Otmanzai would call their enemies.

Thanking him, Esmie took a turn with the mullah to carry Lydia and give the others a short respite.

They were almost past the place where they had left their ponies the previous day, skirting below it, when they spotted movement.

'There's someone behind that wall,' Esmie gasped.

Suddenly, shadowy figures were rushing down the slope, rifles in hand. Esmie's knees buckled. Lydia let out a wail as the men put her down. In a futile gesture of gallantry, the mullah pushed forward to protect them. But they were five unarmed fugitives against at least a dozen armed brigands.

Esmie felt a strange calm as they faced them. She had done her best. It had not been enough but at least she had tried to save her friend. Now all they could do was plead for mercy or a swift death.

Chapter 40

A shout rang out in the dark, ordering the fleeing party to halt. Men swarmed around them, shouting in excitement. Lydia clung to Esmie, too shocked to move.

A bearded, turbaned man pushed his way through. On seeing the mullah, he threw up his hands and said, 'Allah be praised!'

Esmie's breath stopped in her chest. 'Subahdar Khan?'

He peered at her in the dark and his craggy face creased in a smile. 'Guthrie Memsahib, you are safe too, Allah be thanked.'

The next moment, another Pathan was striding into the circle. 'Esmie?' he cried.

Esmie let out a sob of relief. 'Tom!'

He was about to catch her hand when he saw Lydia there too and stopped. 'Lydia!'

She stared at him in confusion. 'Tom, is that you?'

'Yes.'

For a long moment they stared at each other and then Lydia flung herself at him.

'Oh, Tom,' she cried. 'I thought I'd never see you again!'

She collapsed into his arms. Tom held her as she wept, murmuring comforting words. 'You're safe now. It's over. The subahdar and the men of Gardan were coming to free you.'

Lydia was sobbing so hard she couldn't answer back. Esmie was weak with relief.

'Thank you, Subahdar,' she said, her eyes stinging with tears.

'But how did you manage to escape?' Tor Khan asked.

'Thanks to Zakir,' said Esmie, putting her hand on the boy's shoulder. 'He showed us a way out – the hideout was his old home.'

The mullah spoke. 'Zakir was as much a prisoner as we were. We must look after him now. I thought I could reason with those men but I was wrong. They are not true Muslims.'

'They will be punished,' growled the subahdar. 'I'll see to that. But first we must get you to safety. You will stay at my house for the rest of the night.' He turned and started issuing orders.

Within minutes, they were being helped onto ponies. Tom took Lydia on his horse. Esmie stifled the memory of how he'd held on to her in the same way during their journey to Gardan. She avoided his look, too exhausted to work out her jumble of emotions. They were all alive and that was what mattered most.

They spent the short night at the subahdar's, the two women bedding down under a thick blanket in a tiny room off the courtyard. Lydia scratched and couldn't sleep and complained that she should be with Tom.

By the next day, events were moving rapidly. Mullah Zada, on hearing how Mahmud and the women had been mistreated, demanded that the kidnappers be brought before him. Mirza Ali, now denouncing them with vehemence, sent a force to capture them. But by the time they reached the tower, the kidnappers had fled.

All this Esmie heard from the subahdar when he handed over her medicine bag which, to her relief, had been retrieved.

'I don't trust Mirza Ali not to have let them escape over the border to Afghanistan,' he grumbled. 'That man faces both ways. But at least Baram Wali and his brothers have gone and if I have anything to do with it, they will never return to Gardan.'

A message arrived from Sergeant Baz that the prisoners in Taha were being released and would start out the following day.

'Why should they?' Lydia, her confidence reviving, was indignant. 'The kidnappers have run away so there's no need to give in to any of their demands now.'

'We're still in Otmanzai country,' Tom cautioned, 'and these men have kinsmen. We should keep to our side of the bargain and give them no reason to doubt our word.'

'Our word is never in doubt,' Lydia retorted. 'It's these Pathan devils who have shown that they can't be trusted.'

'Lydia, your life has been saved by a host of brave and kind Pathans. Don't forget that,' rebuked Esmie.

'Some of them, maybe,' she conceded. 'But they started it by kidnapping me in the first place.'

Esmie caught Tom's look and saw his reluctance to argue. She bit back the accusation that Lydia should never have attempted to drive to Razmak at all. But it no longer mattered and it wasn't her concern any more. Such things were between Lydia and Tom.

Tom said, 'The good news is that we will start back for the border tomorrow.'

'Thank God!' Lydia exclaimed. 'As soon as we get back to civilisation, I'm going to burn every piece of my clothing. I don't want to keep anything that'll remind me of this terrible place.'

'And you'll see Andrew again,' said Tom, his look brightening as he mentioned his son.

For a moment she looked puzzled and then she smiled. 'Yes, of course. I've missed him terribly.'

It struck Esmie that it was the first time she'd heard Lydia mention the boy. Not once had she asked about him. It filled her with sorrow. Poor Andrew!

Esmie got up from where they were sitting in the courtyard. 'I'm going to find Zakir,' she said and left them alone.

The following day, after an early breakfast of curds, raisins and almonds, they prepared to leave. Both the subahdar and Mirza Ali's son were providing an escort to see them to the border and oversee the exchange of prisoners. Lydia said she was well enough to ride her own pony and that way they would make more speed.

Mullah Mahmud and Zakir came to say goodbye. Esmie was delighted that her young friend was to become part of the mullah's household; it was what she had wished for in Kanki-Khel when she'd first come across them.

Tom shook hands with the mullah and thanked him for his help. Lydia nodded in agreement and went to mount her pony.

'I can't thank you enough for all you've done for us,' Esmie said, her eyes stinging with tears of gratitude.

The mullah took her hand in a gentle clasp. 'You have been a brave and loyal friend to Lomax Memsahib. And I hope you will count me as your friend too. You are one of us now. May Allah protect you and be with you all of your days.'

Esmie was overwhelmed; he couldn't have said anything kinder. She swallowed down the lump in her throat and nodded in thanks. What an unlikely friendship they had struck – the Otmanzai holy man and the British nurse – but she knew that both of them would be the richer for it.

She turned and looked tenderly at Zakir. Yesterday she had helped cut and groom his tangled hair. The boy wore fresh clothes, and his cap – the one Esmie had given him a year ago – had been washed.

She smiled. 'Dear Zakir.'

Abruptly, he threw himself at her feet and clung on to her. She crouched down and stroked his head. 'Don't be upset. You have a new family now.'

He looked up at her with sad eyes as if he couldn't understand why she had to leave him again. She cupped his face with her hands and kissed his forehead. 'We will always be with each other in our hearts.'

Standing up, the mullah gently pulled Zakir away.

On the spur of the moment, Esmie said, 'Wait.' She fished inside the pocket of her woollen jacket and pulled out her electric torch. 'Take this and keep it.'

Zakir's eyes lit up. He grabbed it and turned it on, grinning. In a husky voice he said, 'Thank you, memsahib.'

She smiled. 'It's me who thanks you, Zakir.'

Quickly, Esmie turned to mount her pony, not wanting to break down crying in front of the boy. The others were already waiting at the gateway, Lydia looking impatient to be off.

Within minutes they were leaving behind the scattering of fortified houses and skirting the village with its holy tomb. The air was sharp and pewter-grey clouds were amassing over the mountain range. Rain or snow looked imminent. Suddenly, Esmie was infected with the same restlessness that gripped Lydia. She couldn't wait to be gone.

It was only nine days since she had left Taha but it seemed a lifetime ago. Esmie longed to be home in the cantonment with Karo and Gabina – her friend would be so relieved to hear that Baram Wali had fled and could no longer threaten her. And there was Harold. She had much to tell him – and they had things to discuss about their future. Doubts crowded in again about the state of her marriage. Was she prepared to live with Harold like brother and sister forever and to never have a child of her own?

She allowed thoughts of baby Andrew to steal into her mind. Her insides tugged with a familiar protective longing. Ahead rode Lydia and Tom, getting nearer to their son with every mile. She felt her chest tighten with envy. Perhaps she would never be rid of her maternal feelings. It would be a relief when they took Andrew back to Rawalpindi and she could absorb herself once more in the work of the mission hospital. Driving herself hard at work was always her answer to avoiding upsetting emotions.

With that thought, Esmie spurred her pony south.

Baz was waiting for them at the border, along with a police escort and the three prisoners. There was a swift handing over. They said their goodbyes and thanks to the subahdar. Esmie was touched to see Tom and Tor Khan embrace each other emotionally and without the need for words, each knowing they would probably never see the other again. Then Esmie and her friends were riding on, arriving back in Kanki-Khel before nightfall.

Lydia was persuaded to wash and change into some of Esmie's clothes that had been left there on the way north. The old Lydia would not have been able to squeeze into them, but she had lost so much weight that the skirt and blouse fitted. Esmie was alarmed at how skinny her friend had become.

That night, they opened wine that Baz had had sent up from Taha, and drank to their freedom. Lydia was quickly drunk and grew garrulous.

'I suppose I'll have to endure a terrible fuss when we get back to Pindi. Was my kidnap in all the papers? I can't wait to tell Geraldine Hopkirk the full story – her eyes will be out on stalks.' Lydia laughed tipsily. 'And I can just see Jimmy and Stella pestering me for details. My ordeal beats any of the fanciful stories that the so-called baroness has ever come out with. She'll be speechless – for once!'

Esmie glanced at Tom, waiting for him to probe for answers as to why she had gone missing in the first place. But he avoided her look and said little. Perhaps he had decided for the sake of his marriage and Andrew that he didn't want to know the truth. In a few days, they would be back in Rawalpindi and could begin to pick up the pieces of their lives – to start afresh.

Silently, Esmie wondered how possible that would be. She remembered Lydia's confession in captivity. *'I couldn't bear the thought of going back to Pindi and that bloody hotel.'*

Yet Lydia seemed happy to be back with Tom. Perhaps the lengths Tom had gone to rescue her had made her appreciate her husband once more. Tired out, Esmie left them and went to bed.

The next day they climbed aboard a police truck for the journey to Taha, accompanied by Baz and Malik. Esmie chose to stay in the back with her orderly, leaving Tom and Lydia to sit up front together. She sensed a new awkwardness between her and Tom. As they passed the riverside where Tom had declared his true feelings for her, Esmie felt sadness tighten her chest. She wondered if he felt the same.

Yet the nearer they drew to Taha, the more Esmie hoped that the Lomaxes would not linger in the frontier town but hurry back to the city and the Raj Hotel. She, too, just wanted to resume her everyday life.

As the town appeared in the distance, Esmie said to Malik, 'You've been such a support. Thank you. If you wish to take a few days off – go and visit your family – then please do so. You deserve a rest.'

The orderly gave her one of his rare broad smiles. 'Only if Guthrie Mem' takes a holiday too.'

She gave a wry laugh. 'Maybe the rest of the day. I'm not good at being idle. I'm happier working.'

He nodded. 'And so am I, memsahib.'

Twenty minutes later the truck was trundling under the massive stone archway of the northern gate and into Taha. Word had preceded them about the return of the kidnapped memsahib and crowds pressed around, shouting to catch a glimpse of the rescued woman. From the cries of delight, Esmie guessed that Lydia was waving to the masses.

Malik lifted the canvas flaps so that Esmie could see better what was going on. Slowly, they inched through the throng of well-wishers and those come to gawp and on into the cantonment. The streets were strangely quiet. She had expected a rousing reception from the British to welcome them back. Was this an indication of disapproval at Lydia's rash behaviour? Perhaps McCabe had insisted that there should be no fuss. She was relieved that they weren't being faced with military bands and welcome committees.

But when they pulled up outside Number Ten, the Lines, Esmie saw that there were a couple of uniformed men on the veranda obviously there to greet them; McCabe and Rennell. Malik helped her down from the truck while Tom did the same for Lydia. Esmie felt the familiar queasiness of walking on firm ground while her head and stomach still felt they were being jostled on the road. It was so good to be home!

Alec Bannerman came striding down the garden path to meet them, an odd smile on his face. He greeted Lydia and Tom with warm handshakes, gallantly making no mention of Lydia absconding with his car and map.

Lydia began to chatter with nervous excitement about her imprisonment and escape. But Alec turned from her distractedly to welcome Esmie. He kissed her cheek.

'The heroine of the hour!' he said, with a feverish look in his eye. 'My dear Esmie!' Linking her arm through his, he guided her swiftly up the path ahead of the others. 'We're all here for you.'

She was touched that Alec should be the one to come and meet her. It was typical that Harold should let him do so. She wouldn't put it past her husband to still be at the hospital working until he got news that they had arrived.

Reaching the veranda, McCabe and Rennell jumped to their feet.

'Rupa!' Esmie cried in delight to see that her Parsee friend was also there.

Lydia, avoiding the men, rushed past and into the house. 'I must see Andrew this minute. Where's my darling boy? Ayah!'

Esmie noticed a look of awkwardness pass between the brigadier and superintendent; they were probably just as much at a loss as to what to say to Lydia as her friend was to them.

The servants were lined up too; Draman, Ali and the cook. Karo was behind, with her veil pulled across her face, a fretful Gabina in her arms. Esmie's smile faltered as she sensed their unease. She turned to the padre.

'Where's Harold?'

The smile was gone from his face. He looked at her helplessly. McCabe stepped forward and cleared his throat.

'Mrs Guthrie, we're so terribly sorry. It was so sudden . . .'

Esmie's pulse began to race. 'What do you mean? What's happened? Tell me where Harold is, please.'

Rupa came to her side and steered her towards a cane chair – Harold's chair. 'Come and sit down.'

Esmie shook her head. She didn't want to sit in the chair where Harold should be. She wanted to repeat her question but her throat was too tight to speak. Rupa explained in a calm, professional voice.

'Harold had a cut on his hand. It must have become infected during an operation. He fainted at work. It was septicaemia. He died that night of organ failure. We're all so very, very sorry.'

Esmie stared in stupefaction. 'Harold? Dead?'

'There was nothing that could be done,' Alec added.

'A cut?' Esmie questioned. 'I knew he had a cut. I meant to tend it myself.' Esmie began to shake. 'I should have made him put on a clean dressing.'

'This is not your fault,' Rupa insisted.

Esmie felt faint. 'When did it happen?'

'The day after you left,' said Rupa.

Esmie put her hands to her chest, trying to breathe. Harold had been dead for over a week and she had not known. All this time she had hardly thought of him – at least only fleetingly – and now he was gone. She gripped the back of Harold's chair and swallowed down bile.

'I want to see him. Where is he being kept?'

'I'm sorry, Mrs Guthrie,' said the brigadier, 'but we had to go ahead with the burial. In this climate . . . and we didn't know—' He checked his words. 'We had no idea when you would be back. It could have been weeks.'

Esmie knew he had almost said, 'if you would be back.' They all thought she might never have returned. She so nearly hadn't.

'I'll take you to the cemetery to see his grave,' said Alec gently.

Grave. The word was so final; desolate. Esmie heard a stifled groan. She turned to see Tom's stricken face. His eyes were welling with tears for his closest friend. She couldn't bear his pain as well as hers.

'Oh, Tom!'

She felt her knees buckle. In an instant, he was reaching out to catch her before she crumpled. His arms went around her as he supported her and helped her sit down in a chair that wasn't Harold's. Esmie held onto his hand like a lifeline, too shocked to cry.

It was then that she caught sight of Lydia standing in the doorway with Andrew in her arms, staring at them.

'Esmie, what's wrong?' Lydia asked. 'Why are you holding on to Tom?'

Quickly Esmie withdrew her hand. Neither of them could speak.

It was Alec who told her. 'There's been a tragedy. Harold's dead.'

Chapter 41

Esmie remembered little of the following week. At night she couldn't sleep. During the day she was disorientated with exhaustion and dozed for brief snatches that brought a temporary blessed oblivion. She wanted to work at the hospital but Rupa and Alec wouldn't let her.

'You need to rest,' Alec insisted. 'You've been through a terrible time and now this.'

Rupa said, 'You're in shock and you're tired out. You might make mistakes. Be kind to yourself, Esmie. Spend time with Karo and Gabina or your Pindi friends.'

Esmie listened to Rupa, knowing how she had suffered a similar trauma with her husband's sudden death four years previously. But she couldn't bear to be around Lydia and Tom. It should have been comforting to have them there – Harold's most long-standing friends – but it just made the loss of Harold the more acute. Lydia was constantly breaking down in tears and Tom's stoical suppressing of his grief was even more painful to witness.

The day after their return to Taha, they had all gone to the cemetery together. That had been a mistake. At the sight of the freshly dug grave with its temporary wooden cross, Lydia had crumpled to her knees. 'My darling Harold!' she'd cried and begun to sob uncontrollably.

Tom's face, scored with grief, had been too much. Esmie had left quickly, too numb to cry and wanting to get away from them. Alec was putting up the Lomaxes at his bungalow, but each day they came round to keep her company and to see Andrew. Esmie had suggested that the baby and his ayah stay on at hers.

'Padre's not used to having a baby under his roof – and I'm happy for Andrew and Sarah to be here for a few more days.'

But her real reason for keeping him close was that the six-month-old with his large blue eyes and gummy smile could bring her the comfort that the adults couldn't. If he woke in the night, she would rock him back to sleep and sit with him in her arms, drawing strength from his trusting solid warmth. She knew the solace of Andrew's presence could only be temporary but it helped her through the first dark days.

When the Lomaxes arrived after breakfast, Lydia would fuss over Andrew for a few minutes and then lose interest. She began to talk about Christmas, now only eight weeks away.

'We must all go to Ebbsmouth for Christmas,' Lydia declared. 'I can't bear the thought of you being here on your own.'

'Esmie can come to us in Pindi,' Tom offered.

'And endure another Christmas having to eat soggy samosas with the inmates of the Raj Hotel?' Lydia was scathing. 'Esmie would hate that and so would I. It would be so much better at home. We can all stay at Templeton Hall – and we'll invite Harold's mother and aunt over too so they won't be sad and on their own. What do you think, Esmie?'

Lydia looked at her eagerly. Esmie was at a loss as to what to say. She shrugged. 'I really haven't thought . . . It's too soon to make any decisions . . .'

'I know it won't be the same without dear Harold,' said Lydia, her eyes filling with tears, 'but at least we'd all be together and Mummy and Daddy can make a fuss over us. Please say yes.'

Tom chided his wife. 'Lydia, we haven't even discussed this ourselves so Esmie can't be expected to make up her mind. It's too soon. Don't press her.'

'I'm not,' Lydia snapped. 'I'm trying to think what's best for my friend and being stuck out here without Harold is the worst of all worlds.' She turned to Esmie. 'Don't worry about the money; I can pay for your fare home. When we get back to Pindi we'll book a passage for you too and you can decide in a couple of weeks if you want to go.'

Tom looked aghast. 'Lydia, let's talk about this another time. There might be no berths to be had anyway.'

'If you've got the right money, there's always a berth to be had,' said Lydia. 'I'm not forcing anyone to do anything but I'm going home for Christmas even if you're not.'

Esmie could see from Tom's shocked face that he had not been expecting such a suggestion. Would Lydia really travel back to Ebbsmouth without him?

At the end of the week, Esmie could bear no more of Lydia's badgering her to return to Scotland with her. She told them both to go back to Rawalpindi.

She tried to explain. 'I need to grieve alone – I hope you understand.'

'Of course,' Tom said, his look apologetic.

'I wish you would come with us,' Lydia said. 'I hate the thought of leaving you here at the mercy of these wild savages.'

'I'm perfectly safe here,' Esmie insisted. She kept to herself that she felt more at home among the local Waziris and the mission workers than she did with Lydia's friends in Rawalpindi.

Lydia was baffled. 'Surely you don't want to stay on? You've done your bit for the mission.'

'I need time to think things over,' Esmie replied.

'But what is there—?'

'Lydia, leave it be!' Tom cut her off.

Lydia said testily, 'I really don't understand you sometimes, Esmie. I'm only trying to do the best for you after you've helped me.'

'I know you are,' Esmie replied, 'and I'm grateful. I just don't know what I want to do yet.'

But Lydia grew more agitated. 'Can't you see how dangerous it is for a British woman to be left on her own in this primitive place? It's dirty and full of disease and the men leer at you – and who's to say you won't be the next one to be kidnapped?'

'Lydia, that's enough!' Tom berated.

She snapped back. 'Well, I hate India! I can't believe you're not trying to help Esmie escape this backward place. Harold wouldn't have wanted her to stay on without him.'

Esmie was winded by the remark. Lydia was probably right. Harold had only ever agreed to bring her to Taha as his wife and under his protection. She saw Tom trying to hold on to his temper in front of her. 'That's up to Esmie, not us,' he said. 'Now I think we should leave her in peace.'

To Esmie's relief, Alec offered to drive the Lomaxes to Kohat the next day.

On the morning they left, Esmie found it hardest saying goodbye to Andrew. She held him for a long moment, breathing in his baby smell and kissing his cheeks.

'Goodbye, wee man,' she murmured. 'I love you.'

It was Tom who stepped forward to take him, briefly kissing Esmie's cheek as he did so. 'Come to Pindi when you're ready,' he said, his eyes full of sadness.

She nodded, too heavy-hearted to speak. Lydia grabbed her in a tearful hug. 'Please think about coming back to Ebbsmouth. We'll make it just like old times, you and me.'

Esmie was pained at her words. Did Lydia really believe that they could ever go back to those pre-married days together and their girlish friendship? Esmie was a different person; the experiences of the past fourteen months in India and of the last two weeks in particular had changed her. She had been tested to the limits of her courage and endurance – and yet had come to love and admire the agrarian people among whom she worked and lived. She had struggled to make her brief marriage work but now she was a widow.

It struck Esmie suddenly that Lydia would never change. She would continue to rush through life, charming and hedonistic, loving and hurting people in equal measure. The way she talked about the local people with such disdain caused Esmie the most pain. Had she already forgotten how men like Malik, Mullah Mahmud and Zakir had risked their lives to rescue her? How the subahdar had negotiated on her behalf and Sergeant Baz had swiftly organised the prisoner exchange? It was the Pathans – those wild savages as Lydia called them – who had brought about her freedom, not the British. Esmie did not blame Lydia for wanting to get away from her traumatic experience by going home to her parents for Christmas but her condemnation of all things Indian was hard to stomach.

As she waved them away, Esmie felt a stab of pity for Tom having to cope with his wife's capricious nature and thoughtless comments. But there was nothing she could do to help him.

November came and Esmie's numbness over Harold's death gradually thawed. She took to sleeping in his bed, reading and rereading his battered copy of *Old Mortality*, her face wet with tears. She was guilty at her neglect of his wound. If she hadn't been so preoccupied with Lydia's disappearance and Tom's presence, then she might have paid Harold's condition more attention. She thought now of his glassy eyes and pallid face as they said their distracted goodbyes. They were the signs of sepsis, not emotion. She should have noticed.

It made her doubt her ability as a nurse. She felt useless and desperately alone. She tried to fill the empty hours writing airmail letters to Harold's mother and aunt and notes to his friend Bernie Hudson in Peshawar and the Tolmies in Murree. She wrote a more detailed letter to her dear Aunt Isobel in Vaullay, seeking her guardian's advice on what she should do.

She received letters of condolence from people in India she'd never met – friends and colleagues of Harold's from the mission and his secondment to the army during the War. Esmie was touched by their kindness and of the nice things they said about her husband. But she also thought that she didn't deserve their sympathy. Esmie was wrestling with her feelings. She knew that she was genuinely grieving for Harold and missed him greatly – but she also knew that the guilt she felt was partly because she had never truly loved him.

She and Harold had cared for each other but they hadn't been in love. Esmie knew that if Harold had lived, she would have been questioning whether she could stay with him at the mission and continue in their platonic relationship. In the dark hours of the night she had to admit that the day might have come when she would have left Harold. She could hardly dare admit it to herself but once she had, then Esmie allowed herself to grieve for him properly.

She wept for the kind man whose work she had so admired, for his bashful modesty and genial nature. Yet she knew he had been a complex man who had struggled to suppress his nature and had hidden his unhappiness in a single-minded pursuit of his mission work. She was desolate that he had died so young when he had so much skill and compassion to offer the world – and she grieved that Harold had never been able to love and be loved in the way he had wanted.

A couple of weeks after the Lomaxes had returned to Rawalpindi, a letter came from Tom. She read it with shaking hands.

Dearest Esmie,

I know that there is little I can say to bring you comfort in your grief but I wanted you to know that I think of you daily and hope that you are keeping strong. I know you will be. You have more courage than the rest of us put together. Harold knew that – it's why he chose you. He also admired and loved you, Esmie. I know from what you've told me that it wasn't the way you wanted – or deserved – but he loved you greatly in his own way. He told me as much. So thank you for making my friend happy.

I miss him more than I can say. To me, Harold was the epitome of what a good man should be; moral and upright, hard-working and brave – but also kind-hearted and with a sense of humour. He might have been a little too competitive at tennis but we'll allow him that!

He also saved my life. I've never told this to any family or friends, so I hope you don't mind me unburdening to you now. When we were in Mesopotamia together – towards the end of the War – I reached the end of my tether. I refused to obey an order to carry out an execution of one of the Indian sepoys who had been charged with desertion and sentenced to death. I was court-martialled but Harold spoke up for me – pleaded with the tribunal to spare me from imprisonment or possible execution myself. He cited my good record with the Peshawar Rifles and in Mesopotamia and said he'd diagnosed me with shell shock. Yes, Esmie, you probably won't be surprised to hear that. That was why I was so prickly towards you when we first met – I knew you'd spotted my weakness, just as Harold had.

One of the tribunal wanted to make an example of me, saying it would encourage mutiny among the sepoys if my insubordination went unpunished. Luckily for me, the other two were lenient towards me and I was given a week of field punishment instead. That was all thanks to Harold. He was a true friend to me always. I'm ashamed that I didn't do more to stop Lydia spreading the myth that I was some sort of hero in the War. I was nothing of the sort. Harold was the hero – he never wanted his praises sung – but that is the mark of a truly heroic man.

What a ramble this is, Esmie. I'm sorry – I'd set out to write a note of condolence but find I've been pouring out my heart to you instead. You are so easy to talk to, Nurse Guthrie. I wish I could be with you in person.

I hope you are treating yourself kindly and that Alec, Rupa and Karo are all looking after you. Don't be bullied by Lydia into making a hasty decision about the future. Whatever you choose to do or where you choose to go, I know it will be done wisely.

My warmest wishes always,
Tom

Esmie reread the letter again and again. She could hear his self-deprecating voice as he confessed to his wartime trauma. Tom may well have been under mental stress but his act of mercy on the sepoy was the deed of a brave man, whether at the end of his tether or not. Others in the army might have seen it as weakness of character but she didn't. She admired him for it. No doubt, though, it must have spurred on Tom's decision to leave the army and start a new life.

Esmie wondered what life was like for him now that he was back in Rawalpindi. He made no mention of the hotel or Lydia – or even Andrew. The purpose of the letter was to be able to talk about his dear friend Harold and to tell her that he thought of her. How comforting that was!

As the days passed, Esmie carried the letter with her and referred to it constantly. It was tender and compassionate and yet there was nothing of impropriety about it. He might be critical of Lydia but he wasn't disloyal. It was the letter of a good friend and it helped her through the early days of dislocation and loss.

Aunt Isobel wrote too; a long loving letter that advised Esmie not to rush into any decision about her future but to take her time.

> *'. . . you know that you are always welcome back here in Vaullay whenever you want, whether for a holiday or to live and work. My home is your home.'*

Esmie began to think more and more of returning to Vaullay; a place where she could lick her wounds. She had done so before, during the punishing years of wartime nursing. But would it be fair on her guardian to go back without any clear idea that she would stay there long term? Would escaping to Vaullay just be running away from unhappiness? Then Esmie questioned what it was she would be running away from; was it just the sorrow of Harold's death? The more she dwelled on it, the more she realised that going to Vaullay would chiefly be to put distance between herself and Tom in Rawalpindi.

In mid-November a letter came from Lydia, anxious for her to join them in the Christmas trip back to Ebbsmouth.

> *'. . . you simply must come! Your passage is booked. There is no reason for you to stay. Please Esmie, come with us. If only to give yourself a holiday and allow us Templetons to spoil you rotten! If you like, we could invite your Aunt Isobel down for Christmas too. We sail on the 29th from Bombay to Marseilles. I've booked trains from there so we*

> *get home more quickly and well in time for the festivities. Come, come, come! Please, please, please!'*

Esmie heard the desperation in Lydia's letter. She wondered if Tom would be able to get his wife to return with him to India once she was back with her parents. Lydia was a home-bird and she had had such a terrible experience on the Frontier, Esmie was worried about her. Perhaps she ought to go with her and make sure she was all right. Esmie see-sawed about what to do. The Templetons would be kind to her and part of her longed for their warm-hearted attention – and there would be a chance to see Aunt Isobel too while she was in Scotland.

Yet Esmie did not think she could endure spending several weeks in Tom's company, trying to pretend to Lydia and everyone else that she had no feelings for him. She couldn't do it. In fact, it would come as a relief to think of the Lomaxes leaving India for a while and not having to be faced with subduing her love for Tom.

Esmie wrote back to Lydia, declining the kind offer and explaining that she wasn't ready to leave India.

More and more, Esmie was thinking that she might move somewhere else in the sub-continent to work, far away from the Punjab and Rawalpindi. Standing on the veranda at dusk, wrapped in a shawl and listening to the birds settling in the trees and voices carrying on the sharp air, she knew she wanted to stay in this country. She had come to love India; its mix of people, its smells and sounds. India was a place of bright stars, vivid colours and of living outdoors. There was so much more still to learn about the country and its people. This was what had drawn Harold east – and she too felt its pull.

Having made this tentative decision – and with nothing but a vague plan to stay – Esmie went back to the hospital and began to work again.

Chapter 42

Rawalpindi, November

'She's not coming with us!' Lydia tore up Esmie's letter and threw it onto the fire before giving Tom a chance to read it.

'I didn't think she would,' he replied.

'You would have thought she'd be more grateful,' Lydia said moodily. 'I've been through hell but my best friend has turned her back on me.'

'For goodness' sake! Esmie's just lost her husband,' Tom chided.

'That's right, take her side as usual. I know you prefer Esmie to me.'

'I haven't time to listen to this. There's too much to do at the hotel with Charlie being off sick. I thought you had something important to tell me.'

He had come rushing round to the bungalow in Buchanan Road at Lydia's command. He should have known it wouldn't be a matter of life or death. Daily, she sent chits to say he was needed immediately, only to find she had locked herself into the house because she was convinced there was an intruder in the garden or the tonga driver at the end of the road was plotting to snatch her. But she refused his suggestion that they move back into the hotel where she might feel safer.

'It *is* important,' Lydia said, resorting to tears. 'I need you here.'

'I have a hotel to run. My manager is in bed with bronchitis and we have a railway club dinner to prepare for tonight. You have to let me get on with my job,' Tom said with a sigh.

'But I'm frightened here on my own,' Lydia said tearfully. 'Why do you always choose the hotel over me?'

'If you would agree to move back into the hotel, I wouldn't need to,' he said in exasperation.

At times Tom felt sorry for her; she was often nervy and on edge, refusing to go near the bazaar and suspicious of any man dressed in the garb of a Pathan. Lydia had returned to a flood of publicity and interest in her plight. At first her friends had pressed her for details of her ordeal and Lydia had been happy to oblige, turning the story of her abduction into a lurid drama. There had been articles and interviews in the newspapers about the brave Englishwoman and the plucky Scottish nurse, and Lydia had basked in the sympathy of the men at the club.

But soon the tone of the stories had changed. Rumours began to surface that Lydia had been rushing to Razmak to meet a lover. No self-respecting British woman would have behaved in such a way, said the gossips; the hotelier's wife should take a large part of the blame for her kidnap.

Her so-called friends were proving fickle. After a couple of weeks of notoriety, invitations to dinner parties and club dances had begun to dry up. People snubbed Tom too. They openly talked about his faults, which the more waspish of Lydia's friends repeated to her. 'They say he left the Rifles in disgrace – heard it from someone who'd heard it from a captain in the Victoria Barracks. Is it true? My husband says that's why he drinks too much.'

Tom cared little for the tittle-tattle about him but it gave Lydia yet another reason to berate him for being a useless husband.

'I refuse to go back to that tiresome hotel,' she pouted.

'Well, I have a business to run,' said Tom, striding to the door and wrenching it open.

'Go on! Walk out on me again,' Lydia cried, pursuing him. 'Well, I tell you this, Tom Lomax; I can't wait to leave Pindi and I'm never coming back. So sooner or later you're going to have to choose between that bloody hotel and me!'

He spun round. 'Don't tempt me.'

Her eyes narrowed. 'You'd love that, wouldn't you? Blame me for the break-up of our marriage, when it's you that's neglected me. You promised me this fairy-tale life in India but it's been nothing but a disappointment. Worse that that; it's been the most terrible year of my life! If I hadn't been so desperately unhappy, I would never have gone after Dickie and been snatched by those barbarians.'

Tom's heart drummed. It was the first time she had admitted that it was Dickie she was trying to reach when she'd been kidnapped.

'So you were having an affair with Mason?' he accused.

She looked at him in defiance. 'Yes! All summer.'

Tom balled his fists in anger. 'I've gone out of my way to placate you and please you, and all this time you've been sleeping with another man.'

'Don't play the wronged husband with me,' Lydia railed, stabbing his chest with her finger. 'Ever since we were married you've been lusting after Esmie. Isn't that true? I saw the way you looked at her when she wore my emerald dress – you couldn't take your eyes off her. You'd have turned it into an affair if she'd given you an ounce of encouragement. I know you didn't go all that way across the Frontier to rescue me – you did it because of her. You wish you'd married my friend instead of me. You do, don't you? Don't you!'

Tom ground his teeth.

'Well, I wish you had too!' she yelled. 'I should have married Colin Fleming. He would have taken care of me and made sure I was safe. I'd be living a life of luxury in the south of France if you hadn't won me with false promises.'

Tom looked at her in contempt. 'I never promised you anything more than you got or pretended to be someone I wasn't. I'm sorry if you thought I did.'

'Oh, you did, Tom,' she said, her face red with anger. 'You played on being a war hero – Captain Lomax with an aristocratic pedigree. Of course my head was turned. What a fool I was! You're nothing but a failure – even your own father's ashamed of you. The only thing you've got to your name is a second-rate hotel.'

Tom could not bear to hear any more of her vicious words. He turned away. But she chased him across the veranda.

'Don't turn your back on me,' she shouted.

He stopped and faced her, his jaw clenched. All the months of frustration and heartache over his wife's demanding ways made him snap. 'It'll be a relief when you go,' he retaliated. 'And you'll be glad to hear I shan't be coming with you. I don't mind what you do, Lydia – go to Fleming if it makes you any happier.'

For a moment she stared at him as if she couldn't believe what she was hearing. Had she really expected him to take her vitriol without being provoked? Things had been said that could never be unsaid.

'Well, that's fine by me,' she hissed. 'I don't want you to come. But I'm taking Andrew.'

'Andrew?' Tom felt winded.

'Yes, my son.' Lydia challenged him with her look.

'But he's mine too.'

'Well, you have a choice to make,' she said, glaring at him. 'Give up the hotel and come back to Scotland or don't see your son again.'

Tom's head spun. He was too shocked to move.

'But you don't want me as your husband,' Tom gasped. 'You'd do that just to spite me?' When she didn't answer, he said, 'I won't let you take him away. If it comes to a fight in court, I'll tell them about you and Dickie and it's you who won't see him again.'

Lydia's face suddenly crumpled and she burst into tears. Tom felt wrenched in two. He half-hated her, half-pitied her.

'Please, Tom, don't bring Dickie into this,' she sobbed. 'It's not his fault and our affair is over.' She looked at him beseechingly. 'I just want to go home! Mummy and Daddy are longing to see Andrew. You wouldn't deny them seeing their grandson, would you? That's all I ask. Let's take him home together.'

Tom stared at her, in too much turmoil to speak. How could she threaten him one minute and make him feel guilty the next? He no longer knew what to think. Living with Lydia was as unpredictable and nerve-racking as walking on quicksand. If it hadn't been for Andrew he would have left her by now. But for all his bravado about fighting for his son in court, he didn't want to put his wife through that or use his son as a bargaining chip in their marriage. He would go to the ends of the earth for Andrew – and Lydia knew it.

Taha

Esmie had taken to cycling to work, finding the cold air against her cheeks exhilarating in the early morning. On the 29th of November she cycled to work thinking of the Lomaxes in Bombay embarking for home and felt a mixture of sadness and relief. She had not heard from either Tom or Lydia since she'd declined their invitation to join them in Scotland for Christmas. Esmie hoped that Lydia hadn't taken offence but she had tried to explain that it was too soon after Harold's death to leave Taha. She felt close to him here and drew comfort from being with colleagues and friends who had known him.

Each day, Esmie felt a little stronger and, at times, less bereft. She knew that she was not going to stay in Taha much longer and had asked the mission to find a replacement. She planned to travel for a few months, seeing more of India before deciding where to settle next. Somewhat to her surprise she had discovered that, thanks to an insurance policy she had had no idea existed, Harold had left her well provided for and she could afford to take some time off before seeking work again.

A few days later, Esmie received an unexpected letter from Rawalpindi. Slitting open the envelope, she saw that it was written on Raj Hotel headed notepaper in beautiful copperplate writing. It was from Hester Cussack.

> *Darling,*
> *How are you? Your friends here at the hotel think of you a lot and we worry that you are lonely. We don't like to think of you on your own at Christmas, so the chaps and I would like to invite you to spend it with us. It was Stella's idea, so she must get the credit. She is the wisest eight-year-old I have ever come across, wouldn't you agree?*
>
> *We understand if you don't want to come as it might be a painful reminder of last Christmas when you had your husband with you. But, darling, I too know what it is like to be widowed and I found the best tonic was to surround myself with friends and carry on with life.*
>
> *It's a bit chaotic at the hotel as Charlie has been ill and Captain Lomax isn't here to supervise but Myrtle and the children are marvellous and have been coping. Plus, it will be more peaceful this year without the memsahib bossing us all about!*
>
> *Darling, I know she's your friend but she has been making life quite impossible for poor Captain Lomax. He spent the past month at her beck and call, dashing from the hotel to the bungalow ten times a day. He looked worn out. We're all surprised he's gone with the memsahib*

to Scotland – the servants say their rows were like fireworks at Diwali. I wouldn't be surprised if he tips her overboard on the way home!

The Duboises say the memsahib threatened to take baby Andrew away for good and are convinced that's the only reason the captain's gone with her. You know how much he dotes on the small thing. But between you, me and the gatepost, the Duboises are worried Lomax might never come back and so are the chaps and I. The memsahib is trying to get him to sell the hotel. Hey-ho, as you British say. We'll be parcelled off to the next buyer – if we're lucky!

So, darling, if you want to see us all, you better come this Christmas as we might be scattered to the four winds by next!

Kind regards,

Hester Cussack

Esmie was overwhelmed by the unexpected invitation. She was touched to know that the baroness and her friends had not only been thinking about her welfare but wanting to cheer her up. Yet she was deeply upset to think that the Lomaxes were so unhappy and that Lydia was using Andrew to coerce Tom to do her bidding. How cruel! Lydia had undergone a terrible ordeal but it was unfair to take it out on Tom and make a pawn of Andrew.

Her heart ached for the poor boy. What would his future be like in such an unhappy home? Esmie was alarmed to think that Lydia might get her way and end Tom's dream of a life as a hotelier. Tom had found something he was good at and enjoyed. And it was not just Tom's future that was at stake but the employment of the Dubois family and the home of Hester and her friends.

After a restless night, Esmie wrote back accepting the invitation. The more she thought about it, the keener she was to spend Christmas at the hotel. She had felt more at home there in a short space of time than anywhere else in India. Esmie knew that that was mostly to do with the delightful and eccentric residents and the warm-hearted Duboises.

Having made the decision, it became clearer in Esmie's mind that after her holiday at the Raj Hotel, she would leave the mission in Taha and travel on. She began to make arrangements to pack up the house and her few possessions. She asked Karo if she would like to go with her as her maid.

'I will always look after you and Gabina for as long as you want,' Esmie promised. 'But I'll understand if you want to stay in Taha – I'm sure Desai Memsahib would give you a home.'

'No,' Karo said quickly, 'I'd like to come with you, Guthrie Mem'. I'm not afraid to travel and go where Allah leads me.'

'I'm so glad!' Esmie said in relief. She had been dreading the thought of leaving the Waziri woman and the girl behind. In time, she planned that she would take Karo to one of the major hospitals for an operation to reconstruct her nose. Even though few people saw her unveiled, this would be Esmie's gift to her friend for her bravery and serve as a final riposte to Baram Wali's cruelty.

Before she left Taha, Esmie sat down to write the hardest letter of her life.

> *Dear Lydia,*
>
> *By the time this reaches you, you will be back at Templeton Hall and having a wonderful reunion with your parents. I know how happy you will be and I can imagine your parents' joy at seeing you again and meeting Andrew for the first time. I can almost hear the chatter and popping of champagne corks! Thinking of you all at dear Templeton Hall gives me great pleasure and I hope it*

makes you happy to be home. I know you haven't been so in India.

You once told me to stop prying into your marriage and so it's with hesitation that I write this. But you know how interfering nurses can be – and this one in particular! I tell you this only because it may help you understand things better – and to do so, I must break a promise I made to Tom not to say anything. Yet I know how difficult things have been for you both since your terrible experience in captivity and I don't think telling you can make things any worse.

Andrew is all the more precious to Tom because he lost his first baby, a daughter called Amelia. Mary died in childbirth while Tom was on active service and their baby died a few days later. He was so grief-stricken that he never told anyone. Harold and I only found out because we came across the graves of mother and baby in Peshawar. I always thought you should be told about it so that you'd understand why Tom was so anxious about you during the pregnancy and fearful of losing Andrew. But Harold said it wasn't up to me.

I think Tom is still afraid of losing Andrew. That's why he didn't press you on why you were driving to Razmak to see Dickie and why he's gone with you to Scotland. You have tested him greatly, Lydia. I can say that as your closest friend who wants the best for you. But if our friendship still means anything and you have any love in your heart for Tom, please don't take Andrew from him. Come back to India and try again.

I've decided to stay on, though I'm going to work somewhere else than the North-West Frontier. I don't plan to live near Rawalpindi but you can come and visit me wherever I go. I'll buy a swing seat for the veranda and we'll sit and drink gin fizz and you can tell me all the gossip from Ebbsmouth and Pindi.

Lecture over. Now you can tear up this letter or stick pins in my effigy. (Remember when we did that to Maud Drummond when she banned us from going on the school picnic because we'd defaced a photo of the prime minister for opposing women's suffrage?!)

But I hope you won't take offence. I write about such things because you three are dear to me – and were dear to Harold. He would have shied away from putting such thoughts in a letter but it would have pained him to see his best friends so unhappy.

Please give my love to your parents and have a happy Christmas together.

My friendship and love to you always.

Your best friend,

Esmie xxx

Esmie sealed the airmail letter and gave it to Draman to post. She busied herself for the rest of the day sorting through clothes and books, putting aside a pile of Harold's to offer to the mission. At the bottom of her chest she found the emerald dress. Her eyes prickled with tears as she held it close and remembered the night she had danced with Tom – the only time he had held her in his arms – and she had known for certain the strength of her passion for him. She would probably never wear it again but she couldn't yet bear to part with it. Knowing she was being sentimental, Esmie laid it on the pile she was keeping.

A week later, her possessions – reduced to a trunkful – were sent on ahead to the Raj Hotel. The furniture and furnishings that didn't belong to the mission, she distributed among the servants. On her last evening, Rupa gave her supper and the following morning she got up at dawn to lay flowers on Harold's grave. Her tears made her skin smart in the cold. It was a year to the day that they had left Taha to spend Christmas with Tom and Lydia at the hotel. How much had happened in the intervening time. Esmie's heart was sore with distressing memories. Yet she did not regret coming to work and live among the Waziris of Taha.

'This isn't goodbye,' she whispered over the grave. 'I'll come back when I can to bring you flowers and say a prayer. I'm sorry we had such a short time together, Harold. But you know that I cared for you a lot. Malik is going to tend your grave for me. Thank you for bringing me to this place. I would never have met these special people without you. Karo and Gabina are going with me, so their temporary stay lasted longer than even I thought it would.' Esmie gave a teary smile. 'Till we meet again, my dearest.' She kissed her fingertips and touched the newly carved gravestone, and then turned and hurried from the cemetery.

An hour later, as the houses of Taha glowed golden in the rising winter sun, Alec drove Esmie, Karo and Gabina to Kohat. By midday he was waving them off on the train to Rawalpindi.

Chapter 43

The Raj Hotel, New Year's Eve

After dinner, Stella organised them into a game of charades. Jimmy and Mr Hoffman were acting out the title of a book, trying to convey the meaning of the middle word of a three-word title. Jimmy was jumping about and Mr Hoffman was pulling his lugubrious face in ever increasing expressions of pain. Suggestions were shouted out.

'Anger?'

'Horror?'

'Dracula!' Stella squealed with laughter.

'There's only one word in that title, darling,' said Hester.

'Hoffman looks decidedly ill,' said Fritwell.

'Desperate Remedies!' called out Ansom.

'That's two words,' Hester reminded him.

Hoffman sank to his knees and Jimmy mimed climbing a rope.

'The Ancient Mariner?' suggested Charlie.

'That's a poem,' said Ansom. 'Are you allowed to do poems?'

'No,' said Stella.

'It's not a poem,' protested Jimmy.

'No speaking!' ordered Stella.

Mrs Shankley waved her ear trumpet in excitement. 'Return of the Native!'

'That's four words,' pointed out Hester. 'But a nice try, darling.'

'Jude the Obscure,' said Fritwell.

'How could it possibly be that?' Ansom laughed.

'Well, it all looks dashed obscure to me,' grunted his friend.

'Do the whole title, Jimmy,' Myrtle advised her son. 'Or no one else will get a turn.'

In desperation, Jimmy whispered to Hoffman. The retired policeman went on all fours and Jimmy did the same behind him. They moved about the floor, stopping to wave an arm in front and then continue on.

'The Pilgrim's Progress?' Charlie queried.

Helpless with laughter, Esmie said, 'I think they're supposed to be animals.'

'Could be elephants,' said Fritwell.

'Good thinking, Fritters,' said Ansom. 'What's that one about the elephants crossing the Alps?'

Stella leapt up and waved her hand in the air. 'I've got it, I've got it! It's The Jungle Book!'

Jimmy sprang to his feet, grinning. 'Yes, it is.'

Hoffman sighed in relief and pulled out a handkerchief to mop his brow. Ansom and Charlie helped him to his feet and into a chair.

'Excellent acting, sir,' praised Charlie. 'We should have guessed it long before we did.'

While the next couple were chosen from the hat, Myrtle supervised the handing round of cheese pastries while Charlie made sure that drinks were refreshed. Esmie was so full of dinner that she couldn't manage either. Stella unfurled the strips of paper and read out the names.

'Ooh, Daddy,' she giggled, 'it's you and Mrs Shankley.'

Charlie gave a gallant bow and led the deaf resident to the corner of the room to discuss their book title in loud whispers.

'Daddy, we can hear you,' Stella cried.

'Put on some music, darling,' Hester suggested.

Jimmy rushed over to the gramophone and wound it up. Ragtime music filled the room. Abruptly, Esmie was reminded sharply of Ebbsmouth and Lydia. She wondered how life was at Templeton Hall. There had hardly been time for a reply to her letter to come from Lydia, even by airmail, but she doubted she would get one. As time went on, Esmie had questioned whether she should have written at all. Had she added fuel to the fire of Lydia's resentment towards Tom? Charlie had received a telegram from Tom to say that they had arrived safely in Scotland and wishing them all a happy Christmas. But apart from that, no one knew how the Lomaxes were or when – if ever – they would be returning to Rawalpindi.

Yet, to Esmie's surprise, Christmas had been a happy one. She was deeply grateful for the Duboises and her friends at the hotel for making her one of the family. From the moment she had arrived they had fussed over her, giving her the secluded Elgin room with its charming view of the jacaranda tree in the courtyard.

On Christmas Eve, Charlie had made his special punch and Esmie had joined in the traditional hotel party for a short while. The next morning Ansom and Fritwell had accompanied her to the Scots Kirk and afterwards she had joined all the residents for lunch in the dining room and then taken herself off for a walk around the tree-lined streets. She had avoided the Mall and the cricket ground, not wanting to run into acquaintances of the Lomaxes or be reminded of the previous year. Instead she had meandered in the mellow sunshine, looping back through the Saddar Bazaar, and found solace in the bustle of Indians going about their day.

On Boxing Day the Duboises had insisted on taking her to spend the day with Myrtle's family, the Dixons, in Lalkutri Bazaar. Esmie had been overwhelmed by how she had been warmly welcomed into the home of these complete strangers. Their flat was crowded and noisy with family arriving, bringing presents and food to share. All day there was eating and drinking, sing-songs and party games. Stella stuck close to Esmie, showing her off to her cousins and making sure she was enjoying herself.

'You're not sad, are you?' the girl kept asking.

Esmie had to hold back tears at her concern. 'I'm enjoying every minute,' she answered, pulling Stella into a hug. 'Thank you.'

Tonight, as the old year waned, Esmie was glad to be at the Raj Hotel surrounded by friends, amid their laughter and teasing conversation. It was the tonic her bruised heart needed. She stayed up long enough for them to toast in the New Year.

Esmie caught the look of sympathy in Charlie's eyes as he raised his glass and said, 'To absent friends!'

Her vision blurred as they all repeated the toast. Her mind was full of memories of Harold – of her Aunt Isobel, Jeanie and Norrie – and of Tom, Lydia and Andrew.

Suddenly she felt Stella's warm hand slip into hers. Esmie squeezed it in gratitude.

'To the New Year!' Charlie cried. 'To a happy and healthy 1921!'

Chapter 44

Ebbsmouth, January 1921

After New Year, to avoid his wife's constant criticism, Tom went to stay with Tibby at the Anchorage. It was easy to keep out of his father's way too, as the old colonel was almost bed-bound and rarely left his study. Tom spent his time fraternising with the artists who lodged with his twin sister – doing a bit of painting himself – and visiting Templeton Hall to take Andrew out for wintry walks.

He was sorry for the young ayah, Sarah, who had never before experienced the icy east winds blowing off the North Sea in January. He suspected she was lonely and homesick but she never complained and remained stoically loyal to the Lomaxes and attentive to Andrew's needs.

At first Tom had an ally in Lydia's father, Jumbo, who defended his son-in-law's wish to keep the hotel going in Rawalpindi.

'It has a great deal of potential,' Jumbo told his daughter. 'There's no reason why it shouldn't make a good little business, and maybe expand in the future – other Raj Hotels in some of the more scenic spots.'

Tom was encouraged by the idea but Lydia dismissed it at once. 'It would be throwing good money after bad. I can't see why you can't set Tom up in business here. I don't want to go back to India – ever!'

Tom didn't tell Lydia's parents about her affair with Dickie Mason. All they knew was that their daughter had been through a terrible ordeal. Minnie took her daughter's side and was uncharacteristically forthright.

'I think it's cruel to expect Lydia to go back to Pindi after all she's been through,' she rebuked Tom. 'Your first duty is to your family – your wife and son.'

Soon, Jumbo was persuaded round to the women's point of view.

'Let me introduce you to some of my business associates here,' he offered. 'There's money to be made in the motor industry. Have you ever thought about car manufacture?'

'I know nothing about motor cars,' Tom said in exasperation. He had forgone his inheritance to escape his father's controlling influence, so the last thing he wanted was to be beholden to Lydia's father.

He and Lydia argued over Esmie's letter too. She took it as a personal slight that she'd been kept in the dark about Tom's first baby dying when Esmie knew about it.

'Why didn't you tell me?' Lydia exclaimed.

Tom struggled to find the words to explain. 'I . . . I couldn't speak about it . . .'

'But you could to Esmie.' Lydia grew upset. 'I'm your wife, Tom. I should have been told. Poor Mary!' She became tearful. 'You never confide in me – always in Esmie.'

'She and Harold found out . . .'

'How can you want to go back to such a dangerous place?' she asked in bewilderment. 'Force me to go back!'

Lydia pored over the letter again. 'I can't believe Esmie's taking your side over mine!' she said in agitation. 'How dare she accuse me of taking Andrew away from you?'

'You threatened me with that in Pindi,' Tom reminded her.

'No, I didn't! You were the one who said you'd take me to court over the baby.'

Tom barely held on to his temper. 'She's just trying to get us to stay together and try again for Andrew's sake. Don't you see that?'

'All I see is that my best friend thinks more about my husband than me.'

Tom could take no more arguing. Shortly after that particular row, he retreated to The Anchorage and his sister's uncritical company. He was deeply touched at Esmie's attempt to protect Andrew but wished she hadn't interfered; it had only made things worse. Lydia had shown little sympathy over his loss of Amelia; she'd just made him feel anew the guilt at not being there when she was born or able to prevent her death.

The Raj Hotel

In January Charlie had a further bout of bronchitis. To stop him fretting, Esmie stayed on to nurse him and help Myrtle with running the hotel. Between them, the women decided that there was no need to trouble Tom with news of his manager's ill health. Myrtle confided how anxious Tom had been about leaving the hotel to go on furlough and how they had reassured him they would cope while he was away.

'Charlie told him his family must come first – especially after Mrs Lomax had suffered such a terrible time in the North-West Frontier.'

'Besides, Tom's too far away to do anything about it,' Esmie agreed, 'and I don't mind helping out. I have nothing to rush away for.'

She found herself enjoying the routine tasks of choosing menus, greeting guests and liaising with staff, happy to be making decisions that didn't mean the difference between life and death. It made her realise what relentless pressure she'd been under when she had worked as a nurse and the dangers she had faced.

Sometimes it was the simplest activities that she enjoyed the most; supervising Stella and Jimmy's homework after school, playing backgammon with Ansom or accompanying the baroness on her daily walk along the Mall. Most of all, she relished her time spent with the Duboises who treated her like family and with whom she was now on first name terms.

To her delight, Karo and Gabina had settled well into the hotel compound. While Karo made herself useful mending clothes and making new cushion covers for the hotel, Gabina became Stella's shadow and toddled around after her. The patient Stella was often to be seen staggering around with the small girl balanced on her hip, singing her songs and feeding her titbits.

Ebbsmouth

Tom's relationship with his wife grew ever more strained so her mother suggested taking Lydia on holiday to restore her health.

'It's her nerves,' Minnie said with worry. 'She needs a complete rest and change of scene.'

In February, Lydia and her mother booked a hotel in Nice on the French Riviera for three weeks.

Lydia needed little persuasion by Tom to leave Andrew and his ayah behind. She overruled her mother who wanted the baby to go with them.

'How is that going to be restful for me?' Lydia chided.

After they had gone, Tibby was frank. 'You do know who they'll be meeting up with, don't you?'

'Yes, Grace is going to join them for part of the holiday,' Tom answered.

'Apart from Lydia's sister.' Tibby arched her eyebrows.

'Who?' Tom asked, feeling tense at the pitying look on his sister's face.

'Well, Colin Fleming has a place in Nice. Remember that wine merchant who was courting Lydia before you came back from the War?'

Tibby was right. Lydia returned at the end of the month, adamant she wouldn't go back to India and suggesting a separation from Tom. It wasn't long before Tom began to hear about Lydia being seen at social events escorted by Colin Fleming. Despite the humiliation of his wife's blatant flaunting of her new consort – they began to be the gossip of the county – he felt mainly relief. He swiftly booked a passage back to India for himself, his son and ayah.

That was when he and Lydia had their final row. 'At such a tender age, Andrew needs his mother more than he needs a father,' Lydia decreed.

'You spend no time with him as it is,' Tom said angrily. 'He's more attached to his ayah than his mother.'

'How can you say that?' Lydia accused, resorting to tears. 'I can't be without him.'

For once, the Templetons seemed sympathetic to Tom. Yet they supported their daughter as he knew they would.

'I know you're a good father to our grandson,' said Minnie, 'but you can't look after him while you're running a hotel, can you? Whereas Lydia has us here to help her care for Andrew.'

Jumbo took Tom aside. 'Man to man – best to leave Andrew here – at least while he's so young. Lydia's not acting herself at the moment; I don't condone the way she's carrying on with Fleming but I think it's just a passing phase. Lydia might be persuaded to try again in India given time.'

Tom thought it unlikely. But he was tired of fighting. The more he thought about the hotel and India, the more he was impatient to return. Why waste any more time hanging about Ebbsmouth feeling useless and trying to salvage his moribund marriage? He would prove the Templetons wrong. He would go back and make a success of the Raj Hotel and provide for his son, so that one day he could return and claim him.

Increasingly, he could not get Esmie out of his mind. How was she coping with life in Taha without Harold? He longed to see her and find out what she planned to do. Perhaps in time . . . Tom smothered his yearning for the nurse. He must give her time to grieve for Harold. In the meantime, he would rebuild his life in Rawalpindi alone.

Chapter 45

The Raj Hotel

February came and went. March brought a rise in temperature, some sudden storms and blossom to the city's gardens. Then a telegram came from Ebbsmouth.

'Embark March nineteenth STOP arrive Bombay April eighth STOP Pindi tenth STOP greetings.'

This sent the residents into a twitter of excitement and speculation. Was the captain returning on his own or with his family? Was it a good sign that he was coming back or was it to prepare the hotel for sale?

Charlie, once again in charge, tried to calm their fears. 'Captain Lomax has expressed no intention of selling this illustrious establishment. You must not worry. We carry on as normal. Everything is ship-shape.'

But privately, Myrtle voiced her concern to Esmie as they sat sharing a pot of tea after the children had gone to bed.

'Charlie is worried too. Captain Lomax seemed so defeated when he left – resigned to doing whatever Mrs Lomax demanded. I know I shouldn't speak badly of your friend, Esmie, but part of me dreads her coming back. She's not been happy in India. It might be better if they did sell to someone else rather than make the captain's life a misery here.'

Esmie was deeply saddened at the thought. She put a hand over Myrtle's in sympathy. 'We just have to hope that these past weeks on holiday together have been enough to cement their marriage. I just hope for Andrew's sake that they patch things up.' She sighed. 'But you could be right; in the long term the Lomaxes might be happier starting again in Scotland.'

Unsettled by the anxious talk and the doubt over the hotel's future, Esmie decided that she should be gone by the time the Lomaxes – or Tom on his own – returned. As Lydia had never responded to her letter, Esmie guessed that her words had been unwelcome and she didn't want to exacerbate the situation by being there when they got back, so she began to plan her onward journey.

The residents were full of suggestions of where she should visit in India.

'Taj Mahal is a must,' Ansom declared.

'Oh, yes,' agreed Hester, 'especially by moonlight, darling.'

'Lucknow and the site of the Mutiny,' suggested Fritwell. 'And they say the new Victoria Memorial in Calcutta is very impressive.'

'Jaipur's fascinating,' said Hester, 'and the deserted city of Fatehpur Sikri. I've friends in Rajputana you can stay with.'

'Of course you should go to Simla,' said Hoffman. 'A delight once the snow has gone.'

'And Kashmir,' enthused Hester. 'You must come and stay with me in Srinagar once the hot season comes. I have the use of a houseboat.'

Stella grinned. 'Yes, I went last year with Mrs Shankley. It's the most lovely place I've ever, ever been. Everything comes on little canoes so you can shop in your own house!'

'Shikaras, darling,' said Hester. 'Those little canoes are called shikaras.'

'Oh, I'd love to do that.' Esmie smiled, remembering how Tom had enthused about Kashmir. 'I've been told that swimming in Dal Lake is paradise.'

Hester laughed. 'You can swim if you like, darling. I'll sit and watch and drink nimbu pani.'

Esmie booked a train to Lahore for the beginning of April and a room in Nedous Hotel. She was going to start her tour by visiting the ancient Punjabi city with its mix of Moghul buildings and cosmopolitan grandeur. The Duboises had offered to store her trunk so that she could travel lightly with only one suitcase and a large bag. She was lending her sewing machine to Karo, who was proving useful to Myrtle in running up new curtains for some of the bedrooms. The Waziri woman had chosen to stay in the hotel compound and work for the Duboises while Esmie was away.

On her final morning in Rawalpindi, she took breakfast with the Duboises and waved Stella off to school. Halfway down the path, the girl ran back and threw her arms about Esmie's waist for one last hug.

'You will come back and see us, won't you?' Stella said tearfully.

Esmie squeezed her tight. 'Of course I will, I promise. You're like family to me now.' She kissed the top of her head and gently disengaged.

Before her train, she went for a short walk with the baroness.

'I mean what I say about visiting me in Kashmir, darling,' Hester said.

'And I intend coming,' Esmie replied, smiling.

Arm in arm, they made a stately progress back to the hotel. An hour later, she was being hugged and kissed goodbye by Myrtle and the residents, and then Charlie drove her to the station.

'I thank you with all my heart, Esmie, for helping us,' said Charlie.

'It's me who should be thanking you,' Esmie said, as they shook hands. 'You and your family have helped me through a difficult time – I'll always be so grateful.'

As she boarded the train, Charlie pulled a lilac silk handkerchief from his breast pocket and waved. 'Bon voyage!'

'Au revoir!' Esmie called and waved back, and then climbed on board.

Five days after Esmie left, Tom returned alone to the Raj Hotel. He felt the burden of the past weeks lifting as he paused on the front lawn to take in the dearly familiar sight of the white-washed building with its blue-roofed portico and window frames and welcoming open doorway. It confirmed in his own mind that he had made the right decision.

He turned to Charlie, who had met him at the station, and said, 'We'll have to take down the sign with my name on as proprietor.'

Charlie's face fell. 'But I thought . . .?'

'I want the title captain replaced with mister,' Tom clarified. 'Don't worry, Charlie, I won't be selling the Raj to anyone. I'm sorry if you've all been worrying.'

Tom was greeted like royalty by the residents. They ushered him into a seat and handed him a large whisky as if he were the guest and asked him about his furlough in Scotland. Tom said little about the past months of wrangling with Lydia and was glad they didn't press him on his marital situation.

'Mrs Lomax has decided to stay longer with her parents,' he said, brushing over the subject. 'I'll be moving back into the hotel to live.'

'Delighted to hear it, darling,' said Hester. 'I mean about you moving back in.'

The others chorused their approval and Tom was touched by their delight at his return.

He avoided talking about Andrew for to do so would risk an outpouring of emotion. Even thinking about the parting with his young son brought tears to Tom's eyes. On his final brief visit to Templeton Hall, Tom had squeezed the infant to his chest and kissed his soft dark hair, whispering, 'I'll come back for you, my darling boy, I promise.'

Andrew had beamed, showing his new front teeth, and grabbed at his cheek with a sturdy grip. Quickly, he'd handed the baby back to Sarah. His voice breaking, he'd said, 'I know you'll look after him well.

Please talk to him about me, so he knows that he's loved.' Tom had stridden from the nursery before he broke down and wept.

Jumbo and Minnie had said embarrassed goodbyes and wished him good luck, perhaps feeling a little contrite at not doing more to help patch things up between their daughter and son-in-law. At the last minute, Lydia – contrary as ever – seemed upset to see him go.

'You will take care of yourself, won't you, Tom?' she said anxiously, clutching his arm. 'I'd hate for anything bad to happen to you.'

He had nodded and managed to say, 'Goodbye, Lydia. I'm sorry I haven't made you happy. I hope you find happiness here.'

Tom had left to the sound of Lydia sobbing and calling out his name. His insides still clenched to think of it and he wondered what she would have said to him had he stayed. Was it possible in that final moment, she was having second thoughts? He would never be able to fathom what Lydia wanted – and doubted she even knew herself.

Tom was astonished to learn that Esmie had not only stayed at the Raj over Christmas but had helped out for months. He couldn't stop thinking about it and imagining her being there – chatting to the residents and nursing Charlie back to health. It was tantalising to know she had recently walked these corridors, eaten in the dining room and played cards with the guests. Stella would not stop talking about Esmie and proudly showed Tom each postcard that arrived from the different parts of India where Esmie had last been staying: Delhi, Agra, Jaipur and most recently Benares. Tom was glad that Esmie was coping with her bereavement and forging a new life but it made his heart heavy to think she had left the area and did not intend coming back.

Over the next few weeks, Tom threw all his energies into building up his business. In consultation with the Duboises, he advertised the dining room for hire and offered cut-price accommodation for the coming hot season when many British left for the hills. Building on the contacts he had made the previous year with the railway fraternity and the Chota Club, the hotel began to host children's birthday parties, club dinners and bridge competitions with afternoon tea.

He kept himself relentlessly busy so that he had no time to dwell on either Esmie or the son he had left behind in Scotland. Yet the painting he had done of baby Andrew was a daily reminder of how much he missed him. Lydia had written once to say that Andrew's ayah was growing homesick and so Lydia was thinking of sending her back to India and employing a British nanny instead. Tom wondered if it was really because Lydia – or perhaps Colin Fleming – was embarrassed by her reliance on an Indian servant.

He wrote back cautioning such a move. *'Unless Sarah is so very unhappy that she's not doing her job, I urge you to keep her on. Andrew has known her since birth and the two of them are very close. It would be a shame if that bond were to be broken.'*

Lydia had not replied. Tom did not know if that was because she agreed with him or was intent on sending the ayah back anyway.

May was the hardest month for Tom to get through without his son. He sent a card for Andrew's first birthday and a soft toy; a camel made out of leather and brightly decorated in red-and-gold saddle and harnessing. On Andrew's birthday, Tom took himself off to Topi Park with a bottle of whisky, proceeded to get maudlin drunk and allowed himself to weep.

Charlie came out looking for him and to fetch him home. Once the manager had helped Tom into the passenger seat of the Clement-Talbot, he fished out a brown envelope.

'There's a telegram come for you, sir,' his manager told him.

Tom looked at him, feeling groggy and tired as the effects of the whisky wore off.

'What telegram?'

Charlie shrugged and handed it over. For a brief euphoric moment, Tom thought it might be from Esmie. He fumbled and tore at the envelope. At first he couldn't make sense of it.

'Change of heart STOP please meet boat STOP Bombay June Fifteenth STOP love Lydia.'

Tom was stunned. He gaped at Charlie.

'Sir?' he asked in concern. 'I hope it is not bad news?'

Tom, his mind reeling, replied, 'I don't know. Lydia's coming back to India.'

Chapter 46

Srinagar, Kashmir, late June

On the deck of the houseboat *Queen of the Lake*, Esmie leaned on the balustrade and gazed out across the Dal Lake. The sun was rising over the mountains of the Zabarwan range and small puffs of pink cloud were being reflected in the still water. The lake was ringed by pleasure gardens that Hester had sent her to explore during the past two weeks; beautiful formal gardens of scented flowers, trickling fountains and trees that gave shade from the intense sun.

Esmie took a deep breath and savoured the cool of early morning. According to the baroness, June was the hottest month in Kashmir, but to Esmie it was a paradise compared to the plains of India that she had been traversing since April. Here she could wander the paths of the Shalimar or Nishat Gardens and find a shaded seat where she would read a book or simply contemplate the scene.

After the constant travel and sightseeing, which had given Esmie a greater insight into the country but had been exhausting in the heat, she revelled in doing little. Sometimes she took a shikara into Srinagar to send letters and every day she swam, always returning to the houseboat for meals with the baroness. Hester was amusing company, with a never-ending supply of tales about places she had lived and people she had met.

Esmie made a vague plan for the day. First, she would check on a friend of Hester's who had sprained her ankle three days ago while climbing out of a shikara. Esmie had strapped up her ankle and given her tablets for the pain. Then, before it grew too hot, she would go for a swim. Esmie had promised to accompany Hester to a friend's houseboat for afternoon tea but apart from that her afternoon would be free.

Esmie watched a shikara laden with produce for the market in Srinagar glide across the water, creating ripples in the glass-like surface. How easy it would be to stay here indefinitely, seduced by the lake's tranquillity and the pampered houseboat life of meals, swims, reading, dozing and keeping the baroness company.

But it was all the more precious because Esmie knew it was a temporary respite from the world. Even if she stayed on through the monsoon season with Hester, the baroness would be returning to the Raj Hotel come September. Besides, once Esmie had decided what to do next, she would have to go back temporarily to Rawalpindi to ask Karo whether she wished to go with her. From the short, neatly written letters that Stella sent her and Hester, Esmie doubted if her Waziri servant would want to uproot again; she and Gabina seemed to have settled well at the Raj.

Esmie still hadn't made up her mind where she wanted to live or what work she should do. She had hoped that during the weeks of travel she would come across a place where she would want to settle. But here in Kashmir was the first time she had felt instantly at home. Being next to a large lake and mountains reminded her of Vaullay and the friendly, spirited Kashmiris were akin to the Highlanders she had known as a child. With Harold's money, she did not need to find work immediately but Esmie knew that she would soon grow bored if she did not.

Yet, over the past few weeks she had begun to reassess her vocation as a nurse. She knew her greatest motivation had been to please her Aunt Isobel and honour the memory of her parents; she had become a nurse because of them. But what about now? Was it time to do something different? Esmie had greatly enjoyed her few weeks working at the Raj Hotel. She knew she would always want to work alongside others, meeting new people. Or perhaps she would take a job that helped children . . .? She might look for a position here in Srinagar, for she had fallen in love with the place.

Deep down, she knew that another reason she loved Kashmir was because Tom thought it special too. She felt a familiar pang of longing for him.

A letter to Hester from Ansom confirmed that Tom had returned on his own to the hotel and to everyone's relief had no intention of selling it. Tom was now insisting on being called Mr Lomax and not captain. He was being 'tight-lipped' about whether Mrs Lomax and the boy would be returning too. Hester speculated that they would not.

Esmie was sore at heart to think that Lydia had kept Andrew, knowing how much Tom must miss his son. She felt guilty for writing the letter, wondering if it had riled Lydia rather than helping her to see things from Tom's point of view. Her eyes blurred with tears. Hester had told her not to blame herself and that she was not responsible for the Lomaxes' troubled marriage.

The sun was spilling golden light onto the lake and illuminating the string of houseboats along the tree-fringed bank. For the umpteenth time, Esmie wondered if she should write to Tom and ask him how he was. But she wasn't sure what she could say that might be helpful and she couldn't burden him with how much she missed him. Besides, he had not tried to contact her at any time since leaving for Scotland last November. She had avoided journeying to Kashmir via Rawalpindi, instead making her way there by the southerly route via Sialkot and Jammu. Oh, Tom! How she longed to see him, yet she knew that doing so would only disturb the peace of mind she was managing to find here.

Esmie inhaled deeply to calm her thoughts. She refused to be sad on such a glorious morning. She waved to a young boy paddling a shikara close by and then went inside for breakfast.

Later that day, after a refreshing swim at the club landing where she had lingered until late morning, Esmie returned on the houseboat's shikara across the shimmering lake. The sun was high and dazzled the eyes. Squinting at the *Queen of the Lake*, she thought she saw another shikara tied up alongside. It looked like Hester had visitors.

Her hair still damp, she made a half-hearted attempt to smooth its wavy strands as the boatman steered her towards the houseboat steps and the visiting shikara whose seats were hidden by curtains. She peered with interest at the vessel bobbing gently among the reeds and wondered to which of the baroness's many friends it belonged.

She clambered from the boat, clutching her towel and swimming costume and mounted the steep steps to the houseboat veranda. From the shaded sitting room beyond, she could hear Hester talking to someone.

'Hello!' Esmie called. 'I'm back! Sorry I was so long but the water was perfect.'

'Come in, darling!' Hester cried. 'There's someone to see you.'

Esmie gave a surprised laugh. 'To see me?'

She pushed back the gauze curtain and entered. At first she could see nothing in the gloom after the glare of the sun. A tall figure came towards her and spoke her name. 'Esmie.'

That deep precious voice could belong to no other. Her heart thumped in shock.

'Tom?'

'Yes,' said Hester, 'isn't it wonderful.'

Esmie stared. 'Y-Yes.' Her voice faltered with the emotion of suddenly seeing him. Then at once she was fearful that something was wrong. 'Is everything all right? Why have you come?'

He stood before her, extending his hand. 'I heard you were here so I thought I'd pay a visit.'

Esmie dropped her swimming things onto a chair and grasped his hand, holding on longer than was polite. His smile was full of warmth, yet she was cautious as to why he had come all this way.

'The baroness tells me you swim every day,' he said.

'Of course.' Esmie smiled back. 'You were right about this place being a paradise for swimmers.'

'Perhaps tomorrow I could join you?' he asked.

Esmie's hopes leapt. 'How long are you staying?'

'For a couple of days,' he answered. 'We're staying on the *Golden Horn*.'

We. Esmie felt winded. So Lydia must be with him. Was her former friend still too annoyed with her to come aboard with her husband? At least it would mean Tom would have Andrew with him again and that was worth the pain of disappointment.

Fighting down tears, she asked, 'How are Andrew and Lydia?'

Tom hesitated a moment. 'They're fine, thank you.'

'Good,' said Esmie, 'I'm so glad.' Her throat was too tight to say more.

Tom turned and exchanged glances with Hester. The baroness got up.

'I'm going to freshen up before luncheon,' she said, 'and leave you two to catch up.'

When she had gone, Tom said, 'Sit with me.' Taking Esmie by the elbow, he steered her to the sofa.

Esmie, her legs shaking, was glad to sit down.

'I want to thank you, Esmie, for helping at the Raj – for keeping it going while I was away. Myrtle said you were a godsend, and Stella never stops talking about you. I think she'd have you deified if she could.'

Esmie laughed. 'Dear Stella. I was happy to help. They were so kind to me and got me through those first difficult months without . . .'

She swallowed down the lump in her throat as tears welled.

'Tell me how you've been,' he encouraged. 'I've thought of you often.'

'Have you?' Her pulse began to quicken again.

'Yes – every day.'

He looked at her with his vivid blue eyes in that intense way that always made her feel so alive and desired. She could hardly bear it.

He went on. 'But I didn't want to intrude on your grief for Harold. That's why I didn't write. And also because I was trying to save my marriage.'

Esmie's chest tightened. She nodded. 'I'm glad it's working out for you both. Is this a second honeymoon for you and Lydia—?'

'Esmie!' Tom leaned towards her and clasped her hand. 'Lydia's not with me. We've separated for good.'

'Separated?' Esmie repeated.

'Yes,' he said, relief in his voice. 'She's finally made up her mind to stay in Scotland and not come back to India. If truth be told, she's seeing another man – Colin Fleming – and I'm hoping in time we can divorce.'

'Oh, Tom, I'm sorry . . .'

'Don't be,' he said. 'I'm not and neither is Lydia. We've been wrong for each other from the start.'

'But what about Andrew?' Esmie asked.

Tom let go his hold and drew something from his jacket pocket. 'This is for you – a letter from Lydia. She said I could read it first – I hope you don't mind – and then hand-deliver it. It explains things better than I'm doing.'

With trembling fingers, Esmie took the folded piece of writing paper and opened it up.

Dear Esmie,

I spent a long time being furious with you about the letter you sent. I was so annoyed at you for taking Tom's side and not mine. But I've had a lot of time to think it over and I realise that you didn't mean me harm by it. I knew that the brave Esmie who risked her life to come and rescue me was still my friend. We've been through so much together, you and I. I hope we will always be friends to each other.

Anyway, the point of this letter is to say that I forgive you and want you to be happy. By now you will know that I shan't be coming back to Pindi or Tom. The one thing your letter helped show me was that I can never love the baby as much as Tom does so that is why I'm sending him back with Ayah. Daddy's arranged for the wife of a Bombay banker he knows to be their guardian on the voyage back out.

I hope you might help look after Andrew for me. I know you won't judge me like the rest of Pindi probably will – all the 'mems' will no doubt call me heartless and a terrible mother. But I think you understand that after that horrible birth I don't have maternal feelings for him. I used to watch you holding the baby and think – that's how a mother should look at her child – there was love all over your face.

I know that Tom will go rushing off to find you as soon as he can. He's always been mad about you. I wish I'd known quite how much he loved you before we got married. I don't know if you feel the same way but I'm hoping you do. I don't want him to be unhappy. Whatever you decide, I wish you good luck in all you do.

Esmie, one day we will sit together on a swing seat and chat like old times but it won't be in India.

I still think of Harold a lot and sometimes visit his mother – though I try and go when I think his battle-axe of an aunt is out at her kirk meetings!

I hope you will write to me from time to time.

Your loving friend,

Lydia xx

Esmie looked up from the astonishing letter, her eyes stinging with tears.

'She's sent Andrew back?' she gasped. 'You have him with you?'

Tom smiled and nodded. 'He's fallen asleep in the shikara – Sarah's with him.'

Esmie leapt up. 'Oh, Tom! Can I see him?'

Tom stood and caught her hand. 'Esmie, first I need to know how you feel . . . Whether you could see yourself . . .'

She looked up into his handsome face, seeing the doubt clouding his expression. A weight pressed on her chest.

'Oh, Tom; you must know how much I love you,' she assured him. 'Say what you want to say.'

Tom gripped her hands and searched her face. 'I can't offer you marriage yet but I want to be with you, Esmie. I can't bear the thought of you going somewhere else or living without you. Will you come back with me to the Raj Hotel – live with me and Andrew – or nearby if you don't want the memsahibs of Pindi gossiping about us? I'd see you on whatever terms you wanted.'

Esmie was choked with emotion. 'I don't care about wagging tongues,' she said with a tearful smile. 'I can think of nothing I want more than being with you and Andrew. I'd happily move into the hotel to be with you both.'

Tom stifled a cry. He looked on the point of tears himself.

'Oh, happy day!' He pulled Esmie into his arms and held her tight.

She clung on to him, hardly able to believe how in a few short minutes her life had been turned around so joyously. There was nothing now to stand in the way of their being together – no more obstacles to their loving each other.

She looked up into his face and saw his expression – tender yet passionate – mirroring her own.

'Kiss me, Tom,' she urged.

Jubilantly, he bent and embraced her. The touch of his firm mouth on hers made her dizzy. She could feel the impatience in his kisses as if he wanted to make up for all the time they had wasted not being together. From now on they would be.

As they kissed, she was overwhelmed by love for him. Being held tight in his arms, Esmie felt released from the past – the pain and loss that had marked her life – and huge gratitude to this passionate man. She knew she would make Tom happy, and he her. They would cherish and care for one another as well as fulfil their long held mutual desire.

As they broke away, Esmie's cheeks were damp with tears of joy. Tom fished out a handkerchief to dab away her tears. She saw that it was hers – the one she had made him keep as a reminder of the day they had confessed their love for each other by the river in Kanki-Khel. They exchanged tender smiles.

Abruptly, squeals from outside broke the tranquillity of the lakeside.

Esmie gasped. 'Is that Andrew waking up?'

Tom grinned. 'Sounds like it.'

She felt a rush of euphoria at the thought of holding Andrew in her arms again.

'Let's go and fetch him!' she cried.

Tom took her hand and kissed it fiercely. Then together, hand in hand, they hurried into the bright sunshine to answer the boy's call.

GLOSSARY

ayah	nurse or nanny
bhistis	water-carriers
box-wallah	person in trade
burra	big, most important
caravanserai	desert inn with central courtyard for travellers
charpoy	string bed on a wooden frame
chota	small, young
chota hazri	breakfast
chota peg	small alcoholic drink/sundowner
chowkidar	watchman, gatekeeper, doorman
dak bungalow	travellers' rest house

darzi	tailor
dhobi	washerman
durbar	a public reception held by an Indian prince or viceroy in India
feringhi	foreigner (derogatory)
jezail	muzzle-loading long-arm gun
khidmatgar	table servant/under butler
(old) koi hai	veteran of service in India
mali	gardener
memsahib	a polite title or form of address for a woman
mofussil	countryside
nimbu pani	lemon/lime drink
punkah	a cloth fan that works by pulling a rope
punkah-wallah	man who works the *punkah*
sahib	a polite title or form of address for a man
sahib-log	British in India
sepoy	Indian soldier

shikar	hunting
shikara	small open boat found on Dal Lake, Kashmir
sirdar	person of high rank
syce	groom/stable boy
tonga	two-wheeled, horse-drawn carriage
topee	sunhat
zenana	women's quarters in a house

ACKNOWLEDGMENTS

I chose Rawalpindi, Northern India (now in Pakistan) as the post-First World War setting for the fictional Raj Hotel as my maternal grandparents had lived and worked there in the 1920s. My grandfather's diaries gave some background as to what life was like in the army town and the surrounding hills, including the hill station of Murree. I was greatly helped in my research by Rawalpindi writer Ali Khan, who has written and produced a beautifully illustrated history book of the city with rare photographs: *Rawul Pindee, The Raj Years*. (The book was commissioned and sponsored by Isphanyar Bhandara, the CEO of Murree Brewery.)

The storyline about the kidnap and rescue of a British woman was inspired by true events that took place in the North-West Frontier in the early 1920s – although all the characters and locations in my depiction are fictitious. If you wish to read about the real events I would recommend *Tales of Tirah and Lesser Tibet* by Lilian A. Starr, of Peshawar. The copy I read is housed in the fabulous Lit & Phil Library in Newcastle upon Tyne, in the UK.

Grateful thanks go to my wonderful editor, Sammia Hamer, for her enthusiasm and belief in my writing, to structural editor Katie Green, who has been very helpful in enhancing this novel, to Jill Sawyer for careful copyediting and Swati Gamble for eagle-eyed proofreading. Also, to Lisa Horton for the gorgeous cover, to Bekah and Nicole in Author Support for their work behind the scenes and to all the hard-working team at Lake Union – many, many thanks.

ABOUT THE AUTHOR

Janet MacLeod Trotter is the author of numerous bestselling and acclaimed novels, including *The Hungry Hills*, which was nominated for the *Sunday Times* Young Writer of the Year Award, *The Tea Planter's Daughter*, which was nominated for the Romantic Novelists' Association Novel of the Year Award, and *In the Far Pashmina Mountains*, which was shortlisted for the RNA Historical Romance of the Year Award. Much informed by her own experiences, MacLeod Trotter was raised in the north-east of England by Scottish parents and travelled in India as a young woman. She now divides her time between Northumberland and the Isle of Skye. Find out more about the author and her novels at www.janetmacleodtrotter.com.